PRAISE FOR TRACY SUMNER ...

"Tracy Sumner's stories wrap tightly around your heart and refuse to let go. I was grining to the very end."
"LaVyrle-like!"
—Pam Morsi

"Characters so vivid, so real, they had me pulling for them on every page.
Tracy Sumner is an author to watch."
—Janis Reams Hudson, author of *Winter's Touch*

"Engaging, warm and wonderful."
—*Romantic Times*

"Enjoyable beyond description."
—*Rendezvous*

"*Carolina Rose* blossoms and draws the reader in!"
—Michelle Sawyer, *The Literary Times*

"The battle of the sexes heats up on the pages of this fun and fresh romance
by talented new writer Tracy Sumner. *Carolina Rose* will steal your heart!"
—Susan Wiggs, author of *The Charm School*

"Tracy Sumner brings South Carolina to life with a community of fully developed characters."
—Michelle Marr, Romantic Notions

"A sensual and very enjoyable trip to the past."
—Bell, Book and Candle

BOOK YOUR PLACE ON OUR WEBSITE AND MAKE THE READING CONNECTION!

We've created a customized website just for our very special readers, where you can get the inside scoop on everything that's going on with Zebra, Pinnacle and Kensington books.

When you come online, you'll have the exciting opportunity to:

- View covers of upcoming books

- Read sample chapters

- Learn about our future publishing schedule (listed by publication month *and author*)

- Find out when your favorite authors will be visiting a city near you

- Search for and order backlist books from our online catalog

- Check out author bios and background information

- Send e-mail to your favorite authors

- Meet the Kensington staff online

- Join us in weekly chats with authors, readers and other guests

- Get writing guidelines

- AND MUCH MORE!

**Visit our website at
http://www.zebrabooks.com**

TIDES OF LOVE

Tracy Sumner

ZEBRA BOOKS
KENSINGTON PUBLISHING CORP.
http://www.zebrabooks.com

ZEBRA BOOKS are published by

Kensington Publishing Corp.
850 Third Avenue
New York, NY 10022

First Printing: October, 2000
10 9 8 7 6 5 4 3 2 1

Printed in the United States of America

To Mom and Dad—
Thanks for everything

Prologue

1888, Pilot Isle, North Carolina

Marielle-Claire's father always said misfortune clung to her
like a shadow. As she stared at the diary in her hands, she
knew he spoke the truth.

Crouched under the Garretts' attic staircase, her skin perspir-
ing beneath a flounce and swag poplin dress better suited to a
child than a young woman of fourteen years, she struggled to
understand why God found it necessary to throw her into one
appalling situation after another. Just last week, in front of the
entire town, she had tripped over a misplaced rope and knocked
Preacher Ellis from the ceremony dais. Most vexing of all,
Noah had been standing in the front row. Little wonder he
avoided her whenever he could.

Elle chewed on her already ragged nail and glanced toward
the door. The attic was empty except for two scarred steamer
trunks and a piece of timber from a shipwreck last year on the
Banks. She fluttered the pages of the diary, trying to think.
Hadn't Noah told her every problem could be solved with deep

thought? Hadn't he? Heaven above, she wanted to listen, show him how sensible and intelligent she could be.

Maybe then he would love her as much as she loved him.

She swallowed hard, felt a fingernail sliver catch in her throat. *Juste Ciel,* what could she do? She could hide the diary in the azalea bushes, sneak over later tonight and . . . What? Glancing at the faded volume in her hands, she traced the flowery script and felt a renewed surge of grief. She could not destroy the journal of a woman she had loved as much as her own mother. *She could not.*

But, despite the reverence she felt for Eliza Garrett, she did not want to know the woman's secrets. Noah's secrets.

Elle leaped to her feet, her swag ripping on a splinter in the plank floor. She had only volunteered to pack Mrs. Garrett's clothing because none of her sons seemed able to face the task. Noah and Caleb stayed away for long periods of time, fishing and crabbing, seine nets slung over their sun-kissed shoulders, hair plastered to their foreheads in a salty crust. Meanwhile, Zach spent his days aboard his boat, polishing and scrubbing things that did not need polishing or scrubbing, unloading crates at the dock until his arms swung limp like a puppet's.

Too well, Elle understood the need to escape. After six months, the Garrett house still smelled of sickness, despair. Her family's provincial stone cottage had never lost the scent of death either, even after she and her father buried all her mother's blood-soaked handkerchiefs deep. Sadly, the scent was one of her few remaining memories of France.

She flinched in remembrance, Mrs. Garrett's diary lying open in her hands. Mercy, Elle had only read a few pages because she thought it might tell her some of the things she needed to know. Some of the things her mother would have told her if she had lived long enough. What to do about loving a boy fast becoming a man—a boy who regarded her as a silly child, all scraped knees and loose teeth. What to do about the strange feelings that consumed her when she looked Noah in the eye or touched his arm accidentally. The tingling sensation that spiraled through her stomach.

"Hey, Ellie, whatcha' got?"

Elle wrenched about as Caleb snatched the diary from her hands—she had not heard his footfall on the stair. She stumbled forward, struggling to untangle her skirt from her ankles. "Give that back to me!" A loud tear echoed; humid summer air glided past her knee.

Caleb stared for a moment, then doubled over, broad shoulders shaking from the force of his laughter.

"Give it to me." Grasping the diary in one hand and Caleb's wrist in the other, Elle twisted and struggled to no avail. In the last year, he had gotten as brawny as the Yankee whalers who prowled the docks late at night. And at times, he seemed just as wild. "Please, Caleb."

"Don't waste your time, Frenchie," he said, and squeezed her fingers, not hard, but enough to scare her a little. He lifted the diary out of reach, a grin plumping his sun-baked cheeks. Tilting the book into the shaft of light streaming past the filthy glass pane, he scanned slowly. "Well, lookie here. A journal of some sort. I betcha I know which Garrett you're writing about."

From the corner of her eye, Elle saw Noah step through the shadowed doorway, the ghost of a frown twisting his patrician features. Her stomach unclenched, a flood of relief rocking her where she stood. He would take care of things. He always did.

"Let her go, Cale." With lithe movements, and all the grace his brother lacked, he pried Caleb's fingers from hers and shoved him back a step, but only because Caleb let him. Two years older, Caleb towered over his brother and outweighed him by at least twenty pounds.

Noah's gaze touched her, held for a heartbeat, and slid away. He squeezed her hand, then glanced down, his frown growing. Walking backward, he let her arm flop by her side.

Caleb tapped an impatient tattoo upon the floor, dried mud

flaking off his dirty heel. "Don't go saving her all the time, little bro'. You started it her first day here, and you ain't stopped yet. Let her paddle her own boat now and again. Be good for her." He flicked a lock of nut brown hair from his eyes. "Don't you realize that King Alan stuff keeps her darned idolizing going an' going?"

"King Arthur." Noah sighed and gave his ever-present spectacles a nudge. "Just hand her the book, Cale. God knows, you wouldn't know what to do with one unless you thought to use it as a weapon."

Elle's heart pounded as she crossed her fingers in the wrinkled folds of her skirt, her thumb finding a tattered hole and slipping inside. If anyone could make Caleb do something, Noah could.

However, Caleb's effrontery billowed, full sail, and he skipped around them, coming within an inch of knocking his head on a slanted ceiling beam. Dropping to his haunches beside a portable gas lamp, he skimmed stained fingertips over the page Elle had marked with a piece of pine straw. "I begin with the woeful tale of Elle Beaumont's undying love for Noah Garrett."

Elle fisted her hands, nails biting into skin. She glanced at Noah, standing so close she could feel the heat radiating from his body, smell the hint of sea clinging to his pressed shirt. A weary, terribly familiar grimace tugged at the corners of his mouth.

"Don't, *please* don't," she pleaded, the accent she worked to hide threading her words. Caleb regarded this as another silly prank. After all, hadn't her love for Noah always served as amusement of one kind or another?

Caleb thrust his chin out and cleared his throat. "Ahem. *My husband has left me. Less the beating, if you don't count a slap or two. Lucky for me, I'm left to think. Lucky for my . . . sons.*" His voice wilted; he sat back on his heels. Throwing a puzzled look at Noah, he returned to the diary, which had begun to quiver in the lamplight. "*Everyone believes the baby is his.*

Lucky, because Pilot Isle is too small a town to live in with a dreadful scandal surrounding you. No one knew about my beloved Noah, God bless his soul.''

Elle slammed her hands over her ears, temples beginning to throb, knees to knock. English still came with some difficulty, her mind often confusing phrases. *Mon Dieu,* this was not difficult enough.

Caleb gripped the diary in both hands and brought it close to his face. *''I pray for a boy, one I can name after his father. I cannot help but wonder if I shall go to Hell for also praying Zachariah and Caleb's father never returns.''*

Elle dropped her head to her hands, tears leaking from her eyes. Beside her, she heard Noah draw a choking breath.

Caleb flung the diary to the floor and crossed the room, his brogans jarring the scarred planks. "I grew up without a damned father. Because of *you.* Because of *her.* All those times I wondered what I did to make him leave. I needed him, and I thought I made him leave. Because I'm the bad son. You're the smart one, and Zach's the responsible one. But all this time it was you. Holy Mother Mary, you ain't even really my brother!"

Elle lifted her head, unable to stand another second. "Caleb, you don't realize what you're saying. We don't even know . . . this was before we . . . when you were a child." Her words were lost to Noah's dazed stare and Caleb's red-faced fury.

Noah's jaw worked, his lips parted. He didn't move, just let Caleb take him by the forearms and shake him—something she had never seen Caleb do and mean it. "Mama loved you most," he raged. "And now we know why, don't we? *Don't we?''*

Noah gazed at a point high above his brother's shoulder, looking like he was struggling to piece together shards of shattered glass.

"Dammit, did you know? Did Mama tell you?" Caleb's voice shot into the high ranges.

Elle shoved one hand between them, swiping tears from her face with the other. "Please, Caleb, stop. *Arrête.*"

"How many people have joked with us, Professor? About your lily-white skin and your hair, the color of a dried-up stalk o' corn. While me an' Zach look like two bulls let loose in a muddy field. You, you look like some prince, all scrubbed and sparkling perfect. If it wasn't for our eyes . . ." Mashing his lips together, he gritted between clenched teeth, "You don't look like us. You don't act like us. Who *are* you?"

"I don't know. Not a Garrett, I suppose."

Later, Elle would wonder if Caleb had been begging Noah to admit the opposite, that brotherly love bound them as solidly as sinew and bone, that words in a diary did not have the power to tear a family apart. Later, she would wonder about everything.

Then, she just stared as Caleb snarled and cocked his fist, throwing it forward with more than enough force to knock a grown man off his feet. He wrenched around, not waiting to assess damage, and charged past like the bull he'd compared himself to.

Struggling to his knees, Noah ripped his spectacles from his face and flung them into the corner. Elle crouched beside him, heard him take a ragged breath, his shoulders quaking uncontrollably. Tears swam, pooled, and ran in narrow tracks down her cheeks. She covered her mouth with her hand, wondering if she was going to be sick.

In the distance, dull whacks filtered through the open window. Angry blows, metal against wood, violent. Noah tilted his head, casting his face in darkness. "No, Cale," he whispered, and shoved to his feet. She grabbed his sleeve, but he shrugged free, crossing the room in a drunken stride.

Going after him, she tripped down the staircase, slapped the screen door wide, and dashed across the yard. Blades of dew-soaked grass clung to her ankles, streaks of moonlight struggled past the thicket of pine branches. Noah stood in the doorway of the dilapidated shed he and Caleb spent so much time in, building ship models to sell to the mercantile in town.

Elle stepped behind him, bounced up on her toes. Overturned spools of wire and shelves once holding models lay in a twisted gnarl. A New England schooner and an American block sloop were crushed to bits. Caleb was nowhere to be seen.

Noah's hand gripped the frame as he lowered his brow to the rough wood.

"Caleb didn't mean to do it. You know how he is. Like me, I guess. Acts first, thinks later." She brushed her hand along his arm. His muscles tensed beneath her fingers as he turned his head, looking straight at her. Blood trailed down his face, dripped from his chin to his stiff ivory collar. One eyelid looked mangled, like it had been sliced with a knife.

Her stomach pitched. *"Your eye."*

He lifted his arm, sighed hoarsely, let it drop, and glanced away.

"I'm sorry. Oh, Noah, I'm so sorry."

"Don't be. You and Caleb can't help creating havoc. And, he's right. I'm always close behind, picking up the pieces. Except this time it's me you've destroyed."

"You must know I . . . I never meant—"

His hand shot out, banging against the shed door. "I don't know *anything*. Don't you understand? The people I trusted the most are strangers to me. The only people I ever trusted. My blessed *family*. Zach knew about this. He was old enough to know. I questioned. I did. Why I look so different, why my mother treated me in that delicate way, like I would disappear if she blinked. Zach could have told me after she died. It's been months. If he wanted me to mature enough to be able to understand, blessit, I'm almost seventeen years old. He's ashamed, that's why he didn't tell me. And Caleb"—he swallowed a choked sound—"to *hell* with Caleb." She watched his lower lip quiver and nearly dropped to her knees in agony. "Come to think of it, to hell with *you*."

"Don't say that." Elle took a distancing step from his glacial fury. This angry young man did not resemble the compassionate one she'd loved with all her heart since the first moment she saw him. "You don't mean it." The plea came out a strangled whisper. "You don't."

He slid to his knees, his head still resting on the frame. "Yes, I do. I've never meant anything more." He flicked his hand at her, a clear gesture of dismissal. "I'm tired of protecting you. Of protecting him."

In the distance, a seagull shrieked and a wave crashed against the shore. The sounds struck her, impacts of shocking validity. She would remember those sounds, remember the feeling of being awake during a nightmare, for the rest of her life.

As if he heard nothing and knew even less, Noah didn't move a muscle, just appeared to shrink into himself, squatting there on the ground.

Zachariah. She had to find Zach. Just the thought of Noah's eldest brother calmed her. He would know what to do. "Stay here," she said, and reached. He flinched and withdrew until his body was squeezed against the side of the shed.

Nearing the alley leading to the docks, a glimmer of awareness made her look over her shoulder. One more inch, and she wouldn't have been able to see him. Noah's head lifted, a shaft of moonlight throwing his face into luminous profile, beautiful despite the blood and the bruising. His vacant expression sent a shiver down her spine. Terror unlike any she had ever imagined swept through her, intensifying with each thudding step as she sprinted away. She could not destroy the notion, the grave recognition, that her life had just taken a blind, insidious turn.

Please stay there until I get back, she prayed. She never supposed he wouldn't.

Or that he would stay away for ten years.

Chapter One

1898, Chicago

Noah marked four notches in the top of the ship's keel and pushed up his shirtsleeves, rechecking his measurements. He was adding the figures in his head, faster than he could with paper and pencil, when a knock sounded on the door.

"Coming," he muttered beneath his breath, but didn't rise. He disliked finishing a model section and leaving his materials spread over his desk.

"Garrett, I know you're in there. Open the door. Freezing my jibbers off in this godforsaken warehouse." The door rattled on its tracks, yanked from the outside.

Noah groaned and stretched, crossed the room and slid the metal door wide, allowing Bryant Bigelow, the ruddy-checked fisheries commissioner, to charge inside.

"Dammit, Garrett. Freezing in that hallway." Bigelow blew into his hands and stamped his feet. His pilot coat, sodden from the looks of it, fluttered at his ankles, nearly brushing the floor. The former Navy captain, all bluster and brashness, stood just over five feet tall. "Christ Almighty. Freezing in here."

"Is it?" Noah grabbed a sweater from a rusty hook and tugged it past his head. He smoothed the scratchy wool, let his palm linger over his twitching stomach muscles. He pressed hard, sucking in a furtive breath. *Maintain a calm façade,* he ordered himself.

"Why in God's name do you live here? Never felt a colder place in my life." Bigelow advanced into the center of the enormous chamber, loosening a crimson scarf from his throat. "All this junk. Shells and"—he jabbed his boot against a rusted anchor—"ship models. And books. How many books you got here, Garrett? A hundred? A thousand? A blessed library in a frigid typesetting warehouse. Place stinks of ink, too." He angled his head, fixing his flinty gaze on Noah. His fleshy lips twisted in what he probably considered a smile. "You're the finest biologist I've ever worked with, but sometimes I think you're crazy, you know that?"

The jarring squeal of the Union Loop Elevated kept Noah from having to reply. At first, he'd hated the metallic, ceaseless screeching on the tracks below his window. Now, he found it difficult to sleep without the train rattling the glass panes. Of course, he could live in Jackson Park with the other biologists or on Prairie Avenue with the educated elite. Admittedly, he found it impossible to heat this space during a typical Chicago winter. However, he could not, *would not,* explain his choice to distance himself from his colleagues. It made him decidedly uneasy to account for his idiosyncrasies.

"We have a problem, Garrett."

The blurred edges of Bigelow's face finally registered. Noah reached for his spectacles. "I would offer tea or coffee, as you look like a drowned rat but"—he slipped them on, blinked—"no facilities."

"You can't even boil a cup of water in this joint?"

"Afraid not." He shoved his hands deep in his trouser pockets, stiffening his shoulders, hoping the stance looked properly composed. He wasn't going to ask. Did not want to know.

Unfortunately, the rumors had made their way to his cramped office yesterday afternoon. And, he had been hiding in the flat he'd rented for the last five years ever since.

"I received another telegraph regarding the lab in North Carolina. Seems they prefer to work with a local. Soothe ruffled feathers of the fishermen or some such guff. You're from Raleigh, right? Pretty close, isn't it?"

Circling toward the window, Noah squeezed his eyes shut, forcing down the bread he had eaten earlier. The sheer irony of life never ceased to amaze him.

Bigelow's leather soles cracked as he crossed the room, paused to fiddle with a row of horse conchs resting on a low shelf. "Anyway, we're ready to build. Need someone there to supervise construction. You're a local, which fits nicely and . . . well, to be honest, you're the only man I have on staff who worked on the lab at Woods Hole. No choice here, you see. Our funding agreement contains conditions. Unfortunately, you've become one of them."

Noah watched a streetcar turn onto Dearborn Street, blue sparks spitting in its wake. Licking his lips, he trailed his finger along a dangling electricity wire. "Last week, I received word a stipend has been approved for the trout acclimatization west of the Mississippi. I wanted to start working—"

"Give it to Thomas or someone on your crew. How many trout can one man save? Chrissakes, Garrett, do you remember the disaster at Woods Hole? Had to replace the floor in the main workroom. And the roof caved in when the hurricane hit. Remember the locals howling about the trawling limitations? Didn't we learn our lesson?" Noah heard a match strike, then Bigelow sucking on one of those foul cigars he loved. "You've been pushing for a second lab. Well, here it is. A month or two living a stone's throw from some of the best examples of barrier islands in the world doesn't sound terrible to me. Look at it this way, you can get some fine research done, and you won't have to sleep or eat. Same as here, only warmer. This

Pilot Isle place is perfect for you, really. Somber, dull . . . smallest town I've ever seen. No telephones. Hell, no electricity. Two years shy of the twentieth century and no electricity. Of course, the place stinks of fish and inlet muck, but it's truly not much worse than the stench in this place." He grunted, blew a noisy breath into the air. "I got to admit, this dawdling makes me question your commitment, son."

Noah shivered as ten years of grief and uncertainty, of raw, gut-wrenching fear, descended on his shoulders. *Commitment.* He would do anything to make the laboratory a success, was, in fact, the most devoted member of the fisheries department. And Bryant Bigelow knew it. "When do I leave?" he asked without turning, not wishing to see the victorious light in the commissioner's gaze or reveal the dread in his own.

"Soon as you're ready, Garrett. Soon, better be. Already leveling the foundation." He ground his heel to the floor, his smoking cigar stub no doubt beneath it.

Noah dipped his head, gripped the sill with both hands. A gust of wind off the lake rattled the windowpane in its frame, sent a frigid draft of air across his cheek. After all the years of running, the past had finally caught him.

Noah had once believed nothing less than a decree from God would make him return to Pilot Isle. Long ago, he'd convinced himself of his ability to live without his family, without Elle. Yet here he sat, on a rigid plank, his trousers damp against his bottom, bouncing across whitecapped swells in a sturdy skiff clearly bearing the markings of his brother's design.

"You staying for the heated term, yup?"

Noah glanced over his shoulder. The old man sat at the stern of the boat, tiller in one hand, bottle of spirits in the other. He remembered the face, brown and withered, the pale scar splitting one cheek. Cinnamon Stick they had called him. He remembered the name, too—Stymie something or other. "You're pinching," he grumbled without thinking, then frowned and turned toward the bow, wishing he had kept his mouth shut.

"Pinching?" The skiff rocked with Stymie's abrupt movement. A dry cough, then a slurp that sounded like a swig from the bottle. "I reckon I can get us to the Isle, young fella."

Noah squinted and swabbed at his eyes. The spray of salty water over the side had made it necessary to pocket his spectacles, but he could see well enough. Too well, perhaps. They were three hundred yards from docking, just now sailing past a ship anchored as close as it could get to the wharf. A rowboat loaded with cargo bobbed by them.

"Ready about." Stymie swung the boat into the wind. "Little storm brewing, bit o' rain. Windy all the time, yup. No nor'easter . . . nothing like that. Hope you got a place to stay. Lodgings, what little we got, all crammed tight with goshdarned whalers. Only boardinghouse in the Isle is fuller than a milkin' tit."

"I made the necessary arrangements," Noah said, watching a row of peaked cypress roofs burst into view, upper porches rising above wind-shaped oaks. He grasped the sides of the skiff, the reality of returning stabbing deep, the urge to flee hitting hard.

Stymie altered course, a smooth skip and a light thud against the pockmarked pier as he angled in. Hopping off, he knotted the lines before Noah could get his feet untangled. Grabbing his satchel, he lumbered topside, surprised to find his gait unsteady.

"Only one fella ever told me how to sail."

Startled, Noah straightened to his full height, an action he avoided with much shorter men; the breeze took advantage and ripped his coat wide. "Excuse me?"

Stymie released a whistle-breath through the gaping space in his teeth. "Professor used to tell me how to manage my sail. Pert near right most times. I think I mighta been pinching a smidgen at that."

Dammit. "Nice story." Noah shoved a few coins into Stymie's bronzed hand and took off down the pier.

The first raindrop smacked his face as he crossed the wharf,
shrieking seagulls and pounding waves a seductively familiar
chorus. Stepping off the raised planks, he shouldered past a
throng of whalers, cast-iron try pots slung across their shoulders,
their ribald laughter peppering the air. He skirted a fishmonger's
wagon and stepped over a length of rope. An old man perched
on an overturned water cask glanced at him, lifted a weathered
hand in greeting. Noah returned the gesture reluctantly and
turned behind a concealing wall of stacked oyster barrels.

Humid air arrived in gusts from the east, thick from the
increasingly steady drizzle, the final nod to the question of
whether to wear his spectacles. *Maybe it's better,* he reasoned,
pausing in front of a house facing the bay, the double porch
sagging above a foundation of ballast stone, the cypress shake
roof dull gray. The enticing scent of the marsh on the far
side of the island distressed him enough without clear vision
bringing added misery, transporting him back to a time of
security and love, family and friendship. While he stood there,
trying to remember whose house this had been, the loneliness
inside him awakened, overflowing his heart, forcing aside every
other emotion. Eyes downcast and shoulders hunched, he traversed the shell-paved lane, the owner of the house forgotten.

Shaking rain from his face, he broke into a trot, a fine mist
swirling about his ankles. He must remember the promise he
had made as his train exited Dearborn Station: He would not
be drawn into wondering *what if,* drawn into reliving a period
of his life he wished to forget, drawn into lowering his guard,
allowing the people who had once meant the entire world to
him to mean the world again. He had learned to survive on his
own, after years of agonizing exertion. No one to trust or lose
trust in. No one to risk his heart for.

If he had one to risk.

By the time he arrived at the weed-choked walkway leading

to Widow Wynne's boardinghouse, he had regained his equilibrium but lost most of his body heat to the driving rain. His wool underdrawers stuck to his skin, water dripped off his nose and slid past his collar. Cursing beneath his breath, he made a mad dash for the front porch and a reprieve from the storm.

The woman stepped into his path, or he stepped into hers, her head bouncing off his chest, his satchel landing in a puddle, his arms rising to steady her. "Excuse me, ma'am, terribly . . ." His voice tapered off. Deep green eyes met his, glistening drops of water spiking the long, reddish brown lashes. The fierce ache started deep in his chest and moved to his gut. Only one person had eyes as beautiful as these. *Goddamn luck,* he thought, and sank his heels into the moist earth.

Elle tipped her head, rain washing over her fading smile. She flicked a glance at the hands holding her. *"Juste Ciel,"* she rasped, her throat doing a slow draw down her neck. Her face paled, and she lifted a trembling hand to her forehead. Noah felt the tremor rock her. He braced his knees, fingers tightening around her slim forearms. For a moment, he feared she would pitch into the mud at their feet. Then, she mouthed his name, her gaze again falling to his hands.

Remembering she had always liked them, even impulsively called them beautiful once, he snatched them from her and searched blindly for his satchel, tried to escape the ringing in his ears, the darkness dimming his vision. Coming here had been a mistake. If it hurt this much to face Elle Beaumont, how would it feel to face his brothers? What would that do to him?

She shouted to him, a frenetic edge sharpening her voice, "If you're here about the coach house, there's nowhere else to stay but there. Unless you want to go home."

He halted by the gate, threw his head back on his shoulders, and blinked the ashen sky into view. The first time he had looked at one in years and not seen a tangle of electricity wires and bricks dingy from smoke. *Go home?* God, no. Water trickled in his mouth as he whispered, "Nowhere to go? There must be."

"Whalers. Down from New England. Till the weather gets warmer, they'll be here, making runs all day, brawling and busting up the saloon's tables all night." She hummed an indecisive delay. "I've already refused two fishermen. Widow Wynne returns from her niece's in a month. Then she'll accept boarders. Trust me. . . . I'd tell you if there were anywhere else."

Trust her? Oh, yes, *that* had turned out well before. Sighing, he cut his gaze her way, found her standing in the middle of a shallow puddle, a sack of vegetables hanging forgotten from her fingers, a mannish blouse clinging, somewhat indecently, to her bosom. She had grown up, had curves in places once flat and uninspiring. Blessit, why would he even notice? And why was he standing here, drenched and shivering, wondering how much better she would look if he had his spectacles on?

Shifting his satchel from one hand to the other, he waited for a distant roll of thunder to pass before he spoke. "I could telephone—"

"No telephone. I petitioned the town committee for a public one, like they have in Morehead City. I proposed we place it at the mercantile." Swishing her toe through the puddle, she needlessly splashed her cream-colored jersey gaiters with mud. "Mr. Scoggins planned to install it on the boardwalk post so his mother didn't have to see it. She threatened to move off the island if he did, thinks spooks will creep along the line and into the store." She lifted her gaze, a mix of emotions crossing her face. Delight, caution, even a hint of anger, damn her. He could read them all, like ink stamped on her forehead, same as he could when they were children. "We do have a telegraph," she added.

"Impressive changes. There was a telegraph *before.*"

"Yes, well"—he watched in amazement as she pulled a watch from a narrow slit in her skirt and flicked open the tarnished copper cover—"Impressive or no, the office closed about forty-five minutes ago." She blinked rain from her eyes and pocketed the watch, faltering when she caught his look. "Oh . . . I have the seamstress specially sew the pockets. Practical item to have." She waited a moment, perhaps for his reply, then stamped her foot, splashing more muddy water on herself. "Why should a man be the only—"

For the love of God. "A hotel?"

She shoved a sodden clump of hair behind her ear, brightly colored against her skin. "This is Pilot Isle, remember? You think we've gone this long without telephones but suddenly have hotels?"

A fat raindrop hit his neck and slipped inside his collar, making him shiver. He wasn't about to stand around in a blessed downpour and explore his limited options. "Please, tell me this isn't your house, Elle."

She lifted her chin, a flush sweeping her cheeks. "It isn't."

"Tell me you don't live here. Tell me you're married and you live with your husband and six children. Tell me you're only bringing Widow Wynne her groceries."

She shook her head, an angry circle of white rimming her mouth.

No way, not living in the same goddamn *house,* he vowed, and kicked the gate open. Elle emitted a squeak of panic and caught him by the wrist, throwing him off-balance, against the white pickets rising between them. Her breasts, firm and plump, bumped his chest, and he recoiled, but not much. She had a remarkably strong grip for a petite woman, and perhaps, if he were honest, he didn't want to move badly enough. After all, Elle presented the first tangible evidence of home.

"There isn't another train leaving Morehead City today. Where are you going to go? Don't. Please don't run away. Not again."

Grief and remorse claimed him. "Run? You don't have any idea what's it taken to *get* me here. But you do have an idea what it took to make me leave, don't you?" He raised his hand in apology. "It's only . . . I've agonized for two months about this, waited until I could . . . until I felt sure I could . . ." He tilted his head, icy drops of rain stinging his face. He refused to confide in her, refused to confide in anyone.

"You're the marine biologist we've been expecting? The one I'm holding the coach house for?"

Nodding, he blew out a breath.

"I'll leave it to you to tell Caleb and Zach. I won't say a word. I promise. Caleb is gone for two more days, buying lumber in Durham. And Zach, well, Zach is here."

Noah closed his eyes, felt his skin prickle in anticipation and dread. Caleb and Zach. God, how he had missed them. "Too late for promises, Elle. Stymie Hopkins recognized me."

"Hawkins. Stymie Hawkins." She worried her bottom lip between her teeth. "It *will* be all over town by tomorrow then."

He tugged his hand through his hair, the damp locks immediately flopping against his brow. If he had a moment alone, he felt sure he could ease his discomfort, at least make a list of reasons for his return to Pilot Isle, something tangible to assess.

"Come in . . . out of the rain. The coach house is very private. You have the second floor all to yourself."

A gust of wind pressed damp cotton against his chest, and he struggled to suppress a shudder.

"Some boxes arrived for you yesterday. Rory and I stacked them in the front room. Everything's clean, just a little dusty."

Who the hell is Rory, Noah wanted to ask? Her fiancé, most likely. *Good.* "Second floor?" he asked instead.

"It has a private entrance. Widow Wynne even had facilities installed last year."

"Facilities. Ye gods," he muttered, and took three long strides forward. Concentrating on the clank and rub of boats edging the dock and the bang of the unlatched gate against its post, he made an indecisive halt, a half turn. "I don't know, that is . . . I don't know if I can stay."

"I understand."

She probably did. Elle had always been able to sense his moods, seemed to know when he needed a friend or when he needed to be left alone. As a child, he'd had no choice *but* to keep his distance, when she could read him like a blessed book. How he'd hated that. Every subtle expression, even the ones he worked to conceal, visible to her.

"Noah." Her teeth began to chatter, her labored breath chalking the air.

Wonderful. He shrugged from his coat. Kicking the gate shut, he flung it over her shoulders, careful not to touch her. He rounded the corner of the house, hoping his flat was unlocked. In Pilot Isle? He laughed humorlessly. Of course, it was unlocked.

Elle huffed, struggling to match her stride to his, her hands fisted in his coat lapel. "The bottom floor is vacant, pretty much. Water damage. Needs a new floor before it can be rented. Right now, I use it for my school. Two classes a week. Tuesday and Thursday mornings. The typewriting machine *is* loud, but it shouldn't wake you."

He halted at the bottom of the staircase leading to the second-floor landing. So did she, her feet skidding across slick grass, her body, warm and soft, skidding into him. He set her back, trying to ignore the teasing scent of gingerbread and soap. "*School?* What could you teach a child? How to break an arm rolling off a roof? Better yet, how to shatter the largest pane of glass in town with a misplaced kick?"

He watched her swallow her first reply, the only time he remembered seeing her halt a foolish word from tumbling past those lovely lips of hers. "For your information, it's a school for *women.* Anyway, climbing the trellis was Caleb's idea. How was I to know the roof was still wet? About that pane of glass, if you recall, I worked all summer to replace it." She shivered, possibly more from indignation than chill, and gripped his coat close. The sleeves hung well past her wrists, the bottom edge hitting her just above the knee. She appeared fragile and defenseless, a façade surely, yet Noah felt the familiar compulsion to protect her.

He took the stairs two at a time.

"It'll be quite cold in there, until you get the parlor stove lit," she yelled.

Parlor stove? Chrissakes, he hadn't seen a parlor stove in ten years, wasn't sure he would remember how to light one.

"If it's too chilly, you can come inside—"

He glared over the railing. "I live in Chicago, Elle. In a printer's warehouse. If it gets above fifty in there, in July, I'll eat my hat. So, thank you anyway, but no need to worry."

"Fine, Professor. Freeze your skinny rump off for all I care."

He leaned out, the fragile railing bending beneath his weight. "What did you say?"

"Nothing." She forced a smile, her lips clenched.

He couldn't halt his study of her, the little not hidden beneath his pilot coat. Reddish strands of hair curled about her face, an occasional gust of wind slapping the ends against her cheeks. Tiny fingers locked around his lapel, pallid against the black wool. He denied the urge to squint, see if her lashes were as long and dark as they had appeared. The absence of his spectacles and the misting rain painted a fancifully soft-edged portrait. She even looked—*God help him*—a bit attractive, her face flushed from the cold, her eyes wide and very, very green.

Noah wrenched the unlocked door, ducked inside, and slammed it behind him. Elle Beaumont was trouble and would never be anything *but* trouble. *Forget about how much it hurts to look at her and remember the life I left behind.* Years ago, he had protected her from everyone, including herself, but he wasn't going to do it again.

The woman was on her own this time.

Wait until I get my hands on Zachariah Garrett. Just wait, Elle fumed, fury propelling her across the street at a fast trot.

Noah lived in Chicago. Zach had mentioned sending telegraphs to the people building the laboratory. Telegraphs to *Chicago*. And Zach, town constable, approved all the building permits in Pilot Isle. Elle kicked an oyster shell from her path and watched it tumble, wishing she could do the same to the town constable's backside. He had let her stumble upon, stumble into, the one person she wasn't sure she ever wanted to see again. Much less *touch*.

A biologist. Elle emitted a harsh laugh and dodged a loaded clam wagon. A marine biologist. How perfect. No one loved fish and seaweed, the stink of the marsh at low tide, more than Noah Garrett did.

She banged her fist on the metal door of Zach's office, which doubled as the town jail. Oh, she hoped he was there. If not, she would find him.

The hinges squealed. Zach popped his head around the frame, a delighted smile growing, revealing straight white teeth. "Ellie—"

Brushing by him, she charged into the office, words tumbling free. "How could . . . *je suis* . . . I never . . ."

"Boys," Zach said to the group of men gathered round the wood-burning stove, "how about I meet you at Christabel's in fifteen for dinner. Rory'll be along any minute, and we'll come on over."

With a chorus of agreement and a few wide-eyed looks thrown toward the woman they had all seen in a similar state of chaos, the men shuffled out.

Zach turned to her when the door clanked shut. "What's wrong? Your father? Another attack? I'll get Doc Leland, you don't have to talk to him. I don't blame you for not wanting to. After the engagement pickle, I don't blame you at all."

Elle slumped into the nearest chair, head dropping to her hands, the heat from the stove making her queasy.

"Your face is as red as the fire. Do you have a fever?" Zach crouched before her, his knuckles grazing her brow. "This coat isn't helping. Blamed thing is more suited to the North Pole."

"Or Chicago," she said between splayed fingers.

"Yes, Chicago, I sup—" His heels popped the floor; he rocked back. "Noah's here." He grabbed her shoulders, slid her forward in the chair. "You've seen him? Where is he?"

She shoved his chest with both hands and jumped to her feet. *"You knew.* You knew he was coming."

He nodded, an eager glow in his eyes.

"Mercy above, you could have told me. Warned me, at the very least." She sniffed and wiped her nose on Noah's sleeve. A potent scent, as purely masculine as any she'd ever smelled, clung to it.

Zach tipped her chin high. "Could I? Then what? You move to the mainland until he leaves? Hide in Widow Wynne's basement for a month? *No.* It's enough your father has driven you from your home, forced you into a desperate situation. A situation you've refused to let me help you with. Caleb and I are the only family you have right now. I did what I reckoned best. You must know that."

"I wouldn't . . . I wouldn't call my situation desperate," she said, angling her chin away. She couldn't look at Zach and lie at the same time. "Not really desperate."

"Your father has cut off your finances, forced you to take up residence in a boardinghouse and act as an old woman's nursemaid to survive. All for refusing to accept a loveless marriage. In my book, that's pretty desperate."

Elle turned to the window, pressed her brow against the cool metal bars. She could not marry a man she didn't love—being alone seemed a far better choice than living a lie for the rest of her life. She agreed with Zach about that, but she could not admit it. She didn't feel comfortable discussing marriage with him. Not after he had lost his wife to consumption just over two years ago. Hannah had been the love of his life, the light in his life, and only recently had the light begun to shine again.

"How did he look? Did he"—Zach sighed, his toe tapping on the stone floor—"did he seem glad to be back?"

"Um . . ." Her heart sank. Steadfast, reliable Zach.

"Did he ask about me? About Caleb?" His voice weakened with each word.

Elle pasted on a smile and turned to face him. "Well, he's gotten really tall." She held her hand high above her head. "Six inches, maybe more. He had to duck inside the coach house."

"His head almost brushed the frame? Imagine that."

"And his voice, you remember, kind of rough, like sandpaper? Sounds the same." Lashes long enough to make any woman jealous. "Hair, his hair was a little darker, I think. The color of ripe wheat." A face so handsome she had experienced an absurd rush of anger. "Thin, he looked thin," she blurted.

"Did he seem happy, Ellie?"

Combative, defensive, suspicious. "I didn't get much of a chance to talk to him." She chewed her lip and glanced away.

The stove lid rattled as Zach settled wood inside. "I should go to him. Get this confrontation over with. He can't hide in a town this size for long."

"I don't think he wants to hide. I think he wants . . ." Her lids drifted low as she pictured Noah's expression when he'd stormed through Widow Wynne's gate. Disbelief, certainly, and mistrust, a definite trace of fear. "He mentioned waiting two months before coming back. Maybe he believes he's finally ready to see you again. See Caleb. But, he wants to be the one to decide when you'll meet."

She opened her eyes to find Zach staring at her. "He tell you all that?"

"Of course not. He won't tell Saint Peter that much at the Pearly Gates."

Zach nodded and flipped the stove lid closed. "It's still there between you two."

"No, Zach, it's *not.*"

"I never, though Lord knows I tried, understood him like you did. Even when he was a tiny thing, no higher than my knee, the questions he asked darn near knocked me off my feet. Made me feel kinda funny. As if I had this special person to tend to, to watch over, someone I didn't know how to handle. I was a ship's pilot. What would I know about how shells are formed or how birds stay in the air? To make matters worse, that nonsense, the fishermen treating him like some carnival fortune-teller. Professor . . . what a stupid nickname for a kid." He grabbed his coat from a hook by the door and shrugged into it. "Yet you, you always knew what he was thinking. Heck, I never did. Made me crazy to even try."

Elle trembled beneath wool still holding Noah's body heat. "I, my, that . . ." She wanted to deny the notion, call it a whim, a flight of fancy, but she *had* always known. She threw out her hand, said, "That's over, Zach. He came along when I needed a protector, someone who didn't laugh at my accent and knock me into the dirt in the schoolyard. I guess I loved him for it. It was an immature infatuation, one I didn't manage well." She released a huff of air. "Clearly, I don't need a protector any longer. I'm not going to drink too much cider at the Spring Tide Festival and get sick on my shoes. Or tumble off slick roofs and break my arm. Noah doesn't have to save me from town bullies or carry me to the doctor anymore."

"You don't really believe—"

"Papa!"

A boy burst into the room, filthy coattail flapping past his waist, bootlaces tripping him up. Elle watched Rory fling his arms about his father's shoulders, snuggle his cheek in the folds of Zach's shirt. A swift jab of envy pierced her. If she shielded her sight for a moment, she could imagine he was *her* child, this lovely boy who shared an uncanny resemblance to his absent uncle. Only, she had loved his mother too much to do that. Hannah's smile, the dimple in her cheek, the shape of her nose, all lived in Rory's face. Her warm laughter rolled from his lips, her gentle touch from his fingers.

"Tomorra, Miss Ellie," Rory mumbled around a mouthful of chocolate filched from his father's pocket. Brown-tipped fingers tugged at her skirt.

"Tomorrow?"

"The beach. We're tooking the skiff to the beach."

She fluffed his hair, traced Hannah's dimple. He smelled lovely, like sweets, dirt, and little boy. "Taking. And, I promised, didn't I?" Over Rory's tousled head, she captured Zach's gaze. "Does Caleb know?"

Zach shifted from one foot to the other and popped two buttons loose at the neck of his shirt. Avoiding her question, he grabbed Rory's arm and hustled him through the doorway.

Elle just managed to pluck Zach's sleeve between her fingers. "You have to tell him. Everyone in town will know by tomorrow. The next day at best. And Caleb will be home by then."

"I know," Zach said, tugging his arm free.

"See ya, Miss Ellie," Rory called, racing down the jail's narrow walkway, trailing his father like a pup.

Elle sighed and sank onto a stiff wooden bench, the music of Pilot Isle wafting through the open door, the familiar sounds calming the dull ache inside her. Pounding waves and squawking gulls, the crunch of wagon wheels over crushed shell, ships' flags snapping in the wind. She accepted the meager solace, willing to accept anything but the sight of Noah's eyes, guarded and full of torment. A deep, enduring sadness armored by a wall of restraint.

In his trenchant gaze, she witnessed every misstep, every foible, every foolish poem wrapped around a rock and tossed through his bedroom window. If he cared to differentiate, and of course, he did not, Noah would find an independent woman, not a bothersome child. A competent teacher, an active member of a thriving community, a woman no longer infatuated with a young man who did not return her feelings. Although she liked to think she'd done it for herself, she had become the sensible person he had once encouraged her to be. The proper woman her father demanded. Years ago, she had relinquished her hopes of true love and an education, prudent enough to realize they weren't in the cards.

A gust of putrid air filled the room, signaling a receding tide on the marsh. She wondered if Noah smelled the scent and remembered what it meant. Elle's slick palms slid along her thighs. She gripped her knees and bowed her head. The man she'd encountered this afternoon was a stranger, yet she'd recognized him in a purely elemental way. Detected his wounds, as visible to her as hers were to him. She lifted her head, unconsciously bracing her spine.

She had nothing to fear; the silly child in need of a young boy's acceptance had died years ago. The mature woman who'd taken her place had enough good sense to stay out of trouble.

Only, her *good sense* had come at the price of her dreams.

Chapter Two

Walking along a narrow street, who, oh who, should I meet?
Noah turned his cheek into the hot sand, humming the ditty
he'd sung as a boy. The rush and swirl of the sea rolling in to
shore mingled with the lilting tune. A strange dream, he thought
drowsily, a stinging bead of sweat rolling into his eyes. He
blinked. Darkness. And heat. A film of vapor fogging his spectacle lenses. The warehouse in Chicago never got this warm.
Pushing to his elbows, he knocked his hat from his face.

"No bite yet."

Noah turned to find a young boy sitting beside him, legs
spread, trousers rolled to the knee, a fixed grip on *his* fishing
pole.

The boy gestured to the hat. "Your face looked kinda burnt."

"Burnt?" Noah mumbled, his mind clouded by sleep.

"You come to Devil Island to fish?"

"Um, well, I came out here to"—*hide*—"yes, fish."

The towheaded boy wiped his hand on his leg, fingers spreading across his thigh. "Name's Rory."

Noah stared at the small hand, the crescent-shaped fingernails
pink with good health. *Rory?* The mover of boxes into his

coach house Rory? Elle's fiancé? *Damn.* The kid looked about six years old, tops. Finally, he asked, "You didn't come here alone, did you?"

Rory laughed, the skinny end of the pole dipping toward the sand. "My pa'd likely skin me then." Jumping up, he dashed to the water's edge. "My friend brung me," he yelled and reared, pulling hard on the line. "Cain't swim near the dock in Pilot Isle, with the boats and all anchored about. Devil is the nearest beach." Racing back, the hook a bouncing flash of silver, the boy plopped to the sand at Noah's feet. "Got any more? I had a couple shrimp, but used 'em all." He waved the empty hook in the air, the bait long gone.

Noah passed Rory the bucket sitting behind him.

"Sand fleas? That all you got?" Rory's expression soured. "No wonder nothing bitin'." He shrugged, secured the pole between his knees, and easily baited the hook.

"Did you bring a pole?" Noah plucked his hat from the sand and adjusted the wrinkled brim.

"Nah. I'll just use yours."

Noah coughed behind his hand, not wanting to hurt the boy's feelings. He had not laughed in months. It felt good.

Rory squatted beside him, throwing curious glances at Noah's rucksack. Noah pulled it close, removed a short length of wire and a pair of tweezers. His hook had taken a beating at the boy's eager hands. "Where is this friend of yours?" he asked, curling the metal. A worthless chaperon, this friend.

"Oh, down the beach aways. She tried to do a somsault." He wiggled his tiny toes in the sand. "Pretty wet now."

Noah dipped his head, hiding a smile.

Rory tinkered with the pole, shifting side to side on his scrawny buttocks. "Are . . . are you my uncle Noah? The one I look like?"

Noah dropped the tweezers to the sand. He jerked his gaze to the boy's face and cataloged features as meticulously as he cataloged species of fish. Square jaw. Tousled gold curls.

Conceivably, the jaw could be . . . and the eyes. Gray, like all
the Garrett men. The hair, he wasn't sure who that came from.
But . . . *Noah, the boy had called him Noah.* He felt a sharp
prick and looked to find the wire embedded in his palm. He
winced, snatched it out, and thumbed the dribble of blood.

Rory poked his big toe in a ghost-crab hole, wormed it back
and forth. "I heard them talking once. Real loud. Mad. Uncle
Caleb said it was the same as walking 'cross a ghost, seeing
me." A shoulder jerk accompanied the confession. "Then I
heared my pa talking last night, about you sailing in on Mr.
Stymie's skiff. He reckoned you needed to rest your first night
home."

Noah reached for the small chin, tipped it high. Rory stared,
curious and hopeful. "Where did you hear this?" he asked,
his voice weaker than he would have liked.

"Wharped door at Widow Wynne's. Cain't shut it all the
way. You can listen lots if you're quiet about it. My pa, Zach,
says everything at Widow Wynne's is wharped or busted."

"Wharped . . ." Noah let his hand drop, unable to do the
same with his gaze.

"You a professor?"

Seagulls scurried past, searching for a piece of discarded
bait. Waves surged, nearly brushing their feet. Rising tide. Noah
recorded it in dazed silence as he watched the boy fidget and
squirm, a trickle of love seeping past his hardened heart.

"You a professor?" Rory repeated, tapping the corked end
of the pole against his hip.

Zach's son. Caleb's nephew. *His* nephew. He swallowed,
throat clicking. "That's a . . . a nickname someone gave me a
long time ago."

"Why?"

He shrugged. "I don't remember the exact reason. People
used to come by the house, the house where I lived with your
father and Caleb." Where Rory lived with Zach and Hannah?
"They asked me questions. Questions needing answers."

Rory jiggled the pole, the bent hook dancing a jig. "Where'd you find the answers?"

Noah grabbed the tweezers and made little roads in the sand between his feet. "Books, usually." What year was the cotton gin invented? Why don't the numbers in my ledger add up? Is this a King Mackerel or a Spanish Mackerel? How many miles is it to Raleigh? The questions had been as preposterous as the nickname. "They weren't hard to figure out."

"There's my friend," Rory said, pointing with the tip of the pole.

Noah shaded his eyes and watched as Elle swaggered over the packed sand, her barefoot stride sure and even. In no hurry to reach them, she stopped once to skip a rock, once to stoop for a shell. The same girl, obviously. Head chock-full of mischief and frivolity. She waved at Rory and turned slightly, her stride faltering, sputtering to a halt. Her hand dropped to her side. The other tensed around her basket handle.

She hadn't known he was there.

Noah felt a moment's wicked pleasure in the face of her discomfiture. Hell, she had delivered enough in her day. He had left the coach house before dawn to avoid her; her uncertainty made up for his lack of sleep.

With a resigned shrug, she swiped her curls from her face, smoothed her hand over her shirtwaist, and started forward. He couldn't help noticing how her dress clung in moist patches— a result of her poor gymnastic ability and her immodesty. Clung to her hips, the curve of her breast.

Look away, Noah.

He gave his spectacles a recalcitrant shove. No need to retreat. He didn't care how refreshingly undone she looked, how wet cotton clung enticingly to her curves. Her hair lifted in the breeze, and she captured it between her fingers. Even in Chicago, few women wore their hair that length, just below the ear. Noah preferred long hair.

When she got closer, he saw her skirt was tangled in her

free hand, gathered above any point of decency. Trim ankles. Narrow, fine-boned feet. Creamy skin, smooth knees, he noted before he forced his gaze away. The years had eased the dappled preponderance of freckles.

"Such a surprise," she said, and plunked her basket to the sand, scattering enough to fill a bucket.

Noah frowned and scooted as far as he could without actually moving to a different spot.

"Thank you, Rory, for leaving me wet and floundering."

Rory giggled. "I told ya not to do the somsault."

"Somersault. I agree. The first try was shoddy. Perfectly shoddy. Hence, I tried again, much to the delight of a group of fishermen sailing by."

Noah cut his eyes to her, his jaw dropping.

"Oh, Noah . . ." She wrapped her arms about her stomach and laughed. The only other word he understood was, he believed, "fussbucket."

Fussbucket? He moved to stand, sand squeaking beneath his heels.

She circled his wrist with a finger and a thumb, a gentle appeal. "Stay." She nodded to the basket, curls bouncing against her cheek, smile teasing her lips. "I've brought lunch. Enough for an army."

Yes, he could smell her lunch. He could smell *her*. Honeysuckle and a dash of something woodsy, like moist earth, thrown in. Still, even if she smelled ordinary—perhaps a shade better than ordinary—this woman was still harebrained Elle Beaumont. "I couldn't—"

"Yes, you could. You're too thin. You must be hungry."

Famished, in fact. A cold turkey sandwich in the train's shabby dining car had been his last meal. Still . . . His gaze sliced to her feet, pink toes digging in the sand. Skin as soft as it looked, he would bet. Scooting over another inch, he stared hard at a flock of sanderlings bustling around a beached jellyfish. "I don't—"

She shushed him, so he sat. Completely bewildered, while she chattered and shuffled, unpacking enough food for her army of three. Slices of ham, four chicken legs, a loaf of bread, a small round of cheese, three pickles, two apples, one orange, and a jar of lemonade. The necessities: tablecloth, napkins, forks, plates, cups. Once she'd placed the items in an admittedly handsome composition, she sat, skirt bunched beneath her.

She handed him a napkin. He folded it neatly in his lap, yielding to the surge of relief to see her limbs adequately covered.

"I've brought dessert," she added, tucking Rory's napkin into his rumpled collar.

All at once, the males leaned forward, peering into the basket. A feast, a *child's* feast, lay inside. A chocolate bar, a bag of vinegar taffy, and at least ten different penny candies, everything getting mushy in the sun. Rory released a delighted whoop, which Noah silently echoed. He tilted his head her way, feeling a small smile tug, wondering if she remembered his sweet tooth.

A green-eyed glance, an impish smirk. He didn't know what to make of the teasing look. He had never known what to make of Marielle-Claire Beaumont. He remembered mischief and shenanigans, pranks and rough horseplay, accidental touches and a fierce desire to protect. Helplessly, he glanced at her blotchy bodice, doing its best to dry under fixed sunlight and steady gusts of wind. Sinking his teeth into the chicken leg, he tore off a chunk and looked away.

Same old Professor, Elle noted with little surprise.

Deliberate chewing, measured swallows, a leisurely sip now and again, his napkin swabbing the corner of mouth every third mouthful. He ate like an aristocratic, long legs folded gracefully, hands propped on the edge of the blanket, not a smack or a slurp slipping past.

From the corner of her eye she watched him pluck two apples from the basket, flip one to Rory, who scrambled to catch it, hands cupped. Noah polished his on his creased trouser leg and took a neat bite. Rory mimicked, then attacked with enthusiasm. They shared a smile and a laugh, mouths full of apple bits.

Elle dabbed in the vinegar pooled beneath her pickle. It rattled her to see them together, looking like a matched set. Repeatedly, she turned to find Rory perched atop her kitchen table or squatting next to Widow Wynne's cat, and her vision would spot the hair, the eyes . . . suffering cats, the jaw. The square, handsome little face, the same stoic pout hardening the cheeks. She hated that look. Although she loved—*had* loved— both the faces.

In her youth, when one of Noah's dispassionate displays pushed her fury over the edge—had her fists readying to knock him off his polished boots—she would make the mistake of looking into his face, see a spark of loneliness, or merciful heavens, grief. Solidified her love like a clay pot in a kiln.

Jabbing her finger between her lips, she sucked the tip clean. The scent of wet wool wafted beneath her nose. Wool? Ah, Noah's sweater. She glanced at him, found him staring at her, a pale gray assessment. She popped her finger from her mouth, her pulse hammering. As Rory hummed an off-key tune, a joyful, abstracted chaperon, the world stilled. The sun beat down on their backs, the roar of the ocean a distant rumble. She wanted to know everything about him. Did he have a fiancée, *Juste Ciel,* a *wife?* She searched, trying to read him. She could do it, if he gave her enough time.

With a muttered oath, Noah bolted to his feet, scattering sand across her arm. "Rory, how about a walk?"

Rory jumped at the chance and raced toward the water; Noah followed, a stiff-shouldered stride.

Elle rose also, her heels sinking into the warm sand. Her skin burned from humiliation, not heat. What did he think she was going to do, bite him? Of course, he *had* witnessed her letting the reins of protocol loosen a bit. Devil Island provided the one place she felt free enough to allow that to happen. *And,* she'd been trying to trespass in his feelings. No matter, he was in for a blunt awakening. *Elle loves Noah* might be carved in every tree in the schoolyard, but that didn't make it an eternal decree. He perplexed her, that's all, and if her knees shook, the shock of seeing him after all these years made that happen. She stalked down the beach, determined to tell him what she thought of his haughty presumption. The nerve, the gall, oh what she wouldn't—

Skirting a piece of driftwood, she halted abruptly. Two sets of footprints mashed into the sand. She cut her eyes toward the water. Noah and Rory hunkered near the edge, heads nearly touching. Before she could change her mind, Elle settled her foot in the larger impression, heel over heel. An incredible sensation—partly a tickle at the back of her throat, partly a contraction in her stomach—hit her with the force of a tidal wave. She swallowed, heart thudding, heat racing up her leg.

The smooth tickle to the arch of her foot sent a memory roaring through her mind. Running barefoot along the acorn-studded cemetery path, yelping as a sharp stem pierced her skin. Noah had stopped and offered his lanky back. She'd accepted without thinking twice and let him piggyback her the rest of the way. Accidentally, of course, and for just a moment at most, his fingers had brushed her ankle, circling it and squeezing. He'd stopped and glanced over his shoulder, and something, something blustery as a summer thunderstorm, had passed between them. Something that made him avoid her for two weeks, two weeks of tears and tantrums because the day after the incident, she found him kissing Christabel Connery in the darkened coatroom at school.

Elle blinked and lurched forward. She halted just behind them. Windswept and sun-kissed, they created an enchanting picture.

Her hands itched to touch.

A warning sounded, deep in her mind. Gripping her damp

skirt in her fist, she leaned in, intent on telling Rory they had to leave. *Now.*

"There are two ways to determine its age," Noah said, flipping a bluefish in his hand. A ring-billed gull shrieked and danced nearby, begging for the pungent morsel.

"Deter?" Rory wiped a sandy fist beneath his nose.

"Oh. Tell. Two ways to *tell* its age."

"Is this one old? He's already dead."

"Well, growth rings on scales, or on otoliths, would tell us." He tapped Rory's ear. "Otoliths are bones in a fish's ear."

"Fishes have ears?"

"Of course." Noah's lips parted in a smile as he leaned closer. "Have you ever chopped down a tree and looked at the rings to tell the tree's age?"

Rory considered for a moment, nodded. "Yup, once with my uncle Caleb."

Noah stiffened, just the tiniest bit, but Elle saw it. "These . . . these are the same kind of rings." He drew a circle in the sand, then another around it. "Two circles. The fish would be two years old."

"How old is this one?"

Noah shrugged. "I'd need a microscope to tell."

"Micrascope? Do you have one?"

He nodded.

"Go get it," Rory said, and flipped his hand toward Noah's gear.

Laughter, deep and clear, rumbled from his throat; Noah bent from the force of it. "No, no. At the coach house. The rest of my equipment is being delivered tomorrow. Next time, maybe—"

Rory shook his head fiercely. "We gotta check this fish. I'm afraid he might be so young. A baby without a mother."

Elle held her breath. Noah arrested his movement to throw the bluefish into the sea. He brought his arm to his side, the stiff fishtail brushing his trousers. "No mother, huh?"

"Just like me."

Noah swallowed, working hard to recover from his shock. "I'm sure he's a rather old fish. A grandfather, at least, by the looks of him. I can take him home and check. If it will make you feel better."

"It will," Rory assured him, leaning close to his uncle.

They could have been father and son, two casts from the same mold. Elle sighed and pinched the bridge of her nose. Merciful heavens, how could Zach not realize her fascination with his son? Her body overheated, neutralizing the nip of cool water against her feet. Maybe he did realize after all.

They rose together, Noah's hand clasping his nephew's shoulder, Rory making no move to shrug it off. When they turned to find her directly behind them, Noah took a deliberate step back, Rory an excited step forward.

"Miss Ellie, we got a grandfather! I'll tell you how old tomorra." He waved the fish close enough for her to get a good whiff. She didn't know how old it was, but the putrid smell told her it had been dead a long time.

Pasting a smile on her face, she ruffled Rory's hair, trying to hide the distress Noah's simple rejection brought. "We'd better go. Your father will pitch a fit if we sail home in the dark."

Noah reclaimed the distance. "Do you want me to take him home?"

"I'm quite capable of getting a child home, Professor." She grabbed Rory's hand and tugged him behind her. Halting at the food-scattered tablecloth, she swiftly repacked the basket.

She heard him step behind her. "I only meant—"

"I know what you meant. I always know what you mean." Clutching the basket, grit biting into her palm, she shoved to her feet. Rory stood to the side, jabbing a broken conch shell in the sand. Curling her hands into fists, she welcomed the irrational surge of anger. It kept her from lifting a mutinous hand, brushing aside the strand of hair lashing Noah's cheek.

"You'd better go before it gets dark." He sighed and blinked eyes so pale the edges dissolved into white. His left eyelid drooped, resisting a return to its previous position.

A sick shot of remorse replaced her fury. Caleb's fist *had* done permanent damage. "Yes, I've—I've got to get back," she stammered, stepping forward. "Come on, Rory."

Rory waved, oblivious to the tension crowding the air. "The micrascrap, Uncle Noah. I'll come by tomorra."

Noah's shoulders slumped as he recorded their brisk departure through salt-crusted lenses. He felt tangled in knots, an absolute snarl. Looking at his nephew, he had experienced the first hint of love he had felt in ten years. And, dear God, what had happened to Hannah?

Of course, as always, Elle reappeared, rightfully, as if she owned him. He glanced down the endless stretch of ivory shore, bewildered and forlorn. Being back on this damned island, dense shrub thickets and oat-topped dunes, his childhood refuge. Kneading the ache in his neck, he retraced his path. *Footprints somewhere along here.* He stooped. The larger held another impression. Noah traced the toes, dabs in the sand the size of a dime, and circled the firm imprint of a heel.

He had looked back once—while squatting near the water's edge—and seen Elle placing her foot *in* something. At first, he'd guessed she pricked her sole on a pin shell. Then, the look on her face as she stared at the ground, frightened or confused, maybe even excited, cranked an idea through his mind. A fantastical idea. Impractical and silly. Perfectly, typically Elle Beaumont.

He outlined the mark of a feminine arch, drew his hand back when his fingers started to tingle.

Years ago, he had not been able to understand her fascination with him. Summer heat and winter frost, they were disparate beings. He'd loathed her heedless nature, her inattentive squirming, her frivolous chatter. Laughing during church service, talking during school lessons. Tardy for everything. Most of the time, looking like a tomcat had spit her from its mouth.

How had she found anything to admire in someone as dissimilar?

Their differences didn't mean he had ignored her. Elle made it impossible *not* to notice. Sneaking into his bedroom, stolen apples crammed under her skirt, telling dirty jokes while perched atop a shell slab in the burying ground, gawking at him so often that Christabel Connery carved *Elle loves Noah* into every blessed tree trunk in the schoolyard.

At twelve, her antics had embarrassed him. By sixteen, however, he had come full circle. Disconcerted in an adolescent way, yet speculating, for the first time. Why her eyes flashed in that impassioned way whenever she looked at him, what he had done to warrant it, and, if he remembered correctly, what he could *do* with it. After all, how many times had he seen her crawling out or dropping off? Landing at his feet or in his arms? Skirt billowed around her knees, a bare ankle, or bony shoulder flashing? A healthy young man could only take so much.

He tipped his head toward the sun, calculating. It sat low in the sky, a flaming ball coloring the water cherry. Still enough light to cross the pass, but he would check on Elle and Rory after he sailed in, just to make sure. Old habits died hard.

He glanced at the footprint again and nudged his spectacles. He would have expected this nonsense from the girl with apples stuffed under her skirt, the girl who had made sure Christabel's gibe would last by spending an entire summer scratching the marks in deeper. What did it mean coming from the woman who flaunted surprisingly generous curves, ruby curls and a plump bottom lip he could barely tear his gaze from? Noah dashed sand across the troublesome footprint and sank to his heels.

If Elle thought to tangle him in knots, he would show her he wasn't willing. He wasn't willing to let her read his blessed mind either, even if he believed her talent for it had faded long ago. He entertained women out of necessity. Institute dinners, charity events, and alleviation of his infrequent pangs of desire. He didn't have the former to contend with and could live without the latter for months yet. In fact, maybe he should tell Elle she didn't interest him. In the *slightest*.

Noah watched the sun slip low in the sky, his mood lifting. He always felt better with a plan in mind.

Elle rounded the corner of Widow Wynne's house, mumbling beneath her breath. A brisk breeze, close to cold, sliced through her thin coat but failed to cool her ire. What cheek! Questioning her ability to care for a six-year-old boy. Presumptuous, conceited . . . *man.* Noah Garrett could take his raised brows and his neat-as-a-pin clothing, his fish talk and his stiff backside, and—

"Marielle."

Elle pinched the bridge of her nose and halted in her tracks. Mercy above, would this day ever end? "Magnus."

He sat on the porch's brick steps, long legs encased in striped trousers, ones tailored during his bimonthly excursions to Raleigh. An imported cigar dangled from his lips, the stink recalling memories of their brief courtship. Favorable memories, most of them. Favorably dull. "You seemed to be in another world for a moment there, Marielle. A little flushed around the cheeks. Could that be ire on your lovely face? I don't believe I ever saw you thus, my dear."

She raked him with a caustic assessment she hoped would send him on his way. "What do you want, Magnus?"

He lifted a newspaper from his lap, offered it to her. "Just thought you might enjoy reading this. Tomorrow's edition of the *Weekly Messenger.* I stopped by the office to see if my advertisement had been placed. One I paid for last week, I might add. You understand how unreliable Jewel Quattlebaum can be. What do you know, not only had they placed it, they had reserved a copy for my files. I'm announcing my new location. You remember?''

She snatched the newspaper from his hand and clenched her teeth hard enough to crack a molar as Magnus tapped a manicured fingernail over the right column. Of course, she remembered. She had helped him select the plot of land.

''I think you'll find this of interest,'' he said, his voice wavering as it did when he tried to contain laughter.

Her lips moved as she read, a habit she had never been able to break. *Noah Garrett, brother of Zachariah and Caleb, sailed from Morehead City on the* Adele—

Elle crumpled the newspaper in her fist and raised her head slowly. ''Why are you bringing this to me? What could you possibly hope to gain? You humiliated me in front of the entire town, let everyone know you decided to end our engagement. What more do you want? You have your pride, your infernal medical practice, and whatever sum of money my father paid you to ask me in the first place. One of the few ill-judged investments I've ever known him to make, by the way.''

Magnus's gaze began to smolder, no longer shining civilly for the sake of propriety. ''You really are as unbalanced as some think if you believe the situation to be that simple. You made a fool of *me,* a circumstance I have trouble overlooking, my dear. Do you think anyone in this pitiful excuse of a town imagined you felt anything but relief after I failed to attend our engagement soirée?''

She slapped the newspaper against her thigh. ''A dinner party, Magnus. It was a simple dinner party.''

Standing, he flung his cigar into the blooming azalea bush at his side and descended the steps with a deliberate gait she could see contained a fair measure of anger. ''A particularly fierce look was on your face when you rounded the corner of the house, Marielle. Who were you thinking of? I never witnessed any emotion but that unfocused, albeit attractive, expression of boredom. Pity even. What could paint a rosy bloom on your cheeks? Or, should I say who?" He moved forward, his elbow nudging hers, much too close for comfort.

In her haste, she stumbled over the bricks lining the walkway, catching her balance at the last moment.

Taking advantage of her misstep, he grasped her chin between baby-smooth fingers, forcing her eyes to his. "You must be happier than you've ever been in your life. Noah Garrett back in town, and this time, you're old enough to consummate your love for him. I applaud your efforts to keep yourself ready and available. I hear he's living in the widow's coach house. How convenient."

Her palm cracked his cheek with enough might to send him staggering. *"Get out."*

"Now, my dear—"

"You heard her, Leland. Get out. Before I allow myself to get angry."

Magnus's hand paused halfway to his cheek. He swiveled on a rounded heel, his bark of laugher splitting the air. "My word, Garrett, how *do* you do it? Better yet, how has our little Marielle survived without you for, what has it been, nine years?"

Noah had Magnus by the collar of his studded shirt before Elle could draw a breath. "I'm accosted often on the streets of Chicago, Leland. Trust me, you don't want to know what I've had to learn to protect myself."

Magnus's lower lip quivered, and he sucked it between his teeth. He craned his head, struggling to look his opponent in the eye.

"Watch yourself, Leland." Noah clenched his hand, muscles bunching, lithe forearms at odds with his orderly cuffs.

"You'd better take that advice as well, my friend," Magnus snarled, and shoved Noah's arm aside, storming from the yard without another glance.

Noah watched him go, then stalked in the other direction. Elle heard him muttering beneath his breath.

She snatched his rucksack from the edge of the walkway and ran after him. She had never seen Noah this angry, not even after Caleb busted his eyelid wide open. She had never seen him use his hands for anything violent, either, unless you counted the lists he had made for Caleb detailing ways to solve problems *without* using fists. "I have no idea what bramble is stuck in Magus's paw," she panted, struggling to hoist the rucksack over her shoulder.

He shot her a furious side glance, his eyes doing a slow burn. "No idea? Jesus, how blind can you be? *You're* the bramble." Grabbing the rucksack from her, he climbed the coach house staircase. "You're everyone's bramble."

"Me? Of course, yes, well, it seemed that way this time, didn't it? But, it's been months. Magnus and I broke off our"— she lifted her skirt above her ankles and scrambled after him— "our engagement months ago. Besides, why should he be mad? He made it very public that the decision was his, and his alone. Embarrassingly public." Noah stopped abruptly, her head thumping him right between the shoulder blades, the newspaper she had forgotten she held fluttering to the step.

He stooped, smoothed the newsprint against his knee, his head moving side to side as he read. "Were you sorry?" he asked, his gaze lifting.

"Was I sorry about what?"

He adjusted his silver-rimmed spectacles. Behind glass, she could see his eyes had cooled. "Sorry Leland ended the engagement."

Tell him yes. Let him think you love the man. What better way to show him you haven't been pining after him for ten years? Because you haven't. "I was ... terribly distraught. Nearly broke my heart. I looked so forward to being Mrs. Magnus Leland." Her voice cracked hard.

The muscles in his shoulders tensed; he shoved to his feet.

"You're a terrible liar, Elle. Truly dreadful. Scares me to think you would waste a chance at marriage because of that silly"— he nudged the door open with his elbow and ducked through the entrance—"*infatuation* when we were children."

She slapped the door wide when he would have shut it in her face. "Why you arrogant, boorish—" Her words caught in her throat. Stacks of books covered every surface. The chipped desk, the leather chair and ottoman, the faded settee that had once been dark magenta.

Cautiously, she strolled to the desk. She hadn't seen this many books since the long nights spent in the university library. Rows and rows of chestnut shelves, covert laughter, and the smell of dust. The thrill of learning, of taking control of her life for the first time, sadly, the only time. Burying the burst of longing, she hefted a leather-bound volume as thick as her wrist. *"Depths of the Sea,"* she read and fingered the gold tassel marking page eighty-one. "It's magnificent, Noah." She turned the page slowly. "You know, I had an interest in biology once, but that, well, that was a long time ago." She shook her head, denying the impulse to tell him about her past. Why would Noah care about her dream of finishing university?

"They're books for the laboratory, mostly. The others are for research." Elle felt the heat of his body before she smelled him. A rush of warmth, then the tantalizing scent of sea and man. His arm circled her waist, and he lifted the book from her hand. Brushing his finger across the mark Magnus's cheek had left on her palm, her fingers curled, her body swayed into the desk's jutting edge. "This will bruise, more than likely," he said, his hot breath dusting her cheek.

"It was worth it." She stared at his slim, supple fingers, the nails finely trimmed, the pads slightly callused. She had once pictured them exploring her skin. Troubled, she tossed a careless smile over her shoulder, one she hoped would conceal her trepidation.

Noah blinked, his gaze lowering. To her lips, she guessed,

from the way they started tingling. She licked them nervously, deciding the insincere smile had been a bad idea after all.

Cursing softly, he stepped away. When Elle recovered enough to face him, he had his back to her, palms braced on the frame of the only window in the room. The reddish glow of early evening spilled in, kicking glints of gold in the hair curling over his stiff collar. "What Leland said, about you, about me . . . he was wrong, wasn't he?"

"Oh, that"—Elle rolled her fingers into a fist to stop their trembling—"of course he was. Magnus was always a tad jealous of . . . it's just, he remembered lots of things that happened . . . before. Nothing worth mentioning, things I'm sure you've forgotten by now. You're not the only one to light a fire beneath him. He hated Caleb, too. The proposal business rankled."

Noah slanted his head, a startled part to his lips. *"Caleb?"*

"He proposed at the Spring Tide Festival, four years after you left. He'd been drinking, and when I refused his offer, he bent down on one knee, stumbled into the tent pole, and knocked the fiddler from his perch. Into another tent pole. A crucial tent pole, evidently. The entire length of canvas collapsed on top of us. Christabel took him home that night, something she's been doing ever since, I think."

"Why in the hell did he ask *you,* then?"

Her teeth clicked together. "Get that dazed look off your face, Professor. I've had a number of eligible suitors."

"Yes, I got a firsthand look at one of them today. In hindsight, maybe you should have accepted Caleb."

She swiped a lock of hair from her eyes, wishing for the hundredth time it did not look so bright against her skin. "Caleb never loved me like he loved Christa. He felt an obligation, struggled to be everything to everybody after you left. Instead of being my friend, he wanted to act as my protector. And a woman's protector, at least in his mind, is her husband. You may not want to hear this, but your leaving and us hearing no word from you just about killed him. He was lost. Completely and utterly lost. When he found himself, he had changed from a caterpillar to a butterfly. He grew into a man, a good man, but not the same man.''

His hands dived into his pockets. "Caleb wasn't the only lost soul.''

She closed the distance between them, drawn by his bitter mien. "I always wondered what leaving here, frightened and alone, would do to you. If it would change you against your will, into someone I wouldn't recognize at all.''

"Didn't we establish in that damned attic that none of you knew me? Hell, I didn't even know myself.'' He laughed, but it sounded raw and reluctant. "So, am I still recognizable?''

Elle suspected he did not want to be. He believed change would shield him from his family, from the horrors of his past. But she would not lie. He had to face them, his fears and his family, sooner than he liked. "Yes, I recognize you, because I knew him. Deep down, I *feel* him. I see him. In gestures you make, he comes back to me. Bits and pieces I had forgotten. The curve of your hand when you adjust your spectacles, even the absurdly neat way you roll your sleeves.'' Against her better judgment, she added, "What you did today, sending Magnus away, he would have done that.''

He jerked his head, the light profiling his shuttered gaze. "I lived on the streets for months after leaving here. While struggling to survive, I learned to smell a person's fear, recognize their anger before they turned it on me. I learned the hard way, each bruise a tough lesson I could not afford to ignore. When I rounded the corner of the house''—his shoulders stiffened beneath crisp cotton—"I reacted purely on instinct. Nothing solicitous or benevolent in the gesture, I can assure you. Don't take it for something it's not.''

Her hand lifted, but he flinched before she'd even decided if she would touch him. "Would it be so terrible to find he's still in there? The boy who loved his brothers? The boy who trusted me?''

"He's dead and gone, Elle. These days, I'm the only one I trust. And that's the way it's going to remain."

She tilted her head, her neck aching from the unnatural angle. Behind glass, Noah blinked, eyes narrowing as he watched her watch him. She swayed closer. Ivory flecks swimming in silver. Long, flaxen lashes. Absurdly long. A face fit for an angel.

"Marielle-Claire!"

They leaned at the same moment, banging heads.

A hiss of breath slipped past Elle's lips, and she rubbed her brow. Her father stood in the yard below, hand shading his face as he stared at the upper porch of Widow Wynne's house.

"*Juste Ciel!*" Elle dug in the pocket of her skirt. "Six-thirty," she said, and glanced from her watch to her clothing. Dirt-streaked shirtwaist. Cuffs and collar missing, wadded in her bicycle basket. No belt. Hem dangling in two places. "He'll kill me. Alone in a man's apartment, late for our weekly dinner appointment, and dressed inappropriately. He will simply kill me."

Noah spared her a glance, rolled his eyes to see her smoothing the strawberry mess on her head, licking and slicking the curls springing around her cheeks. "It's no good. You still look like you rolled from bed and sprinted down the street without passing a mirror."

She paused, expression frosting by the second. "Thanks. Thanks a lot." Turning, she crossed to the door, a swift, feline stride calling to mind a panther he had seen in a market in Algiers.

Halting at the door, she squeezed the beveled knob until her knuckles paled and made another pathetic attempt to straighten her clothing—and the damned urge to protect her hit him hard.

"Wait." *Ah, Garrett.* Well, blessit, he never had liked her father.

She glanced over her shoulder, a timid smile tweaking her lips.

"I'll help you this time. But this is it. I promise you, this is it."

Her eyes flashed. "Fine. This is it. What do you think I want from you, anyway?" Her patience drained away like water from a leaky bucket. "Let's get this out in the open. I was infatuated, once, a long time ago. Time to move on, Professor. I've refused marriage, according to my father, the grand opportunity to improve my life. And I don't see any good prospects looming on the horizon. Not to break your heart or anything"— she angled her chin, trained her stunningly green gaze right on him—"but that hasn't changed since you arrived on Pilot Isle."

He felt an odd tightness in his chest, although her pledge was exactly what he wanted to hear. "Good. We understand each other." He lifted his hand, staying her impatient jiggling of the door handle and the anxious glances shot through the quarter inch crack in the wood. "I'll do this, on one condition."

"Condition?" Her brow scrunched, her canvas boot tapping double time.

"No more 'Professor' nonsense. Never again from those lovely lips of yours."

Elle raised her hand to her mouth, smoothed her finger over her top lip. "Of course." She shrugged weakly.

Puzzled by what he'd just uttered, he dropped to his haunches and flipped through a pile of books. He motioned her behind the door as he approached, a burgundy volume in his hand. "Wait until I have your father's full attention, where you can see our backs are turned. A minute or two is all it should take. Then run. Don't think, run." He stepped outside, then leaned back in. "Let me amend that. Think. *Please.* Don't trip crossing the yard or tumble down the staircase and break your leg. Only one doctor in town, I'll wager, and he's someone we want to avoid just now."

Elle glared and kicked the door shut, propelling him onto the small landing. "Fine show of gratitude," he muttered, and yanked his cuffs.

Closing in on Henri Beaumont, Noah reminded himself that Pilot Isle differed greatly from Chicago. No tangle of streets to get lost in, no mad rush of people scurrying along icy sidewalks, too busy to bother with the person scurrying past. He had to get used to being part of a community, tipping his hat and making eye contact, engaging the fishermen he had come to soothe in discussions about the weather or the latest catch. Inane, completely harmless topics. He could do that. He hadn't had much practice in years, but he could do it.

Hell, might as well practice his rusty skills on Henri Beaumont.

Chapter Three

Elle had to struggle to contain the fury she wanted to release in a thunderous, unladylike bellow.

"I must admit, Marielle-Claire, I imagined living in that old woman's home would last one month, perhaps two. The stink of putrefied velvet would have sent me fleeing the first night. Except, my, I tend to forget you are more Felice's daughter than my own. Just like her, stubborn, impulsive, foolish." Henri Beaumont brought his napkin to his lips and belched behind it, the indelicate sound nearly covered by the clink of silver in Christabel's crowded dining room.

Elle slammed her fork to the edge of her plate, swallowed grilled fish, and tasted sawdust. "I'm perfectly happy living with Widow Wynne, Papa. Her needs are simple, and she pays me well enough to attend to them. Anyway, she isn't returning until the middle of May. How difficult a position can it be?"

"A house servant? Is this to be your station in life? Is this how you choose to repay me for a fine education? A superior upbringing?"

"For the year of university you allowed me to complete, I'm able to teach. That's how I repay myself *and* my students.

Washing garments and polishing flatware once a week doesn't alter my being, only my station. I suppose you could say I'm a teacher who washes and polishes.''

He slipped a finger inside the pocket of his double-breasted waistcoat. "Teacher. House servant. Immaterial designations. At twenty-five years old, a wife is what you should be. A mother.'' Tucking a cigar between his teeth, he bit off the end, leaned close to the candle flame, and sucked hard. Lips clenched to hold it in place, he muttered, "Such a simple choice, Marielle-Claire. Marry and I will release your funds. If your husband permits, you can build a new school, buy a decent building. No more lessons on rotting floors of a rank coach house. Teach every woman in this town how to scribble figures in a bookkeeper's journal if this is what you think you must do to make yourself happy. There's money enough for that *and* new clothing.'' He blew a wisp of smoke into the air. "By the bye, the dress you are wearing is pathetically dated.''

Elle flattened her hand over her bodice, her gaze following the movement. A simple tea gown, once a glorious shade of green. She had spent a week bordering the lawn collar with lace and thought it looked rather good for an accessory costing less than ten pennies.

"Marielle-Claire, are you listening?''

Reaching for her wineglass, Elle drained it in one swallow. Her father kept a bottle of Bordeaux in the storeroom of Christabel's restaurant and insisted on drinking it from his own crystal.

"Daughter, are you *listening?*''

"You cannot force me,'' she said, a kaleidoscope of color glittering across the tablecloth as she lowered the beveled glass.

"Force you? *Grands Dieux!* If I could have forced you, I would have. Long ago.''

She let her lids drift, smelled smoke, fish, and Macassar oil. Strong enough to make her think every male head in the room was heavily slicked.

"You let Dr. Leland slip through your fingers, Marielle-Claire. Absurd, especially for a man, but I believe he wanted your love. Would not have *you* unless he had *it*, which, of course, he did not." Henri's lips parted on a sigh, a puff of gray drifting forth. "Let there be only honesty between family. Your love is not available, now is it?"

She blinked and coughed, her eyes stinging. "Available? I've never loved a man enough to get married, if that's what you mean."

He flicked his hand in the air, ignored the ashes drifting to the floor. "Why do you have this antiquated ideal stuck in you mind? Forget about a marriage based on love. I didn't love your mother. And she did not love me. We had a sensible relationship, a solid partnership. Love would have thrown a kink in a well-oiled piece of machinery," he said, candlelight revealing flaring nostrils and plump cheeks. Except for a hint of plumpness in her own cheeks, she and her father shared little. "If your mother had not been dead all these years, I would curse her for putting such nonsense in your head."

Elle dug her heels into the pine planks beneath her feet and prayed to God she could hold her tongue. She counted to ten, then whispered, *"Grandmère* Dupré filled my head with nonsense, if you must know."

"Ah . . . cela n'a rien d'etonnant." Henri stabbed his cigar in the clump of creamed spinach on his plate, lips curling back from his teeth. "Not a surprise, to translate for you since your French is much like a child's. This news makes me regret, not for the first time, sending Marie our address after we moved to America. Is this what she wrote about in those cumbersome letters she sent every month? Cautioned you to marry for love? As she did, but, alas, as her beloved daughter did not? Imbecilic drivel from an old woman."

Elle swallowed her ire, wishing for another glass of wine to soften her father's cruel counsel. "Marie Dupré bore seven children with a man she cherished more than life. She believed in the power of love and urged me to hold on to it if I found it, no matter the cost." Of course, years ago, not long before Marie's death, Elle had made the mistake of writing to her about Noah. Every cumbersome letter from then on had mentioned his name, asking if he had returned to Pilot Isle. As if she somehow knew he would. As if it mattered.

"Don't look at me with blatant hostility on your face. You are my only child, a beautiful woman, and I love you. However, you tend to dream far too much, Marielle-Claire. Life is for those who grasp it in both hands." He made a fist. "Who *do*, not who dream. Sad but true, but you need a man to grasp life for you. You cannot do it alone. It's impossible. I made a mistake allowing you unlimited freedom. University, the disruptive group of women who encouraged you to attend those ridiculous rallies. The trouble you got into was easy enough to rectify. After I assured them you were going home, the officers released you without complaint. But the ideas, they remain a wall around you. *Grands Dieux!* Ideas of independence and feminine freedom, as if there were such a thing." He rolled the rim of his glass along his bottom lip, took a measuring sip. "Caleb would have put up with your nonsense. After all, he continues to."

"He's in love with Christabel. A tad late, I'm afraid." Elle smothered a yawn; she had heard these complaints many times.

"Well, well. Gossip travels, does it?" Henri shifted, his bulging stomach slapping the edge of the table.

Elle's shoulders lifted beneath her faded dress. She felt calm, overly calm. She wondered if she could blame her father's Bordeaux.

"Christabel Connery is nothing for you to worry about. I could talk to Caleb, if you wish. If you changed your mind, I could be persuaded to change his."

Elle gazed through flickering candlelight—across an incongruous setting of chipped porcelain and gleaming crystal—into a stranger's eyes. At times like these, her mother's comforting smile returned, and Elle felt pain greater than any she could imagine. If only . . . *oh, damn and blast with if only*. "Papa, I don't care about Caleb and Christabel. I don't care about Magnus and Anna Plowman. That's the problem, *don't* you see? If I married a man, shouldn't I care if he loves another woman?"

Henri reared, his thumbs snaking beneath the braided edge of his waistcoat. "I imagine you would care if it was young Noah. He asked me to translate a science text this afternoon. Mentioned he's living in the widow's vacant dwelling. How opportune."

She slid her glass in a slow circle on the table. Would she care if Noah loved another woman? Kissed another woman? The naive young girl would have cared plenty and gone after them, claws sharpened. Elle rubbed her hand across her stomach, the sudden ache warning her the young girl still resided inside her. *No.* A woman could not possibly experience the unconditional love of a child. And, it had been unconditional from the first moment. She could still see Noah shoving Daniel Connery from her path and turning to escort her inside the schoolhouse. Her mind had not understood every word spoken that day, but her heart had.

Her father's fist cracked down, upsetting a tin saltshaker and her wineglass. "Marielle-Claire, you must get that boy out of your mind. I would be happy to hand you over to him, believe me, but be reasonable. He does not want you. He never has."

Elle righted her glass and reached for the bottle. "Our relationship does not include sharing my mind, Papa. What's there is mine and mine alone." Commending herself for pouring with a steady hand, she took a long sip before she looked into eyes that scaled and stored. Exposed, she buried her anguish deep.

Henri leaned forward, wadding stained cloth beneath each elbow. "Forget him, daughter. Right now, right this *minute*. You made a perfect ninny of yourself, but you were a child, and people will excuse a child's impropriety. They will not excuse a woman's.''

Anger bloomed hot and fast in her cheeks.

"I can see by your intractable expression I will have to unveil harsh truths to make you understand your position. A scented letter was waiting for young Noah at the post office this morning. From a Mrs. Bartram. Caroline, I believe. Return address somewhere in Chicago. Unfortunately, he retrieved it before I had a chance to intercept. Written proof would work wonders in convincing you.''

"That's despicable," she gasped.

"Is it?'' His shoulders lifted in a careless shrug. "Dear girl, I no longer presume where you're concerned. I learned that lesson long ago.''

"I no longer presume where you're concerned either, Papa. Those lessons blistered.''

He vaulted to his feet, his chair skidding back. "Daughter, you set yourself on a perilous course. '' He stuffed his crystal wineglasses in his coat pocket. "A direly perilous course.''

Knowing it would fuel his ire as mere words could not, Elle flicked her fingers in a dismissive gesture. It worked, she thought, watching him storm from the restaurant, cursing the tables crowding his path, cursing his daughter, cursing America.

"Whew . . . that was a good one.''

Elle propped her chin in her palm, watched Christabel Connery sweep her maroon skirt to the side and plant her ample bottom in the chair her father had vacated.

"Some quick-tempered male, I tell you.''

"At least he didn't break any crystal this time,'' Elle said.

Christabel pulled a dented cup from her apron pocket, emptied the rest of the wine in it. "Oh, he's just getting sick of ordering those fancy glasses every month. Sees it's cheaper to flounce outta here spitting curses rather than throwing things. For the love of Pete, at least that's free.'' She swished wine from cheek to cheek and swallowed. "Have a fit if he saw me drinking his premium hooch from a tin cup, wouldn't he?"

Elle laughed, or tried to, and dipped her head low. Her father's tantrum hadn't left the sick feeling in her stomach. Oh, no, what he'd told her about Noah's love letter had done that.

"That bad, huh?"

Startled, she glanced up, taking note of the compassion in her friend's dark brown eyes. Not able to stand anyone's sympathy just then, Elle dropped her gaze to the tangle of blond hair trailing past Christa's shoulder, frayed ends jutting from her round breast. Her father called Christabel a floozy. Elle called her a friend. Just another disagreement on a long list of disagreements. "He's never going to sign my money over to me, Christa. Never. He has no right to do this. My mother planned to give it to me for my education. She and Papa talked about it before she died. He promised her, promised me. And now, it's been so long. I'm too old to return to university."

"Honey, it seems he has every right, fair or no. Didn't your momma leave anything in writing? Anything at all? I don't know much legal, but I do know you have to get it in writing."

Elle shook her head. Her mother's death had been sudden, three weeks after the headaches and dizziness started. There had not been time to sign papers and legalize things her mother had never dreamed would have to be legalized.

"Maybe you should marry—"

Elle's hand shot on, coming close to knocking the bottle to the floor. "Please, don't say it, Christa. Please, anyone but you."

"Honey, what are you gonna' do? Your school ain't a money-making business. Not enough, anyway. And what if Widow Wynne, bless her heart, passes on? You could open a shop, a millinery or something, like Carol Hudley. Except you can't sew worth a lick. And your cooking ain't good enough for even *me* to hire you." Christabel raised the cup to her lips, her words a hollow echo inside it. "You could still go back to Magnus."

Elle slammed her elbows to the table. "You must be joking."

Christabel lowered the cup, revealing flushed cheeks and a half grimace.

"Mercy above, you're embarrassed to even suggest it. How could you think ..." The words turned to a growl low in her throat.

"He still loves you, Ellie. Anna Plowman is a blind fool, I guess, not to see. You could lie, tell him you love him and didn't realize it before. He'd jump like you lit a firecracker under his tail end."

"I won't do it. Something deep inside tells me not to do it."

A dreamy smile rounded Christabel's lips, and she took a lazy sip.

Elle leaned in, and whispered, "Get that look off your face. It's not going to happen." She looked over her shoulder, but no one appeared to be listening.

"Like your granny always foretold. Past time, if you ask me."

"Yeah, yeah, so Noah's returned. Fat lot of good it will do me. My father just told me a woman is writing him from Chicago. Scented letters, of all things."

"Chicago's a long way, honey. Miles and miles. She's there, and you're here. Seems you have the advantage. Not so hard to make him fall in love with you if you put your mind to it."

A ragged laugh burst from her lips before she could stop it. "Noah Garrett, in love with me? Rich, Christa, really rich."

"Listen, from one woman who loves a Garrett to another who loves a Garrett but won't admit she does, it ain't that hard. You just got to make 'em see what's already there, honey. Caleb never knew what hit him. Plain as the writing on a chalkboard most times. Men are just too stupid to read it."

Elle shoved a spiral of hair behind her ear, wondering why her chignons never held for more than an hour. "Let me say this once, so I don't have to repeat it. I will never make a fool of myself over him again. I loved him, yes, I admit it. *Loved.* A young girl's infatuation that's a faded memory now." She plucked at her bodice. "As pathetically faded as this dress. Can't you and the people in this town understand? I avoided the post office this morning, because everyone is watching me, expecting me to swoop down, snatch Noah between my teeth, and fly off with him. It's ridiculous."

"Can you say you wouldn't enjoy flying off with him in your jaws? Can you *really?*"

Elle dropped her head to her hands and groaned. "Oh, Christa."

"I say you can't, 'cause I saw him today, walking back from the docks. He didn't recognize me or didn't see me one. Still the same ole Professor, absorbed in his thoughts. When I saw him, I darn near dropped my sack of potatoes. He grew up mighty fine." Christabel clinked the cup against her teeth. "Taller than any man on the street, a head fulla hair the color of good scotch whiskey. Fancy fishing pole thrown over a broad shoulder. Picture spindly Noah Garrett having broad shoulders? Not broad as Caleb's, mind you, but a surprise considering what a scrawny scrap of a boy he was."

"He was never scrawny."

Christabel threw back her head and laughed, bosom jiggling beneath twisted apron straps.

"Stop it," Elle whispered. "Do you want the whole town to know what we're talking about? Heaven, that's all I need."

Christabel pressed her hand to her mouth, her head bobbing. "Sorry, sorry."

"I can handle this, I'm telling you. I can handle *him.* Don't go making a scene about it."

"Uh-huh. Did you see the clothes he wore? Slicked sharp as Sunday, neat as a pin. You always liked him spot-shined, didn't you?"

Elle pinched the bridge of her nose, a nagging headache

creeping up on her. "Sure, I loved feeling fit for the rag box compared to him."

"Rag box? Naw, just a handful of trouble every now and then. Still are, I guess. But a man forgets all his arguments real quick when he looks into a face pretty as yours. Rag box? That's a new one." She gazed into her empty cup, her voice gone soft. "Ellie, you and Noah were the sweetest things I ever saw."

"*Sweet?*"

"Oh, he acted like you rubbed him the wrong way, or acted like you didn't rub him at all, most times. Maybe he wasn't acting, but once or twice, not long before he left, I know I caught him looking at you, a spark of interest showing." Christabel dabbed the frayed edge of her apron against her lips. "You see, honey, I recognize the spark of interest in the Garrett grays."

"Good for you. Good for Caleb. Just leave me, leave Noah, out of your spark-of-interest, Garrett-gray theory."

Christabel shook her head and sighed theatrically. "Sure a shame. Imagine the children you two would have had. Smart as whips with a dash of spunk thrown in."

Elle's stomach twisted. Would they have had green eyes or gray? Hair the color of a burst of sunlight or dull, stringy red? Elle lifted her head, discovered a shrewd smile crossing her friend's face. "Damn and blast," she muttered, and wrenched to her feet.

"Wait, honey, your daddy left this," Christabel said.

She grabbed Noah's textbook and skirted the crowded tables, ignoring the amused glances burning into her back, the whispered comments filling her ears.

All the way home, the book pressed to her bosom, Elle wondered how many people believed she still loved Noah Garrett.

* * *

She gave the dangling front doorknob a gentle twist, fearing it would fall off and roll into the tangle of shrubs surrounding the porch. Another chore to add to an unbearably long list. Tossing her shawl and gloves on the hall-tree shelf, she eased the door shut with the heel of her boot and made her way along the darkened hallway.

Sliding the pocket door aside, Elle twisted the gasolier switch, murky light flooding the parlor. Sinking to the edge of the tattered love seat, Elle turned her attention to the leather-bound volume in her hands, a flattened cigar ring jutting from the pages. She read enough to see the red-and-gold slip marked an essay about coral erosion. Unfortunately, she could not read it well. As her father had bluntly pointed out, her French equaled a child's.

Remarkably devious way of diverting her father's attention, especially for a boy who had once dragged her into the mercantile and made her apologize for stealing apples.

Propping her feet on a tasseled ottoman, Elle hoisted the book against her ribs. She flicked her finger over the dog-eared page, the scribbled notes in the margin. Noah had always managed to age a book quickly.

An hour later, the case clock chimed; the book thumped to the floor. She reached for it, then sighed in dejection. Noah's accomplishments were buried in the index at the rear: doctoral research, expeditions in the Pacific. He had even lived up to his childhood nickname. Heavens, she had eaten lunch with a professor with her skirt hiked around her knees.

She kicked the book, then curled her toes in pain. She hated this feeling of . . . inferiority, of envy. If she had finished university, maybe she could converse about science or literature, history or mathematics. A semester of domestic economy wasn't likely to help her there.

Elle let her gaze stray to the pilot coat hanging over the arm
of the love seat, drew her hand back before her fingers brushed
the sleeve. She and Noah did not have one interest in common
except a thirst for knowledge, something he did not even recognize.

She wasn't sure who he was anymore. The person in the
book, the biologist who had traveled the world and written
research papers, the man who received perfumed letters from
a married woman and stood so tall he had to duck through
doorways . . . She didn't know him.

She didn't think she would ever know him again.

Noah felt the stare burning into his back a full minute before
he turned. Shading his face, he squinted into the sun, seeing
only the darkened silhouette of a woman. A jolt of undesired
anticipation tore through him, then trickled away when he
caught the scent.

Fruity. Banana? Somehow, he knew Elle Beaumont would
never smell like banana. An angry sea or a fistful of dirt, maybe,
but never banana.

The silhouette hopped up a step, going from sunlight to
shade. Flashing blue eyes tipped at the corner. Hollow cheeks,
full lips. Young and blond, very blond. Noah shrugged away
his discomfort.

She took another step, her pleated skirt brushing his trouser
leg. "Hello," she said in a laughing, breathless rush.

"Hello." He caught the nail that dropped from his lips. "Can
I help you with something?" He perched his hip on the railing,
which wobbled precariously. Another addition to his repair list.

"No." The young woman bounced on her toes, buckling
her boots where the patent leather cap cut in. "My name's
Meredith. I'm waiting"—she giggled and glanced over her
shoulder—"for Miss Ellie to finish her other lesson. I come
twice a week from three to four. She's teaching me to do my

daddy's accounts. He owns the mercantile. I wasn't too good in school. Numbers and all, I mean. But Miss Ellie says I can do anything if I set my mind to it. Even add my daddy's accounts and not tangle them up worse than two tomcats in a feed sack. My daddy would rather have a son do it, if he had one. But he doesn't, so he's stuck. With me, and with Miss Ellie, who he thinks is tetched.'' She emphasized this by drawing a circle around her ear. "But it's only 'cause she's smarter than he is.''

Noah swung his gaze toward the coach house. The metallic ping of a typewriting machine had woken him from restless slumber, dreams idling just below the surface. Zach and Caleb . . . and Elle, circling a campfire on Devil Island, youthful faces glowing in the amber light.

"I remember you," Meredith cut in, before he had time to refocus on her face.

He glanced back slowly, raised a brow as he tugged his leather glove off with his teeth.

"You used to stop in my daddy's store when I was real little. Bought a lot of cotton handkerchiefs, for ship's sails you told me. Your brother Caleb even let me see the models one time, in his shed out behind your momma's house.''

Noah loosened his fist, dabbed the fleck of blood where the nail had pieced his palm. Not much of a shed, more of an enlarged privy. He'd spent many hours in that dusty old shack, watching Caleb work his magic on piece after piece of wood, threading sail for his favorite model, the American block sloop. The old shed stood less than a mile from here, if he wanted to see it. He frowned and shoved the notion of returning from his mind. Caleb had likely smashed it to bits—along with his block sloop.

"Your name's Noah, right?''

Tilting his head, he found Meredith watching him, marked defiance clear on her face. "Yes, that's right,'' he said, and tugged the other glove free, a trace of unease at her predatory look mounting.

"The Spring Tide Festival is in two weeks." She flashed a crook-toothed smile, the first imperfection he had witnessed. "I didn't know if anyone told you about it. Who you might be squiring."

Squiring?

Meredith bounced and giggled. He almost reached out, fearing she would topple down the staircase. "The committee decorates a stretch of beach on Devil. A big tent, lots of pretty ribbons and white clematis, daisies and carnations if they bloom early. Old-time oil lanterns. Sailboat races during the day. Music and dancing at night. It's wonderful." She twisted her hands together and released a dreamy sigh.

Oh, yes, he remembered running after Caleb and Elle, struggling to divert some catastrophe. Pocketing the nail, he offered a tight smile. "I have a lot of work—"

"Work?"

"The fisheries laboratory. Out on the point."

"Oh." She slumped, heels slapping hard.

Across the way, the door to Elle's *school* opened, and a young woman stepped outside, glanced their way. No sign of Elle, and it looked like Meredith would soon be on her way. Shrugging a bead of sweat down his neck, Noah barely harnessed a sigh of relief.

Meredith cupped her hand around her mouth, and whispered loudly, "I have to go. Miss Ellie is a stickler for punctuation."

Noah laughed; he couldn't help it. "I'm sure she is."

"Bye, Noah. Maybe I'll see ya later." Lifting her skirt, she danced down the stairs, a wad of peach cloth clamped in each fist. "Maybe even at the festival," she added, tossing a bold look at him.

He followed her through overgrown grass, all the while marveling at the peculiarity, the sheer fickleness, of women. With his toe, he located the nail Elle had snagged her skirt on yesterday. Lifting the hammer, he pounded the nail in. He pounded again, hard, the nail already embedded deep.

Elle settled her shoulder against the doorjamb, took advantage of her luck. Dove gray clouds crowded the sky, dimming the flood of sunlight streaming over Noah. He shifted, knee flexing as he put his weight on it, and clamped a nail between his teeth. As he skimmed dirt-streaked fingers along the step above him, the muscles in his shoulders flexed beneath pressed blue cotton. She smiled; he looked dressed for church, not fixing. Swiping his wrist across his brow, he tilted his head enough for her to study his shaded profile, to determine the changes ten years had brought.

An air of masculinity, to be sure. Grooves chalked alongside a mouth she would call virile and beautiful in the same breath. Little white lines spreading from eyes the color of woodsmoke. Lower, firm ridges of muscle in his arms and his thighs. Looking away, she drew a breath of humid air and leaned in to see Meredith diligently working on her assignment. A pretty girl, a tad young, but not *too* young. Elle had seen Noah laughing with her. Maybe he would ask her to the Spring Tide Festival, and Elle would have to watch him hold her against his chest and—

You must get that boy out of your mind, Marielle-Claire.

The warning pounded through her mind, mixing with Noah's hammerblows, the voice clearly her father's. She recognized the danger. For her, Noah would always be a swift route to heartache. Corroborating the warning, he leaned to the side, the play of movement stretching his trousers across his firm buttocks.

"What are you doing?" she shouted, climbing the staircase with the grace and speed of a madwoman.

He shouldered a bead of sweat from his cheek and spit a nail into his gloved palm. "Hammering."

"Yes, I can see that. No need. And if there is, I can do it."

A gust of wind raced in from the ocean, slapped a loose

shutter against the house. Noah lifted a tawny brow, the edges of his lips curling slightly. "You're doing a fine job."

"The school takes most of my time. Besides, I'm not really very handy ... well, Widow Wynne can't afford them and neither can—"

"A deal, Elle."

"Deal?" Clearing her throat, she forced the nip of suspicion aside. Deals created by men never seemed to get her anywhere.

He braced his elbows on his knees, dipped his head, and laughed. A curl on the crown of his head fluttered like a flag in the wind. Elle twisted her fingers in the folds of her skirt to keep them from wandering where they shouldn't. "What kind of deal?"

Noah's head lifted, his eyes warm and clear. "Don't look so dubious. This isn't one of Caleb's deals. You don't have to worry about it biting you in ..." He laughed again and rubbed his hand over his mouth. "You don't have to worry, that's all I'm saying. I worked as a laborer to put myself through university, so I'm qualified. I'll purchase the supplies and complete the repairs in exchange for help I'm going to need for the next month. Someone to transcribe my notes. A student of yours, possibly. It'd be a good assignment."

"There is one student." She worried her lip between her teeth. "Annie's trying to improve her penmanship, but her reading skills are middling at best. Besides, this sounds like a lousy deal for you. You pay for the materials *and* do the work."

"Let me worry about that. You can't ignore the repairs any longer. This blessed place is collapsing around you." He nudged his spectacles absently. "And my notes aren't complicated, simple details concerning the lab's construction. I have to wire Chicago once a week with a report. I took it by this morning, and the telegraph operator wasn't able to read my handwriting."

"It's not that bad."

He paused in mid-motion, the hammer dangling from his fingers. "How do you know?"

A gust of air swept her hair into her face. She brushed it aside, concentrating on the shadows pooling at her feet, the distant rumble of thunder signaling an afternoon storm. "I have your book, the one you gave my father. He left it in the restaurant, and I, I brought it home with me. I thumbed through it last night. You made notes in the margins. Notes I could decipher . . . easily." She shrugged.

"You read some of it?" He sounded incredulous.

She planted her hands on her hips. "I can read, you know."

His thoughtful gaze skimmed her face. "I know that, Elle. I just had no idea you would be interested."

"A long time ago, I had books similar to yours, but I"— no need to tell him she had been forced to sell her precious textbooks to raise money for the school—"don't have them anymore."

"Which essay did you read?" He propped the hammer against his hip and stretched his long legs, his shoe polish cloaked by bits of grass and dirt. The eager expression on his face struck a deep cord, and she forgot his question. "Elle? Which essay did you read?"

"Um, something to do with average catches . . . the number of fish breeding. Nothing much."

Surprise widened his eyes; a faint smile curved his mouth. "By calculating average catches, we can demonstrate reduction in stock and generate an estimate of the number of fish breeding in a given area. It's what we call a skeleton study, time-consuming and exhausting, and basic. I'm going to conduct one here. God knows, I have the time. I went by the lab site this morning and Tyre McIntosh, the master draftsman, told me to stay away for the rest of the week." He flicked a blade of grass from his shoe. "Said he didn't need some fish specialist hanging over his shoulder, telling him how to hammer."

"Sounds like Tyre. Interference doesn't sit well with him. Nor with the fishermen."

He grinned, the first truly genuine smile she had seen since his return three days earlier. "I'll use my considerable charm to persuade them."

Wondering if the time was right to discuss what he could no longer avoid, she said mildly, "Caleb has daily contact with the fishermen. He designs and builds their boats. You could—"

He shot to his feet, sending the hammer tumbling. *"No."*

"Noah, he's your brother. You're going to have to face him." Sooner than he imagined. Caleb would return on the afternoon skiff.

"I'm not asking him to help me." His hands closed into fists, his voice dropped, clearly a man preparing for battle. "Never again."

The oak branches above their heads cracked together, nearly obliterating Elle's words. "You could. For anything . . . anything at all."

He flinched, his face losing color. "I found out just how much I could rely upon Caleb."

"He loved you, you must realize that. He still does."

She witnessed a wealth of emotion: remorse, uncertainty, and rage. "I don't know what to think. About myself or my family." Grasping her shoulders, he dragged her forward, the grief he fought to contain rising to the surface. "After ten years, I still don't know what to think."

A bolt of lightning struck, rattling a loose windowpane above them. They glanced up, then warily, at each other. Her skin burned where he gripped her. The air she drew into her lungs grew heavy, filled with the promise of rain and the threat of an emotion she feared.

She wanted to ease his anguish but could not form the words when he stood so near she could see the curl of his lashes, the flecks of black in his eyes. Fear sharpening every angle of his face. She could only watch as his lightly whiskered jaw clenched, his hands leaving her so quickly that she staggered. "Keep out of my life, Elle. For once, just keep the hell out of it." He thundered down the stairs and shouldered past the shrubs separating Widow Wynne's yard from the next.

Elle gripped the railing, a splinter jabbing her hand. *Keep the hell out of my life.* Unfortunately, she couldn't. Not when he headed for the docks—and the skiff anchored there. She couldn't say exactly how she knew. She just *knew.* The loose shutter whipped against the house, a startling reminder of the danger of sailing during a storm. She forced a brisk stride, but not reckless, which would draw attention she neither needed nor desired.

As she turned onto Main Street, the oyster shells crunching beneath her boots, a cold raindrop struck her cheek. She shivered and dabbed at her bodice, thinking she would be happy when summer began, be even happier when Noah returned to Chicago. Her heart gave a little jerk, exposing the bald-faced lie. She slapped her fist into her open palm and cursed beneath her breath. He had broken her heart once, sailing away without a backward glance, a slight that still pained her if she let it. She must bear in mind, he had not contacted her in all those years, and, in a few short weeks, he would leave and never think of her again. She would help mend the rift between the Garrett brothers, because she had played a major role in the skirmish. That was only fair. But nothing more.

Solving this mess wouldn't be tough if she put her mind to it. The stubborn fool still loved Zach and Caleb, loved them with a depth of feeling she had often wondered if he even possessed. With Noah, you could never be sure just how much he would *let* himself feel. She'd never seen someone hold a tighter rein than he did.

Running, she didn't see the puddle but felt the grimy water seep inside her boot lacings. She could see the pitched roof of the jail and a glimmer of light glowing in the window. She lifted her hand to her mouth, worrying her thumbnail between her teeth. Noah would be angry with her for meddling although he shouldn't expect anything different. Except, with a sudden mingling of pride and fear, she realized this *was* different. This time *she* would do what Noah had always managed to do for her.

She would save him from himself.

Chapter Four

The turbulent weather had driven everyone from the docks by the time Zach arrived. *Nearly* everyone, he noted, shoving his hands deep in his pockets. Icy raindrops streamed down his face, cooling his skin but doing nothing to relieve the furious pounding in his head. Whitecapped swells lashed the pier as he moved forward with a cautious step, the worn planks rocking beneath his feet. Through the dense fog rolling in from the sea, he saw the vague outline of a man standing in a flat-bottomed skiff moored next to the ferry bell. A tall man calmly working the sail's lines. For a brief moment, Zach wondered if Elle had been mistaken about Noah's distress.

Anxious to reach his brother, Zach stepped heavily, the thump rising above the storm's steady cadence. With a start, Noah glanced to the side and, before he recovered, his unguarded expression reflected such stark loneliness that Zach's throat closed. *Why,* he questioned, *why did this happen to* my *family?*

The wind ripped the slack line from Noah's hand, the sail billowing wide. He muttered an oath and rubbed his palm. "Damn her," Zach thought he heard.

"Don't," Zach yelled above the clamor. "Ellie did what she figured best."

Noah's shoulders stiffened, and he yanked the line taut.

Zach halted beside an overturned water cask and propped his elbows upon it. It had been ten years since he had seen his little brother, and he wanted to ask everything, see everything, know everything. *Hold on, Zach. Don't want to scare him off.* "Weren't thinking of sailing in this, were you?" he asked, throwing a glance at clouds the color of wet ash.

"Of course not," Noah replied, struggling to batten the sail.

Zach coughed and steadied his voice, though his words still came out rougher than he'd planned. "Good thought. I have enough souls to save running the lifesaving station without having to go after yours. Had a shipwreck last month on the shoals, lost twelve sailors."

Noah turned his head and presented a glacial stare, as if, that night he chose to stay on Devil Island and observe nesting sea turtles instead of coming home, he had not been yanked across Zach's lap and spanked within an inch of his life. A wild gust billowed his sleeves, flicked his hair into his face, and the stare turned to a squint. Zach fought hard to contain the urge to lean in or tell him his spectacles sat in his front pocket. After a long moment, Noah pressed his lips tight and averted his gaze.

Lids fluttering low, Zach let a breath shoot from his lungs, not sure what to say or what to do. Except for the hostile expression and the deeply hollowed cheeks, Noah looked much the same. A good bit taller, skin pallid from months spent in a harsh winter climate, hair a shade darker, Zach would guess, although it clung to his head in wet slicks, making it hard to tell for sure. But his eyes looked the same as the ones Zach saw each morning in the mirror, his nose reminded Zach of their mother's, long and perfectly sloped, and his chin jutted forth, firm and sculpted—Caleb's, no doubt about it. The shape of his face belonged to his father, most likely, and his height, it would seem. A nice combination. He had always been on the edge of pretty, to Zach's way of thinking, but he would have suffered mightily before admitting it.

Many times, Zach had searched his memory for the face of the man who had loved their mother. Maybe he had passed him on the dock or spoken to him in the mercantile. At times, crazy as it seemed, he wished for this memory more than he wished for one of his *own* father. That he and Noah shared only one parent had never mattered to him, and he had known the truth since the day of Noah's birth.

A horde of men shuffled past, rattling the rotted planks he stood on. Whalers, Zach guessed, from the sound of jangling try pots. He looked to see Noah halfway down the pier, skirting the boisterous group and disappearing into a thick shroud of fog. Zach strode forward until they walked side by side, pleased to see Noah only had a couple of inches on him. He felt a smile break. Caleb would hardly reach his shoulder.

Noah halted abruptly and wrenched around, hair plastered to his brow, eyes dark and watery. "What the hell are you smiling about?"

Zach ignored the warning, disregarded the air of wariness, and threw his arms about Noah's shoulders before he could step away. He inhaled a breath of salt air, soap, and the slightest trace of ink. A familiar combination. "I missed you," he whispered, because he could think of nothing else to say.

Noah stiffened, yet his hands rose to clasp Zach's shoulders, for one brief moment, before he mumbled a denial and shoved hard.

"You didn't have to come." He turned toward the sea and tunneled his fingers through his drenched hair. "Elle made a mistake running to you. I wouldn't have gone out in this mess. I just needed to think ... not have everything crowding in. Sailing during a storm isn't sensible, and you know me." He glanced back, his smile flat, his eyelid drooping. "Always the sensible one."

Zach's heart thumped, dulling the slap of waves against the

jetty. Letting emotion seize him, he forgot his pledge to go easy. "Three years, Noah. For three years I watched the mail, the telegraph, reviewed every crew roster thinking you might have sailed in on a merchant ship and were hiding somewhere in town. Then I gave up, not knowing if you were dead or alive. Can you understand how that tore me apart?"

Noah tipped his head and blinked furiously, considering before he spoke, always considering. "Did you think it was easy for me? Everything I loved was in this godforsaken town."

Suddenly too weary to stand, Zach dropped to the edge of the dock, resting his elbows on his knees, his legs dangling over the side. "Why, Noah? *Why?*"

Silence reigned for a long moment, making Zach imagine he would have to chase his brother down the street to get him to speak. Surprisingly, with a weary sigh, Noah settled beside him, impractical shoes skimming the water as he swung his feet. "I couldn't stay here. Things were . . . different. I didn't know who I was. My family didn't know who I was. I felt out of place, belonging to nothing and no one. Sometimes, I still do."

"You're my brother, Noah, and nothing will ever change that. Not a thousand miles or ten years or sharing half the blood you thought we shared. Do you think it matters if our mother loved another man? Who cares if the bastard who sired me didn't sire you? I don't know why she chose to stray outside her marriage to my father or even if she loved yours enough to make up for her husband leaving. All I've ever known, clear to me as the sun rising every morning, is you and Caleb are my family. Nothing else matters."

"It mattered, Zach. It mattered more than I knew. You and Caleb were all I had, and I lost both of you that day." Noah dipped his finger into a gash in the bleached plank, his gaze fixed on the white-capped swells. "The damage to my soul, my pride, my sense of family, was too much to overcome." He kicked his leg angrily. "Is still too much."

Zach splayed his fingers across his stomach, the unshakable conviction in Noah's voice making him feel sick, and frightened. No way would he let his brother slip away again. "Did you love us any less because we shared only one parent?" His expression as steady as he could possibly keep it, hand gripping the dock edge like a lifeline, he waited. Finally, Noah felt compelled to look him in the eye.

Love? Noah swallowed past the knot in his throat. He had forgotten the Garrett propensity—evident in both of his brothers—to blurt what they were thinking without thinking first. Delaying the inevitable, he slipped his spectacles from his pocket and wiped them on the front of his shirt, pleased his hands shook only a little. He wanted to ask about Hannah, but if Zach fell apart right now, he was doomed to follow.

"Did you, little bro'?" Zach's voice rumbled through the air, air seasoned with his peppery cologne. God, that smell had haunted his brother's pilot coat like a ghost, reminding Noah of the many times he had pressed his tear-streaked face into it, and just now, reminding him of everything he had worked to forget, then feared because he couldn't remember.

"No," he said, and jammed his spectacles into place, wishing he could lie.

Zach rocked forward, clasping his knees. "After Caleb had time to mull everything over in his rusty can, read Mama's blamed diary from cover to cover, he wanted to die. He felt so protective, so responsible, and Lord, Noah, we had no idea where you'd gone, how you were surviving." His voice cracked, and he paused, hitched a noisy breath through his teeth. "When Caleb found out about your father, about his father leaving because of it, he let his anger control him. And he ended up punishing the person he loved most in the world. It's his way. Act first, think later. You knew that. How could it have been a surprise?"

Head beginning to ache, Noah gazed across a turbulent, blue-black sea, watched a pelican swoop and settle on a weather-beaten piling, its distinctive white coloring telling him it was no more than six months old. "The look in his eyes ... this gaping void, some horrible absence of attachment. Like I was a stranger ... or worse, his adversary." He flicked a hardened shrimp tail from the pier, where it plunked beneath the waves. "I *felt* like a stranger, weighed down. Shame on top of devastation on top of despair. Not knowing whom to trust or where to turn. I ran because I didn't know what else *to* do. I couldn't go to Caleb, and I wasn't sure I could go to you. You knew. I know you did, and you never told me. I figured you wanted to keep it secret, hide it because it shamed you. That made me feel tainted and dirty." He swiped the specks of salt water from his brow, the day he'd left Pilot Isle appallingly clear in his mind. Chrissakes, he dreamed of it often enough to keep it fresh.

"Are you still running, little bro'?"

Little Bro'. "What an asinine question. I'm here, aren't I?" He slammed his palms to the pier, shaken to the tips of his toes.

"In a way, yeah, you're here. For the blamed laboratory on the point. But I can't help thinking it's a weak link at best. Tenuous, Ellie called it, and I think that's what she meant." He picked a splinter from the worn plank and twirled it between his fingers. "I have to admit, she could always read you better than I could, so I'll take her word for it."

Noah snorted derisively. "Tenuous. Pretty big word for Elle to be throwing around."

"She's a very bright woman, Noah. Incredibly dedicated to her school. If you weren't so darned gifted, maybe you would have noticed."

"It was hard for me to notice anything besides the broken arm and cracked teeth, the torn clothing and stolen fruit. Jesus, she and Caleb created chaos, day after day, and kept me busy repairing the damage. I never had time to stop and consider whether Elle Beaumont was an intelligent girl or not."

Zach sighed. "Not everyone pauses to consider every move in life before they make it, every word in life before they say it. Besides, all that happened a long time ago. Ellie is a woman now, not some silly kid. Haven't you noticed?"

Oh, he'd noticed, all right.

"Funny, I reckoned the tide was turning about the time you lit outta here," Zach said, not even trying to hide the amusement in his voice. "Thought Ellie might finally get a chance to snag you. Lord knows, she worked for it long enough."

"You're absolutely insane."

Zach raised his hands in defense. "Hey, just telling you how I remember it."

"Well, *big bro'*, your memory is shot to hell."

Zach tilted his head and laughed, fueling Noah's discomfort and igniting a rare burst of recklessness.

"Listen, I admit to wondering a few times"—Noah's foot shot out, spraying water—"wondering how she would look wearing a proper dress, some fancy ribbons in her hair, maybe." Not to mention the times he'd pondered how she would look beneath the proper dress. He grunted. "Dammit, she was always *touching* me. What was I supposed to think?"

Zach drew his hand across his mouth, but not before Noah saw his wide smile. "Maybe you should have given it a go. A fast smooch under Mama's towering oak, lots of shade and privacy under the thicket of branches. Only, I reckon that would have been hasty, knowing you."

Noah jumped to his feet and growled low in his throat, "Don't try to push me toward her. It won't work."

"I'm not pushing anyone anywhere. Clearly, Ellie is over her juvenile crush. After all, she has her life, her school. Calm down. I think your virtue's safe this time."

"Virtue," he muttered, and stalked along the slippery dock, hoping he didn't slip and tumble into the blessed ocean.

"Have time for dinner? Looking a bit on the wiry side, little bro'."

The use of the nickname literally stalling Noah in his tracks, Noah glanced back to find Zach dusting the seat of his trousers, shaking loose drops of rain from his collar. A gull flew past them, squawking and diving into the wind. "Dinner?" he repeated, certain Zach would be hungry if he thought about it long enough.

Zach smiled carelessly and ambled toward him, a lock of black hair flopping over his brow. The raw yearning in his gaze and the answering pang of guilt in Noah's chest made the decision simple.

Noah felt the Garrett net tightening about him, and he wasn't sure he minded.

Rory sat to his right, legs dangling above the floor, gravy smeared on his cheek, a dab of mashed potato clinging to the end of his nose. Zach sat to his left, waving a butter knife like a wand as he talked about the tribulations of being the town constable. They smiled and laughed often—something he certainly wasn't used to. Their behavior better suited a family kitchen, not a public restaurant. Some restaurant, Noah thought, and surveyed the crowded dining room. Dented tin chandeliers dripping wax to the floor, chipped porcelain atop tattered cloths, bowed chairs surrounding tables of all shapes and sizes, the stink of fried fish, whiskey, and hair tonic.

A hoarse bellow from the adjoining saloon jarred him from his deliberation. "What the"—he threw a quick glance at Rory, then lifted his gaze to Zach's. "What was—" The shatter of glass cut into his question.

"Uncle Caleb." With a vague motion, Rory sucked a lump of sweet potato pie from his spoon. "In the Nook and mad about somethin'."

Noah didn't take time to think, the conviction in Rory's

voice enough. Plus, in the deep recesses of his mind, the bellow had held a familiar ring. Shoving his chair back, he pocketed his spectacles, and took the narrow hallway leading to the saloon at a near run. It was, if he remembered correctly, simply a battered shed Christabel Connery's father had attached to the restaurant after the New England whalers started flocking to Pilot Isle in the early seventies. The same place Caleb had given him his first lesson in drinking. Rum, he recalled. The next day a fierce headache and the flat of Zach's palm against his bottom had given him reason not to try it again.

The crack of wood and a husky grunt of pain had Noah shouldering past the crowd blocking the doorway, the fracas getting worse if the escalating uproar meant anything.

"Hey!"

"Wait a darned minute, fella."

Ducking inside, he knocked at the clutching hands and the groping fingers, understanding these men wanted to sustain their entertainment. Hands curled into fists he hoped he wouldn't have to use, Noah shoved into the central circle. Flickering light cast shadows across a multitude of besotted faces and wrinkled clothing reeking of sweat and toilet water. He squinted, then took a lurching step forward. It had been a long time, but he instantly recognized Caleb. The hunched stance, the way he held his shoulders, blessit, even the coal black cowlick sticking up on the crown of his head. Surprisingly, bitterness didn't rear its head. Instead, the warmth filling his heart felt akin to devotion.

Devotion bowed to fury when Caleb's head jerked from the impact of a blow. Loathing the part of his mind that sanctioned action above reason, instinct above logic, Noah nonetheless stepped into the fray. It wouldn't be the first time he had taken a hard knock because of his brother's recklessness.

Clearly taking a beating, Caleb stumbled to his knees. Fist cocked and ready, his opponent advanced. Noah got a close look at the face—and time slipped away, until he watched his brother retrieve his spectacles from beneath Magnus Leland's boot, straightening them with clumsy fingers and resting them on his nose.

"I'll be damned if you aren't begging for a drubbing, Leland," Noah said, his voice relatively calm considering that his pulse pounded in his head. He held his arms by his side, figuring he could still reason this out, avoid using his fists. *Maybe.* If he avoided looking at Caleb, who lay in a dazed heap on the floor.

Magnus's arm dropped. He tilted his bloodied face into the light, ejected a whiskey-scented breath and a bark of laughter. "Well, well. You actually *are* everyone's lofty savior, aren't you? Imagine, rescuing your brother after you neglected to mention your arrival to him. He was overwhelmed, to say the least, much to my enjoyment." Lifting his hand to his mouth, he frowned at a smear of crimson on his fingers. "What happened, Garrett? Your dearly devoted little admirer couldn't keep you occupied? Admittedly, there's not much in the way of feminine solace in this town, but perhaps you might find something effortless compared to Mari—"

The first punch he threw split his knuckles. The second sent a shaft of pain up his arm. Ah, it felt *good,* the violence justified. The scales of justice had shifted into balance.

Magnus tottered, launching a wild swing that caught Noah just under his left ear. His teeth came down hard on his tongue; a flash of blue lit his vision. He blinked, felt a warm trickle slide down his neck, swallowed the metallic tang of blood.

Without warning, hands gripped his shoulders, propelled him through the kitchen, out a back door and into the night. The peppery scent told him exactly who led him. Shrugging free, he placed a steadying hand on the Nook's rough-hewn wall and dragged a breath of crisp, salty air into his lungs, releasing it in a ragged chop.

"That was goddarned perfect! The two of you absolutely

amaze me," Zach said, and kicked a wooden bucket into the wall.

Noah shook his head and tapped the heel of his hand against his ear. "What?" Chrissakes, he'd forgotten how deafening a blow to the ear could be.

Zach leaned in, whispered through clenched teeth, "I'm the little bit of law in this town. I should throw both you idiots in jail. Lord help me if one of you needed a doctor. He's out cold, draped over the only table left standing."

Noah rolled his head to the side, waiting for the wave of dizziness to pass. Zach stood before him, face white as chalk, brow beaded with sweat. Moonlight flooded the alley, throwing everything into silvery relief. "Good," he said, then ducked his head, and spit a mouthful of blood onto the ground.

"Good? *Good?*" Zach spun around, paced to the edge of the building, hands propped on his hips, foot tapping a frantic rhythm.

"You've . . . learned a lot . . . little bro'."

Hair prickling the back of his neck, Noah stared at the blurry shape slumped against an overturned oyster barrel. He dug in his pocket, slipped his spectacles on. Broad shoulders stuffed into a bloodied sack coat, one eye swollen shut, the other roving Noah's face, hungrily. "Yes, I learned a great deal, thanks to you," he finally said.

His words appeared to knock the wind from Caleb, who dropped his head and flexed his hands, outwardly intent on his injuries. "I'm sorry," he finally whispered, his Adam's apple bobbing.

Noah sent his fist into the wall before he could think to stop himself. "Don't pull some damn remorse act on me, Cale. I can live without your sorrow, your recrimination. I have for years," he said, and took a wild step forward.

"Hold up, there." Zach grasped him by the shoulders, set him against the wall with a shove.

The kitchen door creaked, a dim shaft of light and the scent of baked apples spilling into the alley. "Zach? All clear? I have alcohol and bandages, if you need em'."

"Yes, all clear," Zach replied.

Gathering her pleated skirt in her fist, the woman stepped out, closing the door behind her. Noah had trouble piecing together names and faces, but something about her seemed hauntingly familiar. She knelt before Caleb and placed her supplies beside her, whispering softly and turning his hands in hers, her touch decidedly intimate, gentle. Ah, yes, Elle had mentioned Christabel Connery and Caleb ... well, they had been together for a long time. Since Elle had refused Caleb's impulsive proposal.

Noah exhaled raggedly and stared at the puddle of water beneath his feet.

"Where's Rory?" Zach asked.

Christabel tilted her head, glanced at each doggedly set face before returning her attention to Caleb. *Stubborn fools.* "With my brother. Daniel's ship docked earlier. You know how he's always chasing after Ellie, asking her to have dinner." She pressed a cloth against a gash on Caleb's knuckle, knowing she could have used a lighter touch. "Cornered her this afternoon at the mercantile, didn't leave her much choice, I reckon. Poor dear walked in as you went tearing out, Zach. She's in the kitchen, chipping ice. Should be here any minute."

"I have to go." Noah shoved from the wall.

Caleb staggered to his feet, blocking Noah's path. "Go on, get outta here. Scurry away like always."

Facing each other, they squared off like two hungry mongrels, the air around them humming with painful emotions. Still, the wounds needed to be poked, so all the resentment and hurt could drain out. Christabel had believed that for years.

She discreetly shook her head when Zach started to move between them. Might be a fair fight, she guessed, calmly squeezing the damp rag, scattering drops of water on her patent leather slippers. Noah stood a head taller but Caleb's arms were twice as thick.

After a moment, they eased back, cautious and unsure, muscles in their shoulders jumping. She watched Noah duck his head, his throat working, his lips parting, closing, and parting again. Watched Caleb studying him, longing etched in each groove of his face. Heck, it all looked clear as daylight to her, the blind nitwits.

But, in the end, Noah turned and walked from the alley.

"Let him go," Zach said, and raised his arm to hold Caleb in place.

"Holy Mother Mary!" Caleb spun to face them, swollen lips curled. "I did that once, remember, and he never came back. I shoulda hauled him home by the scruff of his scrawny damned neck, made him understand."

"I thought I was doing the right thing, letting him think. You know how he always wanted time to consider every little happening. How was I to know he wouldn't come back? How the hell was I supposed to know?" Zach asked.

"Yeah, he's thinking real reasonable, all right. So reasonable, he about knocked Leland's head off." Caleb's voice softened to a tone Christabel had only heard him use in bed. "And . . . he did it for me."

Zach tugged at his collar. "When he was a boy, I never did know what to make of him. Now, he's a man, and it's even worse. I don't know how to handle this, this . . ."

Christabel handed Caleb a rag. He pressed it against his cheek and winced. "Well, you better figure it out. If you leave it to me, I'll go to that stiff-backed widow's right this minute and drag his—"

"*No.*"

"What then, Constable? He can't stand to be in the same room with us for five minutes. How in the world are we ever gonna resolve this mess if we can't even talk to him?"

"This isn't a room, Cale."

Caleb flung the rag to the ground. "Oh, hell, you know what I mean."

She covered her mouth, but a laugh burst forth anyway, had Zach and Caleb twisting around, identical twists of confusion on their faces. She was beginning to enjoy this almost as much as she'd enjoyed seeing little Noah Garrett slug that high-nosed doctor in the jaw. "Noah didn't go tearing outta here because of you two. Not wholly, anyhow."

"What are you talking about?" Zach asked, impatience narrowing his eyes to slits.

All at once, the door banged against the outside wall, and Elle burst into the alley, washing bowl in one hand, strips of white cloth in the other. Her hair had come loose from its slapdash knot, bronze curls framing a face both ashen and flushed. Christabel smiled; she couldn't have been timed better if she'd planned it.

"Where is he?" Elle paused before she reached them, glancing wildly into each darkened corner.

Zach's gaze locked with Christabel's; she nodded faintly. Figuring she needed to give Caleb an extra prod, she dug her elbow into his ribs.

He groaned and massaged his side. "Not there, darling."

"Where is he?" Elle repeated, panic accenting her speech.

"Gone, honey." Christabel grabbed the washing bowl and rags and turned Elle toward the kitchen. "Noah can take care of himself. A little blood and a thump in the head ain't gonna kill anyone, specially a Garrett."

"Blood?" Elle jerked to a halt. "*Juste Ciel!*" She whipped back, green eyes glowing, face devoid of color. "What did you do to him, Cale?"

Caleb threw his hands in the air, then groaned and lowered them. "Not a darn thing, I tell you. It was *your* former betrothed doing the damage. Angrier than a swatted-at wasp. And drunker than . . . well, than *me.* Some doctor, that one."

"*Magnus.*" Elle stalked to the door, practically ripping it from its hinges.

"Good Lord, Cale, go get her. Honestly, I can't handle any more havoc tonight." Zach dropped his head to his hands.

Caleb jabbed Zach in the chest. "You and I are having a long talk later, Constable. I'm not so stupid I don't realize you knew Noah was coming."

"Yeah, yeah," Zach muttered, as the door slammed behind Caleb.

Christabel perched her hip against an oyster barrel, the washing bowl cradled in her arms. "Whatcha think about this, my friend?"

"Be darned if I know what to think."

"Could work out pretty good. Love would keep Noah here, sure as Moses parted that sea. Give him and Caleb plenty of time to mend fences."

Zach lifted his head, exhaustion shadowing his face. "I don't know, Christa. True, there's *always* been something"—he made a vague motion—"between Ellie and Noah. Some kind of understanding, a keen insight into each other's feelings. I know because I saw it many times with my own eyes. I'll even admit I think it's still there. But love? Dadblast, love doesn't take this much figuring."

"Honey, what you and Hannah had was a diamond sitting atop a pile of rocks. You knew right off she was made for you, and she knew it, too. I see lovesick idiots every day, drinking and searching for answers, and I can tell you, it ain't easy for most people. Bury deep what they don't want to see, go blind to what they're scared to feel. Decide what they want using their heads, not their hearts." Christabel trailed her finger around the rim of the bowl, the sharp scent of alcohol stinging her nose. "Remember the first time we saw Hannah? Her daddy brought her to preaching just after they moved here from Atlanta. She wore one of them bonnets with all the ribbons trailing down, practically to her fanny. And some kind of yellow frock with lots of lace.''

"Pink." He paused, stared into the distance. "It was pink."

"Pink." She coughed to regain her voice. Strange, how sorrow lingered after all these years.

"I'm terrified, Christa."

"Why?" she asked, shocked to the core. Zach wasn't the kind of man to fear much.

"In one split second, I lost my wife, my unborn child . . . and Rory, dear Lord, for a long while I lived just to make sure he got to bed on time and brushed his blasted teeth. I wasn't much of a father for months after Hannah died and''—Zach drew a shuddering breath and paced to the end of the alley—"I almost failed him like I failed my brothers. Like I'm afraid I'm going to fail them again."

"You didn't fail nobody, Zachariah Garrett!"

"Somehow, I did, Christa. Yet, I can't for the life of me tell you what I would do differently if I had the chance to do it all again." He settled his palms on the wall and leaned in, shoulders hunched, head hanging low. "My mother didn't leave me two boys needing protection and a switch against their behinds now and then, she left me two young men needing I don't know what, changing and growing in ways that confounded the tar out of me. One with a temper I couldn't control, the other with a mind I didn't understand. I did my best by them." His voice dropped to a tortured whisper. "Honest to God, I did."

Christabel stepped forward, a healthy gust of wind trapping her skirt between her ankles. "It will all work for the best, Zach. You've just got to give it time."

"Time? Ten years hasn't helped. Did you see their faces? Made me sick to see how much it still hurts them."

"Maybe Ellie could heal some of—"

He knocked his boot against the wall, sending a flutter of caked mud to the ground. "I don't want her causing Noah to run away again and''—he threw a sidelong glance at her, a tight smile locked in place, sorrow and self-hatred riding high in his face—"you see, I asked him about her today. Pestering him, 'cause I remember him looking interested a time or two. Watching her when she didn't know. He admitted it, said he did wonder about her, but mixed in his confession was this hunted look, like I was the hound and he was the fox. After giving it some thought, I figure it might be better to keep that chest sealed."

"What are you saying?"

"I'm saying I think Noah's better off staying away from Ellie. And she's better off staying away from him. She says she doesn't care about him any—"

"And you believe her?" Christabel laughed outright.

"Of course, I believe her. Why would she lie?"

"Why, indeed." She slammed the bowl on the barrel and began folding the strips of cloth into needless squares. "Oh, could be because the entire town teased her, always laughing and calling her the professor's assistant or no-beau-Beaumont. Or, could be due to Noah never showing a smidgen of encouragement, telling her blunt as can be he wasn't ever going to come around." She grunted and waved a cloth in the air. "Would be enough for me. Forget about the heartless drivel her father's been telling her for years."

Slowly, Zach turned his head, his concerned gaze finding hers. "Are you saying she lied to me?"

"Good heavens, no." Christabel dropped the last pleated square in the bowl and sighed. Men could be so feeble-witted. "Ellie's not lying to you." Supplies in hand, she paused before the door. "Honey, she's lying to herself."

He was lying to himself.

It *definitely* bothered him to watch that blessed seaman, Daniel Connery, crouch in the corner of Elle's porch for the third time this week, making last-minute adjustments to a wrinkled lapel, dusting the thin layer of pollen from poorly creased trousers. Why would she want to go to dinner with a man who dressed so slovenly?

Tipping his head against the coach-house wall, Noah observed the spill of indigo across a twilight sky, the cool breeze bringing Elle's laughter to his ears.

Surely, the bastard's ship would sail soon.

Powerless, he looked in time to see her step outside, Daniel holding the screen door, rumpled hat in his meaty fist. A broad band of dying sunlight revealed the scuffed toe of a maroon boot, gloved fingers tying her satin bonnet ribbons, then a half turn as she secured the latch he had repaired two days ago. She tended to use the back entrance after dark, presumably because it sat right next to Widow Wynne's bedroom, although the old woman wouldn't return for a month. Ever a circumspect man, Noah had recorded this decidedly considerate habit. In the past eight days, he had recorded far too many of lovely Miss Beaumont's habits.

She liked to sit on the porch steps and watch the sun rise, fresh sunlight sparking bursts of cherry in her tousled locks. She preferred to leave the door open while she taught, her patient instruction and affectionate regard floating through the rotting boards, upsetting Noah's equilibrium, disrupting his exacting schedule. In between lessons, she volunteered to assist repairing broken latches and rusted hinges, her enticing scent making him snarl and snap, then berate himself for his lack of control, his cruelty. He also berated himself for not being able to ignore the charming dimple marking her left cheek, the intelligent gleam in her eyes as she discussed politics or fashion or bicycles, one of a hundred different topics she retained in her ravenous little mind. She craved information in any form— from collecting plankton using tow nets to tagging certain species of fish—and possessed a zest for life that amazed and confounded him.

He'd never had a student listen as attentively, grasp topics as quickly or as eagerly. Come to think of it, he had never talked as freely, and never, *ever,* about subjects he held close to his heart.

"Hell," he muttered, and snatched a conch shell from the railing. Placing it next to his ear, he held himself from straining for a better view of the widow's porch.

Elle left the porch at a boyish jog, striding down the dirt path a full step ahead of her escort, striped cloth tapping her fine-boned ankles. He worked his way up the threadbare dress that gently hugged each curve to perfection. Stopping at the side of the house, she took her coat from Daniel, a beautiful, plump breast outlined in shadow.

Noah sucked in a breath, then felt his lips curl in gloating, masculine satisfaction.

He could not deny the possessive wallop to his gut as he watched Elle slip her arms into *his* coat, bulky cuffs hitting her mid-thigh, notched collar bunching beneath her chin. She should have returned it a week ago; he should have asked her to. Only . . . the thought of her scent overriding his made him hesitate, and he was damn sure he didn't want to examine *that* too closely.

As Noah debated calling out, telling the idiot sailor just whose coat she wore, Daniel offered his arm and Elle wavered, glancing to the side, a wide straw brim concealing most of her face. Noah stiffened and pressed against the wall, praying deepening shadows and blooming dogwoods concealed him.

She tipped her head, her face flooding into view, bottom lip slipping between her neat, white teeth. Noah groaned and slammed his eyes shut, categorizing the marine specimens he had collected on Devil that morning. In between razor clam and ribbed mussel, Elle's plump bottom lip intruded. Pink and soft, slightly moist.

Chrissakes, I'm going mad, he reasoned, and pitched the conch shell over the railing.

Scrubbing his fingers beneath his spectacles, he counted to

ten and looked to find heightened darkness and an empty yard. His frustration only increased the throb in his temples, the ache in his back. Recompense for hunching over the desk in his poorly lit flat, reviewing sketches of the laboratory until sunlight spilled across the floor. He completely neglected the narrow bed wedged in the corner of his bedroom.

His skin tingled from a week spent knee-deep in muck, specimen bag a heavy weight by the end of the day, the sun roasting him through his clothing. Rotating his shoulders, his gaze dropped to the recently dirtied plate by his side. Sometime last week, Elle had begun bringing him dinner. He had taken to eating on the coach-house landing, delighting in the lingering warmth, the animated fireflies and the boisterous crickets, the endless shush of waves rolling into shore. Vastly different from a spring night in Chicago. Elle had even eaten with him once. Over a dessert of sugary apple cobbler, he had shown her how to trace her way from the Big Dipper to the North Star.

At the end of the lesson, she had traced her way back across the heavens.

Noah nudged the plate aside, wanting to do the same to Elle's hospitality. Only, coming home to find a palatable meal waiting on the step felt—he searched his mind. Good, it made him feel *good*. After years of living in a city where he cared for no one and no one cared for him, he could pretend he had a real home here. Laughable, but the scent of fried chicken and black-eyed peas had transformed Widow Wynne's musty coach house into a place where he resided in moderate serenity.

Perhaps Elle brought the food to repay him for securing loose shutters, tightening wobbly doorknobs, and promising to replace the rotten floor in her schoolroom. Perhaps not. Scooting forward, he settled his arms on the uneven railing, let his legs dangle over the side of the stairs. He stared at nothing, yet saw Elle in her striped dress, a tender smile dimpling her cheek.

Dropping his chin to his arms, he inhaled the scent of honey-suckle and recently trimmed grass layered beneath the cloying stink of the salt marsh. Underneath that, if he really concentrated, he could smell whatever Elle sprinkled all over her skin, her clothing. Moist earth and fresh rain, the slightest hint of something sweet sealing it in gossamer wrapping. Nothing particularly feminine about it, yet the fragrance muddled his senses like no other could. Clouded his mind with ambiguous images. Tattered silk hiked past a shapely knee, a round bottom lifting off a worn leather bicycle seat, blazing green eyes and a dimpled cheek, plump lips parting on a sigh—

Noah's palm connected with the railing he needed to shore up, the unwelcome rise in his trousers making him question, for the first time in his *life,* if a trollop could ease his troubled mind, make him sleep better at night, think clearer during the day. He didn't even know if they *had* trollops on Pilot Isle.

Blessit, he didn't enjoy imagining a woman—the *one* woman he had no intention of touching, ease of mind or no—could throw him off his strict course by the way she smelled, the way her lips formed certain words. Dammit, he had an established plan, a definite trajectory, one not allowing for a wife. Or a lover. It allowed for the occasional tussle beneath scented sheets, a balanced, natural hunger that never bowed to control. Rather dispassionate, he supposed, but he carefully considered the circumstances before making love, deciding years ago he would avoid sexual encounters if they created the turmoil he found so repellent. Governing his impulses had never been a problem before—he gave his body what little it needed and it quieted. He shifted, trouser buttons digging into his groin. Usually, anyway.

Perhaps a written list of reasons why he could not afford to react in this fashion would resolve it in his mind. Then his mind could send the signal to the rebellious part of his body. Nodding, he started to rise, then he cursed and sank back. No, he could handle this trifling, sophomoric physical response, easily manage it, and put it in its place. Of course, he could. Besides, he had already made a list.

Blessit, he had made *two*.

A dull whack broke the silence as a gust of wind pitched a salt-thickened clump of hair into his face. A shutter dangling from one of Widow Wynne's second-floor windows. He had missed that one. Actually, *missed* wasn't exactly correct. He had climbed the ladder and innocently glanced into a bedroom that looked like a tornado had blown through it. Dresses hanging from the bedposts, magazines and books stacked on a grained pine dresser, scattered cologne bottles, framed portraits, and undergarments. A lacy, frilly, stiff-looking contraption, yellow with slim black edging. Leaning in to get a better look, he had cracked his brow on the glass and nearly tumbled off the ladder.

"What a mess," Noah whispered, and peeled a strip of paint from the railing post, imagining peeling one of those faded dresses from Elle's lovely body. Finding a corset or chemise— the delectable undergarment he had spied—clinging to each lush curve. What would it feel like to sink into her as deeply as he could sink into a woman, suck her skin between his teeth, have her breasts swell beneath his fingers and her nipples pebble beneath his tongue?

Spontaneous, uninhibited.

He knew that's how it would be with Elle, recognized it as easily as he recognized his face in the bowed mirror above his basin. The woman leaped headfirst into everything. Always had. Making love would be no different. Passionate, impulsive. Didn't sound similar to anything, or *anyone*, he had ever experienced. Passion had always seemed rather tepid to him, a glass of tea left too long in the sun.

He didn't know why he wanted to control his life to the point of wringing it dry. He had analyzed this predilection many times. Since he had left Pilot Isle, alone, frightened, and bewildered, he had not been able to get close to anyone. A few friends here and there, people he could easily hold at a distance. Every time someone reached out to him, in friendship or affection, his thoughts, his feelings, crawled deep inside.

Caroline Bartram was the one person who knew about his childhood, his struggle to forget his brothers, and what had happened to make him run. And, he had only told her in a fevered delirium. She had found him, bloodied and shivering, lying between stacks of stripped pine outside a lumber mill. He had left Pilot Isle little more than six months before, his anger too raw for his mind to subdue and far too savage for his hands to defend. She had dressed his wounds and listened. Simply listened. He remembered the relief it had brought to tell someone.

Flicking another chip of paint loose, Noah sighed. Every day, he struggled to make room in his heart for his brothers, although it scared the hell out of him to let them in. He recoiled every time Zach touched him, yet, deep in his gut, he suppressed this powerful urge to return the touch. *Crazy,* when he and Caleb had barely gotten past gruffly spoken greetings as they passed each other on the street.

This would have to change. Had already changed. This morning, Noah had done the unexpected—he had asked Caleb for help. In an impulsive attempt to reduce the amount of time he and Elle spent together, he had sent his brother a note requesting his aid in getting the fishermen to take him on their daily runs. He had asked every captain and received only suspicious glares and offhand rebuffs. With Caleb's assistance, the captains had agreed, if Noah, in turn, agreed to salt fish and drain nets. In plain truth, if he agreed to work like a mongrel. He welcomed the challenge, welcomed any excuse to leave the coach house before dawn and return after dusk, too exhausted to eat Elle's meals, much less eat them *with* her.

Noah's stomach cramped imagining how he could thank Caleb. Especially after he had vowed never to depend on his family again.

He'd broken that vow easily enough. The only other one he had made since returning involved avoiding Elle. He cocked his head, listened for her lively step on the path, her buoyant laughter giving life to a hushed night. He heard the spiked chirp of a cricket and the crash of waves in the distance, and felt a sharp, brief stab of disappointment.

Noah angled his spectacles and pressed his knuckles beneath his eyes. The *Elle Vow*, as he liked to think of it, he must keep. Because he had no room for a woman in his life—in his heart, most particularly.

He wasn't entirely certain he'd left room for anyone.

Chapter Five

Elle slipped on the stair's worn edge, banging her shin. She groaned, grimacing in pain. Two more to the coach-house landing, then a quick check of her dressing gown. Ties tied, buttons buttoned. Covered to the neck, albeit inappropriately. *Oh.* She wiggled her toes, tried to shake off the grass and dirt. Frowning, she drew a salty breath of courage and pounded on Noah's door. No time to worry about him giving her the evil eye over such a minor detail as bare feet.

"Suffering cats, Professor, be home," she whispered, and pounded once more. A rumble of thunder sounded; she threw a frantic glance at the sky. *That's all I need,* she thought, and gave a good tug on the doorknob. *Locked.* Merciful heavens, if Sean Duggan found them—Annie said he was staggering drunk—he would kill them both.

"Please, if you're there, Noah, let me in."

The door flew inward, the gas lamp in his hand revealing tousled curls and a muscled chest lightly sprinkled with hair. "Elle? What the . . ." Noah squinted drowsily and fumbled for his spectacles. His eyes narrowed, his gaze lingering on her unbound breasts before lifting to her face. He mouthed one word—*inside*—and hauled her in by the wrist, her damp feet skimming the floor.

Elle jerked from his grasp before he could close the door. "I need your help," she gasped and dropped the wadded bundle of clothing she held to the floor. "Annie Duggan . . . oh, Noah . . ."

He raised his head, his fingers halting their buttoning. "The student who's been transcribing my notes?"

"Sean, her husband"—she clutched his arm, dug her fingers into firm muscle—"he hurt her. I knew—I knew it was happening. Bruises on her arms, her wrists. I begged her to let me help her, but she protected him, always refused. *Why?* Now, it's gone too far and . . . I have to hide her, somewhere, but not at Widow Wynne's. He'll look for her there. I jerked some of my clothes off the line. Hers are bloody and torn. I have to get her out of Pilot Isle on the dawn skiff. I have to."

"Take a breath and tell me where she is."

"Downstairs. In the school. When I got home, I noticed the door was open. I figured it might be Rory hiding from Zach, might be you, fixing the floor or something. After Daniel left, I went inside. Under my desk, she was crouched under my desk, crying and moaning. I'm not even sure she recognized me. Sean will know to look at Widow Wynne's, but he won't think—"

"Calm down, Elle. I'll go get her."

"Thank you," she whispered, voice cracking, shoulders slumping in relief.

He studied her face, reading her like a book. "Stay put." As an afterthought, he pressed a soft kiss to her brow. Then he turned and strode through the doorway, his footfalls thumping on the staircase.

She wedged her shoulder against the wall, bringing her fingers to her brow. *Grands Dieux.* Had Noah just kissed her? She swallowed slowly, felt her heart thud against her breastbone. Had she imagined the graze of whiskers across her eyelid and the marked smell of soap on his cheek?

Annie's shrill scream jerked her from her contemplation and she forgot Noah's command. Slowing as she entered the schoolroom, she threw a quick glance into each darkened corner, not knowing what she would find. Moonlight struggled past the grimy pane of glass set high in the wall, colored Noah in weak tones of silver where he knelt on one knee before her battered desk.

"Come on, no one's going to hurt you here." His words were softly spoken, his arm stretching toward Annie in a calm, gradual motion.

"No," Annie whimpered and shifted, her worn cloth slippers and the ragged border of her lavender dress disappearing beneath the desk.

"Trust me," Noah said, conviction in his expression, protection in the hand he offered. Elle did not have to see his face or grasp his fingers to know it. When Annie remained hidden, he glanced over his shoulder, drawing Elle into silent consultation. That they could communicate in this way shook her to the core, a telling glow of pleasure heating her cheeks.

"Dear"—Elle stepped in behind Noah, cursing the creaking planks—"I promise, we won't let anything else happen to you. I'll help you get home." This much, she *could* promise. She had just enough money hidden beneath her misshapen mattress to see Annie returned to her family in Atlanta.

"Home? Mother?" Annie scooted forward on her bottom, her frantic blue eyes seeking, searching. A thin band of light slashed her face, highlighting the rapidly darkening circle around her eye and the streak of blood on her chin. The raging wind and a brawny fist had matted her hair close to her head. She rested a hand on her protruding belly, glanced at Noah, and whispered, "I had to run, Professor. My baby. He'll kill my baby."

Noah's fingers curled into a fist behind his back, but the hand he offered Annie did not so much as quiver. "Of course, you did. Come on, now. You're not doing the baby any good sitting here on a cold, damp floor, shivering to death." With careful movements, he lifted Annie's tattered shawl from her waist to her shoulders. "Elle brought clean clothes for you to change into. Come upstairs. I'll light the parlor stove, warm it up, nice and safe." Moving prudently, he leaned in, slipped his arms beneath her. "I won't hurt you," he crooned, lifting her high against his chest and standing easily. Elle stepped aside as he gently maneuvered his swaddled bundle through the doorway. She followed, blind to everything but the sound of Annie's pitiful whimpers and the tone of assurance in Noah's voice. Reaching the landing, he ducked into his set of rooms.

Gripping the railing, Elle mounted the staircase, searching the overgrown shrubs for a wild-eyed man with whiskey on his breath. At the top, she rushed inside and slammed the door, flipping the metal latch. Crossing the room, she watched Noah brush a pile of papers to the floor and settle Annie in a towering leather chair. The girl's bones seemed to melt, and she slithered to a half sit, head lolling, arms dangling.

Elle knelt before her, tucking a lock of matted brown hair behind Annie's ear. "Noah?"

He appeared by her side, the gas lamp in his hand flooding light past the etched glass globe to shimmer in his pupils. "I have few medical supplies here. Do you think I should get Dr. Leland?"

Unchecked, she flicked a glance at his right hand, the knuckles marred by yellowed bruises and scabbed gashes from Magnus's teeth. "No, um . . . I don't think Annie would want to involve him. I can handle this."

"Fine." He appeared relieved. "What do you need?"

"Blankets, a towel, soap, water." Using a gentle touch, she

probed the swollen skin circling Annie's eye. "Liniment?" she asked, catching his gaze.

He paused, reviewing the list in his mind, then nodded. Placing the lamp on the desk at her side, he left the room.

Briskly, Elle tugged Annie's ruined dress from her shoulders and hurled it to the floor. The one she had snatched from the clothesline would hang on her student's gaunt frame, but at least it was dry. And absent of bloodstains. Elle swallowed a swift burst of rage, lightening her touch as she slipped the peach cotton over Annie's head and smoothed it past her thickening waist. She finished securing the bone buttons, then chafed her student's blue-tinged hands until her own stung, pleased to hear the girl's whimpers quiet to soft mews.

Noah reentered, a tarnished serving tray in his hands, a frayed towel looped over his arm, and the scent of coffee clinging to him. "Here," he said, and shoved the towel and loaded tray at her. In a moment, he returned holding a musty patchwork quilt, which he wasted no time in tucking around Annie, who mumbled and shifted restlessly. Elle sloshed coffee into a chipped blue mug, drops stinging her skin. Forcing Annie to take a sip, she heard desk drawers being opened and turned to find Noah standing behind his desk, holding a corked bottle high like a trophy.

"Got it." He shoved drawers closed with his knee. The flickering light reflected red-gold on the metal instruments and glass beakers littering his desk, blue-black on the tidal charts and detailed oceanographic maps tacked in neat alignment to the wall behind him. "Alcohol." He thrust the bottle toward her. "I couldn't find liniment."

Setting the mug aside, Elle jerked the cork loose and soaked the grayed edge of the towel, the sharp scent stinging her nose as she swabbed Annie's lacerated skin. Using the soap and water Noah had provided, she washed Annie's face, her neck, her arms and hands, slipped the ribbon from her own hair and secured the girl's in a damp lump, off her face and neck, at least. Abrasions doctored well enough for the time being, she forced Annie to drink the rest of the coffee. She blinked sleepily, winced in pain, then slid into a restive slumber.

Rain began to plink against the window, a comforting distraction from the tense silence. Elle glanced at Noah, who sat quietly by her side. His calm façade didn't fool her in the least. His unlaced leather boot tapped in rhythm to the mantel clock, and his breathing sounded a tad harsher than required by sitting still. Arms hooked around the back of the chair he straddled, a pad of paper in one hand, a gold-tipped fountain pen in the other, he frowned in concentration and scribbled, paused. Light bounced off his spectacle lenses as he tilted his head to stare at her through round wire rims. His gaze was thoughtful and shrewd . . . and held the slightest edge of anger. He'd collected himself, she noted, taking a hasty sip of Annie's coffee. Floppy hair finger-straightened and shoved off his brow, modestly wrinkled shirt buttoned and tucked in. He wore no belt. Before she looked away, she saw that his trousers were faded at the knee, frayed at the waist . . . probably threadbare in the seat.

Hands shaking, she tried twice before managing to jam the bottle cork in place. *Juste Ciel,* for a room sealed tighter than a water cask for two years, a room that should have smelled of dust and decay, it smelled fresh and alive, of pine needles, salt air, hair tonic, and *him.* The scent swam past her defenses and made her, for a brief moment, imagine racing into Noah's arms, pressing her cheek next to his heart, her lips to the hollow beneath his ear. She wanted to accept the protection he had just offered another woman and hold it close.

Making room beside an aromatic horseshoe crab carcass and a textbook opened to the last page, Elle slammed the bottle to the desk. She had to remember her objective—to face Sean Duggan if he came looking for Annie, send him on a wild-goose chase if necessary. She had to handle him. Somehow, she had to.

Giving her skirt a casual shake, Elle shoved the bloodied

towel at Noah. Courage, she reminded herself, sometimes felt a great deal like fear.

"Don't even consider it." Noah yanked the towel from her and threw it to the floor.

"Consider what?"

"You're not going to wait for her husband alone." His voice lowered to a hoarse whisper as he glanced at Annie. "Look what that bastard did to his *wife*. Do you want him to get his hands on *you?* Have you completely lost what's left of your mind?"

How had he known? Frowning, she kicked the towel underneath the desk. She hated it when he used undeniable logic and left her with nothing to say.

He slammed the raised legs of his chair to the floor. "Blessit, do you think I'm stupid? Do you think I would let you walk into a situation like that without, God help us both, my devoted protection?"

She laughed thinly. "Never in my life have I thought of you as stupid."

"Never mind," he said, his face flushing beneath a look of somber chagrin.

Elle had to curl her fingers into a fist to keep from cupping his cheeks, the charming blush making him look all of sixteen. Her heart must have remembered what it felt for him then, because it started thumping eagerly, reminding her there had been a time when she would not have hesitated to touch him.

"I'm assuming this is not the first time her husband has beaten her." He slapped the pen and paper to the floor. Straightening, lamplight played over the muscles in his shoulders and his chest. With a gleeful flutter, Elle realized her mediocre cooking had chased some of the hard edges from his frame.

"Well . . ." Lifting her thumb to her mouth, she nibbled the nail, directing her attention to the pad of paper sitting by his feet.

He nudged it beneath the desk. "Not the first time you've come between Annie and her husband, either, is it?"

She nibbled harder, wondering how to avoid this line of questioning. A sensible, rational explanation might do it. Then, she would not have to involve him any further in this mess. She tilted her head. Maybe she could say—

"Quit trying to concoct some suitable reply. How about it?" His heels dug into the varnished planks, pulling his long body forward in the chair.

Flustered, Elle spit a sliver of fingernail from her mouth and promptly forgot her objective. "Twice. It's happened twice I know of. Sean twisted her arm behind her back the first time, left some nasty bruises on her wrist. The second"—she lowered her hand, felt a frown tug—"he split her lip, knocked a tooth out, loosened another. I begged her to go home, to her family. I offered to pay for the ticket to Atlanta. Or to let her stay with my friend Savannah, in New York, if she'd rather not go home. But, Annie had just figured out she was pregnant ... and he frightened her so." Elle forced a smile, quaking inside. Sean Duggan had made threats she wasn't about to repeat to anyone—especially a man who had turned out to have a surprisingly ready temper. When he continued to stare, she snapped, "To put it plainly, because I can see you're waiting for me to dig a ditch and crawl into it, *everything* I've done for Annie has been against her husband's wishes. Including teaching her to read and write."

Noah bumped his spectacles up, drawing his knuckles across his eyes. Laughing, he said, "Isn't it just like you to make an enemy of every bully you encounter? Congratulations. This makes two in a week."

"You think I'm still that silly little girl, don't you? Getting into one predicament after another. Begging for your help, your blasted protection. How incredibly insulting."

"You slip into trouble as easily as a warm bath, Elle. Be insulted if you like, but yes, that's what I think."

"For your information, Professor, not every problem has a solution. Sometimes people have to go by gut instinct, sheer, candid *emotion*. Fight fires when they catch a whiff of smoke in the air, not wait until they trip over the burning building. Maybe my actions are a tad precipitate"—she bent down, jerked the towel from the floor, and snapped it into sloppy folds—"but at least I know how liberating it is to act without planning every little move."

He lowered his hand, the spectacles resting on his brow stark against his sun-kissed skin. His left lid sagged lazily, giving him a reckless, rakish, thoroughly undeserved air. "How liberating"—his gaze traveled the length of her and back—"does it feel, sweet?"

"Don't call me that," she said, and swallowed hard, her fingers digging into the damp cloth. *Trapped.* She felt trapped, her ankles chained to the floor. When he looked at her, grave and probing, she forgot her avowals of indifference.

Damn and blast! She didn't love him, this tall, well-formed man gripping the chair with bulging knuckles, his square jaw tense with frustration. If she loved anyone, it was the self-possessed boy who had wiped tears from her face and blood from her knees. She certainly didn't love this enigmatic, unreachable man.

Sometimes, she didn't even *like* him.

She lifted her chin, prepared to tell him, but her lips parted and no sound passed. His expression had gone hot. She couldn't think of another way to describe it. Eyes dark as a stormy sky, nostrils flaring as they caught a scent. Her scent? His hands uncurled, and he lifted enough to bring their faces in line. Her fingertips tingled, her arms inching toward him.

Noah met her halfway, his breath hitting her cheek, warm and sweet. She made a low sound in her throat and he stilled. Cursing once, he shoved from the chair. It rocked from side to side and finally flipped with a crash. He stood by the door, holding a black pilot coat in his hand when she reached him, looking dazed for no reason she could fathom.

"Put this on," he growled.

"But—"

"You can't go running around in"—he tossed the coat over her shoulders, their skin never making contact—"your underwear."

"I'll be back—"

"I'm going with you."

"Annie—"

"She's safe here. Safer than you are at Widow Wynne's." He grabbed a rumpled fishing hat from the hall tree and stuffed it on her head. "This door will be cinched as tight as any on Pilot Isle. I should know, I installed the lock."

She tipped the hat, glaring at him from beneath the stained brim. He glared right back. Clinching her teeth, she said, "Now look here—"

"I have the only key, Elle. I'll be watching the coach house the whole time. That bastard won't get past me. And he won't get in here, I promise you."

"But—"

"If you say no again, I'll sit on your front step and wait for him there. Do you want that?"

"No, of course n—"

"Keep the hat pulled over your face." He placed his hand in the middle of her back and gave a firm shove. "All I need is for someone to see you leaving here in the middle of the night."

She sputtered and stumbled onto the landing, "All . . . all *you* need? Do you think it would do wonders for me, Professor?"

He swung her to face him. "Thought we had a promise," he whispered, his fingers cupping her jaw. "No more. I don't want you to call me that." She watched his lips settle against his teeth, opened her mouth to reply, and inhaled his breath. The sweet scent again. Peppermint.

His half smile settled into a flat line of she didn't know what. "You don't have to agree, sweet. Just move it." He jerked the coat lapels close to her chin, took her hand, dragged her down the stairs, and across the dew-slick grass.

She stammered, French tangling with English and gibberish coming out. Noah ignored the chatter, flinging her hand from his as soon as Widow Wynne's door closed behind them. Resigned to his interference, she mashed her lips together and fought a fierce surge of fury, praying she could get through the night without killing him.

Look what my damned illogical sense of duty has gotten me into this time, Noah groused, flicking the maroon-velvet drapery aside and glancing into a sober, rainy night.

Turning, he prowled the length of Widow Wynne's gaslit drawing room, wishing his thoughts were as surefooted as his stride. What had just happened in the coach house? Definitely wasn't a belated sense of duty that had made his body heat like a skillet over a flame. He'd simply been watching the wheels in Elle's mind spin, cataloging the emotions crossing her face because he could, and then something, a tender, warm expression had sent a jolt of raw need right to his heart. Making matters worse, he'd inhaled her scent, and *goddammit,* leaned in to kiss her. The longing to touch her had all but brought him to his knees.

He fingered a frayed hole in the sleeve of his shirt, distancing his mind from his body. The wind shrieked outside, rattling the windowpanes and shooting a moist draft of air past his face. He brushed his fingers past his cuffs, checking the buttons. These were work clothes, not ones he generally wore in the company of women. Then again, Elle had not even thought to throw a coat on over her *nightdress.* His coat—the one neither of them had the nerve to discuss—would have done well enough.

Now, blessit, she had both of his coats.

Suddenly, a vision of Annie spreading her hands over her swollen belly flashed in his mind. The metallic smell of blood lingered in his nostrils. Returning to the window, he searched the dark street again, almost hoping for a sign of Sean Duggan. If that bastard *ever* got his hands on Elle, Noah would kill him. And Annie, dear God, what would happen to her if they didn't get her off Pilot Isle? Somehow, they must. Noah had seen what years of abuse could do to a woman, eroding her confidence and her dignity, leaving a vacant, pitiable shell. Caroline Bartram had denied her husband's mistreatment for years because she had felt indebted to him. Her previous occupation had not garnered many proposals, and the first one she received, she accepted. She had denied Noah's offers of assistance many times, until she finally understood that her husband would destroy her if she did not leave him. Annie's situation felt chillingly similar.

The door clicked shut, and he glanced back, releasing a relieved breath. Elle had changed into decent clothing, thank God, although the blouse looked tattered beyond repair, fit for the rag box, too wash-worn to do more than cling to her lush bosom. The skirt looked much the same, hanging in temptingly gentle folds from her hips. Why the hell couldn't she wear all those layers that normally kept a man from seeing a woman's true shape?

"Any sign of Sean?" she asked, her voice surprisingly controlled. He had to hand it to her—the woman was made of stern stuff.

"No." On his second pass around the parlor, he paused by the mantel, a dab of color catching his eye. "What is this?" He plucked a faded yellow ribbon from a brass hook.

"Oh, that." Elle cleared her throat and from the teasing scent invading his senses, took a step closer. "A suffrage bazaar ribbon. Widow Wynne let me put some of my things in this parlor when I moved from my father's house. He offered to let me keep them there, but . . . I didn't trust him with, well, not with that.''

"World's Congress of 1893, Department of Women's Progress. New York City." Noah turned it over and back. "Where did you get this?"

"At a rally."

"You've been to New York?"

He saw her chin angle and her shoulders stiffen, then she nodded jerkily, offering no further explanation. Stepping forward, she took the ribbon from his hand and hung it on the hook. "I was a student delegate, not a full member," she added, before he could think to ask another question.

He considered her for at least a full minute, trying to firm his slack jaw muscles. "Student?"

"Yes." Crisp as a fresh bill, no hint of inflection.

"You went to university, Elle?"

Bringing her mouth close to the mantel, she pursed her lips and blew dust from a ceramic clown figurine. "For one year." Their arms brushed; her tattered hem flapped against his ankles. She drew a breath, and he wasn't sure if he heard it or felt it. "There was trouble at the rally"—she gestured to the ribbon— "the university called my father and . . . that was that."

"Trouble?"

She made a show of slipping her watch from her pocket, checking the time. "I got arrested."

He jerked to face her. *"Arrested?"*

She snapped the cover and returned it to her pocket. "For two hours. The police herded us into the rear compartment of three baby blue wagons, not much more than grocer's carts. They only did it to clear the streets they told us, quite apologetically. The jail cells were clean. Not bad if you ignored all the things etched in the walls." She frowned, remembering something unpleasant. "And the catcalls from the other cells."

He mouthed the word.

"Yes, a *jail* cell. They put all the women into two directly across from each other, crammed us in, fish in a tin. I wasn't scared. I guess I knew from the astounded look on the lieutenant's face he had no idea what to do. I feared my father's reaction much more than I feared a stranger's. Silver badge or no." She turned toward the window, thrusting the velvet back just as he had. Then she laughed, the sound both anguished and amused. "Actually, I found it rather exciting. A once-in-a-lifetime event."

"You call being arrested an event?"

She dabbed at a drop of moisture on the glass, shrugged. "I can't explain it, but I felt an incredible sense of freedom. Watching the crowd of women marching along Fifth Avenue, I realized life offered more than I could ever attain, if I only had the courage to grasp it. For the first time in my *life*, Noah, I altered my destiny. My life finally took a turn I had chosen. A turn that did not require my father's sanction. Or society's." She rubbed her finger and thumb together, weighing what she would reveal to him, he could tell. "Though it didn't turn out well in the end."

"Your father forced you to leave the university?"

"Oh, heavens, yes. He telegraphed the dean after the rally, threatened them with endangering my safety, letting me run wild. They were glad to see me go, and I can understand. Many universities hesitate to start women's programs in the first place because of the additional responsibility for female students." Elle cut her eyes his way, the pain in them making him wonder if she had talked about this with anyone else. "My father forbid me to attend university, refused to discuss it, vowed to withhold funds. I wrote to every eastern school accepting women and requested information. Had it all sent to a postal box in Morehead City. After a few months, he figured I had forgotten about it. He didn't know I had funds stashed in a spectacle case in my closet. Money *Grandmère* Dupré sent the year before she died. And what little I'd managed to save taking in darning here and there, delivering groceries for the mercantile, anything

I could do without my father's knowledge.'' She began a gradual circle of the parlor, her memories setting her in motion. "In June of 1892, I got a letter from Byrn Mawr that I had received a stipend for the fall term in exchange for working in the library four afternoons a week. I sent a letter of acceptance in July, took the train north in August. I stayed with Savannah, my roommate's family, until the term began in September. I returned to Pilot Isle a year later, without my degree.''

My degree. Noah swiped hair from his brow and felt the pinch of realization. Her voracious appetite for knowledge suddenly made sense. "Elle—''

"Oh, I know what you're thinking,'' she blurted, and bounced on her toes, adjusting the gas fixture on the wall. The flame heightened behind etched glass, sparking a bright orange blaze in her curls. "I would have graduated if I had not gone to the rally . . . you may be right. I've turned that over in my mind a thousand times, until I can't stand to think of it anymore. But, I would have missed my one, true moment of completeness, standing in the middle of a crowd of strangers, all of us experiencing our own sense of purpose. Also, I can't help but long for her, the girl who believed''—she tilted her head to the side and a smile much older than her years graced her lips—"she was braver than people who fear the future because it's uncertain. I just acted, figuring it would all work out for the best.'' Using the edge of her sleeve, she swabbed the brass arm, injecting a cool tone into her voice. "I lost that naïveté, that self-assurance, when I came back here. I still have no fear of the future, I just loathe it because it *is* certain.''

Noah propped his elbow on the mantel, a deck plank salvaged from one of Pilot Isle's many shipwrecks. Watching Elle pace the length of the Aubusson carpet brought a startling revelation to mind. *He did not know this woman.* This engaging, puzzling, and entirely too attractive woman he denied desiring even as desire pulsed in steady jolts. He watched her frown and glide her worn slipper across the floor. The impulse to ask what made her brow crease was so powerful he gave in to it. "What are you thinking?"

She drew her head up, her foot stilling over a stubborn wrinkle. "About the school. Why, if I didn't have it, I would have nothing," she said, as casually as she would recite a recipe.

Noah brought his hand to his neck and attempted to knead the pressure away, feeling something like what he'd felt when Caleb sat on his chest as a child. Dread, breathlessness, dependency. Blessit, he did not want to know her this well, recognize her fears, understand her dreams, witness her vulnerability. Liabilities he would use to bring the balance to his side if he grew desperate enough.

And he might be getting there. Elle Beaumont packed enough force to knock him from his pragmatically grounded feet.

Crossing his ankles in what he hoped passed for casual lassitude, he pretended interest in straightening his cuffs, covertly studying her. She twisted her hair into a careless knot and raised her arm to slide an ugly hair clip—decorated with what he thought looked like calla lilies—into place. The elbows-out posture thrust her breasts forward against the worn cotton blouse which, he decided again, belonged in the garbage bin. He would bet a gold eagle against her wearing an item of consequence beneath it. He would just bet.

As unsought images intruded, he suppressed a groan and dug his nails into the mantel's jagged surface. This was not the time to let lust, a response he had learned to subdue years ago, gain the upper hand. All because a girl who had once been a thorn in his side had turned into a beautiful, intelligent, exciting woman.

I'm losing my mind. He shook his head, denied it, but the evidence chafed against his buttoned fly. Imagine me, Noah Garrett, man of rational science and precise procedure, contemplating an action as mercurial as kissing Marielle Beaumont. More specifically, of sucking her plump lower lip between his.

Without even pausing to consider the ramifications, perhaps make a detailed list of pros and cons and reviewing it to decide if he should act or not.

Which, of course, he shouldn't.

He didn't need another damned list to reinforce it. Why, he could easily think of five reasons against touching her just then, would have recorded them if he had pen and paper. He tapped his finger on the mantel. One, he would return to Chicago in another month, six weeks at best. Two, children and marriage were not on his agenda before the turn of the century. He simply didn't have the time to attend to a woman the way he supposed a man must if he intended to court her. And if he pictured getting married, it wasn't to a woman who could make the blood boil in his veins. *No, thank you.*

Elle brushed past him, her enticing, woodsy scent trailing behind. He sniffed, then let his arm drop, hiding his bulging trouser fly. A brief affair, maybe. Elle claimed to be a modern woman. She said she didn't want marriage, and he certainly didn't want it with *her.* He envisioned a marriage of respect and . . . restraint. He did not want to invite this loss of control into his life for the remainder of it. No, no, he shook his head, affairs always resulted in lies and seduction on someone's part. Things he had not had much experience doing, which led quite logically to number three—

"Merciful heavens!"

Startled, Noah reached the window in two long strides and ripped the drapery aside. A drop of water smacked his face. Craning his head, he wiped his cheek, let the musty velvet settle into place. "The roof leaks."

She smacked the heel of her hand against her brow. "Is that why this water is puddled beneath my feet? I can see why everyone thinks you're sharp as a fresh blade."

He shot her a hot look but didn't reply.

She snatched a wooden bucket from behind the threadbare love seat and shoved it at him. "Make yourself useful and put this by the chaise longue. Where the bleached spot on the floor is. That's the worst leak."

He centered the bucket precisely over the spot and returned to Elle's side. "Why don't you have the roof fixed?"

"It only happened once before. Last month, I think. I hoped it wouldn't happen again," she said, crouched on all fours, mopping the floor with a dirty rag. He felt his restraint slip another notch. Of course, her dress was bunched beneath her knees, slim ankles peeking out, round bottom perched in the air.

"Hoped it wouldn't happen again?" He went to one knee beside her, slipped a handkerchief from his back pocket, and did what he could with it. Anything to keep his hands occupied, keep them from seeking her. "How like a woman to think a roof leak would just disappear," he muttered, and twisted, wringing the cloth in a potted fern sitting atop the marble pedestal by his side.

"I'm not sure what you mean but"—she swabbed furiously, then paused to rub her wrist beneath her nose, splattering drops of water on her chest—"Widow Wynne hasn't any family in town to help her. I do what I can, in exchange for board and use of the coach house, but I can't repair the roof." She glanced at him from beneath long, thick lashes, a lazy smile spreading. "You remember my luck with roofs, don't you?"

A bark of laughter slipped out, loosening the tightness in his chest. He and Elle were *friends*. They could laugh and cross wits . . . even eat dinner together occasionally. Friends did those things all the time, innocently. Relieved, he said, "I'm not suggesting you repair the roof. Hire someone to do it." Get that lovesick idiot, Daniel Connery, to do it, he wanted to say.

She leaned across him, twisted her rag over the fern's pot, then leaned back, taking the warmth of her skin and a thoroughly seductive aroma with her. "Repairs take money, Noah. Widow Wynne doesn't have much, and I don't have much either. In fact, sending Annie to Atlanta is going to take everything I have.''

He straightened, dropped his hand to his knee, and watched her fingers skim the floor. Another drop of water smacked the blemished pine and she frowned. "I thought you had, I mean . . . I remember talk of a modest inheritance. From your mother, wasn't it? You used to tell me you were going to build a home for stray cats."

She swiped hard, spotting Noah's trousers. "My father controls that, and he won't let me have it." The accent coloring her speech and her energetic scrubbing presented the only signs of her agitation.

Before he comprehended his action, he'd captured her rag hand. "Why would he do that?"

She jerked her arm but not hard enough to pull it from his grasp. "Mercy above, Noah. I'm an unmarried, twenty-five-year-old woman running a school which makes no money and is shunned by every man in this town. My father looks at me and sees a dismal failure, a frivolous woman holding no prospects for the future, a dreamer lacking even an ounce of common sense." She swallowed, her voice dropping to a whisper. "He sees everything he hated about my mother."

Noah felt a reflexive tensing in her arm; the quiver reverberated along his. He dropped his handkerchief to the floor, uncurled her knotted fist, and kneaded her palm until her hand sprawled open on his knee. Her skin was work-roughened in patches, marked by light blue veins and freckles, fingers long and slender. He traced the bones in her wrist, her pulse thumping beneath his fingertips. "Does it matter what he thinks?"

She hung her head, considered for a moment. "It shouldn't, but it does," she finally said.

"I understand." And he did. His brothers' respect had always meant more to him than anyone's. Colleagues, professors, students. Accordingly, their criticism cut the deepest and scarred the worst. He should know.

The fingers around her wrist tensed, and she glanced up, slowly tugging her hand free.

A strained cognizance circled as rain pinked against the glass panes. Turning, she arched her back and swabbed the floor in a burst of intensity. The knot of hair at the base of her neck had begun to unravel. A lone curl brushed her collar; another lay just beneath her ear. He watched his hand lift, felt the bright spiral twist about his finger, felt the stroke of her skin, moist and warm, across the pad of his thumb.

A shudder rippled through her; her shoulders lifted in slow degrees. The delicate shush of air from her lips parted his on a strangled sigh. He could feel the heat radiating from her, see the light sheen of perspiration on the nape of her neck. Taking a deliberate breath, he let his senses savor the fragrance that lingered in his dreams night after night. Earthy and vital, the scent drew him. He wanted nothing more than to satisfy the reckless longing in his heart, ease the desperate hunger in his mind.

Giving in, Noah groaned low in his throat and curled his arm about her waist, slowly pulling her against his chest. She gasped and dropped her head, exposing a patch of radiant skin above her collar, an invitation he could no longer refuse. At the touch of his lips, the salty essence of her flowed into him, surging to the tips of his toes and back, leaving a mass of exposed nerve endings in its wake. He had never, never in his *life,* been crowded by as many images—sensual, spicy, enthralling. Not a single lucid thought remained to suppress them.

"Sweet," he whispered and tangled his fingers in her blouse, her stomach gently rounded beneath his palm, her skin searing his. He pressed light kisses along the edge of her lace-trimmed collar, following the silky curve of her ear to her jaw. His mouth parted over the hard ridge, desiring more, and moving toward it.

Elle murmured and sagged against him, giving him the opportunity he needed. Swiveling her around, he cradled her face in his palms, bringing her eyes to his. A fire burned in the green depths, one to match his.

A wave of virile self-satisfaction consumed him. *She wanted him.* Passion lived in each shallow breath she took, in the steady flush sweeping her cheeks. His hunger grew as he watched her lids flutter, her chin tilt, unwittingly bringing her lips closer. She had no idea the level of desire he felt for her, the crude images he entertained. Ones he could hardly believe, for somewhere, deep inside, he knew the touch of her lips would never be enough.

How could it be enough when she has belonged to you since the first day you saw her?

Noah reeled, the appalling thought a punch to the back of the head. He opened his eyes to find hers fixed upon him, hooded and sleepy with desire. Moonlight trickled in through a slit in the curtains, a golden glide across her slender shoulder, a fine-boned cheek. Her breath caught, body jerking beneath a tattered blouse so revealing in its simplicity he had imagined ripping it from her and taking her on the dirty *floor.*

A flood of emotion engulfed him, the weakest of which he could not contain.

Fear had him releasing her in a sudden wrenching movement; anger shoved him to his feet. Blindly, he made it to the entrance hall, his hands trembling, his gaze stealing back to the enticing sight of her kneeling in a pool of silver, her hair unbound and surrounding her lovely face, her eyes luminous and seeking. Blessit, didn't she know what it did to him when she looked at him like that? He forgot his plans for the future, his strict code of honor and his decency crisping in the blaze. He needed to remember she was an innocent woman, even if she stared at him like a courtesan.

He jerked a muddy boot on, then fumbled for the other. He'd struggled to create a life from nothing. To let Elle into his heart would demand examination of a past he had already paid the price for. Facing his brothers provided enough anguish and self-doubt for a lifetime. Not her too, dammit. He grabbed his pilot coat from the hall stand and jammed his arms in the sleeves. She roused everything he'd spent years burying beneath layers of self-sufficiency and detachment. He couldn't allow her to hold such power over him, no matter how much of a coward it made him.

Her fingers grazed his arm and he flinched, turned to find her standing directly behind him. He felt a renewed burst of desire; he wanted to touch, kiss. Battling the beast inside him, he backed away.

The beveled doorknob slid from his grasp. Wiping his hand on his trousers, he snatched the door inward and charged through it, ducking just before he hit his head on a low beam, boots skating across the damp planks. The sharp pricks of rain against his face were welcome. Hell, he would welcome anything that washed the salty-sweet taste of her from his lips. "Close the door, Elle. I'll be right here," he croaked.

"Noah." His name on her lips sounded thick and tender, heavily accented, the same way it had years ago. Starting to turn, he checked it before he had a chance to see her face. Tears might be enough to defeat him. Clenching his hands at his side, he stared into a sky dense and black as his soul, and counted the few stars he could see.

Let her cry. Let her despise me until the end of her days. Let her think I'm heartless. Cruel. A bastard. Just let her close the damned door and put something tangible between us.

With a faint click, she did.

Noah released a tense breath he had not known he held and leaned wearily against the porch railing, his trousers snug in places he did not want to consider, his heart aching because he had hurt her.

He relaxed his fists with some effort, fear holding him in its grip. Sentiments born of emotions deeper than lust bullied him: *Go back. Finish what you started.* Enduring sentiments.

Friendship, respect, admiration. How he had come to feel so much for Elle Beaumont in such a short time loomed far beyond his reasoning.

Worse, how in the world could he conquer his feelings?

Elle slid to the floor in a boneless, breakable heap. Oblivious to the rattling panes of glass in the door or the steady drip soaking her shoulder, she dropped her head to her hands and prayed for the first time in months. Surely, God wouldn't let her . . . didn't plan for—

She slammed her fist against her bent knee, recognized she held a damp rag in her fist, and flung it halfway across the entrance hall. What did everyone on Pilot Isle expect her to do *but* fall in love all over again? Why should God be any different? Noah was handsome and brilliant and honorable, everything she had known he would be. She clenched her teeth. He was darn close to perfect.

Knocking her head against the wall, she listened to his heavy footfalls. Six steps forward . . . a stagnant pause . . . six steps back. It provided some level of malicious comfort to *hear* his confusion. He would never love her, but at least he coveted her. She understood enough about that from Magnus's inept groping and Christabel's candid clarification of men's motives. Elle had held Magnus off effortlessly, never worrying about her ability to deny him.

She pinched the bridge of her nose, cursing the sudden headache. Easy to do when you didn't covet the person right back.

Reaching, she rubbed the tingling spot on her neck. He had sucked her earlobe between his lips, then swirled his tongue inside—something she would have guessed felt similar to a dog's sloppy kiss. Heaven, nothing could be further from the truth. Burying her fingers in her hair, she felt her skin flush.

Admittedly, the attraction they shared could pose a problem What did one do about it? Was there a way to reduce it, like the flame on a gas lantern? She had no idea. She had loved Noah with a young girl's heart, never experiencing this, this ... *physical* yearning that made her knees go all watery and puckered her nipples beneath her shift. Nothing but a wintry gust or a swim in the ocean before June had ever caused that before.

Strangely enough, she wasn't angry. The blatant terror on Noah's face had brought only embarrassment ... and, admittedly, a trifling twinge of anger. *All right,* it nipped a woman's vanity to close her eyes to receive her first real kiss, then open them to find the lover in question tugging his boots on like he had a fire to put out. Only a fool would be pleased by *that* reaction.

She thumped her chest and stiffened her posture. Marielle-Claire Beaumont was no longer a lovesick fool.

No, but she recognized her limits. Kissing Noah stretched those limits to the breaking point ... threatened to plunge her into the throes of unrequited love. And this time, she would want more than friendship. She might go as far as demanding the delicious things Christabel had explained in vivid detail.

A cold drop of rain struck her flaming cheek, and she sucked in a startled breath as Noah continued to pace outside. Scooting across the floor, she captured the rag beneath her heel and dragged it into her waiting hand. She wasn't some pathetic schoolgirl, she reasoned, and viciously scrubbed at the water stain.

For once in her life, maybe the first time, she planned to follow Noah's advice and think. Use her head and not her heart.

Chapter Six

"Well, daughter, you've definitely landed in trouble neck-deep this time."

Elle turned, dropping the bundle of files she held to her father's desk. Horrified, she could only wonder how he knew about Noah touching her.

Henri slammed the office door behind him and crossed the room in three angry strides. He stubbed his cigar in a crystal dish of rose petals Elle had placed in water that morning. A thin streak of blue-gray smoke wafted past her face, the honeyed stench turning her stomach. "You had to help the little Duggan urchin, didn't you? Had to make sure you protected her. Feminine freedom for all. From whom has she gained independence, Marielle-Claire? May I ask you?" His lips clenched, a white ring circling his mouth. "Her husband, daughter, who has every right to do whatever he pleases to her, which includes applying a firm hand if he chooses. Did you know she is carrying his child? *Grands Dieux!*" He slammed his fist to the desk. "Did it ever occur to you to remember Sean Duggan is the best pilot I have? My shipments are rarely delayed. He can navigate every inlet and shoal in the Banks with his eyes closed. Or should I say he is the best pilot I *had*. He tendered his resignation today, left to work for Elias Benton. When I requested a reason, he said he could not continue to work for a family aiding in his wife's departure.''

''I—''

Henri leaned as far as he could, belly digging into the dark mahogany edge. Before she could react, he grasped her chin between his fingers. ''Elias Benton is my competitor, Marielle-Claire. A ruthless competitor, who does not need the assistance of my only child to make a success of his business ventures.''

She tried to open her mouth, but he lifted her chin, forcing her lips together. ''Do not speak unless it's to inform me you did *not* help Annie Duggan leave Pilot Isle, in which case you will apologize to Sean for his dilemma. He is worried, beyond measure. His wife has been missing for five days, and it appears as if she is not returning. The man has searched Morehead City thoroughly with no luck. Except to find a receipt of his wife's passage on the express train bound for Atlanta. He refuses to go chasing after her if she has run home to her mother.''

Elle jerked her chin from his grasp and shoved to her feet, knocking the chair against the wall. ''I did help her, and I would do it again. Tomorrow and the next day and the next,'' she said roughly, her throat dry from fury and frustration. ''Think highly of that monster while you think poorly of your own daughter, if you wish, but I would do it again. Again and again. And I will never, I can vow this on Mother's grave, apologize for helping Annie leave.''

The slap rocked her head to the side with less strength than he could have used. Calmly, Elle walked around the desk, the pain in her cheek fading to a dull throb. However, the shock of her father's brutality had her pulse pounding in her head.

''Marielle-Claire, come back here,'' he called, but she was beyond hearing, or caring. The last, fragile vestige of family had been robbed from her, and she found herself racing down the staircase to escape being so alone.

* * *

The lively confusion of the harbor crowded round Noah as he maneuvered the slick gangplank leading from the *Nellie Dey*'s deck. He rotated his aching shoulders, wondering how he would ever get in good enough condition to work the nets without his muscles screaming for relief. Stepping onto the wharf, he tossed a scrap of fish to a shrieking gull and watched it seize the morsel in a swooping dive. Men dressed much as he was, in grimy bib trousers and muddy brogans, bumped past, gill nets in hand, barrels hoisted upon their shoulders, crab pots clanking at their sides. All of them, him included, reeked of fish and hard labor, the stink worsened by the scorching afternoon sun.

"Aw, look at her, willya."

Noah shouldered his satchel of research materials and moved next to a group of fishermen circling a corked barrel of ale which would, no doubt, be recorded as damaged in transit.

"Wonder what the French bastard said to her this time?" Fat Jack asked in a singsong alto.

Effortlessly, Noah looked over their heads, to the top of a staircase leading from Henri Beaumont's warehouse. His breath caught. Elle descended at a dangerously breakneck speed.

Her skirt flipped about her ankles; bright curls danced about her head. He squinted, imagined he could see a flush staining her cheeks. The sudden image of his lips pressed against her smooth, slightly moist skin pierced him like a hook beneath his.

"She looks to be in a fine fury, don't she?" This from a young New Englander who had sailed south aboard one of the whaling ships.

Jeb Crow, who claimed to be half Cherokee, but looked rather Nordic to Noah, laughed and ejected a stream of tobacco juice from his chapped lips. Noah grimaced and glanced at his feet. Whether he wore dirty brogans or polished oxfords, he preferred not to have his shoes spit upon.

"She gave the worldly toad the business end of a stick, I tell you. Trying to get her hitched, he is, and she ain't agreeing," Jeb said and spit again, this time closer to the New Englander.

"Can't blame Beaumont. Never married, never close, even. If that was *my* daughter, I'd skin her alive," Walt Pepper stated, seeming to forget his daughter had run off with a Scottish sailor and nobody knew for sure if marriage had been part of the deal.

Jeb crammed another wad of tobacco in his cheek. "Yep, Miss Ellie's 'bout near thirty years old. Way past time to marry, birth some babies. Make her forget that women's school nonsense."

Noah's gaze traversed the group. *Chrissakes, what a bunch of idiots.* He started to turn when, as often happens, the conversation degenerated.

"Look at her twitch. Put together nice, she is."

"Yessiree."

Noah glanced back in time to see Elle hop to the boardwalk. He wouldn't call it twitching, but she did jiggle a little.

"You know what they say 'bout orange-haired women."

"Maybe she ain't found the right fella, yet. Maybe I should go calling." Crude sniggers and hard backslaps accompanied this suggestion, then the conversation halted. They turned in unison to stare at Noah, snickering beneath their ale-scented breaths. "Or maybe she *has* found him, but he just won't find *her.*"

Noah's hands closed into fists. What did these men know of Elle? Would they have been willing to defy an enraged, drunken bully who beat his wife? Had they fought for freedoms they believed in and lost their dreams as a result? She had more courage in her pinkie finger than the whole lot of them put together. Wrenching around, Noah forced his feet to move before he did something ridiculous, something completely out of character. Before he allowed a quintessentially masculine response to overpower intellect. It seemed he fought this battle too often lately.

He sidestepped a muddy rut in the center of the shell-paved road, navigated a crush of lumber wagons and vegetable carts, and raised his hand in greeting three times to the call of "Professor" before increasing his stride.

The edge of Elle's skirt was mud-stained, the hem dangling. It flicked the front of his brogans as he reached her. He struggled to ignore how the worn cloth clung to her hips, swayed with her brisk, rolling stride. She didn't walk like a lady, and she obviously didn't care who knew it.

Just when he caught up to her, she halted, dead in the middle of the street. He had no choice but to plow into her, grip her waist to steady himself.

"Noah, what are you doing?" She made no move to pull from his grasp.

Doing? He had no idea. He woke each morning, his mind full of images he couldn't shake, desires he didn't want any part of. Physical labor served as his only savior. The captain of the *Nellie Dey* had even offered him a job for the season, telling him he had never seen a man work so hard. If the captain only knew about the tangle of conflicting thoughts crowding his mind, driving him to labor until his hands cracked and bled, until he collapsed in a leather chair each night, too exhausted to do more than stare at Tyre McIntosh's sloppy notes regarding the laboratory's progress.

"Hello, Noah?" She tapped his head with a slender finger. "Are you in there?"

"I'll be damned if I know," he muttered, and dropped his hands.

"Don't you have some young woman waiting at the corner to walk you home? Why then, in the name of heaven, are you hounding me?" Elle took a step, then stopped, and he almost ran into her again. "If I could only scream what I really think about life at the top of my lungs. Oh, if I had only been born a male, I could drink a bottle of whiskey and shuck my clothes off while I screamed and it would be just fine and dandy.''

Noah shrugged, evading the image of Elle shucking her clothes off during a drunken binge. He rocked back on his heels, properly chastised. Perhaps *chagrined* better described the itch beneath his collar. Not for following her or watching her little show on the staircase, but because Meredith Scoggins probably *was* waiting for him on the corner. She had been there every day this week.

"That's right, shrug and wonder what possesses women to rant and rave like they're deranged. Hunch your shoulders like a boy who wants to crawl under his bed and hide. Go ahead. Congratulate yourself for your mighty, masculine restraint. Your superior intelligence."

"Elle." He patted her shoulder in an awkward gesture of peace, opposing emotions battling for advantage. To comfort, to flee. Only, her voice, though filled with fury, held a frantic, alarmingly ragged, edge, which rallied right through the hardened walls of his heart. "What happened?" he asked softly.

He watched her back rise and fall on a deep breath. "My father asked me to apologize to Sean Duggan for helping Annie leave town. He summoned me to his office this morning, and it was stupid of me, I know, but I reasoned it might be because he wanted to call a truce for our argument last week. I showed up early, did his records for the past week, and filed the invoices. He probably won't even notice. Every time I offer him a part of myself, he throws it away like an old shoe. I should know after all this time not to trust him. My father doesn't give his love freely. He never has." She touched her cheek, her face hidden from view. "The discovery that nothing will ever change, that, in fact, things are worse than I imagined"—she shrugged—"oh, never mind. Certainly none of your concern." She whirled right into the path of a dray loaded with crates of squawking chickens.

Noah grabbed her shoulders and hauled her against him. "Hold on there," he whispered in her ear. He could feel the tremors shaking her body, molding tightly, *perfectly* to his.

"Watch out, Miss Ellie," the driver shouted, and jerked the reins, bringing his nag to a stumbling halt, chicken feathers drifting to the ground.

"*You* watch out, Homer Crawford!" She slapped the side of the wagon and wrenched from Noah's grip.

"Women," Homer grumbled, and plucked a feather from his lap.

Noah dodged the end of the wagon as it shuddered forward. Racing to catch Elle, he shoved her into the nearest place they could talk without interruption, the darkened alley between the mercantile and Christabel's saloon. "Do you want to calm down and tell me what's going on?"

"Please, Noah"—she tapped the toe of her boot against a broken bottle, her voice wavering—"just leave me alone."

"What happened?"

She shook her head in denial.

"Tell me what happened," he demanded, his voice rougher than he'd intended. "I'm a part of it, if you care to remember. I escorted Annie to Morehead City, not you." He pressed his elbows into his ribs, determined not to touch her. His attraction, he had decided, was perfunctory, nothing more. Just then, with her honeysuckle-scented hair tickling his chin, he had trouble remembering.

She straightened her shoulders and slowly lifted her gaze. It disturbed him to see the grief behind a wall of ragged vigilance. But nothing disturbed him as much as seeing the round bruise purpling her cheek. Something shifted. In his stomach. In his chest. Something unrecognizable, something he felt sure he had never experienced before. "Did he hit you?" His hand lifted, traced the mark gently. A dull wash of red clouded his vision. "Did your father hit you?"

She swallowed. "It doesn't matter."

"The hell it doesn't," he hissed, and tipped her chin high. "Why, Elle, why did he do this?"

"Sean Duggan resigned today. The best seaman on Pilot Isle, according to my father. And because of me, he lost him to Elias Benton."

"He did this to you because of a business deal?"

"Yes."

Noah stepped back, folding his arms. Rage made him think terribly ugly thoughts. "Is he in his office?"

She grabbed his wrist, pulled him close. "You have to let me handle this. He's my *father*. Anyway, it didn't hurt, except in here." She pressed her palm over her heart. "And, sadly enough, that's mostly gone. You see, I *left* him, actually left him, when I moved from his home two years ago. Besides having dinner with him once a week, he gives me nothing, and I give him nothing. We share nothing. Heavens, sometimes it's hard to believe I'm his flesh and blood."

"You don't have to ask him for anything. Not after this. I can help you. I want to help you."

"I told you no before."

"Elle, be reasonable. You used your savings sending Annie home, gave her the last penny you had. Take the money. I told you I made some very wise investments in Chicago. There's more in my accounts than I know how to spend. I could give you enough to see you through the year, get the leaky roof fixed, *and* buy a new floor for the school."

She shook her head. "Knowing I can talk to you is more than enough. Maybe I was waiting for you to find me. Who knows? Old habits die hard, or so they say. It's nice to speak honestly for once in my life. I admit, I felt the weight slip from my shoulders the minute you stepped behind me."

A chill raised the hair on his arms. "How did you know I was behind you?"

"Oh, Noah." She laughed, a mixture of impishness and frustration. "I would know if you entered a room if the door was behind my back, and I had a blindfold tied over my eyes. I used to sit in school, waiting. The air changed temperature, closed in around me the second you walked in. The hair on my neck would prickle. I knew, I just knew." She considered a moment, then shrugged, clearly stating it didn't matter if she acknowledged it. "I still do."

He took an unsteady step, grinding crushed shells beneath his boots. "Hush," he rasped, a full dose of panic trapping his breath in his chest.

"If I can't tell you, whom can I tell? I get tired of pretending. I don't know why, I mean, I've never quite understood it, but it has always been there, this connection between us. At least for me it has." She sighed. "Don't deny it if you know it's there. Why bother?"

"I don't know what you're talking about," he said, and glanced at a cobweb dangling above her head.

"How can you lie when we each need a friend so desperately?"

His hand shot out as his gaze snagged hers. "What if I *do* lie? What the hell difference can it make to reawaken issues best left dead? How can it help either one of us?"

"Dead *issues?* Is that what you think of your past, your family, your childhood? As something dead?" She searched his face, observing too much. "You carry this grief around like baggage. It's foolish. Your brothers love you. You're blessed to have them, to have Rory, and yet, you have no perception of the miracle of family. Love is a gift. Not an obligation, not a burden."

Ignoring her penetrating stare, Noah paced the length of the alley. She had twisted him into a knot, as usual. Strong words and high-minded ideals. Brutal honesty. And what had he been trying to do in the first place? Comfort her. Protect her from harm because of the damned *connection* she spoke of. "I'm trying to repair the damage I've done to my family, you know that. I'm doing it in my own way, in my own time." *Without completely ripping my soul from my body,* he silently added. Pausing in front of her, he said, "What would you have me do? Cut a vein and let everything inside rush out?"

"Yes, if it brought you some level of serenity."

"Serenity?" He ripped his spectacles off and rubbed ink-stained fingers beneath his eyes. "Don't I look serene to you?"

"You look haggard."

"There was a problem at the lab yesterday, the freight company lost a shipment of materials. And, I took beach patrol with Zach and Rory last night." Slowly, he shook his head. "They're trying so hard to reach me and . . . I don't know what to do about it."

"What did you expect? None of this disappeared when you left. It's been frozen for ten years." She brushed a lock of hair from her brow. "Have you attempted to face it? Visit your mother's grave? Ask where her diary is?"

He shoved his spectacles in his pocket and stumbled forward, her chin meeting his chest, her skirt brushing his knuckles. *"No."* He wanted to clap his hands over his ears. Her words held the strength of a sharp knife, slicing past his restraint, his calm sense of purpose. "I told you once to stay out of my business."

She smacked into the wall. Bits of flint sprinkled her feet. "Quit looking at me like some wild animal, cornered by a predator. I'm not that lovelorn girl chasing you down the docks. Dear heaven, she has been gone for a long time. How can I make you believe I only want your friendship, which I would think you would be willing to give? You can talk to me, even if you don't think you can talk to anyone else. You always could."

She innocently spoke of love and friendship, but what he wanted from her had nothing to do with those things and everything to do with her melting like butter over him. Didn't she understand? The cherished boy in her memories wouldn't be contemplating throwing her to the ground in a disgusting alley, tangling her hair around his fingers as his body covered hers. Knotting his fists together, Noah fought the urge to run.

"Don't shut me out."

"I *want* to shut you out. Better yet, shut you up."

A small wrinkle appeared between her scrunched eyebrows. "I don't know how to help you with that."

He expelled a ragged hitch of laughter. "Yes, well, makes two of us." Pacing from her, a confusion of emotion bombarded him. Did she honestly think what happened in Widow Wynne's parlor occurred between *friends?* Blessit, was she that naive? He'd wanted one brief taste of her, to see if she would equal his dreams. Similar to an experiment, he reasoned.

Sudden relief flooded his mind, and he smiled. An experiment. So damned simple, he couldn't believe he had not thought of it before. Most of his torment the last week had been self-induced, pure conjecture. He had taken an instinctual sensual response of adolescence and transformed it into a man's carnal desire. He could not draw from past experience any of the images crowding his mind. In all probability, they were as spurious as a storm cloud that never brings rain. To disprove them would force them from his mind. Touching Elle the way he had the other night had obviously not disproved anything.

Before he could change his mind, he dropped his satchel to the ground and turned to her. Elle flattened against the wall, chin angled high, frightened but defiant. She would not run. And for once, neither would he.

The muddled humming in his ears the only sign of his discomfiture, he leaned in, pressed his palms to the rough brick on either side of her head, effectively blocking her exit. He had no choice, could no longer live at the mercy of his emotions. To expunge the temptation, he must yield to it.

"Noah," she said, half question, half plea. A warm breath skirted his cheek, one smelling faintly of apple. Her gaze skimmed his face, lingering on his mouth before lowering. She made a faint sound of protest.

"Friends, Elle." He lifted his hand and outlined her bottom lip with the tip of his finger. Sealing his lids, he concentrated on the way the moist skin clung to his. Soft, but not as soft as he had dreamed. Chapped, like she worried the skin between her teeth. She exhaled, her nostrils flaring beneath his fingers. The silky curve of her cheek, the crescent of hair above each eye. Expelling a strangled sound, she stiffened and left his hand dangling before her face. "Friends," he whispered before he dipped his head. He paused, savoring the sweet scent of her. With her next apple-breath, he guided his mouth to hers.

He felt her tremble from the effort of stemming her response. "Trust me, sweet," he coaxed. He dug his palms into the gritty wall, thinking only of his goal, intent on ending his fascination with this woman. Today, right this minute, he would find out how good she tasted. Find his dreams were simply dreams.

On a sigh of surrender, a shared release of passion, her mouth parted. Seizing the opportunity, he plucked her generous bottom lip between his teeth, held it steady as his tongue memorized the delicate texture. He moistened and suckled, skimming back and forth. Grasping his forearms, she groaned into his mouth, and his mission dimmed, a light at the end of a long tunnel. Deepening the kiss, he fell prey to the sensations pricking every exposed nerve. The scent of scorched rose petals . . . the rough edges of her front tooth . . . her tentative forays. She edged up the wall, soft breasts chafing his chest, eager hands tangling in his bib straps.

His heart slammed hard, out of control. "No," he said, and twisted away from her.

A rush of humid air shot between them, and Elle blinked, looking into an impossibly young, unguarded face. Eyes closed, lashes curled against his sun-kissed skin, lips parted to allow throaty breaths free. She captured the image, realizing she would never see it again unless she caught him sleeping.

Merciful heavens, he looked like the boy she remembered. Her first day of school, a classroom smelling of chalk and vinegar. Herman Stanley apologizing for making fun of her accent. Noah giving her a slow smile of acceptance and unwittingly propelling a warm tide of love between two beats of her heart.

He had touched her with his beautiful hands before he had touched her with his mouth. His fingers had stroked her face with the intent of enlightenment. Some of the gentle-hearted child had to be left inside him—and *he* pulled away from her.

She curled her fingers around his straps and tugged him off balance; a word of protest slipped free.

This is your chance, Elle. Take it.

She ignored his alarmed expression and bounced onto the balls of her feet, silently thanking her father for the ballet lessons. Slanting her head as Noah had done, she fit her mouth over his, pliant but not eager. She would use him for her own purpose, just as he had done. Her hands stroked his chest, his face, recording each ridge, each crease. She threaded her fingers through the damp curls at the base of his neck. Not sure how to ask for more, she gingerly touched her tongue to the corner of his lips.

Uttering a low groan of defeat, he crowded her into the wall, arms stealing around to cushion the impact. His heat scorched her skin; the taste of butterscotch filled her mouth. He had a sweet tooth, she remembered, dazed and dreamy.

Raising his hands to her face, he cradled her head, held her steady as his mouth truly captured hers. Her body slumped, a gradual melting. Caution, fear, logic, her father's cruelty, all liquefied, roaring like the ocean at high fury in her head.

Lightly at first, then using greater pressure, he teased, raising the point of pleasure to heights she had not imagined. He angled his head, drew his tongue across her lips, showing her what he wanted. She didn't care if it was right or wrong, foolish or wise—she opened. And he took.

It was unlike any kiss she had known before. His mouth aggressive, his whiskered cheeks rough, his hands eager, gliding past her neck, her shoulders. She felt his control slip as he delved, bending, wrapping her in a gossamer web of need. *His need.* Of course, he would deny it later. But right now, *this minute,* his body joined intimately with hers, the scent of her clinging to his clothing, his salty-butterscotch taste heavy in her mouth, she knew. She had wondered the other night but now she knew.

He wanted her.

She did not mistake it for love or consideration, kindness or respect. This blind ferocity, wild and physically undeniable, amounted to nothing more than overwhelming urgency. So be it.

Hesitant but earnest, she followed his movements, flicking her tongue against his, then swirling. A battle of hunger. A tortured sound rumbled deep in his throat. His lips trembled, his hands snagging impatiently in her hair. Her knees weakened, and he steadied her, fit her to him.

Desire. Christabel had explained in vague terms what it meant to want a man so much you would do anything to have him.

"Closer," he whispered against her lips, his sweet breath skimming her face.

Juste Ciel, she wanted to get closer. Already, his back bowed to accommodate for their disparity in height. The notion burned: They would not have this problem lying flat. She stretched, trying. Almost ... she could almost—

He caught her under the arms, lifting and settling her astride his hard thigh. Her dress snagged between her legs, his knee wedged against the wall. His lips never left hers. Not once. *My, how ingenious,* she thought.

She explored freely everything accessible to her hands, her mouth. His arm muscles felt bigger, from hauling nets and icing fish, his chest broader, harder. Her mouth traversed the hard edge of his jaw, nipped lightly at the skin below his ear.

How could a man who smelled so strongly of fish taste so wonderful?

She wiggled on his thigh, heat pooling between her legs. Whatever she searched for, she couldn't find.

"Let me show you," he breathed against her ear, and grasped her waist, moving her gently forward, then back—a tantalizing abrasion. *Oh, yes.* She buried her face in the crook of his neck, the muffled moan escaping before she could stop it.

A rusty creak penetrated the haze surrounding her, and she lifted her head. Noah's mouth traveled to her cheek, to the corner of her lips. Elle fought the urge to close her eyes, drift on a cloud of moist, fervent kisses.

A gentle cough. Then another. Elle pushed on his chest. "Noah." She forced the word between gasping breaths, took his face in her hands. "We're not . . . *alone,*" she said, mouthing the last word. Gradually, the music from the Nook filtered past desire. His eyelids flickered, flipped open, widened. Smoldering, charcoal gray. His nostrils flared on a rush of released air.

"Chrissakes," he whispered, throat clicking on a hard swallow, chest rising and falling in a frantic rhythm as he fought for air.

Equally bewildered, Elle could only stare, wondering if she looked as disheveled as he did. As appealingly undone. Gaze unfocused, lips swollen, hair plastered to his forehead in locks of wet gold. Another burst of heat lit her. She wanted nothing more than to pull his mouth to . . .

"Stop looking at me like that. Do you want to end up beneath me, dammit?" He spoke harshly, but he was slow to release her, even slower to lift her from his thigh. The whole time, he shielded her from view, waiting for her to stand firmly, her palm braced against the wall to hold herself up. Expelling a weary sigh, he slipped his spectacles on and turned.

Elle peeked around him to find Christabel, hands fisted on her hips, her expression vacillating between amusement and a healthy dose of curiosity. "Sorry to come across you in an indelicate state, but better me than some horny fisherman."

Elle frowned, unfamiliar with the term. Maybe Noah knew it because he tensed.

"You'd better take the back way, Noah. Honey, you come through the kitchen with me," she instructed.

"What the hell do you have to do with it?" he all but snarled.

"I'm the woman who's gonna keep every gossip on the Isle from making your life a damned ordeal, that's what I have to do with it."

"Christabel Connery, you remember. Daniel's older sister. She owns the restaurant." Elle laid her hand on Noah's arm to diffuse his rigid stance and . . . honestly, she couldn't stand so close and not touch him. Not when his had brought her body to life.

"I own the Nook, too. Trust me, the men will be streaming in from the docks any minute, ready to drink now the sun's set. Some are already in there raising the devil. End of the week and pockets full of money. No need to advertise you've been here. Poor man's bedroom, they call it."

Noah growled and spun to face Elle. His somber gaze captured hers, shadows slithering down his face. He drew air into his lungs and let it loose in a harsh rattle. "I'm sorry, Elle. Sorry for this."

She stared at his lips as they moved, watched them flatten, helpless to do anything but remember them covering hers. "I don't want you to be sorry. I'm not sorry."

"You will be" he promised, and stooped to grab his satchel from the ground. Rising slowly, he frowned, fiddling with the leather strap, his lips parting as if he would say more. His hand hovered near her bruised cheek. "I'm sorry," he repeated, and let his hand drop. The snap of shells beneath his brogans rang hollow and final in his wake. The mystical appeal of the alley departed with him, leaving only a slight chill, deepening shadows, and the stink of whiskey and fried fish.

"I waited as long as I could, but you don't need nobody seeing you tangled up like two cats in a sack. Believe me, I know. It don't do any good," Christabel said from the doorway.

Elle had no idea what it would be like to be caught *tangled up* with a man. Although Christabel was right, of course. It wouldn't be good. Well, it wouldn't be *wise*. Her father, Zach, Caleb. All of them would find out, not to mention the entire town. She dropped her head to her hands, inhaled a ragged breath. Her skin smelled of him, her mouth tasted of him. How did a woman get past that?

"I didn't know he would stalk outta here. Boy, he has a nasty temper. Do you reckon he remembers I carved *Elle loves Noah* into all those tree trunks?"

Elle laughed through her laced fingers. "Oh, Christa, however it ended, he wasn't going to handle it well. For a brief moment, the appalling happened, and he lost his beloved control. It's not your fault he's . . ." Scared. Stubborn. Churlish. She wagged her head, frustrated to the core.

"Do you want to come inside? Have a cup of coffee? I make a mean pot, you know."

"No." She glanced at Christabel. Blond and robust, she carried a lot of responsibility on her broad shoulders. Elle never underestimated her wisdom, no matter the packaging. "Thank you. I know you did what you thought best. And you're right. I know that, too."

"Makes no difference if I'm right. Don't lessen the wanting. Anyway, no need to fret. I'll take care of him when he comes in tonight."

Executing a feeble half turn, Elle swayed against the wall. *"What?"*

Christabel gave her a sympathetic look. Never had the contrast in their upbringings been more apparent. "He'll be back. Not a man alive who can walk away from what he walked away from here and not seek a little relief." She winked.

"Unless he comes knocking on your door, I provide the only relief in town."

Jealousy curled Elle's fingers into fists, stiffened her spine until she feared it would crack.

Christabel snorted and slapped her hands together. "Oh, honey, not *that* kind of relief. Whiskey is all I'm talking about. Sure, he could find the other if he wanted it bad enough, but Noah's not that kinda man. Trust me, I can pick the scamps a mile off."

Elle chewed her lip, her suddenly tight clothing making her hot and itchy. "I didn't mean . . . without doubt, I don't care what he does. This was simply a—a slip."

"A slip? What proper women call it, I guess. Okay, honey, a slip." Christabel flapped her apron in the air, her lips pressed to hold in a smile. "Now, get going. Just in case Noah decides to *slip* with you again, dabble some toilet water or some nice-smelling perfume between your breasts and put on a pretty dress. Maybe comb your hair."

Christabel's laughter, and her blasted advice, needled Elle the entire walk home.

Chapter Seven

Elle angled the letter into a shaft of moonlight and read it for the fourth time.

April 2, 1898

My Dearest Friend:

I have enclosed an application for the scholarship program I mentioned in my previous letter. As you can see, each year the fund lends money to permit a promising young woman to attend college. Our last recipient chose to attend Cornell. I know you had previously considered returning to Bryn Mawr, but just look at the marvelous number of universities included in the program.

I admit to rallying behind you at the scholarship meeting last month, but dearest Elle, who could be more deserving? Many on the committee feel your extremely high entrance scores are an added benefit as well as your proven dedication to furthering women's education. I am confident a completed application is all that is standing in the way of your dream.

Now, my friend, I can see you right now, shaking your head and telling yourself your school could not survive without you. Actually Elle I have felt a fair measure of discontent lately, an urge to accomplish more than I possibly can in New York City. I hope you consider my offer to manage the school in your absence a serious one. I would be proud to work with your students.

I am speaking at a reform meeting tonight and hope to encourage the audience members to contribute generously.

> *To friendship,*
> *Savannah*

The letter provided a grand opportunity to change her life, Elle guessed, folding it and slipping it into her pocket. The scholarship application lay on her marble-top washstand, four pages of essay questions and personal queries. If she could find some additional means of income, she could survive.

In her entire life, she had only wanted *one* thing more than she wanted an education. Glancing at the darkened window of the coach house, she knew no hope of that remained.

Reclining on the bed of grass, she hooked her arms beneath her head and stared into a sky ripening from pitch-black to predawn blue. Birds had just begun to twitter, the only noise besides the distant roar of the ocean. No, not the only noise. She tilted her head, heard the thump of barrels being unloaded on the dock, the ring of a bell announcing a ship entering the harbor.

She rubbed her hand beneath her nose, the fragrance shooting a dart of chagrin through her. Sentimental absurdity to dab perfume between her breasts, behind her ears, beneath her wrists. A lone tear trailed past her cheek, and she scrubbed it away. How could she do this? Hadn't she learned her lesson years ago? For her, Noah Garrett would always mean heartache.

Obvious he would not be coming home. Christabel had said he would go to the Nook. *To seek relief.* Elle could not picture Noah dousing his confusion in whiskey and cheap cigars. Nonetheless, Christa understood men better than she did.

Frankly, it surprised her he had not removed his possessions from the coach house. Fled to safer ground, as he would in preparation for a deadly hurricane. Losing control posed as grave a disaster in his mind. It would be easy for him to sneak away, apart from the multitude of glass tubes, research books, and curious gadgets in the coach house. In a sorrowful testament to her weakness, she knew they still littered every vacant surface. Darkness had provided the courage to climb the flight of stairs and peer through the grimy pane. Unfortunately, a shift in wind had startled her, causing her to turn too quickly, knocking a jar filled with murky water and a piece of gnarled driftwood from the landing. The driftwood she had put back in its place, the jar lay in pieces in the bottom of her garbage bin. She hoped she had not ruined some important experiment.

What had she been thinking? She twisted the damp edge of her dress in her fist and pounded her thigh in frustration. To let him kiss her as he whispered "friends" in her ear, to kiss him back, starved for his touch. Exposed, her mouth eager and open. It didn't make sense. She had let him go the other night, stressing she would not fall in love with him again, telling herself she was finished with men. In fact, she had told Daniel Connery the same thing not a day before. And she had meant it.

She had not even considered rejecting Noah. Had, in fact, raced recklessly into his arms. A reckless, gullible fool hoarding a vestige of absurd hope—imagining a twenty-seven-year-old man was innocent. Oh no, not after, not after the little—she groaned, but it loomed terribly clear—*rubbing* incident. He had known exactly where to focus his energy, setting her atop his hard thigh, grasping her waist, and . . .

She squirmed. Her memory had not only recorded their performance in vivid detail, it had salvaged her feral response. She plucked her clinging bodice from her hardened nipples. A fresh morning breeze lifted loose tendrils of hair from her neck, her forehead, yet she felt as wilted as a cornstalk during a summer drought, her face swollen and feverishly warm.

The image of Noah touching another woman made her queasy. He had obviously touched many. Mrs. Bartram of the scented letters, for one. He simply knew a woman's body too well. Living in a depraved city, possibly hundreds had shared his bed. Elle closed her eyes, a sharp pain seizing her, riding hard from her toes to the top of her head. She gasped and coughed, rolled to her stomach and heaved. Her stomach churned but emptied nothing.

She rested her cheek on the prickly cushion of grass, images of Noah's hands upon her spinning round and round her mind like the phonograph in Christabel's parlor. What they had done represented only a trifling part of what they could do. Even in her ignorance, she realized that. And, she understood he had done much more at some point in his life. The presumption only made her sob and bury her face in her hands. *Damn and blast,* she didn't need to wallow in the dirt when she owned only three decent dresses, and this represented the best of the lot.

Tears had never come easily or often, and they dried quickly. Crying answered no questions, abated no fears. It only made Elle feel sticky and weak. Swabbing her face, she rolled to her back and watched the first delicate streaks of red and gold spread like a blush along the horizon.

I wish Noah had come home, been here to share it with me.

"I still love him," she whispered. "You fool, after all this time, you still love him."

Wrenching to a sit, she pressed hard on her chest and willed her heartbeat to return to normal, the world to right on its axis. *Oh, blast. I still love him.* A man armored against love.

Her hand shaking, she slipped her fingers into her watch pocket and fingered Savannah's letter with a renewed sense of anticipation and dread.

The pounding ripped Zach from sleep. Shoving to his elbows on the bunk, he drew a hitching breath and let his head flop back. The muscles in his arms quivered, and his heart raced in his chest. The dream returned in a series of gray flashes. Blood staining the sheets . . . Hannah's shrill, weak cries . . . his lungs burning as he raced for the doctor . . . lifeless blue eyes and cold, stiff fingers.

A dream, Zach. A dream. The salty burn of tears stung, and he swallowed thickly. *Oh, Lord, am I going to dream about her dying for the rest of my life?*

Another round of knocking shook the metal door in its frame. "Coming," he said, praying a ship had not gotten beached on Diamond Shoals. He would have to check his list to see whose turn it was to patrol. They had been lucky lately, but luck, Zach well knew, always ran out. His certainly had.

Flinging the thin woolen blanket to the floor, he found his coat hanging on the back of a chair and was just pulling his arms through the sleeves when he reached the door.

"Cap'n Garrett, open up."

The door swung inward, hardly a squeak cast from her well-oiled hinges. The smell of smoke and whiskey drifted in, attached to Bigby Dixon, Christabel's manservant, for lack of a better description. The hulking man stood beneath the jail's narrow lean-to, broad shoulder braced against a timber post, hooked grin riding his freckled face. Zach's shoulders slumped in relief. Bigby helped him organize the safety drills and scrubbed salt from the breech buoys on occasion, but he did not patrol the beach on a regular basis, and never alone.

"You might better come, Cap'n." Bigby dabbed his boot in the circle of light cast onto the scrubbed planks. "Miss Christabel sent me for you. All I know. Honest."

Captain. Zach had ceased being a captain before Hannah died, but Bigby would hardly know it. "Who is it?" he asked, digging in his pocket for his ring of keys, knowing exactly who it was.

Bigby's held tilted quizzically. "Ah, you know, Cap'n. Your brother."

"Of course." Zach crossed the street at a fast clip, Bigby trailing in his steps. They stopped twice. To look at a frog flattened by a wagon wheel and to count the masts rising above the peaked roofs of the warehouses. Zach reminded himself, gazing into Bigby's joyful face, that all the excitement and innocence of Rory's world filled this man's and always would.

When they arrived at the Nook, he sent Bigby to fetch coffee with a promise to let him sleep in the jail cell one night next week. Sidestepping scarred tables scattered with cigar butts and half-filled glasses, he halted before Christabel's parlor doors. She settled Caleb on the striped horsehair sofa after he'd gotten particularly rambunctious, separated from the temptation angry words, cheap whiskey, and flirtatious women presented.

He knocked once, hard and furious.

"Zach?"

"Yes."

One of the doors slid into its pocket, a flood of light spilling across his boots. He strode past her, pulling his sleeve from her grasp.

"Zach, you might . . ." Her words faded to a whispered sigh.

The uncharacteristic hint of caution in her voice threw a wrinkle in his stride. Zach halted, his gaze drawn to the mammoth chestnut desk occupying one corner of the room. "Damn," he said and raised his hand to his face, wiping grit from his brow. "Damn."

"His spectacles." She tapped them against his wrist. "Didn't want him to break them."

Zach took the wire frames from her. "Lord knows, this isn't what I expected."

She tilted her head to the side and twitched her shoulders, a halfhearted shrug. "He's a man, Zach."

An inadequate explanation for finding his *sensible* brother slumped over her desk.

Zach stepped forward, his knees knocking against the heavily grained wood. Noah's arms sheltered his face, his hair tousled and bright against rumpled black shirtsleeves.

"What happened?"

Christabel stepped beside him, the opposing scents of whiskey and flowers surrounding her. "Things were pretty quiet last night, most of the men summoned home by their wives long before Noah got here. He'd been sailing, from the look of it. Had a wild glow in his eyes. Honest, I never figured he looked much like Caleb until then. I reckoned for sure he would bust up one of my tables before the night ended." She stacked her fingers along the desk and leaned her weight on them. "Anyway, I brought him here right away. With a bottle. I knew, I just, well . . . oh, I probably shouldn't say, but good gracious, I wanna tell someone." She knotted her hands together and recounted a story that left Zach feeling like he'd stumbled into a burning building.

"You found them *what?*"

She raised her hand to her heart and made a swift sign of the cross. "Kissing. And no sweet, decent kiss, neither. Singed the air, it did. I swear, plain as day that's what I saw."

"Maybe, maybe . . ." He slid a thoughtful gray gaze her way. "Are you sure?"

"Sure? Honey, they were practically clawing at each other."

Frowning, he watched Noah's chest rise and fall in a steady rhythm. "Do you think he loves her?"

She considered a moment, took in Noah's condition in one

sweeping glance. "Whatever he feels, looks to me like he don't want to."

"What should I do?"

Christabel cocked her head toward the heavy footfalls on the floor above, Bigby's childish laughter, and the sharp clink of silverware. "Take him home," she said simply.

Zach dragged his hand across his mouth, then crossed his arms over his chest. "What about Ellie?"

"What about her?"

"Doggone it, Christa, she's like a sister to me. I don't want Noah to hurt her again."

Christabel trailed her finger over the desk and laughed, a sound full of womanly wisdom. "Honey, how do you know she won't hurt *him?*"

"Christabel told you, I know she did," Noah said, an exaggerated drawl lengthening each word.

Zach tugged the spread as high as he could while keeping his brother's feet covered, although they dangled off the end of the bed. He nudged a wooden bucket across the pine floor, banging it against the bed frame. "If you feel sick, all you have to do is lean over." A trick he had learned from Rory.

Noah laughed, thin and worn. "I told you, I didn't ... eat dinner. There's nothing"—he patted his stomach—"nothing."

Zach frowned. No dinner. He glanced at his brother's wrist, angled high on his flat belly. Sun-buffed skin covered lean muscle but bones protruded where muscle was scarce. "I put a pitcher of water on the table. A glass beside it," he instructed, tucking the blanket around Noah's shoulders, amazed, again, by how much Rory resembled him.

"She did, she told you. Don't try ... deny it. Always a meddler, that one. I remember what she carved in those tree trunks."

"Yes, she did tell me." He unbuttoned Noah's collar and

dropped it to the table. The starched cuffs followed, rasping against skin as Zach tugged them free. Thank goodness, Rory had gone fishing with Jason and his father. He didn't need to see his beloved uncle Noah like this.

"I"—Noah's fingers fluttered, tangling in his black brace, the bones in his hand dancing—"I'm not sure why I kissed her. It's fuzzy . . . the reason I did it."

"I'm sure everything is fuzzy right now." Zach grabbed the chair he had shoved from their path when they stumbled into the room. Straddling it, he leaned his arms on the back, hooked his thumbs below each elbow. Contradictory emotions tugged at him. He wanted Noah to sleep, knew he needed to sleep. Already, morning light colored the end of the bed; birds twittered and darted outside the window.

Another part, the part that had grieved—wondering if he would ever see his little brother again—rejoiced at the chance to talk to him without the blasted wall standing between them. Zach had fought to destroy it. Two dinners at Christabel's. Unplanned visits in the guise of dropping off Rory at Widow Wynne's. Heck, he had even sailed on the *Nellie Dey*—the first shad run he'd been on since the year he turned twenty. Watching Noah—feet planted wide, body swaying with the roll and pitch of the ocean, recording figures in a book as thick as his arm, eyes faithfully scanning the horizon—had brought home how much his brother had matured. Drifted away. Become a stranger. A marine biologist who lived in Chicago. A man Zach often wondered if he would ever know again.

"Why do ya suppose she does this to me?" The scar on his quivering eyelid showed white against his skin. "Makes me all confused and wobbly. Never gotten wobbly before."

"The whiskey's making you wobbly." Zach tapped his palms against the slats of the chair and rocked forward on the front legs.

"Oh, no, she's more potent than liquor. Too beautiful. More than any woman I've ever seen. Intelligent . . . fascinating."

Zach felt his lips slide into a smile. What the heck, he decided, Noah probably wouldn't remember the conversation anyway. "You're the scientist. What's your hypothesis?"

"Lust."

"Hmm, could be." He paused a beat. "Or . . . maybe you love her. Maybe you always have."

Noah's eyes flipped open, watery and bloodshot. He raised an inch off the mattress. "I don't love her. Impulsive, headstrong *woman.*" He scowled and sank back.

"Would it be so bad if you did?"

His hand popped up on his stomach. "Disaster . . . a disaster. Like everything Elle involves herself in. Schools that don't make money and leaking roofs. Watch pockets and pocket watches. A nymph's body. Thanks, but I'll take a rational . . . judicious woman if I ever marry. No power over me. Disrupt my well-organized life. A proper wife's the ticket."

"Rational and judicious? Proper? Sounds like a goddarned judge to me."

Noah waved this away. "You don't understand. I have a precise . . . plan."

"For what?"

"Everything."

Zach banged the chair legs to the floor. "You have a plan for love?"

Noah nodded, a weak smile blooming. "Since university."

"Then what are you doing kissing Ellie? Part of your plan?"

His smile dimmed, one eye slit open. "Course not. Unexpected bit of, rather . . . a circumstance I wasn't expecting. Blessit, she has lips . . . made for kissing. So, I decided to conduct an experiment, a kissing experiment . . . which failed horribly."

"A kissing experiment? You think you can control falling in love with a women like you can control one of your fishy experiments?"

"When I have time to devote to marriage, I'll find the perfect wom—"

"Perfect?" Zach sputtered.

"Someone sensible. Someone who doesn't expect me to lasso the moon, who doesn't look at me with big ole green eyes full of emotion."

"What about not being able to take *your* eyes off her when she enters a room? What about cherishing the sound of her laughter, the way she whispers your name in her sleep? If you love someone, you'll want those things, you'll crave them as much as you crave the air you breathe."

"When I said I had a plan for love"—Noah jammed his thumb under his brace and jerked it clumsily past his elbow—"I guess I meant she would love *me*."

"Elle would love you, if you'd let her."

Noah's fingers clenched around the brace. "I don't want her kind of love."

"What other kind is there, little bro'?"

"The kind I'm not tempted to return," he answered hoarsely.

Zach gripped the chair, Noah's pain hurting him as badly as his own would. "That's not love at all, then. Noah, you have to let what happened fade into the past. You can't live your life watching over your shoulder, afraid to feel something in your heart. Afraid of what it will cost you."

Noah dropped his arm across his eyes; Zach puzzled over what he sought to hide. "I loved you, both of you, more than anyone could love his brothers." He swallowed, his throat doing a long draw. "I never wanted, I never wanted to hurt Cale. I couldn't think rationally . . . when I left here, and I hated that. I made too many mistakes, following my heart instead of my mind. I lost both of you. I won't . . . can't risk it again. Ever again."

"You didn't lose anybody." Gently, Zach lowered the other brace from Noah's shoulder and slipped the top button loose on his shirt. As usual with *this* brother, he felt helpless, didn't know what to say, what to do. Before the night they stumbled upon their mother's diary, the only emotion Caleb had ever shown Noah was love. Protective, fierce love. Zach could just imagine how Caleb's hostility—and it could be brutal—must have hurt him.

Zach waited until Noah's brow smoothed and his lashes lay motionless against his skin. He rose from the chair, stretched.

"Home. I should be home," Noah murmured.

"You *are* home."

Zach turned at the sound of the softly spoken words. Caleb stood in the doorway, shoulder propped against the frame, legs crossed at the ankle. The wretched look on his face belied his indifferent stance. He watched the bed for a sign of movement, twisting a worn hat in his blackened hands.

Zach held a finger to his lips. "Not here," he said, and jabbed his thumb over his shoulder.

Their boots thumped on the carpeted staircase, echoed off the sun-streaked kitchen walls, the door swinging shut behind them. Zach poured coffee into two cups and sat with a fragile façade of composure.

Caleb slumped into a chair and dropped his hat on the floor. "Is he drunk?" he asked, gazing into his cup as he spooned in sugar.

Zach released a ragged bark of laughter. "You should know the signs of that well enough."

The spoon hit the table with a crack. Coffee splashed over the sides of Caleb's cup, staining the white tablecloth. "Holy Mother Mary, Zach, give me a chance."

"Give you a chance to what? Run him out of here again?" He pressed his tongue against the back of his teeth, counted to ten. "Did you see the scar on his eyelid? Is that what you want to do to him again?"

Caleb plunged his fingers into his hair, cradling his skull. His skin looked as filthy as the tangled strands. "You bastard. Do you think guilt doesn't eat at me every day without you prodding it in the rump? How can you do that? When you know how much"—he pounded his fist on the table—"how much I loved him."

Mist drifted from the hot liquid, collected in moist beads on his chin. He scrubbed the heel of his hand over the damp stubble. How *could* he do it? Caleb had mourned Noah's disappearance until Zach had believed he'd lost both of them. "I'm sorry. I had no right."

Caleb grasped his cup with both hands, staring into his coffee. Sooty streaks sullied the chipped white china. "Don't apologize for speaking the truth."

"Let's cut the self-pity bull, how about it? It's time this family set things straight."

"Dammit, Zach! I've been to that old crone's back house, or whatever the hell you call it, three times. I talked to the fisherman and got him on the boats, figuring he would come to me then. Honor and all the bunk he holds dear. Got me nothing. What more do you want me to do? Kidnap him?"

"You don't have to kidnap him. I've done that for you."

Caleb's head lifted, his eyes shining like polished silver. "I guess you have more courage than I do, brother." Pushing from the round oak table, he dropped his cup in the sink and paced to the window. He shoved the curtain aside with a blunt motion, his broad shoulders as unyielding as his stubborn pride.

Zach looked closely at the curtains for the first time in years. Yellow with little daisy things sewn around the edges. Funny, he remembered Hannah saying she liked them. Must be why they still hung there. "Where have you been?" he finally asked, skimming his cup in a gradual circle.

"The warehouse. A delayed shipment of sails. Fisherman coming down from New England for a boat next week." Caleb's gaze sliced toward Zach, a half smile twisting his lips. "Where'd you think?"

Zach shrugged, chagrined to admit he usually thought the worst.

"Obviously, Noah was keeping my space warm at the Nook." Caleb turned his head toward a window, thumping his knuckle against the pane. "At least two of the Garretts enjoy the entertainment Christa's has to offer. Remember those lovely creatures, Zachariah old boy? Called women?"

Zach ignored the familiar jibe. "I have to work this afternoon, so I won't be here. Could you stay, talk to him after he wakes up? I'm not sure he's going to remember walking home."

Caleb stiffened. "How do you know he'll wanna talk to me?"

"I don't."

"You'd love it if he blew outta here after telling me to go to hell, wouldn't you?"

"Oh, for pity's sake, Cale, don't be ridiculous." Zach's hand flexed around his cup. "For once in your life, just think before you go charging in like a blasted wild bull. That's all the advice I can offer."

Frowning, he flicked a glance over his shoulder. "What went on last night? Something happen to upset him?"

"Make that your first question. Should get the ball rolling."

"Not going to make it any easier on me, are you, Constable?" Caleb leaned in, his breath fogging the glass.

"Nope."

"I saw him yesterday, on the boardwalk with Ellie. They were fussing, if I had to make a guess. I considered going on up to them, but the look on her face stopped me. She loved Noah so much. You remember. Heck, the whole town remembers, she made such a goose of herself." He swiped the heel of his hand through the smudge of vapor. "And you know old tough-hide Professor. If he did feel anything for her, he never let it show. I always reckoned he just found the whole mess irritating, a nagging rock in his shoe. Ellie sure never let his dawdling stop her. Not for a minute. We were only kids but"—he shrugged— "if the drinking spell has to do with *her*, I think I'm too much of a coward to ask."

"Just talk to him, Cale. Nothing more, nothing less."

Caleb braced his hands on either side of the window frame and propped his brow against the pane, a long sigh his only reply.

Noah reached for her, his hands betraying him. He managed to grasp a lock of hair between his fingers, a cinnamon streak across his skin. His lips tingled; roaring blaze consumed him. Elle laughed and kicked her feet, sailing higher and higher, back straight, breasts forward, legs wide. She smiled, and he felt a catch in his chest that could easily be called an ache.

In a slow backward arch, the old wooden swing whizzed by him. He grabbed the rope in his hand and jerked it to his side, trailed his fingers along the empty seat.

Noah blinked, squinted.

Where was he?

He lifted his shoulders from the mattress and groaned, a roaring headache nearly splitting his head in two. His shoulders quivered as he struggled to sit, cradling his face in his hands, imagining that would halt the crew building a modest structure in his brain. Maybe a few deep breaths would help. No . . . only brought dust up his nose. The sneeze proved unavoidable, and painful.

He had been dreaming of Elle, he realized, noting the effect the dream had had on his body. The blanket was puffed like a tent. Cursing, he flung the scratchy cover away and swung his feet to the floor, the bed swaying. Gingerly, he touched his nose. No spectacles. Not on the table, either. Or in his shirt pocket. He squinted and glanced down. Maybe they had fallen to the floor.

Sliding to his knees with a groan, his hands searched the smooth pine. He jerked to a halt, fingering a six-inch gash running as deep as his knuckle.

"Mama, what's that chip in the floor," he asked. A sugary

smell from the cookies she had made earlier in the day scented the fingers she brushed across his cheek.

"A Union soldier thought to chop wood in this room. I set him straight after one swing of his ax," she said and pressed soft lips to his brow.

Noah swiped at the gash, an ineffectual erasure of the past. Had he gotten so drunk he had come *here?* He shook his head, trying to remember. Elle . . . the alley . . . sailing . . . the Nook . . . a woman's hand on his knee . . . Christabel pulling him into her parlor.

Zach, she must have called Zach.

Noah slumped against the bed frame, his head pounding with every beat of his heart. *Damn you, Elle, you wanted me to face them, and here I am, doing just that.*

Even at that moment, when he was dying, he could taste her on his lips, as if he had pressed a kiss to her mouth before rolling from the sheets. The tormenting image that had prompted him to guzzle an entire bottle of Christabel's rotgut whiskey returned, vivid and tangible. His hands propelling Elle's body across his thigh until the very core of her scorched him through his trousers. Blessit, he must have been out of his mind. Never, never in his *life*, had he handled a woman in a reckless, improper manner. And they had been standing in an *alley*.

The images were so vivid that he questioned—feeling a faint twinge of desperation and a strong dose of fear—how he could erase them. He dropped his head to the mattress and groaned in misery. Why had he bothered getting drunk for the first time in years if it left everything intact, a damned painting in his mind?

Glancing toward the window, he struggled to his feet. Murky, late-afternoon light flooded the room. Had he slept all day? Swearing, he straightened his braces and smoothed the wrinkles from the front of his shirt. He had missed his morning meeting with Tyre McIntosh, and he certainly couldn't go to the lab site stinking of whiskey, his eyes bloodshot and bleary. He brought his sleeve to his nose and sniffed, the action throwing him off-balance and into the bedside table. God, he was a mess.

Feeling his way, he shuffled along the hallway and down the staircase. Familiarity eliminated the need for his spectacles. Caleb had chipped the bottom stair throwing a bowl to Noah that he hadn't caught. His mother had always complained about the kitchen floorboard creaking if you stepped on it on the left side. He knew the house as well as he knew his face in a mirror. Luckily, his blurred vision kept the memories from swallowing him whole.

He entered the kitchen hesitantly. The smell of coffee and sausage greeted him, but no brothers. Swallowing hard, he rushed outside and inhaled a clear breath. *I'll never drink again,* he vowed. It hadn't done any good, anyway. Elle still lingered.

What was he doing, stumbling around his family's yard, waiting for a confrontation he didn't want, didn't need? Or maybe he did want to face them . . . oh, hell, face *Caleb.*

Gathering his courage, he took a halting step. The shed, vague but tangible, tin roof vivid against bleached, half-rotted wood, sat in the back corner of the yard, sheltered from direct sunlight by a snarl of pine branches. Noah had always wondered if Caleb, in an irrational bout of fury, had chopped it to bits with the ax he'd used to destroy their models. The door creaked when he put his elbow to it, a harsh, forsaken sound reverberating in his head.

A bird screeched and darted through a hole as he ducked inside. He mopped a cobweb from his face and turned in a slow circle. The smell of glue and raw wood had been replaced by the stale scent of abandonment. Smoothing his hand across the pine workbench Zach had made for them one Christmas, he found a tiny paintbrush tucked into a split in the wood and rolled it out with the pad of his finger.

A grinding creak fractured the silence. Noah turned more swiftly than his body could adjust to, and bumped against the bench.

"Noah?"

He shaded his face. A muscular shape outlined by a thin halo of light, shoulders stretching the width of the doorway. Could be a hundred different men. But the voice called to him in his dreams.

"Caleb," he said, sounding as rusty as the shed's hinges.

"What the heck are you doing out here?"

He searched for an even tone, the stiff bristles brushing his palm. "Call me a sentimental fool, but I just had to see the place you redecorated with an ax. My, you've done a lot since then."

"Dammit, Noah." Caleb stalked into the weak stream of sunlight flowing in through a gaping chasm between two planks, his haunted expression materializing.

Noah rolled the paintbrush between his hands, his palms warming. He bent his head, shielding his expression from clumsy inspection. Beside his knee, a fat black spider hunkered in a web spread delicately between the bench legs. A hapless deerfly struggled in the lower corner. He watched the spider crawl toward its prey, experiencing a strange kinship with the luckless insect. "I was just looking for my spectacles. Have you seen them?"

"You and Zach are both heartless. Fine, if you want to be that way." Caleb drove his fingers through his hair, leaving it sticking up in a half dozen places. The face in Noah's memory altered to the one before him: nose crooked near the top, shallow grooves chalking the cheeks, a tiny patch of gray at each temple. It was the first time he had been this close to his brother in ten years.

He inhaled deeply to return his breathing to normal. "I hate to tell you this, Cale, but there's a big black spider spinning a dazzling web right next to me. Probably babies scurrying across this rotted floor right this minute. You know they hatch thousands at a time."

Caleb cocked his head, gingerly lifted one booted foot, then the other. He glanced timidly into each corner of the shed. A shudder shook his broad shoulders and rippled down his muscular arms. Uttering a growl and a curse, he curled his hands into fists and turned on his heel. The door slapped against the inside wall, flooding the musty enclosure with light.

Lowering his hands to his knees, Noah hung his head and laughed, gasping for breath, his head pounding until he feared he would be sick. Swaying, the barrier he had constructed in a blind panic years before crumbled.

"Get out here you skinny bastard!"

Strangely, the jagged slivers of wood scattered beneath his feet—fragments of models he and Caleb had constructed, their knees scraping the underside of the bench and glue coating their fingertips—flooded his chest with tender emotions. Devotion and security, hope and concern. He regretted the past, profoundly, but for the first time in years, he did not fear the future.

He stepped from the shed, a gust of wind right off the sea pressing his shirt against his chest, lifting his hair from his brow. He tipped his head, watched a puffy white cloud skim a sky of deep rose and blue . . . and green. Emerald green.

"Noah?"

Wagon wheels clattered over crushed shell, and a dog yipped in the distance, but he only heard Elle's accented, dulcet whisper. The paintbrush snapped in two in his fingers.

"You okay?" Caleb stripped a piece of bark from the tree he leaned against and gave Noah a worried frown. "How about coming inside and having dinner? I caught two flounder and four blue this morning. We can"—he coughed, shrugged—"talk."

Noah slipped his hand into his pocket, concealing the evidence of his frustration. "How big are the blue?"

"One's a good five pounds, at least. They were running like crazy in the edge."

"Bleed and ice them yet?" Noah lifted his finger to his nose, forgetting his absent spectacles.

"I'm not some blamed ocean scientist, but I reckon I can clean fish well enough to suit most folks," he grumbled, and pushed away from the tree.

Noah forced his feet to move until he stood by his brother's side. Registering the jolt of surprise, he realized the top of Caleb's head barely met his chin. "We'll see. Cleaning them never was your strong suit. Or cooking them, for that matter."

"Heck, little bro', you can do the cooking." Caleb winked and strode along the worn path with the same reckless energy Noah remembered. Ejecting a labored sigh, he followed with the beleaguered step of one being coerced, but he could not deny the swell of happiness in his heart.

Noah flipped the fish and leaned back, a bubble of oil bursting in the sizzling iron skillet. A drop struck his hand, and he cursed, sucking the singed skin between his lips. Behind him, the screen door squeaked and a small projectile slammed into his legs, throwing him off-balance and into the counter.

"Oh, you're here," Rory said, the delight in his voice bringing a wide smile to Noah's face. "Uncle Caleb said you would never come here, ever again."

Noah turned and pressed Rory's cheek against his hip, running his fingers over his nephew's downy tufts. "What does your Uncle Caleb know anyway?" A prickle of awareness intruded; he lifted his head. Elle stood in the doorway, reddish brown locks tousled by the wind or impatient fingers, her eyes dulled by exhaustion. He snatched his hand from his mouth and willed his heart to stop banging inside his chest.

Ignoring him, she smiled at Rory. "Go wash your hands. Wouldn't hurt your face to hit some soap, either."

Rory lifted shining eyes and fairly danced in place at his uncle's side. "Are you staying for dinner? Are you, huh? Guess what? I caught a sheepshead fishing with Jason. I told him what you said, about how they use those pointy teeth to chew barncycles off rocks. He called me a liar, so I slugged him.''

"*Rory.*" Elle stepped forward and lightly swatted Rory on the behind. "Upstairs. Now. And, I think you should apologize to Jason tomorrow or your father is going to find out what happened today."

Rory shuffled his feet. "Do I have to, Uncle Noah?"

Noah lifted his head, his gaze seizing Elle's and holding. His fingers itched to wipe the smudge of dirt from her nose, slip the loose tendril brushing her cheek into her hairclip. He tightened his hand into a fist and turned, before his regard strayed to other parts of her body. "Miss Elle's right. You *will* apologize to Jason tomorrow." Grabbing a spatula, he scooped the fish from the skillet. "Just because someone doesn't believe something you've said is no reason to slug them. Hitting never solves any problems. Trust me."

"Yeah, all right, I'll trust you," Rory mumbled, clearly unconvinced. "But I still think Jason is a poop." Before Elle could get to him, he raced from the kitchen, his feet pounding on the stairs.

Elle's step was light and brisk, the swish of her skirt gentle music to his ears. Let her go, he ordered. *Let her go.*

"Elle, wait." He tossed the spatula to the counter and wiped a bead of sweat from his temple. Glancing over his shoulder, he found her with one hand on the door, glancing over hers. "About yesterday ..." Grabbing a dishrag, he turned, wiping his hands, his eyes everywhere but on her. "I don't know—"

"Save your awkward apologies, Professor. Merciful heavens, it's clear you don't know."

He knotted the rag between his fingers. "What do you want from me? I let myself get out of control. I take full responsibility, and I'm sorry."

"I never asked you to take responsibility. Or be sorry. In fact, I told you *not* to be."

"Well, I am." A rush of apprehension threatened to buckle his knees. "Aren't you?"

She swallowed—a long, slow pull. "Of course."

A pause. A full second pause. He had seen it. "You're lying," he breathed. "What did you do, Elle? Oh, God, you didn't . . . did you wait for me to come to you last night?"

In reply, a rosy streak grazed each cheek.

Her blush mirroring his desire and the perplexing feelings they shared, he spun around, all at once afraid to look at her, yet obsessed with imagining how she looked. She had waited . . . wanting him and knowing what it would lead to.

Skin blazing hot as the skillet by his side, he said, "So, that's the smell."

"Smell?" she whispered.

"A different scent on your skin. Perfume. Real perfume." He slapped the rag to the counter. "Roses?"

"Honeysuckle. I usually put it in my hairwash."

He gripped the counter edge and prayed for restraint, his mind trying to fool him into believing it had been years since he'd touched her instead of hours. "Elle," he said tightly, "you play a dangerous game."

"Yes, I've been told before."

He had her by the shoulders before either of them could speak or breathe. "What do you mean?" If Magnus Leland had touched her—

"My father. He . . . he told me once."

Noah closed his eyes, shamed and infuriated by his reaction. He inhaled, then wished to hell he hadn't. Who knew a man could be thrown off his feet by honeysuckle? "Elle, I wish things were different . . ." He halted. The squeaky floorboard just inside the kitchen. Turning his head, he watched Zach pile into Caleb, who stood stock-still in the doorway, jaw so slack it touched his chest.

Elle growled in French and used both hands to brush past him. The screen door banged behind her. Noah glanced out in time to see her turning the corner, her hips swinging crazily beneath another delightfully tattered dress. He pressed his brow to the rusted screen and sighed.

"What the heck—"

"—is going on between you two?"

"Nothing," he said, then dared his brothers, with a severe, hooded look, to dispute him.

Chapter Eight

A sunset blaze of red and gold had seized the sky by the time Noah made it to the dance. He hitched his hip on the edge of the skiff and slipped on the black canvas shoes he had purchased the day before. He scanned the crowd of people gathered round the campfires, some dodging the sizzling flash of dripping meat, others using driftwood to bury potatoes deep in gray ash.

Lifting his head, he scanned the horizon, noted with a faint sense of unease the thin layer of mist drifting in from the east and the listless breeze carrying nothing more than the scent of roasted chicken and pork. Glancing at the line of flower-bedecked skiffs, all waiting for steady hands to sail them home, his apprehension heightened. Only the gentle slap of water against the hull of his boat calmed him.

As he made his way along the packed sand, music, laughter, and snatches of conversation flowed free of a tent constructed of hastily sewn-together blankets, yards of mosquito netting, and eight dented poles jammed in the sand. Swirling couples floated by, silhouetted by the glow of oil lanterns swinging in time to the whim of the wind. Was Elle inside, dancing with

Daniel Connery or some other young man? Smelling of honey-suckle, perhaps, or bright sunshine and damp earth? Stooping to grasp a scallop shell, he traced the ribbed edges and wondered in astonishment if the hot flare in his chest could be jealousy.

There had been no mention of their passionate kiss or his brusque apology. In the three days since, there had been no conversation at all. An abrupt greeting in front of the post office and a lengthy stare across a packed mercantile shelf. Did the empty ache inside mean he missed her?

Noah neared the tent, the hum of sound increasing. A group of drunken whalers dodged by him, pouring from the V-shaped exit. Hesitating before the draped opening, he observed the joyful display of camaraderie with a sense of detachment. Here he was, twenty-seven years old, a man of considerable means and education, yet he found himself seeking refuge in an emotional storm. Zach, Caleb, Elle. The three people in the world he had always been completely at ease with. Maybe *that* laid bare his childhood protection of Elle, not to save her but to save himself.

Bunched sprays of daisies and carnations brushed his shoulder as he made a reluctant duck inside. Telling himself he looked merely for the sake of curiosity, he searched the outer circle. Standing a head taller than everyone else made his task easy. That, and the undeniable cognizance he experienced whenever she was near. A whisper of air leaked past his lips and his body warmed. She stood just inside the tent's triangular back entrance, a crush of people whisking by her.

For days, he had been unable to erase it from his mind. *She had waited for him.* Put perfume on her skin and actually waited for him. Knowing he would take her virginity and . . . leave.

Then again, Elle had always had the courage to grasp what she desired.

She laughed and tossed her head, exposing the lithe arch of her neck. Smooth and sweet beneath his lips, he remembered. She tucked a stray wisp of hair behind her ear, and he marveled at his ignorance. Elle Beaumont was simply radiant, validated in the golden wash from the oil lamp by her side. It was not wholly physical, this radiance. It flowed from her lively green eyes, from the hands she moved so exuberantly in conversation, from the confident stride which carried her along the boardwalk.

Noah admired her vivacity, her innate sincerity, yet he *hated* the loss of control it brought. Averting his gaze, he corrected his thought: He *feared* it.

Immaculate black canvas in a sea of dirty leather and sandy buck. Elle concentrated on those shoes as they moved through the crowd. She laughed at the appropriate pauses in conversation and nodded her head often, hearing absolutely nothing.

Covertly, she peeked. Noah spoke to each man who stopped him, a slap on the back or a punch to the chest the common greeting. He accepted each masculine gesture of friendship, a calm smile hiding his faintly bewildered look. She recognized his discomfiture as if it were her own.

"Ellie, dear, what do you think?"

Startled, Elle flicked a glance at the group of women surrounding her. Forcing a smile, she said, "I think that would be lovely, of course."

Heads bobbing, they agreed.

When the conversation lagged, Elle searched. Her fingers curled, nails digging into her skin. Meredith Scoggins stood next to Noah, her hand on his arm, her head lifted toward his. Blatant interest shone in her cornflower blue eyes, in the teasing curve of her lips. A group of Meredith's friends circled, shifting Noah's cohorts to the outer circle.

A hulking, red-faced seaman tapped Meredith on the shoulder and she turned, giggling in delight. Immediately, Noah's charcoal gaze captured Elle. He shoved his spectacles up, a scowl crossing his face.

What? Elle shrugged with a passiveness she certainly didn't feel.

Stop staring.

Me? She patted her chest.

His gaze lowered then jerked to her face. *Yes. You.*

I'm not staring. Elle gestured to the oblivious, jabbering group of women.

He pursed his lips—an appealing pout, part-boy, part-man. A wave of desire surged from the tips of her fingers to her knees, leaving her gasping in astonishment. Elle glanced around, frantic and fragile. The women chatted and fluttered, never noticing the fire in her cheeks.

Daniel Connery, in the most fortuitous action of his life, chose that moment to ask her to dance.

She raced into his arms.

"See the way she stares at him, Doc. All dopey-eyed." Stymie shifted a wad of tobacco from one side of his jaw to the other, his watery gaze focused on the dance area. "Loony woman still loves the professor better 'an Peter loved the Lord."

"Shut up, you old fool," Magnus snarled, and stalked off.

Stymie scratched his head and spit. "Wonder what put him in a stew."

Henri Beaumont linked his fingers over his bulging stomach, watched one besotted idiot stumble toward the nearest whiskey bottle, the other toward the exit. Leland had gotten exactly what he asked for, expecting Marielle-Claire to love him. That stinking fisherman, well, unfortunately Henri could not argue with his verdict.

For he had also recorded his daughter's impassioned display. *Mon Dieu.* After all this time, she still looked at young Garrett like a lovesick pup. A blind pup. Made Henri realize he had been too lenient. By half. Waiting for Marielle-Claire to make up her mind, properly secure a promising future. Absurd to imagine a woman making a choice, *any* choice, and choosing correctly. Twice, he had allowed her to go against his wishes. Against his better judgment. Evidently, a weakness of paternal love. University, for God's sake. What good had that done? Sprouted ideas of independence in her mind. His second mistake had been allowing her to live in a dilapidated house and act as housemaid to a crotchety old woman. Her mother would collapse if she had lived to see it.

What did Marielle-Claire think? He would live forever? Provide for her after she came to her senses and moved back home? Didn't she realize she needed a man to guide her? Protect her? Didn't she realize *he,* Henri Beaumont, wanted grandsons to carry his blood if not his name?

Now this. *Merde.*

He had prayed the boy would never show his face on Pilot Isle again. Though he would have gladly kissed young Garrett's feet if he had shown an inkling of interest in marrying Marielle-Claire. Unquestionably the most handsome member of his family. Intelligent. Successful. Immediately upon hearing of the boy's return, Henri had made it his business to discover which of the circulating rumors were true. Discreet inquiries, of course, but he'd had no choice. He clearly recalled his daughter's impulsive carelessness.

Henri watched the boy shrug free of a clutching female hand. A marine biologist. True. Garrett taught a biology course at a well-respected institution in Chicago. Furthermore, he had done research aboard a government fishing vessel and written essays for a scientific manual.

Tapping his fingers on his belly, Henri struggled to recall the description the investigator had used in regard to the boy. Ah, yes. A rising star in his field. A rising star would have suited Marielle-Claire very well indeed. Exceptionally bright, his daughter. And she had never lacked beauty, although that had caused more trouble than it was worth.

Henri followed Noah's progress through a sea of simpering pouts, fluttering eyelashes, and broad smiles. Yes, young Garrett would have forced the hand. Henri's grandsons would have been assured of possessing intelligence *and* good looks.

Remarkably, in this instance, his daughter had been a good judge of character. She'd recognized the boy's value long before the others. Yearned for him when he was no more than an ashen, bespectacled lad.

Maybe it was just as well that Marielle-Claire's mother, Felice, had not lived to witness this impasse in their family. She might have sided with her daughter, for she had once loved a man as well. What an imbecile *he* had been. Jacques Montreau. Of course, Felice's father had rejected the union. For good reason. As Henri had done for his daughter's benefit. Her funds, for instance. Given time, he would break her, he knew he would. Using her love for her useless school appeared cruel, he knew. He could be a cruel man when forced.

Henri stepped outside the tent and headed in the direction of poor Leland, who stood facing the ocean, his back to the festivities. Henri wished he were home drinking a glass of Bordeaux instead of standing outside a homespun tent, sand lodged beneath his fingernails, sweat sticking his tailored shirt to his skin. *Mon Dieu,* how he hated the ocean. If not for his business interests, he would move inland as far as he could get.

It was brutally clear from tonight's performance that young Garrett didn't want Marielle-Claire, would never want her. Nothing had changed. Oh, Henri didn't doubt the boy lusted after her. After all, she probably threw herself at him. Time had apparently changed little. If only Henri had figured a way to force the issue of marriage, it would not have been necessary to involve the woman his investigator had located. Regrettably, the situation grew dire and required him to use what little he had been given.

Strange, but Henri found it hard to believe the boy had it in him to take a married lover. Not that he objected. Celibacy was reserved for feeble men and unmarried women. His daughter, for example.

His fingers clenched over his paisley waistcoat. He would

be damned to the eternal fires of purgatory before he'd let her falter over a man who did not intend to marry her.

As Daniel laughed and spun her through a wide turn, she tilted her head and returned his laughter. He liked her, she supposed. She also recognized ... Elle chewed on her lip, trying to remember the word Christa had explained to her. *Horny.* Daniel was horny. Who cared, he was safe. He made her feel attractive without consequence. If he held her a little closer than she liked, the church committee members perched in chairs surrounding the dance floor weren't inclined to titter behind their hands about it. Moreover, he didn't hold her close enough to make her heart miss even a beat. Hence, carelessly confident, she flirted.

Until she caught sight of Noah leading Meredith into the circle of dancers. The girl giggled and simpered adoringly, seeming to shimmy in her satin slippers.

Elle lost sight of them on the turn.

Truly, she found it hard to record one man's movements while locked in another man's arms, but she managed. Noah bestowed a slow, sweeping smile upon his eager dance partner, his tanned fingers splayed across her back. Elle watched and pondered and felt sick inside.

"Daniel, can we stop for a moment? I need a breath of air."

"Sure, Ellie," he said, and halted in his tracks. Cupping her elbow, he escorted her outside the tent.

The night was pitch-black, the crescent moon's glow dulled by a layer of fog. The wind kicked at her skirt as she searched for a source of light. Saffron flames from one of the campfires dancing against a dun backdrop, a ray of moonlight, anything. Worrying her lip between her teeth, she began to think she might have made a mistake asking a horny man to walk alone with her.

"Um, Daniel—"

"Excuse me, I'm afraid there's some sort of problem with the flowers."

Elle turned suddenly, stumbling over a burrow in the sand. "Flowers?"

"Come along, flower girl." Noah grasped her wrist and yanked her behind him, contradicting his absurd pretext by dragging her away from the tent and any flowers to be found. When they neared the dunes, he halted and flung her hand away. His back rose and fell on a ragged breath. "Elle, do you have any idea how long that man has been confined to a ship? With no women in sight."

"Six months, I believe he told me. I know, I know"—she dipped her toes into the sand—"he's very horny."

Noah's head whipped around. *"What?"*

Elle shook the sand from her foot. "He's horny. Christabel said it was the same as being lonely, except a special way a man feels lonely. She said it makes men confused."

"Dear God," Noah muttered beneath his breath.

"Well, does it?"

He dropped to the sand with a resigned sigh. "Yes."

Elle plopped beside him, crossed her arms behind her head, and rolled flat. Noah sighed again, but after a moment, he followed.

For some time, they lay silent, gazing into a sky absent of stars, listening to the piercing warble of sand locusts and the ceaseless wash of the ocean, the sand cool and solid beneath them. It seemed a perfect, crystalline moment in time. She feared a movement, a sound, a breath, would shatter it. The completeness flooding her heart was a delusion. Surely, it was a delusion.

"Close your eyes," he whispered, close to her ear. "Listen. There's so much."

She did as he asked, opened her mind to the enchantment of a peaceful night, the allure of the sea. She wanted to see the world through him. "I hear a bird. It sounds far away."

"An oystercatcher. She's sounding an alarm because someone is nearing her nest."

Elle waited, more sounds coming together. "Scraping. The hull of a skiff against the sand as it's shoved off. A crackle. Driftwood burning on one of the campfires."

"Good." She could hear the smile in his voice.

"I can hear . . . breaths slipping from your lips."

Sand shifted as he turned toward her, shifted again as he lay back. Finally, he said, "I can hear yours, too."

A wisp of wind carried his soapy, masculine scent. She drew it in and held it close, tucked it in the secret place where she tucked all her memories of Noah. Her love for him.

"Tell me about university, Elle."

Her arms stiffened beneath her head. "What's there to tell?"

"Did you ever consider going back?"

A hundred times. A thousand. "Once or twice."

He paused, seemed to consider. "Was it lack of funds that stopped you?"

She laughed. "Oh, Noah, only a person with a surplus of funds would ask such a question."

"If it's purely a financial concern, I could help."

"You offer from a sense of duty. The same sense of duty you curse for getting you into every pickle involving me." She blinked, startled by the haze of fog enclosing them and the clear notion she had of his thoughts. "I know it would be easier for you to leave Pilot Isle believing my future is all wrapped up in a nice, proper package. Check an obligation off your list and move to the next."

"Dammit, you twist everything until I'm not sure what I meant." He stirred restlessly. "Someone once offered me what I offer you. I didn't want to, but I took it."

She turned to her side, propping her chin on her hand. "Who?"

"It was a long time ago. It doesn't matter. I paid it back when I could. By any means possible." He rolled his head toward her, a fierce light in his eyes. "Elle, I wouldn't expect—"

She pressed her finger to his lips, ignoring the way their skin melded. "You're the first person to understand an education meant something to me besides the chance to leave Pilot Isle, and for that, I thank you. Sometimes, I think, people have to fight their own battles. *Need* to. I let you fight mine before, and it shot a gaping hole in my judgment." She considered a moment, then nodded. "I'd like to take the next step, whatever it may be."

His expression grew pensive; his gaze darkened. Beneath her finger, she felt his lips parting, his tongue—

Leaping to her feet, she followed the edge of the dune, her gait sluggish in the ankle-deep sand. She walked briskly, forcing her heartbeat to calm, letting the incessant gusts of wind dry the dampness from her brow. Her fingers lifted to her lips, smoothed over them, her hand shaking so badly she couldn't hold it steady before her face.

"If you follow this path"—quietly settling in beside her, Noah gestured to a break in the dune—"it runs through a forest of loblolly pine, to the southern edge of the island. I noticed some artificial light coming from the lumber wharf when I was collecting plankton samples last week. Loggerhead turtles will be attracted to the light come late July. It'll be a good place to take Rory to see them deposit their eggs. You can't miss the flipper bites in the sand. Just look for a broad V-shaped impression leading to the dunes."

Cocking her head, she watched him jerk his shirttail from his trousers and swab his spectacle lenses. "You can show him, Noah."

"I'll be gone by then," he said without looking up.

"I don't understand. If you love this"—she gestured to their surroundings—"how can you stand to live apart from it? If you love your family, how can you stand to live apart from them?"

He jammed his spectacles in place and climbed the dune, his attention centered on the sea. A gray layer of mist settled about him, giving him a ghostly appearance. "I have responsibilities. A calling I'm dedicated to, one I treasure. It demands most of my time and my strength. I've gotten used to making sacrifices."

Lifting her skirt, she clambered after him. She peered but could not see the water's edge for the thick haze. "Will leaving be a sacrifice?"

He waited so long, she thought he wasn't going to reply. "Maybe," he finally said.

"Stay, then," she whispered, shocked to hear it come from her mouth. *Stay, and I'll rip up Savannah's application, I'll run my school and . . .* She shook her head, confusion robbing her of breath. For the first time, she did what Noah had been begging her to do her entire life. She listened to her *mind,* not her heart. One desire shone bright and clear. *I want to finish university.* She did not want to destroy the scholarship application. Not even for the sensitive, passionate, intelligent man standing next to her.

Not even for him.

Intent on telling him, she turned. Before she could open her mouth, he had her chin between his fingers. Regret and torment darkened his eyes. "I can't stay, Elle. Please don't—promise me you won't ask again."

With a nod of finality, she promised.

"Thank you, flower girl." He trailed the back of his hand along her cheek. His smoldering gaze followed.

"Flower girl?" The words came out in a hoarse choke.

His knuckle skimmed her jaw. "The other night. The scent of honeysuckle on your skin." His lips parted. A wisp of breath touched her cheek. "I haven't been able to erase it, or you, from my mind." Languidly, he leaned in, his lids drooping low.

A jolt of awareness shook her to the core. Heart and lungs

and mind, every inch of her readied for his touch. *I love you,* she vowed. *I won't ever kiss you again and not tell myself, tell you if you'll listen. You can fool yourself, Noah Garrett, into believing it's simply passion we share, but I'll know better.*

Just before his lips captured hers, a raw-throated scream broke them apart.

The situation at the edge of the surf came as close to complete and utter chaos as any Noah had ever seen. People shoved past him, stumbling toward, or over, the beached skiffs. Men grappled with lines and dug oars from the bilge, swaying from drink. Hoarse shouts of alarm and hands raised to the heavens in befuddled prayer became the pattern in the matter of a minute. He didn't have to ask what had happened. He could hear the distant, savage groan of a ship's hull being fractured against the shoals. A sound you only had to hear once to remember forever.

"Shipwreck," Elle breathed by his side.

Half-turning, he gripped her shoulders. "Don't even think of getting near the water. I mean it, Elle. Don't even *think* of it." He let her go—before he did something stupid like kiss the woman he had wanted all night to kiss—and plunged into the throng.

Rolling his sleeves high, he scanned the beach for a sign of Zach. The fog made it impossible to see more than twenty yards. Blessit, what a night to put the test to the lifesaving crew's preparedness. Noah had not seen one sober man yet. Pausing, he snagged Daniel Connery's arm. "Zach? Have you seen Zach?"

Daniel jerked the length of rope in his hands, tightening the square knot. "Hundred yards down. By the edge. Where the wreckage is washing up. You'll see the flares."

Noah kicked off his shoes and sprinted, lungs near to bursting, eyes tearing behind his lenses. He caught sight of Zach, then

Caleb, standing in the middle of a small group of men he recognized as being members of Zach's patrol. When he reached them, he found his brothers involved in a heated exchange.

"The blasted ship's too far out to fire the breeches buoy, Cale."

"You can't go." Caleb shoved Zach in the chest. "I found you sleeping on the damned beach and now, you wanna be some hero? Nobody here is fit to sail. You wanna lose one of your men, Constable?"

Wavering flares splayed a blazing ring of light across the sand, casting the men in brushstrokes of gold. During a shift in wind, Noah noted the potent stench of whiskey drifting from them. "I'll go," he said and shoved inside the circle. "Do we know the location? What kind of ship? How many men?"

"*Noah, no.*" Caleb flinched, equal measures of fear and fury etching his face.

Noah met Zach's startled gaze. "Instead of standing here arguing about what man in this group of six is fit to sail, you'd better worry about the group of fifty down the beach who aren't and are preparing right now to capture their moment of glory."

Zach yanked an unsteady hand through his hair. He looked from Noah to Caleb to the ocean and back.

"Go on, Zach. Take your men with you. Someone needs to control what's going on." Noah tipped his head in the direction of the tent.

Zach nodded and said to the man next to him, "Get Seaman Bennett." He placed a hand on Noah's shoulder, squeezed once, then shouldered through the group.

"Dammit." Caleb slammed his fist against his thigh.

A boy no older than sixteen appeared at the edge of the circle, a ragged blanket fisted at his neck, a mop of red hair standing at stiff angles about his head. Shivers shook his gaunt shoulders and rocked him where he stood. "Si-Sir?"

Noah stepped forward. "Tell me what you can, son. Anything you can. Quickly."

"I'm a seaman on the *Queen's Jewel,* sir. A wooden clipper, eleven on board. No passengers, praise be. Headed to Charleston with a cargo of woolpacks, printing paper, and ironmongery. We sailed past Hatteras without incident and the cap'n, he said making it past the watery graveyard should be cause for celebration. So he opened a crate of fine brandy, of which two hundred cases was stored below. The cap'n, he was the worse for drink lots of times"—the boy glanced around nervously and wiped his nose on the edge of the blanket—"but this time he was staggering before the breakers was even sighted. We wasn't concerned, sir, reading the calm weather and all. Then the fog, she rolled in heavy as a mama's teat, and the cap'n, he mistook the Cape lighthouse for something it weren't." The boy shivered, his throat working rapidly.

"Go on," Noah coaxed.

"At half past, the fog was swelling and the night getting darker and darker. Then, sudden like, the *Jewel,* she bounced hard on the shoal, sir. The man on lookout, he began signaling. We tried to wear around, almost got it when she swung, broadside on, with her head to the southward. The after port and starboard boats were cleared and lowered, both hitting water about the same time." The boy's lids fluttered and he quaked violently. "I was in the . . . lee boat, sir. Me and Deck O'Malley. The boat on the weather side, sh–she got caught by a swell. Dashed under the ship's counter like a finger . . . shoved her there. They screamed. Oh merciful Lord in heaven, they screa–screamed. And the sea . . . She just roared."

Noah swallowed past the rise of sickness. "Get him out of here. Someone get him out of here. Keep him warm and get some food in his belly."

Jeb Crow seized Seaman Bennett's arm and led him away. The boy turned and yelled, "O'Malley, he washed over the side. I tried to help him. Clinging to debris the . . . last time I saw him, sir. To a scrap of skiff, sir."

"A skiff." Noah closed his mind to the distant sounds of destruction. "Someone's skiff got tangled with the clipper."

Caleb wrenched him around by the shoulder. "I'm going with you, little bro'."

"I've done this before, Cale. Remember?" He slipped his spectacles in his pocket and strode down the beach, the wind whipping his hair into his face. "I'd simply forgotten how ghastly looking for survivors is."

"How good can you see without those things?" He nodded toward Noah's pocket.

"Well enough."

"Goddammit, I'm going. You can't stop me."

"Cale—"

"You need me on this one, little bro'."

Noah halted by the boat and cocked his head, looking directly into stubborn gray eyes exactly like his. "Maybe I do. Maybe I do, after all."

Chapter Nine

"You let them go?" Elle pinched the bridge of her nose and hurried alongside Zach, trying to contain the quiver in her voice.

He stopped abruptly and waited for her to backtrack before he answered. "Do you think I wanted to send them out in this mess? Fog so thick I could carve a design in it. My brothers lost for all I know." Swishing his foot through the bubbly froth at the water's edge, he said, "I can't allow anyone standing on this beach to go. I was lucky to find six capable volunteers. Lucky we're only searching for ten seamen. Plenty of space to bring them back if they're found. Maybe they'll even locate some of the cargo."

Elle seized a scrap of wood that washed against her boot. A perfectly planed, smoothly varnished splinter of wood. "Part of the hull," she said dully, and let it fall from her fingers.

Zach dropped to his haunches and covered his face with his hands. The wind tossed strands of coal black hair against his fingers. "I'm resigning this post. I don't want it if it makes me feel so responsible for every shipwreck that I put my family at risk. How can I control what happens on those blasted shoals? How can anyone but God?''

Sinking beside him, she hugged her knees to her chest. Waves lapped at her feet. "I'm sorry I said that, about letting Noah go."

"Oh, Ellie"—he shook his head sadly—"have you told him?''

She laid her cheek on her knee and stared into the fog, searching. "What?''

"That you love him.''

She tightened her arms about her legs.

"Tell him before he returns to Chicago. Tell him when his skiff lands on shore. Give him a chance to—''

"To cringe and back away as if I had the plague?''

"He's not that frightened of you.''

"Close.''

"What about Christa's—''

"She *told* you." Elle's hand shot out, a shower of water drenching his trouser leg.

"A little," he admitted, and plucked at the damp cloth.

"Wonderful. Everyone in town knows I kissed Noah in the alley behind the Nook. Of course, they imagine I hauled him there. Poor beleaguered man.''

"It's not like that. She only told me because . . .'' His lids slipped low.

"Told you because of what?''

He stood and dusted the seat of his trousers. "I've got to get back. Make sure Jeb is keeping the boats anchored.''

She yanked him off balance. "Tell me.''

"All right! I had to get him at Christa's.'' He tugged his arm loose. "He was a mess. Almost as bad as Caleb at his worst.''

"The parlor? Was he in the parlor?''

Displeasure hardened his jaw. "How do you know about *that?*''

"Who cares? Was he?"

Huffing once, he strode away.

Lifting her skirt, Elle raced after him. "Zach, *please*."

"I don't think he would appreciate me telling you all this." He flicked a nervous glance at her. "I mean, he didn't say, not in so many words. Not to give you some idea he said anything like that. Blast, I just don't want to betray his confidence. He's always been ..." He waved his hand in a circle at his side, rummaging.

"Private."

"Yes. Private."

She averted her eyes, refusing to beg. She'd done enough of that to last three lifetimes. A few feet up the beach, Seaman Bennett slouched against an ale barrel, the glow from a campfire revealing a face aged by tragedy. "I'll go to him," she said, and headed the boy's way.

"Ellie?"

She glanced over her shoulder.

"Since the first day Noah brought you home, I've loved you like a sister. You know that. Caleb and I have never made a secret of it. But, this"—his gaze shifted—"I'm torn in two about it. I don't know whether to push you two together, shove you apart, or stick my blasted head in the sand and mind my own business. I've never understood what the heck Noah was thinking, and I guess this time, I don't have a good clue about you, either."

As his words battled past her bewilderment, a burst of love flooded her heart. "Zach?"

He abandoned his study of the sea, his eyes bright with fear.

"Noah's safe." She placed her hand on her chest. "I would know if he weren't."

"The other night, Ellie, I saw a flicker of something when he—when he talked about you. I don't know, maybe it was a reflection of light or something to do with the plentiful amount of whiskey he'd imbibed. Only, well, I think you should tell him how you feel, give him a chance to make good on it this time. Because"—he returned his regard to the sea—"I believe he wants to."

For the next hour, she comforted Seaman Bennett and watched the sea for a sign of Noah's skiff. The seed of hope Zach's words had planted in her foolish, forgiving heart flourished with each breath she drew.

"Starboard, Caleb," Noah yelled, hand cupping his mouth to elevate his words above the deafening roar of the clipper's hull splitting apart, seam by seam. He swabbed his spectacle lenses, practically useless from the salty spray kicking into his face. However, if he could see better, it might save another lost soul.

Shoving a flop of dripping hair from his brow, he glanced at the two seamen huddled in the stern. They looked all of sixteen, tear-streaked faces and pink noses. He and Caleb had come upon them clinging desperately to a section of the hull.

"Where?" Caleb bellowed.

He squinted, a dull ache beginning to pound behind his eyes. If only the moon shone brighter, and the blessed fog rolled out to sea. Still, something . . . a flash of color, fifty yards ahead. He swabbed his lenses and pointed.

With a deft torque, Caleb circled the skiff and rowed like the devil, muscles bunching beneath the dark material plastered to his chest. His mouth curled in anger, and he brushed at a fleck of blood on his cheek, the result of a slap from the flat side of an oar. "Dammit, Noah," he shouted, maneuvering through the litter of debris surrounding them.

"One more pass, Cale!"

Caleb slapped the oar to the water, his voice rising above the shrieking wind. "The fog . . . thicker . . . sucked under."

Noah stared at what remained of the clipper, knowing his brother spoke the truth. It lay port side to shore, a doomed position. Coupled with the dense fog and the hunks of debris keeping them from moving closer, the chances of finding anyone alive were slim. He and Caleb had already had a fierce argument in front of the shivering, wild-eyed young seamen. Afraid to terrify them further, Noah had relinquished the oars and agreed to leave. Only, some thread of recognition or . . . ah, he didn't *know*, but he had to try again. Holding up his finger, he mouthed, "Once more."

Caleb scowled and dug in, sending the boat in an angry skip.

Jagged fragments of wood cracked the hull as they cleaved the water in two. Pages from a book and a leather boot floated past. A pair of men's trousers. Noah gripped the sides and swallowed past a parched throat. God, why did he insist upon searching? Death surrounded them. He could sense it, imagined he could smell it, sour, like the scent of rotting meat. If only he could erase the image of Seaman Bennett watching Deck O'Malley float away on part of a skiff.

The boat slowed, and Noah looked back to find Caleb dragging the oars.

"No more . . . too dangerous . . ."

He shifted on the hard bench, the wind pressing his shirt against his chest. Searching the hazy distance, he could not understand his urgency. That blessed speck of color would not leave him be. Sighing, he tucked his spectacles inside the black canvas shoe sitting by his bare feet. Catching Caleb's gaze, he dipped his hand down, then up—*I'm going in.*

Caleb wrenched an oar against the side and cursed loud enough for him to hear.

Balancing his movements, Noah slipped over the side. Stretching, he lengthened his stroke, shoving debris from his path, the water a cool glide against his skin. Caleb had offered to swim out each time, but Noah excelled in the sport, an advantage that had given him hours of adolescent glee. Besides, he wasn't midway to intoxicated.

Treading water, he lifted his head. Just ahead part of a skiff bobbed free. The stern. And atop it lay a body. Noah paddled forward, lungs near to bursting, legs kicking frantically. *Too late, he'd arrived too late.* Closing in, he slapped his hand against the stern, brought his lips above the surface, and gasped for air.

"I thought your brother . . . had this skilled group of . . . sea rescuers. All I get is you."

Noah reared and swallowed a mouthful of water. Grabbing the skiff, he hauled himself atop it, coughing violently.

"Please don't drown . . . on me, Garrett. I'm afraid I left my . . . medical bag at the office."

"Leland?" Noah croaked.

"Who does it . . . sound like?" Ruining the show of bravado, his teeth began to chatter.

Noah dropped his cheek to the notched wood, gulping for breath. "I risked my life for *you?*"

Magnus laughed raggedly. "I'm sorry, Garrett. What does one do . . . when they helplessly watch men drown, screaming . . . as their ship is sucked into the sea? As it sucks them into the sea? You may think I'm a . . . bastard, and I suppose I can be," he rasped, his voice cracking. "Yet, I am also a doctor. I prefer to save lives, not watch them . . . being extinguished in front of me." He groaned, and Noah felt the skiff rock with the force of his shudder.

"Can you swim? Because I don't think I can carry you." Noah blinked rapidly, his eyes stinging as if he had shoved a fistful of lye soap in them.

"Of course . . . I can swim. I wasn't sitting here . . . waiting to c–catch my breath. Look around you. I didn't have . . . anywhere *to* swim. Because of the fog, I have no idea how . . . f–far we are from shore."

Noah hitched to his elbows. Magnus's bewildered gaze slid his way, and he felt the first real stab of fear. "Who else sailed with you?"

The man's shoulders shook. "Oh, dear Lord. We came upon

it so suddenly, I couldn't . . . t–turn. A slow sail . . . not much wind.''

Noah could not grasp Magnus's shoulders, so he put the strength in his tone. "Who, Leland?"

"The clipper's mast, the main one, I think . . . crashed and caught''—he choked on a sob—"caught us right in the middle of the skiff. A–a clean break.''

"Leland!" He elbowed Magnus in the ribs.

Magnus's head lolled to the side, as he stared blankly into the distance. "She'll never love me now. Not when her father d–died in my skiff.''

"Oh, Jesus.'' Noah pressed his stomach into the curve of the stern to keep from heaving. "Tell me Henri Beaumont isn't out here somewhere.''

"On the other side of the skiff,'' he whispered, his lips tinged blue. "I've been holding . . . his arm so he doesn't drift away. He's not heavy. Floating, he's floating.''

"Holding his . . .'' Noah wrenched back, plunging into the icy water. "Cale!'' he screamed at the top of his lungs.

Caleb returned a hoarse shout.

He screamed his brother's name again, his thread of control snapping.

A rumble and a shudder. The clipper going under. Noah felt the answering quiver along the surface of the water and the strong tug near his feet. "Hang on, Leland,'' he advised, his teeth beginning to chatter. It sickened him to admit he meant, *hang on to Henri.* He watched the wave swell and braced against the edge of the stern. It roared over them, washing him into a large fragment of the clipper and washing Leland into him.

"We're going to die,'' Magnus cried, and circled Noah's wrist.

Noah shoved Magnus toward the skiff. He nearly retched at the solid bump of another body. "Climb up, Leland. Do it. Caleb's coming.'' If Caleb's boat hadn't overturned. *Please,*

God, no. Starting to shiver, he kicked his feet and grasped the underside of the skiff between numb fingers. "Leland, don't let go—don't let go of Henri."

"Still got him," Leland returned in a singsong voice.

Hurry, Cale, he prayed. His head had started to pound, his stomach to churn, and his right side stung from the collision with the hull fragment. Additionally, the frigid water and the biting wind consorted to drive every bit of heat from his body. He never wanted to swim again, yet he dreaded having to step on shore and face Elle.

"I can see you, little bro'. Just hang on."

He opened his eyes, never realizing he had closed them. Sluggishly kicking his feet, he felt the surface of the water ripple, smooth and gentle this time. The knotted end of a rope thumped the skiff, emitting a startled cry from Magnus. "Get us in the boat, Cale." He slapped his hand upon the stern. "Leland take the rope."

"Leland?" Caleb said and leaned out. "What is he doing . . . Holy Mother Mary!"

Noah groaned. Water lapped against his chin and into his mouth. He coughed and spit it out.

"This is going to kill Ellie." Caleb's voice was rough.

"I won't let it," he whispered, wondering if he could do anything to stop it.

Along the shore, the occasional chip of quartz glittered in the dim moonlight. At the water's edge, a crowd of people gathered. Near the dunes, flickering bursts from a campfire danced across the sand. Long ago, Noah had stopped noticing the rancid smell and Leland's corresponding whimper at each crest and dive of the boat. Long ago, he had stopped feeling his teeth banging together or the searing pain in his side.

Now, Elle's pain consumed him.

Standing waist-deep in water, the men greeted them, voices

raised in jubilation and relief. Caleb released the oars as they dragged the boat close to shore. Someone slapped Noah between his shoulder blades and he pitched forward, scraping his palms on the bilge.

The joyful laughter ceased when the men got a look inside the skiff. No one proved quick enough to keep her from meeting them.

"Keep Elle away from here." The crashing waves smothered Noah's hoarse plea.

He watched her drop to her knees in the edge of the surf, the hull smacking against her, waves striking her beautiful body. He struggled to hold her back.

Her scream, Zach's curse, the boat shifting crazily as she threw herself against it. His lids lowered, obscuring the sight of her face, the horror and revulsion, the devotion. Brave and honest, Elle possessed a fullness of heart that gave her the faith to love when the odds went against it ever being returned measure for measure.

He and Henri Beaumont shared this betrayal, Noah realized.

Swaying forward, he flailed, meaning to protect her. A barbed pain, violent and sudden, cut down the right side of his body. He felt a gush of liquid heat, then nothing at all.

Chapter Ten

"Cale, get off . . . my chest."

The groggy whisper had Caleb lurching against the bedside table, nearly dropping the pitcher of water in his hand. He hadn't sat on Noah's chest, threatening to let the long string of drool drop from his lips, in fifteen years or more.

He hesitated, then took a step closer, gazing at his brother. Noah's hair lay against his brow in a tangle of gold. His gaunt cheeks were beaded with sweat, his usually clean-shaven jaw lined with stubble. He had kicked the sheet off his feet, and the frayed edge of Caleb's work trousers caught him mid-calf. He probably wouldn't be pleased knowing he looked . . . sloppy. He'd never liked looking sloppy, Caleb recalled, and sighed.

Gingerly perching his rump on the edge of the chair, he reviewed the list of things Leland had told them to do. *Change bandages daily.* His gaze flicked to the strip of white peeking above the faded linen. He tugged it to Noah's neck and tucked it in for good measure. Thank goodness, Christa had promised to change the bandage when she returned.

Apply cold compresses. Releasing a strained breath, he snatched a rag from the basin at his side, and wrung it with a twist. As carefully as if he placed flowers on a grave, he laid it on Noah's brow. His shoulders slumped in relief. Not a flicker of pain had crossed his brother's face.

Chair wobbling beneath him, Caleb dug in his pocket. The least he could do was straighten his brother's hair. His hand shook as he began to comb. Not much experience with nursing. He and Zach were fit as fiddles, never any need for doctors and sickbeds. Course, they'd never been slammed upside a splintered hull, either.

Leaning back in his chair, he studied the combing job, deciding it would do. This wasn't as frightening as he'd believed it would be. Sorta gave him a warm feeling in his chest. With a renewed burst of confidence, he plucked the damp rag from Noah's brow, dumped it in the basin, and grabbed another. Turning, he slammed into a wide-eyed stare.

"Holy Mother Mary," he yelped, and dropped the rag on Noah's chest.

Noah blinked weakly. "Cold," he said. His throat worked in a slow swallow.

"You're cold?" Caleb raced to the closet. Stretching, he tugged at a blanket on the shelf above his head. It smacked his face, and he wrapped his arms around it, hurrying back to the bed.

Noah grimaced and lifted the rag to his brow.

"Oh, you meant . . . I see." Caleb slumped into the chair, the blanket still wadded in his arms. "Yeah, we've got ice in there to keep 'em cold. Doc's orders."

"What time . . . how long have I been . . ." He coughed, trying to strengthen a voice frail from disuse.

"In and out for two days." Caleb hurled the blanket to the floor. "Would it have been too much to holler and let me know you'd split your side open getting washed into something?"

Slowly, Noah lifted the sheet. *"What?"*

Caleb rested his hands on his knees and leaned in. "You

got slammed into a jagged piece of wood, looks like. Cut into your side like a knife.''

Noah let the linen drop. ''I just figured . . . the pain''—he flicked his fingers—''a bruise.''

''A *bruise?*''

His eyes closed, and Caleb thought he had slipped into sleep. ''How is Elle?'' he finally asked.

''Not so good.''

''Funeral?''

''Today.''

Noah's lids lifted. He struggled to raise to his elbows.

Caleb subdued him with one finger on his shoulder. ''No, way, little bro'.''

''Someone needs to . . . be with her, Cale.''

''I know you think that someone should be you, but Zach and Christa will have to do.''

''You''—his throat clicked off a dry swallow—''why aren't you there?''

Caleb poured a glass of water—belatedly remembered another of Leland's orders—and quickly stirred in a pain powder. Shifting, he slid his arm beneath Noah's shoulders. ''Because I never liked him. He treated Ellie as poor as a fistful of dirt, and she loved him too much to return the favor. Zach was scared I wouldn't be able to hide my *distaste for the man.* I think that's how he put it. A pretty way of saying I hated the bastard. So, here I am playing nursemaid to you.''

With a pained grimace, Noah wrenched from Caleb's hold, sending the rag from his brow to the wall. Clumsy as a baby, he grabbed the glass and emptied it in three long gulps.

''Easy, partner.'' Caleb frowned and snatched the glass out of his hand. ''If you vomit all over yourself, Christa will hang my butt in a sling.''

''Typically vulgar,'' Noah muttered and slumped to the mattress, his skin pallid beneath a fevered flush. ''Whatever you put . . . in the water tastes like—''

"Just hush and lie there, grouchy little man." Caleb slapped a new rag in place, using more force than necessary.

Noah edged the cloth from in front of his eyes. "What kind of . . . nursemaid are you?"

"You scared us to death, Professor." He drew a breath of air stinking of camphor and rubbing alcohol. "Do you realize that?"

Noah waved away the concern, his lids drooping. The jagged white scar held Caleb's attention, a beacon signaling their rocky past.

"Do you think it's a joke, what we feel for you? Watching you topple over in that boat, a river of blood gushing down your side?" Caleb's chair skidded back, and he stomped to the window. Flicking the lacy curtain aside—ones they'd always detested but kept to spare their mother's feelings—he glared into a blustery charcoal day that completely suited his mood. "Ellie was raving mad. You bleeding on one side of her, her father all mangled on the other. Stymie sailing in with three bloated bodies piled in the stern. It was a holy mess, the likes of which I never wanna see again."

Noah's body screamed in agony, a sizzling burst of pain with each drawn breath. It had been a long time since he had witnessed his excitable brother having an emotional outburst. He ached to the depths of his soul, but it was not a physical ache. Elle had lost her father, and he couldn't protect her. Through a wealth of pain and confusion, he searched for the part of her living inside him. It came to him slowly, then in a swelling tide of sensation.

Alone. She felt alone.

"I need a drink," Caleb growled.

"Go find one," Noah challenged in a weak tone.

Caleb stalked to the side of the bed and stood, feet braced, glaring at him. "Let's get this done with right now. No more secrets, no more tiptoeing around. Acting like a couple of frightened sissies. I'm sorry for what I did to you, hitting you in the attic. Not understanding what my anger would do to you. I'm so damned sorry, I can't tell you how much. Every day since then I've puzzled about it, worried over it. I was just"— he plunged thick fingers through his hair—"stunned and . . . hurt. And mad. But not at you. At *him*, for leaving. Mama tried to make up for it. I know she did. But I wanted a father. I needed one. I hated him for leaving. Then I hated him more for making me crazy and making you leave."

"I chose to leave, and I'm sorry. I wish I could change it."

He punched his bulky fist in the air. "You don't have nothing to be sorry for. That's what I'm trying to tell you. If you're still angry, if you can't forgive me, I just wanna know. Right now, I have to know."

A wave of dizziness swept over Noah. "Cale, I was very . . . lonely for a long time. Maybe angry. But I forgave you long ago." He felt his lids slip low. "I did it to myself. Stupid to run away. Coward's way out."

He heard Caleb's boots strike the floor, then the soft creak of the door. "You're part of this family, little bro'. That isn't ever gonna change. Quit expecting it to."

"Cale?"

"Yeah?"

The church bell chimed, signaling the lowering of Henri Beaumont's casket into sacred earth. Noah sought to distance his mind from Elle, but she slipped inside his heart and his mind, and he shivered from the impact.

"Noah? You okay?"

He tangled his hands in the sheet, ignoring the stab of pain beneath his ribs. "Has Elle . . . been here?"

A minute ticked by. "This morning." Caleb coughed. "Only, she left. . . . She had to leave in a hurry."

Noah slipped into a deep, drugged sleep before he could ask what Caleb meant.

* * *

Caleb slammed the door before Noah could ask more and backed straight into Christabel. The tray in her hands tottered, and he grabbed it to keep it from crashing to the floor. "Darn it, Chris, what are you sneaking around for?"

Christabel smiled and tapped the edge of his jaw, as always, dismantling his wrath with her touch. "How's he doing?"

"He woke up, thank the Lord. Seems to be in some pain and really, really grouchy."

Christabel nodded. "Men make lousy patients. Why, do you reckon?"

Caleb shuffled from one foot to the other. "Chris, I, well you see, we had lots of other things to talk about, me and Noah, and . . ." He glanced at the tray, saw his apprehensive expression reflected in tarnished silver.

She perched her hands on her hips. "You didn't tell him?"

He shook his head, hating when she treated him like a child. "Chicken."

He lifted his chin. "What do you want me to say? How you feeling, Noah? By the by, your married lady friend, the one none of us knew the first damned thing about, decided to pay a visit. Oh, and guess what else? Elle walked into the room to find her holding your hand and lit outta here like she'd seen a body hanging from the ceiling."

Christabel stamped her black boot against the floor. "Honey, if that's what you would have said, I'm darn glad you waited."

"Thanks." He stalked down the hallway, the tray clutched to his chest.

"You gotta tell him before that Bartram lady appears on the doorstep again, Cale. I saw her in town on my way to the funeral. Plainly, she ain't leaving. In my mind, this is a delicate situation."

Caleb cursed beneath his breath and wondered when exactly

the tables had turned. For the first time in his life, he had to
rescue his little brother from trouble.

Elle slumped against her father's mahogany desk and kicked
at the scattered papers by her feet. The ticking echo of a grandfather clock provided the only sound beyond her shaken, terse
breaths. She hated this room. Despised the shelves of leather-
bound books, hypocritically untouched except for a yearly wax-
ing, the emotionlessly amassed collection of art and antiques,
the costly poplar-paneled walls, even the explosion of naked
color on the ceiling.

She had perched on the edge of the silk-covered horsehair
sofa, caught between apprehension, rebellion, and love, during
more dreadful paternal encounters than she cared to remember.
From the time he caught her sneaking out her bedroom window,
Noah and Caleb hidden in the shrubs below, to the time she
quietly informed him she would not marry Magnus Leland,
each episode had been a battle of wills, a contest of strength.
Even now, his hostility held as heavy a presence as his blasted
cologne—a potent reminder of what she had lost.

Lost? She laughed raggedly and knocked her head against
the desk. What had she lost today, watching the stooped
gravedigger shovel moist soil atop her father's casket? Evidently, not his love. You could not lose what you had never
possessed.

Elle grasped the official-looking document, the crisp parchment stamped and sealed and signed in all the right places.
This scrap of paper had done more to sever her affinity for her
father than all his cold-blooded words and threats. She rolled
it into a cigar-shaped cylinder and blew a breath down the
barrel. His betrayal, quite simply, left her numb. His body had
started to rot in a casket constructed of the best wood money
could buy, and she could not summon a tear for him.

Swaying to the side, she sloshed brandy in the crystal goblet by her hip, and swabbed at a spill using the sleeve of Noah's coat. Her father would chastise her for using a goblet instead of a snifter, for sitting cross-legged on the floor, for being foolish enough to wear young Garrett's coat and, worse, leaning in to sniff the sleeve with unerring consistency. She rubbed the prickly wool beneath her nose, breathing in the warm embrace of Noah's smile, the heartfelt compassion in his eyes, the gentle caress of his fingers.

She needed him as much as she'd ever needed him, and yet, he could be in Morehead City or Chicago or, for that matter, on the moon.

Clinking the goblet against her teeth, she took a gulp of brandy, then choked and coughed. *Damn and blast,* why hadn't Noah's betrayal—in truth no betrayal at all—left her numb? Why, why, *why* could she still feel everything? She had known he corresponded with a woman. He'd made no secret of it, sending off the letters pretty as you please, fodder for the town gossips. Nevertheless, to see a woman sitting beside his bed, the bed he had tucked Elle into the night she'd broken her arm, the bed she and Caleb had hidden a garden snake in, a garden snake that later ended up in *her* bed, the bed she had dreamed of him one day returning to sleep in—

Wrenching forward, Elle flung the goblet against the wall. An amber trickle trailed down the poplar paneling and dripped to the Wilton rug.

Moonlight spilled through the window, a wash of silver across the rolled document crumpled in her fist. She flattened it on her thigh and skimmed the lines of wrinkled text. Her father had left her penniless, or close to it. Enough for his burial and the employment of a solicitor to arrange for the sale of his business and his properties, the antiques, the art. In the bottom paragraph, he addressed the issue of his only child, Marielle-Claire. She would wed by May of 1899 or lose any entitlement to his estate. If she did not meet the terms, the estate would be transferred to a Banque National de Paris account in the name of Gerard Claude Beaumont, the deceased's cousin.

Elle tossed her father's last will and testament to the floor, watched it glide beneath a tasseled footstool. She hoped Gerard Claude Beaumont, whoever he was, appreciated his good fortune.

As usual, her father had misread her. She didn't care about his money. Of course, she would have liked to control the modest amount her mother had left her, use it to complete her education and make the necessary repairs to the school. Perhaps repair Widow Wynne's roof. The rest, the estate of Henri Paul Beaumont, did not concern her in the least. In fact, the idea of groveling the way she would have had to grovel to get it repulsed her.

The savage cruelty of her father's last communication stung like a thousand needles pricking her skin. He had actually dictated a marriage clause to his reed-thin, hawk-faced solicitor, a stranger who stank of Macassar oil and aided in sending paternal threats from the grave. A threat preserved in black ink for everyone to see. Elle felt humiliated, furious, and very disappointed. Again.

These emotions gnawed at her, negating the grief that had bubbled forth when she stumbled past the arms holding her and gotten a good look at her father's mangled, lifeless body. Grief swiftly turning to horror as she watched Noah collapse, a crimson streak slicking the side of the boat, following the path of his descent.

There could be no greater fear than she had experienced at that moment, thinking she'd lost the one man who would never be hers to lose. Much greater than the nagging uneasiness she'd felt long before Caleb rowed their boat toward shore. She had known something had happened and had lied to Zach and Rory about it.

She drew a ragged breath and twisted her hands in the folds of Noah's coat, picturing the wash of blood down his side.

He's not going to die. No, but he would leave. And, sooner or later, he would touch another woman as he had touched her. For all she knew, he could be touching one right now.

Elle wrapped her arms around her stomach, threw her head back, and laughed until her lungs burned. Caroline Bartram. Another of her father's arrogant, asinine errors in judgment. Unquestionably, he had not expected his daughter to be in his library at dawn, cleaning before a rush of consoling visitors stormed his house. The file had been open on the desk, a pen lying on top to hold his place. Two large circles had caught her eye, the pen pressed hard when they were drawn, ripping the paper. Printed in block letters inside the circles was a woman's name.

Smaller print below the vicious circles had given a great many particulars about Mrs. Caroline Beatrice Bartram. Age, family history, known associations, close friends, and presumed lovers. A detailed and rather fascinating report; Elle had had no idea you could buy a written account of someone's life. And Mrs. Bartram had led an interesting life, to say the least. It seemed a frightful intrusion, and she wondered, lacking any genuine interest, which drawer in her father's desk held Noah Garrett's life printed on cheap bond paper.

Noah and this woman knew each other well enough that an investigator—Elle assumed this was the most reasonable means of buying a person's past—had connected them. She dropped her head to her knees, swallowed past the choke of tears in her throat. Would she be listed in Noah's report? She doubted it.

She sniffed and wiped her nose on Noah's sleeve, his scent sending a warm jolt of—*oh, God, she knew*—desire to the pit of her stomach. Desire and the foolhardy love she wished to crush like a stick of chalk beneath her heel.

This morning, confused by her father's final thrust of cruelty and eager to talk to Noah, more eager than she had ever been to talk to anyone, Elle had impulsively decided to take Zach's advice. She would tell Noah she loved him. After all, he could have died the other night. She could not forget the sight of his blood on her hands. She would never forget. She loved him, and she wanted him to know it.

She had put on her nicest dress, which wasn't saying much, pinned her mother's brooch on her collar, arranged her hair in a shabby imitation of a French twist, and topped it off with a narrow little nothing of a hat she had had her eye on for months. Lilian Quinn, Pilot Isle's seamstress and milliner, had taken the hat from the window and wrapped it in pink paper while instructing her to tilt it forward and dip the brim, then tie the narrow velvet ribbons at the back of her head.

Following everyone's advice but her own, if she'd taken the time to listen, Elle had twisted and tilted and dipped, and for good measure, dabbed a tad of the honeysuckle fragrance Noah liked behind each ear. Her knees had knocked with every step, two hundred at least from her father's house to Zach's. Beneath the haze of grief and uncertainty, she had felt joyously relieved.

Joyously relieved, grieved, and uncertain, she had opened the door to his childhood bedroom and had her world tilt on its axis. A complete, soaring tilt. Closing the door, she walked into town, and telegraphed Savannah.

My father has died. Stop. No change in dire circumstances. Stop.

If anyone found a visit to the telegraph office on the day of her father's funeral a strange occurrence, they didn't say anything. As for the odd looks, who cared? She had been receiving those since the day she set foot on Pilot Isle.

She pulled a lock of hair through her front teeth, tasting the lemon rinse. Noah *desired* her. No honorable intentions. No connection to their childhood. Just forthright, if somewhat reluctant, lust. She understood because, after sifting it around in her mind, she decided she felt it, too. If she looked past the love dwelling deep in her heart, past those silly, childhood fantasies of knights on white horses, it all came down to a persuasive mouth, manipulative hands, and a pair of long, long legs.

She'd wanted more the afternoon in the alley. And the night on the beach.

She wanted more right this minute.

Ashamed to admit feeling emotions other than grief, she jerked Noah's coat off and plucked the clinging bodice from her breasts. Would it be so foolish? One chance to make love to the man she loved. *Juste Ciel,* one night in exchange for years of icy sheets and vivid dreams.

Very foolish, her mind answered, because Noah would react just like he did after he kissed you. Dear heaven, how sorry would he be if he made love to you?

Marielle-Claire, you must get that boy out of your mind. He does not want you. He never has.

In a final act of paternal mastery, her father had proven his statement, presented the evidence in the form of a tall, dark-headed woman holding tightly to Noah's hand. At least sending for Caroline Bartram, which Elle did not doubt, had saved her from humiliating herself. Again.

Sometime during the last few nights, she had discovered a solution to her problem. She didn't think she could bear to watch Noah walk away from her life again.

Therefore, she would have to walk away from his.

Chapter Eleven

Caroline Bartram did not consider herself a person of exemplary moral fiber. She had grown up in a mill village in Solitude, West Virginia, in a squalid one-room shack. No running water, just a creek out back, newspapers stuffed into every hole and crevice, four children to a bed and three stretched beside it on the floor. It had been a long time since she had recalled Solitude's rolling green hills and undeniable stench. A town her father had laughingly called a hillbilly holler, a town her mother had called Hell. Caroline had done things she was not proud of to escape.

She took a sip of tea, her pinkie angled away from the chipped handle. She remembered Ruby Garnet's lessons and used them well. She glanced from one man to the other, smoothed her hand across her bodice, and balanced her cup perfectly in its saucer. Her presence troubled them, Noah's brothers, that much she could tell. The broad, rough one shuffled his feet and drank from the cup using both hands. The tall, thoughtful one alternated between staring at her and staring out the window. Troubled, indeed.

Patience waning, she asked, "Do you think a short visit would tire Noah too much?"

The thoughtful one, Zachariah, jerked his head up. He pinned his brother with a hard glare. "Did you announce Mrs. Bartram, Caleb?"

The rough one's gaze flicked to her, to his brother, to the floor. He shook his head.

Zach sighed and swiveled toward her, his face set in lines of a serious nature. In her former business, Caroline had rarely seen seriousness on any man's face. Lust, greed, and anger, but never this kind of solemn concern. "Of course, Mrs. Bartram, since you've come all the way from Chicago. I just wanted"—he threw another heated glance at his brother—"to let Noah know you had arrived so it wasn't a big surprise. Might wear him out, you understand."

"Is he all right?"

The serious one halted, studying her.

She placed the cup and saucer on the end table and tugged at the button on her glove. "I would love to see him." Vaguely, she questioned whether it constituted a breach of etiquette for a widow to visit a man in his bedroom. Ruby Garnet had never covered this lesson that Caroline could recall.

The serious one nodded and rose to his feet. "Right this way," he said, and started down the hallway.

She brushed her gloved hands over her skirt and stood with a whisper of silk and crinoline. "Good day, Mr. Garrett."

"Mrs. Bartram," the rough one said, averting his eyes.

What they must think of her, she wondered, and climbed a narrow staircase in desperate need of a woman's touch. A spot of color would do nicely, a flower or two, a picture. She almost tapped on Zachariah's stiff shoulder and told him. Such rigid posture. She frowned. After all these years, people's derision still hurt. However, this time, she had lumped the scorn on her own shoulders. She'd begged for this, in a way, by accepting an offer to come to a place she didn't belong. Belated, perchance, but she hoped Noah would not be angry with her.

Zachariah halted before a door at the end of the hall. Touching the dented knob, he said, "It's only been three days since the accident, and he might be sleeping. If he's not, he won't last long. The doctor gave him these pain powders and they snuff him out like a candle . . ."

"I won't stay long, I promise. A quick hello, and I'll be on my way."

He pressed his lips together and peeked inside. "Awake, I think."

She thanked him and entered the bedroom, instantly recognizing the stale stench of illness. Caroline had doctored many sick women in her life, mostly for ailments hospitals shied from.

He lay on his back, gazing through the window, his lids sleep-heavy. His hair was longer than she ever remembered seeing it, curling over his brow in streaks of color. She suppressed the maternal urge to sweep it from his face, instead, clutched her hands together, and slid into the battered chair by his bed.

His chest crested and dipped. "What are you doing here, Caro?"

"I came to see you, darling. What else?"

Gingerly, as if it pained him, he turned his head. Skin shadowed and cheeks gaunt, his gaze was clear and observant. "Are you in trouble?"

She laughed and yanked at a button on her glove. "You know I don't get into trouble anymore." Not terrible trouble, anyway.

He smiled but it didn't reach his eyes. "Why, Caro?"

She shrugged and tapped her fingers together. "Maybe I wanted to see the place you've talked so little about. The family you've told me nothing about."

He laughed, then made a pained sound, and rubbed a spot

below his ribs. "Now you've seen it, seen them, do you think you might like to tell me why you needed to leave Chicago?"

"Well"—she unbuttoned and buttoned her glove—"you remember my gentleman friend, Russell?"

"The lawyer."

"Yes, well, ends up Russell had his fingers in some sticky business. Something to do with whiskey and illegal importation, if I understood the agreeable magistrate correctly."

"Good God, did you get arrested?"

She laughed and fluttered her hand in the air. "Oh, gracious, no. But they searched my house. Russell apparently stored a felonious reserve in my basement. Quite a stink on Prairie Avenue, I can tell you. None of those silk stockings want a former madam for a neighbor. Even if I keep my lawn neater than theirs and drive the grandest carriage on the block. Anyway, the magistrate suggested a short respite until they had Russell, bless his dear heart, locked away."

Noah's lids slipped a notch. "Do you have a place to stay?"

"My, yes. A kind whaler gentleman offered to bunk with his friend and give me the largest bedroom at the boardinghouse. Decorated in lovely shades of pink and ivory. Kind of reminds me of a child's room, but lovely just the same."

"That's it? You ran here to escape Russell the whiskey swindler."

She frowned and clicked her back teeth together.

"I can hear your teeth clicking, Caro." He yawned. "Dead giveaway you're withholding information."

"How about we have a nice, long chat tomorrow?"

"Hmmm, tomorrow the . . . mystery unfolds."

Caroline shook the wrinkles from her skirt and walked to the window. A shaggy-headed boy raced along the street, a brown-and-white mutt on his heels. An unbalanced wagon crept past, loaded high with round barrels and crates of vegetables. A faint breeze ruffled the branches of a massive tree in the middle of the yard, whipped the long stalks of grass into a verdant frenzy. Long ago, Carrie McTavey might have known what kind of tree it was, what to call those red-and-white flowers surrounding the house. She might have known how to let the simple joy of life overcome the everyday pain of living.

She had been a kind, sweet girl, Carrie McTavey. Gentle and trusting. Completely happy to share a bed with three sisters and plug the holes in the walls with scraps of salvaged newsprint. Life had been shiny as a new penny, even if the edges were dull. Then, her father's foreman put his hands on her on her twelfth birthday. After that, men touching her became commonplace. Expected. She shrugged and let the curtain slip from her fingers. It had not harmed anyone to earn money for the expected.

Noah mumbled in his sleep; she glanced back. He looked so young. Worry lines smoothed by slumber. He tugged at her heart, just like the first time she'd seen him. He was the only man she had ever known, besides her da, who wanted to help her and didn't seem to want her body in return. Of course, she had helped him once, the paltry loan for college. He paid it back in less than a year. Oh, well, just another reason for people to assume they had an intimate relationship.

He had *never* touched her in a disrespectful way. At first, Noah's reticence hurt her, because she'd come to understand men wanted her or else they didn't know she existed. Somehow, over time, Noah had changed her view of herself.

She tugged at the button on her glove and thought about what Mr. Beaumont had offered, although he had no idea he'd offered it. Oh, she understood the man's reasons for sending her the telegraph. Nothing to do with her happiness and everything to do with his daughter's.

However, Caroline liked Pilot Isle, the picturesque avenues and earthy smells. Reminded her of Solitude, with friendlier people. They didn't scrunch up their noses when she smiled at them. Besides, Chicago had lost some of its charm, and more important, Justin would love it. He hated the boarding school in Michigan. He wanted her and, gracious, she wanted him. In Pilot Isle, she could have him. She could be a true mother to her illegitimate and much-loved son.

Hesitant to face another dinner alone, she glanced out the window, watched a young woman walk up the drive, a boy about Justin's age holding her hand. The woman shoved a swatch of lovely rust-colored hair from her face and gave the boy's arm a firm hug. Over the boy's shoulders, her gaze lifted, and even from a distance, Caroline could see them, green as the grass beneath her feet, spiked by long lashes the color of her hair. Not exactly sure why, she moved out of sight. Through a slit in the curtain, she witnessed the play of emotions across the young woman's face. Confusion, anger, and ultimately, love.

Evidently, this was Marielle-Claire Beaumont. It had to be. The description matched well enough. A beautiful little thing. Exquisite face, lavish body. Caroline laughed softly. She could have made a fortune in the Pink House.

She looked back at Noah, his chest rising and falling beneath a bleached sheet. Frayed holes dotted the edge. She sighed. *Men.* Had Mr. Beaumont been wrong about Noah and his daughter? In the telegraph, he had presented his plan in brusque terms. He'd wanted Caroline to put a stop to his daughter's ruination. Of course, he assumed she and Noah were lovers, and he obviously knew about her past, probably figured she had some naughty sexual tricks up her sleeve. Enough to stop a man in his tracks.

Russell's untimely hoarding of liquor in her basement had convinced her. Foolish perhaps, but she'd imagined she did Noah a favor. Because women pestered him. Often. She'd seen it on the occasional evenings they had dinner. A smile, a wink, a touch. One had even lifted her skirt, showing off a dimpled ankle. Noah had jerked forward in his chair and grabbed Caroline's hand. She had played her part and given that teasing coquette a look to crack rock.

A private man. Part of his attraction, she'd always believed. She remembered what little he'd told her. Beaumont's daughter had been part of the discovery of his illegitimacy, which wasn't the worst development, Caroline thought. Maybe he didn't want to have anything to do with the girl because of it.

She looked back to find the yard empty, the sun sinking low and throwing all kinds of vivid colors against the clouds. She could see more of the sky on the island than she could in Chicago. She liked that.

Caroline knew from personal experience that small towns bred rumors faster than an alley cat bred kittens. A walk about town, a smile, a subtle question or two. She would ascertain enough to know if she'd made a mistake coming here. Noah sure as tomorrow morning wouldn't tell her.

Elle did not anticipate having Jewel Quattlebaum crash into her as the reporter tripped down Zach's front steps. Grabbing the porch column for support, she turned to watch the crazed woman kick a rock from her path and shake her fist at a nest of squawking blue jays, her back rigid enough to crack.

"Merciful heavens, what's gotten into her?"

"Noah, that's what."

Elle snapped her head around, found Zach leaning against the screen door, a yawn parting his lips.

"You look exhausted," she said.

He stroked his bearded chin. "Frustration over tangling with a six-foot-two baby."

Elle sputtered, surprised to hear laughter. She had not felt like laughing in days.

"You won't believe what he just said to Jewel. She came here looking for details about the accident. Said Noah was a hero. Make a good story for the *Messenger*. Blast it, I assumed he would at least talk to her."

"And?"

Zach scowled, thoroughly disgusted. "He told her to climb aboard her gnawed-off pencil and ride it straight to hell."

Elle dropped her free hand to her knee and bent over, her eyes overrunning with tears.

"It's not funny, Ellie, he's driving us crazy."

She nodded, struggling for breath, trying to agree. She had never known Noah to be impolite.

"Go talk to him. *Please.*"

She straightened, the laughter dying in her throat. "No."

"What have you got in your hand?"

"The book you asked me to bring from the coach house. The one you said Noah needed."

"Give it to him, talk to him. I beg you. Before I kill him or Caleb does. They've been going at it as fiercely as they did when they were children. I'm ready to run away from home, no lie."

"Zach, I—"

"I really believe you're part of this temper tantrum he's having. You haven't been to see him since the day of the funeral. Not that he's said anything, you know Noah. I told him you ask after him every day, and he just grunts."

"Me? Why would he care if—"

"What are you going to do? Avoid him until he leaves because of this woman? We don't even know what to make of her, Ellie. Maybe they're just good friends."

She hugged Noah's book to her chest, her father's file tucked inside. Good friends, indeed. "How is he?" she asked, unable to stop the question.

The door hinge squeaked as Zach stepped inside the house. "You've asked me a hundred times in the last few days." He smiled at her through the torn screen. "This time you'll have to find the answer yourself. By the way, he's out back."

"Thanks a lot," Elle said, and hugged the book. A fine wind blew past, scattering her hair, tugging at her divided skirt. For a moment, she considered leaving the book on the stoop and riding away on her bicycle. Except, she couldn't leave that despicable report for just anyone to stumble upon. For purely malicious reasons, she had decided to let Noah stumble upon it.

I really believe you're part of this temper tantrum.

Had her avoidance hurt him? Was that possible? Elle had figured Mrs. Caroline Bartram would keep him entertained. What did she care anyway?

"Oh, the nerve of the man," she muttered, and marched down the steps. She would give him his blasted book, make sure he felt better, and then leave.

Sunlight and dew sparkled on the tousled blades of grass she crushed beneath her boot. A bout of rain the night before had cleared the air and hastened the transformation of spring. The scent of the ocean lingered, and through an open window she passed, the aromas of bacon and browning butter.

She rounded the corner of the house and halted, damp fingers sticking to the book's leather cover. Noah sat in a rocking chair beneath the oak they had climbed as children, in a stretch of shade provided by a copse of branches. Wavering bursts of shadow and light swam across his profile, the pensive tilt of his lips, the taut line of his jaw. A table sat next to him, piled high with papers and books, and the box of shiny metal instruments she had delivered two days earlier.

His hand swept the page of his notebook with rapidity she found hard to follow. He nudged his spectacles, then tapped the pencil against his straight, white teeth, staring into the distance. As she stood there, torn between love and dismay, Noah stiffened, the pencil sliding from his fingers. He cocked his head and looked straight at her, his reflective, unguarded expression hardening into the detached one she knew well. For a long moment, he stared, the look on his face almost anticipatory. Then he blinked and glanced down, a calm shrug of indifference his only reply.

Elle tipped her hat back and filled her lungs with a strong

dose of courage. A gust of wind shook the thicket of branches as she stepped beneath them and flattened a stray curl against his brow. She swallowed. He'd fastened nary a button on his shirt, leaving just an open tangle of faded, blue cotton trailing past his waist. White gauze circled his ribs and a swatch of hair, darker than the hair on his head, peeked out above *and* below.

Juste Ciel, she thought, a warm pool of heat unfurling in her belly. Stunned, she dropped the book to the ground and plopped her rear end upon it, burrowing her fingers in the cool dirt.

Eyes still glued to his notebook, he asked, "Which one of my textbooks are you sitting on?"

She didn't answer, just watched the wind ruffle his hair and lift the floppy shirttails, exposing more of a man's body than she had ever seen except for an intermittent drunken fisherman on the docks. Drinking him in, she felt him invading her soul's chilled nooks and crannies.

He snatched the pencil from the grass, then drew a hissing breath.

She rocked forward onto her knees, the stance bringing her between his outspread legs. The scent of rubbing alcohol and soap filled her nose. "Noah?"

He lifted a finger and slumped, jaw flexing, face pale.

"Do you want me to go get—"

Before she could finish the question or rise to her feet, he had her by the wrist, his grip strong and convincing, his gaze centered on her. "No. Don't go." He glanced at his hand and abruptly released her.

She sat back, missing the book and bouncing to the ground. She tried again and said, *"Depths of the Sea*, I think it's called. Isn't that the one you asked for?"

"Yes. First textbook on oceanography published in English—1873."

"Mercy, I'm sitting on *that*." She tugged it from beneath her bottom and thumped it on the table.

Noah dropped his head and laughed weakly. "Oh, Elle," she imagined she heard him say. He dragged his fingers through his hair, his pale eyes traveling from her jersey gaiters to the tip of the feather sticking from her hat.

A leisurely stroke that set her skin aflame.

"What is this outfit you have on?" He propped his chin on his thumb and forefinger.

She glanced down. A calf-length divided skirt, a double-breasted jacket edged in black braid, a white blouse with detachable collar, a man's necktie. She would admit to affecting a masculine appearance, although the style was quite fashionable. Her father had berated her once too often, and she had hidden the clothes in the bottom of her wardrobe, forgotten, until she found them yesterday while packing. "I rode a bicycle here and traditional clothing doesn't work ... because of the spokes." She shrugged, her cheeks heating. "I know they're kind of ridiculous."

Noah stroked his finger across his lip, studying her. "I like them," he finally said.

Life tasted angelically sweet at that moment. *"You do?"*

"Very practical, trousers. For a bicycle trip, certainly."

"Yes, yes, they are."

"The hat is nice, too."

Independent of her mind, her hand went to touch it. A burst of feminine pleasure bloomed in her chest. "It's new."

"Ah," he said, and raised a brow.

Suddenly bashful, she pulled a weed from the ground, trying to think of something clever to say.

"Where have you been, Elle?"

She peeked at him through her lashes. He studied the pencil in his hand as earnestly as she studied the weed in hers. "Been?"

"I just assumed ... you would stop by more often." He shrugged lackadaisically, then slid forward in the chair, rubbing his chest.

"Quit squirming." She rose to her knees.

He clamped the tattered end of his bandage between his teeth and struggled to untie the knot below his ribs.

"Here, let me help you." She leaned in, brushing his hands aside. She tapped his lips with her finger, and he parted them enough to let the tattered end fall into her palm. "Too tight, hmmm?" She loosened the knot as carefully as she could. "I bet Caleb tied this one." Her eyes met his, and her fingers stilled, her palm settling over his heart. The gentle rhythm warmed her; his intense look captured her, clear into her being. Her fingers curled in response, sinking into the springy hair on his chest.

She lowered her gaze and loosened the bandage. Hands shaking, she struggled to retie the knot. "I thought . . . you were sick and"—she swallowed—"I thought I'd wait for you to get stronger." *For me to get stronger.*

"Your cheeks pinken when you lie."

"I don't lie." She jerked the knot, avoiding his scrutiny.

"You just did. I would bet my life on it and . . . I don't know why."

She curled her fingers into fists, the desire to touch him nearly overwhelming her meager supply of common sense. "Thank you for"—she glanced into solemn eyes difficult to delude—"for bringing in my father. I know . . . I know there was no way to save him. Magnus told me everything. He said you were helping them when you got hurt. He told me he apologized to you for everything. I'm glad he did."

"Are you all right, Elle?"

She slid to the ground and let her hands dangle between her knees. Blades of grass poked through her skirt, gentle pricks to her skin. She listened to the faded rush of waves to the shore, the mad dash of a squirrel along the branches above her. "My mother used to tuck me into bed and tell me how special I was. Her dear girl, *ma chère fille.* She told me she had prayed for me. And I believed her. Then she died and my entire world twisted inside out." With her pinkie, she recorded the plodding progress of a ladybug. "I tried to love him as much as I'd loved her. Heaven, I wanted to love him that much. But he never let me get close enough. I was a useless female, undeniably silly. Always, no matter how hard I strove to be responsible . . ." She shrugged, having no way to describe the person she had attempted to become.

Sighing, he reached for her. She didn't see the movement, but she pulled back in time to avoid the touch.

"Don't." She lifted her chin. "I'm trying to tell you I can survive if I survived my mother's death. Don't you understand? I loved her more. I always did. And I felt extreme guilt." She shook her head, slinging strands of hair into the mouth. Plucking them out, she said, "Truly, I don't need you confusing the issue by touching me and listening to my problems, making me think I can depend on you."

His lids flared wide. "You *can* depend on me."

"Oh, yes, of course." She leaped to her feet, paced forward, pinching the bridge of her nose.

A baffled look crossed his face, so little-boy-lost her knees threatened to give way. His lips parted, and he appeared to search for words. "You can depend on me."

"I can depend on you to *leave*. The lab is nearly finished. I've seen it."

"Be fair, Elle," he said hoarsely.

Damn and blast, she *wasn't* being fair. Accusing and belittling when she planned to leave as well. "You're right—" A whisper-soft tread rustled the grass behind them. Elle half turned, her heart plummeting to her toes.

"I hope I'm not intruding. I'm Caroline Bartram, an old friend of Noah's." Noah felt a responding nip of unease. Caro could be quite mischievous if presented with a suitable opportunity. "And you must be Marielle-Claire. I've heard a lot about you."

Elle jerked her watch from her pocket, then spared it a nonexistent glance. "I've got to go. Teaching a reading lesson in ten minutes." She nodded to Caroline. "Mrs. Bartram, I left something of yours in Noah's book." Looking frightfully composed, she stalked across the yard, her stride, in his mind, comparable to a panther's.

Caroline turned her head, following Elle's progress as she made an angry pivot around the corner of the house. "Well, well. A little firebrand."

Noah knocked his head against the back of the chair and inhaled a honeysuckle-laced breath. "What the hell was that about?"

Caroline presented an impish grin and settled gracefully by his feet. "For such an intelligent man, you can be terribly dull-witted."

"Dull-witted?"

"Severely preoccupied, blissfully ignorant." She tugged her gloves from her hands, finger by finger. "Please, choose whichever fits."

He rolled his head to look at her. She smiled in reply, a flash of white teeth and sympathy.

"Read what's in your little book, Noah. Unfortunately, I'm afraid I can guess what it is."

Hefting the volume to his lap, he flipped through the pages. Near the middle, a folded sheet caught his eye. He shook it open with the help of a healthy gust of wind and read quickly, line after glaring line, his stomach sinking. In the distance, he could hear the roaring tryst of land and sea, the piercing call of ravenous seagulls. How he wished he were there instead of where he sat. Anywhere else. An image of turbulent green eyes, agony and disbelief spilling from them, stained his vision.

Noah lifted his head and hurled the paper at her feet. "She thinks we were lovers."

Caroline smoothed the paper over the cushion of grass and bent her head to read it. "No, darling, she probably thinks we *are* lovers."

"Blessit," he said, and rubbed the spot on his chest that

burned from the brush of her fingers. "Now I understand why she didn't come to see me. She's had this sordid report since the day her father died, more than likely."

"Or, it could be because she walked in the other day while I was holding your hand."

"*What?*" His head lifted. He blinked slowly.

"Why, darling, if I didn't know you better, I would think you actually cared about this girl."

"Of course, I care about her. I've known her since she was ten years old."

"Sounds like more than childhood affection to me."

"I'm not in love with her if that's what you're trying to intimate. Nothing even close."

"Intimate?" Her brow arched. "Is it the same as hinting at?"

He rolled his eyes heavenward. "Yes."

"Then I will admit to intimating you are in love with Miss Beaumont."

"I'm not, I said," he growled, and thunked his heel in the dirt. "Don't you think I'd know?"

Caroline licked her fingertip, smoothed a wispy curl, and pursed her lips thoughtfully. "Unfortunately, no, I don't. In any event, would it be so bad if you were? She's a lovely little thing. Absolutely lovely. Wild-eyed. Somewhat ferocious in a kittenish way. And, darling, if you could only see how she *looks* at you." Caroline's lashes fluttered. "I would give my soul to have a man look at me the way the little hellcat looks at you. Hot enough to turn wood to cinders." She laughed slyly. "Stumbling upon the two of you, I admit to feeling the voyeur."

Noah's heart gave a violent twist in his chest. How *had* she looked at him?

In answer, an image surfaced. Elle, kneeling in the grass, her full trousers spread around her, one delicate, stocking-covered ankle exposed. Her mannish jacket molded to her breasts.

"Poor, darling, you have it bad."

A scowl tightened his lips. "Granted, I might have it bad, depending on your precise definition, but I'm not in love with her. Chrissakes, don't frown like you don't believe me. Don't you think I would realize something so significant?" Through gritted teeth, he said, "Quit grinning."

Her lips curled wide, her gaze straying to the front of his trousers.

A fever-hot flush swept his face; he shifted the book to his lap. "Blessit, Caro, surely *you*, of all people, understand the difference."

Caroline lifted a slim shoulder, an elegant shrug. "Fine. You don't love the little hellion. Perhaps, then, you should consider . . . other offers. The offer in those feline eyes. A woman like that could challenge a man's imagination. Tempt his mind. Rouse his soul."

"Stop reciting poetic verse, please. I don't want my imagination challenged." To his surprise, he lied calmly, having pictured Elle in this fashion many times. No less than a hundred torturous times. Impulsive nature. Unrestrained enthusiasm. Instinctive sensuality. Blessit, it frightened him to imagine losing control. What would a woman like Elle do to a man? Brand him for life? Noah couldn't afford to be branded for life.

"Afraid to take her up on it, darling?"

A gust of wind blew in from the sea, ripping at his stiff collar. "Completely terrified."

Caroline emitted an unladylike snort of laughter. "Oh, Noah, I *like* this girl. She's the first woman I've ever seen twist you in a knot. Gracious, the first I've seen even make you look twice. Saints be praised, it's about time."

"I see we've moved to the Irish blarney."

"Stubborn fool, you wouldn't know a good woman if she kicked you in the head."

Noah slid low in the rocking chair and crossed his hands over his stomach. "You said you suspected what was in the book."

Caroline pleated the hem of her skirt between her fingers, then stilled, realizing she clicked her back teeth. "You remember the other day, when I stopped by to see how you were?"

"Vaguely. Those pain powders didn't do wonders for my memory."

"Well, I, that is . . ." She circled her hand at her side and blurted, "Henri Beaumont telegraphed me and asked me to come to Pilot Isle. To keep you away from his daughter. I did it because I knew you weren't interested in staying here, I mean, at the time, I thought you weren't interested in staying. And, because of Russell and his sticky fingers—"

"How the hell did Henri Beaumont know about *you?*"

Caroline flashed a sad smile. "Darling, you really are naive. I must have seen ten similar communications about myself over the years. Someone wants a piece of your past, they pay to have it dug up. Simple as can be." She shook her head. "Don't you realize Henri Beaumont paid for your past, too? The little hellcat probably suspects it. She's just afraid to go looking in her papa's desk."

"That bastard paid to have someone investigate *me?*"

"How else do you think he got hold of my name?"

Noah whistled through his teeth. "Chrissakes."

"A good account." Caroline turned the sheet of paper over and back. "It's not entirely factual, but I've seen worse."

Noah slid forward, his hands still linked. "Did he offer you money, Caro?"

"Of course he offered money."

"Did you take it?"

She leaned in, her nose bumping his. "I'm not a prostitute anymore, Noah Garrett, which you well know because you helped me leave the profession. So, wipe the affronted look off your face. I could sell my house on Prairie Avenue and buy this whole town if I wanted to. To heck with Henri Beaumont's niggling offer.''

''I'm sorry. I didn't mean it,'' he said, and relaxed, concealing a grimace of pain.

''You know, you're the only man who has ever respected me. I don't want to think I've lost that.''

''Oh, Caro''—he sighed—''you haven't. I'm simply mired knee-deep right now. I don't know where to turn.''

''Make a list. What you usually do, right?''

''I have a list. A growing pile of lists. One right there, on the pad beside you.'' He rubbed his fingers beneath his spectacles. ''They're not helping.''

She grabbed the pad of paper and tilted it into the light. ''Well, well, would you look at this. A list of reasons to stay clear of dear Marielle-Claire. Not exactly the list I had in mind, but . . .''

He snatched the pad from her hand and shoved it behind his back.

Caroline flopped to her elbows and hooted. ''Saints be praised, this is the best time I've had since that no-account Russell took me to the fancy horse race in Kentucky. Watching you squirm is about as much fun as seeing those huge beasts tear up a muddy track.''

Covering his face with his hands, he mumbled between his fingers, ''Hush, will you?''

''I have just the stuff to ease your troubles, darling.''

He felt a firm tap and glanced down to find a leather-covered flask resting on his knee.

''I keep it tucked in my garter. For medicinal purposes. Fainting spells and the like.''

He uncorked the flask and lifted it to his lips, the metal still warm from being pressed against her thigh. The bitter liquid rolled past his throat, and he coughed, throwing a quick glance toward the house. The last thing he needed was Zach's censure for drinking in the middle of the day.

"I heard the story about you and Marielle-Claire. Her idolizing you, you protecting her. A smelly old fisherman even took me to see the tree trunks in the schoolyard."

"Wonderful," he said around another gulp.

"I found it a charmingly sweet testament to a girl's undying love."

"Elle didn't carve those in the trees, by the way." He grimaced. "But she went back later and dug the marks in deeper."

Caroline smiled knowingly. "And you think Marielle-Claire is the same willful, devoted child."

"Of course not. But she's still too impulsive, too . . ." Intelligent, interesting, vexing, beautiful. *Ma chère fille.* He shoved the cork into the flask, the taste of whiskey heavy on his tongue. Those few sips had softened the impress of Elle's torment, making it easier to catch a full breath. "She isn't the kind of woman to dally with, and when I decide to marry, *if* I decide to marry, I'll marry a woman who will not disrupt my well-organized life. Elle doesn't fit my plan, Caro. In fact, she'd blow it straight to Hades if I let her." He tossed the flask at her feet. "Regardless, I'm returning to Chicago once the laboratory is finished. I have a shellfish study to initiate and biology classes to teach. I don't have a life here anymore, and I'm not going to make one."

"Do you miss Chicago so much?"

He crossed his ankles and scowled. "Who said anything about missing Chicago?"

"Hmmm."

"Mind your own business, Caro. There's no future. Elle Beaumont and I are too different. We always have been."

She didn't answer, just clicked her teeth and hummed a soft tune.

Her silence annoyed the hell out of him.

* * *

"Uncle Noah, why can't you keep your hands offa Miss Ellie?"

Noah dropped his fork to the plate. He glanced at Rory, who dabbed his spoon in the pool of gravy inside his mashed potatoes, and Caleb, who buttered his bread, a guilty flush reddening his cheeks.

Rory mopped his fist beneath his nose and rocked the table as he swung his legs beneath it. Flaxen hair stuck to his brow in sweat-darkened clumps. "Huh, Uncle Noah? I love Miss Ellie, but she's still a *girl*. Have you kissed her? Johnny-Bob says you have to open your mouth for a real kiss. Yuck."

Noah lifted his napkin from his lap and wiped a dab of gravy from Rory's chin. "Where did you hear this?"

Caleb shifted in his chair. "Rory, you're just playing with your supper. How about you go upstairs and wash up. I'll take you to Scoggins for ice cream."

"Yippee!" Rory raced from the kitchen, his chair swaying from side to side, his napkin fluttering to the floor, the subject of yucky kisses forgotten.

"Noah—"

"You know, you and Zach need to develop some other interests."

"Ah, come on." Caleb cracked a smile. "He musta heard us talking today. We were just pondering a piece about you two."

His chair skidded into the wall. "I think I'll spend the night at the coach house. There's a textbook I need to review before I make my next research trip to Devil Island."

"Don't have to go getting your feathers all ruffled," Caleb called. "Heck, little bro', why are you blushing if you *can* keep your hands offa her?"

Noah slammed the door in reply.

Chapter Twelve

Noah left the laboratory site, head bent, gaze fixed on the wet planks beneath his brogans, waves whipping against the pilings almost crushing the sound of Caleb's mockery. The promise of a storm scented the humid air and threw a solid punch into the wind coming off the sea. A fine, salt-laden mist struck his face and slicked his shirt to his chest. Crossing the deserted street, he passed beneath a spherical yellow glow and stopped to observe the gas flame wavering behind a dingy globe. Elle had mentioned petitioning the town committee for twenty streetlamps and the insufficient approval for eight. Her cheeks had gone wild with furious color just talking about it.

He released a shout of laughter that echoed off the warehouses looming on each side of him. No matter how much Elle troubled him, he could not deny her uniqueness, her inherent strength—or his fascination. Jocularity dwindling, he slipped his spectacles off, yanked his shirttail from his trousers, and swabbed the spotted lenses.

As a child, how had he missed those things?

He frowned and forced his spectacles into place. Blessit, he'd squandered half his childhood fleeing her lovesick embrace and the other half rescuing her from some farcical disaster. Who had time to wonder about—well, just to *wonder?* He had been doing enough of that, ceaseless amounts of reflection, since their passionate kiss behind the Nook. He touched his lips, imagining *her* fingers, her touch.

His heart picked up speed as his body betrayed him.

Cursing, he pulled the tattered scrap of paper from his shirt pocket, tipped it into the light, and reviewed the list for the hundredth time. Five solid, irrefutable reasons to avoid Elle Beaumont, starting—

Lightning arced. A drop of rain pelted his cheek. Another smacked his chest, soaking to the skin. With a muttered oath and a shiver, he shoved the list in his pocket and broke into a run, the storm rising to full glory. His rubber-bottomed brogans skimmed over a patch of shells, and he struggled to maintain his balance, his side beginning to throb in an impressive rhythm.

Relief poured through him when the next bolt of lightning illuminated Widow Wynne's pitched roof. Whipping off his spectacles, he slapped the gate back on its hinges. The heavy rainfall had unfurled a silver blanket, obliterating his view of the widow's house. Better that, he mused, taking the coach house stairs two at a time.

The key slipped from his hand twice before he jammed it into place.

Water streamed down his neck, absorbed by sodden cotton and chest hair. He licked raindrops from his lips, the taste of salt invading his mouth. Shivering in the small entranceway, he ripped his shirt and undershirt over his head, and heeled his boots from his feet. Stretching his shoulders, he stepped onto the landing, and flipped the wet clothing across the length of twine he'd tacked between two posts.

A rumble splintered the dense air; a chill claimed his body, raising the hair on his arms. Tugging loose a strip of bandage, he turned his head, searching.

A whisper of movement . . . a hiss of breath. Elle perched

in the corner of the landing, a panther ready to pounce. A
nightdress of cream muslin, drenched in all the right places, or
hell, all the wrong ones, clung to her curves.

She might as well have been naked.

Noah reared into the railing, and pressed hard, his hands
going to grip the cragged wood. The curtain of rainfall sheltered
them from the world as they stared, immobile, seeing each
other in a state neither had known existed.

Noah watched the flashes of light illuminate the expressions
on her face: shock, curiosity, and deep inside, *greed*. She shoved
her hair back, revealing brilliant eyes. Her lids fluttered, her
gaze lowering to his chest. Her tongue peeked from between
her lips, a promise intensely desirable in its innocence. In
response, Noah exhaled, the sound muffling a distant thunder-
clap and the fierce thumping of his heart. Passion scorched the
air around them.

"What are you doing here?" he asked in a voice he hardly
recognized.

When she continued to stare, he rocked forward, flustered
and angry. His chest ached—longing, hunger, and pain.
Repressed until he felt like a tin can ready to explode. "*What*,
Elle?"

Trembling, she hooked her arms beneath her breasts, unconsciously raising them above the drooping neck of her nightdress.
"I wanted . . . wanted to make sure the roof wasn't leaking"—
her chest rose and fell, adding fuel to the fire—"on your, your
beautiful books."

"Blessit." He dragged his hand down his face, feeling her
goodness seep into his forlorn soul. *I'm doomed*, he realized,
and to prove it, effortlessly located her dark nipples beneath
muslin. As he stared, they pebbled, tight and hard, as directly as
if he'd stroked his tongue across them. He swallowed, masking a
groan, desire tensing every muscle in his body, then melting
in a leisurely slide to his groin.

Some of the lewd images spinning through his mind must

have shown because broad spills of rose, much lighter than her nipples, stained Elle's cheeks. Her skin glowed, in a way he had never seen skin glow, how he imagined a newborn's would look.

Rejecting honorable intentions and prudent reluctance, he took a step closer, near enough to catch the hint of fragrance on her skin. "Honeysuckle." He trailed his knuckle along her jaw, then slipped his finger behind her earlobe. "Did you put it here?"

She swallowed and made a low sound of fear or pleasure.

Noah discarded fear. Fear wasn't driving her to explore his naked chest, her look hot beneath a mask of innocence. "How about here?" He moved past her shoulder, circling her elbow, making a gradual sweep to her wrist. Her fist uncurled beneath his gentle pressure. Her pulse skittered beneath his fingertips. She gave a low gasp of surprise and stared at him.

Rain coursed down her cheeks, a lock of cinnamon—hair he wanted spread beneath them while he plunged into her lithe body—lay tucked in the edge of her mouth. If he moved closer, he could use his teeth to peel it from her skin.

Take her.

"I want to make you mine, touch you everywhere, in every way," he said, surprising himself with the thread of need, the brutal honesty. His lips met her cheek, his tongue working the silken strand between his teeth, the taste of lemon filling his mouth. She arched and lengthened, dragging his mouth over her jawbone to just below her ear. He brought his hand to her back, spread his fingers, and drew her near. "I want to explore your body in ways I've yet to explore, in ways I've yet to allow another to explore mine." The words rang true, yet he could scarcely believe he voiced them. As it was with Elle, as it had always been, he could not hide behind a wall of indifference.

"Caroline," she choked, and turned.

His arm circled her waist, and he hauled her back against him. "Never," he vowed, his lips brushing her ear, skimming the nape of her neck. The faultless feel of her, the *completeness,* colored his desire in dark shades of alarm. Even more terrifying, a dizzying ribbon of anticipation wrapped itself around his mind and yanked, choking his fear. Defeated, he leaned into the railing, bent low and cradled her, her buttocks coming to rest against him, cradling.

"Never?" Her breathy sigh captured him, tugged him deeper. Turning her head, her cheek met his chest. Her jaw worked, and she released a ragged inhalation across his chest.

"Never." He tightened his hold and fit her to him. Like pieces of broken pottery, they slipped into place.

"I'm frightened."

His desire to protect her roared to life. "Don't be. Not of me," he murmured, fitting his fingers in the groove of her ribs, her heart pounding beneath his thumb as he swept it toward the rounded weight of her breast. Lightly, he kissed from the sloped arch of her neck to her shoulder. A haunting chorus of sound, pelting rain and howling wind, mixed with their gasping breaths. A shiver shook her, her head lolling forward, inviting more. Unable to stop, he drew her skin between his teeth and sucked, hoping to mark her, a primal urge. She melted into him, her hand rising to cup his jaw. In turn, he drew her in, her fragrance delicious and decadent on his lips.

"Sweet, oh, if you only knew how much I want you." She had no idea. Could have no idea how reckless he felt, how savage and uncontrolled, to the exclusion of reason and rationale, the mainstays of his structured existence.

"How . . . much?" A shift of her bottom accompanied her question.

"Too much," he whispered, and returned the motion, rocking his hips into her. Leave it to this woman to find the precise movement to drive him mad. Tilting his head into her hair, the scent of citrus filled his nostrils, made him picture clear drops of pulp glistening on her lower lip, her dusky pink nipples.

Closing his eyes, he pictured licking her clean.

Muttering an oath he neither heard nor cared to hear, he kissed what he could reach, the edge of her mouth, her cheek, her jaw ... starved, desperate, and impatient. He slanted his head, trying to seize her lips completely, thinking only to have more, much more.

Rising to her toes, she tangled her fingers in his hair and urged him closer.

A burst of liquid heat, passion in its most potent form, sparked and ignited. Bringing her with him, Noah swayed against the railing. He could hardly take it in. Could hardly believe his luck.

She hungered for him as desperately as he hungered for her.

Trust me, he thought. Or did he say it? With the roar in his head, who knew? Lifting his thumb, he rolled it over her nipple. Once, twice, until it puckered and protruded, ready to suckle. He groaned in a mixture of frustration and pleasure, the angle he held her insufficient for delving as he wanted. As he must.

Taking her waist in both hands, he propelled her forward. Kicking the coach-house door closed, he turned her to face him, dipped his head, and seized her lips, his fingers tunneling through her hair. They were *alone,* utterly, temptingly alone. The gleeful knowledge seared the edges of his consciousness. Images of the woman of his dreams swirled, dulling reason and firing his senses. Pleasures he dared share, pleasures he had never wanted to share with another materialized.

He traced the front of her teeth, a brazen invitation. "Like before," he said, beseeching her to remember their kiss in the alley.

She hesitated for only a moment, then showed him she, indeed, remembered. She flowered; tongues tangled, a kiss of promise, earnest and absorbed. It smoldered, then exploded, guttural sound and fervent motion. Mindless, Noah dragged his mouth to her cheek, bent low and wrapped his arm beneath her buttocks, the other across her back. Lifting her against his chest, her toes striking his shins, he recaptured her lips. Holding her in his arms, claiming every inch of her as his own, made it worth the dull ache in his side.

Ducking through the doorway, he halted by his bed, and let her slide down his body. Before her toes touched the floor, he laid her across the mattress in a gentle sprawl.

Her hair, bright and sleek, contrasted sharply against the linens, a seductive flame on a sea of ivory. Her unblinking regard revealed a frantic hint of desire that further unmanned him. Raw and intimate, emotions a husband should see, but a lover would.

Lightning slashed outside the window, a burst of brightness. Through thin muslin, her generous curves stood in shadowed relief. He fought to stay focused on her face. Every tiny crease, every smattering of freckles. She shifted under his perusal, her legs falling open. Down a more dangerous path than he had planned. Truly, he couldn't possibly govern *this* urge. Hadn't he wondered—even at the decidedly naive age of fifteen—if her hair was red all over? With a boy's uncontrollable provocation guiding him, he found her ... dark and glistening, like the inside of a newly split tree trunk. Heart hammering, he swelled to an irreparable length, straining against his trouser buttons.

Exhaling raggedly and finding no rational explanation for his actions, he wedged his knees inside hers, maintaining her immodest posture. "Do you know what I want from you?"

She licked her lips and nodded. Her gaze dipped low, searching. A burst of air left her as she centered on his arousal.

His pulse pounded in his ears, hard and furious. He didn't recognize himself at that moment, a man who stood there thinking only of what he could do to this woman, not what it would cost him.

Or what it would cost *her.*

He traced her delicate arch, then brushed his knuckle over each tiny, perfect toe. "If you're ever going to deny me"— he cupped her heel and raised her foot to his mouth, a delicious impulse—"deny me now." Leaning, he drew the smallest digit into his mouth, laved it with his tongue, warming it as it curled against his lips. The same way he would suckle her nipple, though she might not know it.

She gave a gasp of alarm, perhaps just realizing the man doing these wicked things to her was not her beloved protector. Wiggling from his grasp, she clawed at the mattress, digging her heels in. Her nightdress gathered in a sloppy roll at the bottom of her thighs. Unable, despite his warning, to restrain the movement, Noah slid his hands behind her knees, lingered a moment to caress the rain-drenched skin, then stooped and jerked her forward. She glided across the sheets, legs dangling from his hands, muslin creeping higher, scarcely covering the magnetic triangle between her thighs.

He knew he should flee as quickly as his quaking legs would take him. Instead, he tugged the last bit, the mattress edge cutting into her bottom. He angled his hips and burrowed. Warm velvet folds enveloped the hardest erection he'd ever had.

"I know I asked you—" He swallowed, the words catching in his throat. Helplessly, he shifted a fraction to the right ... to the left. So slight a movement, but he throbbed with each measure.

"Ask me again," she said, her hands sliding toward him. Her gaze snagged his, the fevered eagerness in them stoking his hunger.

"Can I, sweet?" He ran his hand along the outside of her thigh, fingers hesitating over wadded muslin. He would never be able to sleep in this bed, he surmised, curling his hand possessively around her hip. Not with the scent of lemon and honeysuckle and rich, brown earth driving peaceful slumber out, inviting carnal dreams in. "Can I touch you like I've dreamed of?"

In answer, her lids skimmed low.

He inserted his thumb under the tattered hem and gave her thigh a languid stroke. "What would you do if I stripped this from your body?'' He drew a deliberate circle. ''I want to, if you're wondering. *Desperately.*'' He raised the nightdress an inch—an inch closer to ruin for both of them. ''What would you do? What do you think I would do?''

A rushed breath, a raspy, meaningless sound. She tried again, a teasing accent threading her words. ''I . . . I don't know . . . for sure. But, I think I'd like it.''

He snapped his head up and slammed into a sizzling, emerald wall. A powerful surge of lustful abandon, privilege inspired by her reckless words, ripped every remaining shred of prudence from his mind.

Elle felt the mattress dip as Noah washed over her. Knee, hip, stomach, chest. Points of startling, scalding, rain-drenched contact. His hands skimmed her arms, her back, fingers tangling in her hair. She made a noise he must have mistakenly interpreted, because he halted, shoulders quivering, his face hovering an inch above hers. His jaw tensed, flushed skin stretching over high cheekbones. With a willful shake of his head, he leaned in.

She prepared herself—*oh, heaven,* she really did.

Then, he claimed her—possessive and wild—and her preparedness vanished.

A hoarse groan rumbled from his throat, rattled beneath her fingertips. His shoulders tensed. Breathless gusts of air pelted her cheek. Pricks of sensation, a provoking, restless intensity. Heat pooled in her belly, between her legs, flooded her thighs and her buttocks. She pinched them together and burrowed into the mattress. Noah followed, pressing his hips against her. Her legs disengaged at pressure from his knees, embarrassingly weak pressure.

Then he fell into place.

Oh, merciful heavens, this was what she'd imagined in the alley. Height mattered little. And he knew it. Rocking from side to side, perfecting the fit, he knew it *all.*

"Sweet Jesu, you feel amazing," he whispered against her cheek.

In response, she explored with a vague, indefinite movement.

"This is what you're looking for." He tilted her hips and shifted between her thighs. A sense of fullness, one she didn't know how to describe, pervaded her, in a part of her body she knew next to nothing about. Saturated, a sponge filling with scalding water, while he, all angles, rigid and impenetrable.

Not understanding why she felt compelled to, and never considering she'd shouldn't, Elle skimmed her hands down his back, grasped his buttocks, and arched against him.

In return, he attacked. Mouth demanding, hands appealing, he seduced everywhere at once.

"Open for me, sweet," he said hoarsely, kissing his way along her cheek. "Only for"—he drew her earlobe into his mouth and sucked—"me." His tongue swept inside, sending a bolt of heat to her toes.

A ragged sigh slipped from her. He moved quickly, covering her lips and swallowing the sound. Color, sensation, exploded behind her sealed lids as he invited her to play. Returning the kiss full measure, she traced the edges of his teeth, and finally, touched her tongue to his. Mint and the faintest hint of whiskey. Delicious desire.

The occasional boom of thunder and the soft tap of rain against pine shingles intruded little. Moist, openmouthed kisses, impatient bites, fierce sucking. Whispered sighs and ragged groans. His hands and lips worked, in faultless accord, to whip her into a wild frenzy. A smooth nail skimming her cheek, a long finger dipping into her bodice. Muslin lowered; a rush of cool air crossed her breasts.

His breath warmed her. Then his tongue circled. An abrasive, skin-clinging stroke, a lazy rotation. Her nipple fairly sizzled.

Why she craved *this* loomed far beyond her meager scope of knowledge. That she would beg if he stopped astounded her.

She attempted to speak but found she could utter nothing more than a dazed moan of entreaty.

Releasing a pleased growl, he shifted to the other nipple, his fingers finding the spot his mouth had vacated. Arching, she presented her body to him, hearing her tortured whimper break free, the sound echoing off the bedroom walls. Her need swelling, she wished to ask . . . wanted . . . wanted him to use his mouth to . . . but she wasn't sure how to ask.

With a teasing flick, he pulled back, the cessation she had feared. She blinked and found his seething gaze fixed on her. An engrossed expression shaped his features, severe and rigid. The same look he wore when she caught him with his head buried in one of his textbooks.

Slipping his spectacles from his face, he swung them in a deliberate circle. Then he frightened her by smiling, a mischievous quirk of his lips. Wicked, and very, very sensual. Licking her own, she fought to regulate her breathing by counting to ten in French, then in English.

Shifting to the side, he stroked his toe up the inside of her calf. She could not suppress the weak sigh. His smile widened, and in a wonderfully inventive, astoundingly impulsive action, he circled her nipple using the rounded end of his spectacle frame.

A shudder racked her body. "Please."

He leaned in. So close, his breath grazed her mouth. "Please, what?"

She twisted her head from side to side, wadding linen behind each ear. "I don't know."

"This?" He brushed the cold lenses against the protruding nub.

"No," she panted.

"This?" His thumb fondled, circled once, fondled again.

"N—no." She placed her finger over his lips, then lowered her hand to her breast. Blinking past the passionate haze surrounding her, she looked to see if he understood.

As she watched, his controlled blankness slipped away. As

did his smile. His spectacles clattered to the floor. His hands cradled her face; his mouth captured hers. Parting her lips easily, his tongue swept inside. She could not fight, did not care to try.

The kiss grew rougher than any before. Swirling tongues and clicks of teeth, and a singular taste, one to dwell in her mind for eternity. Passion had never played a commanding role in her life, and she questioned, vaguely, if she would be able to live without it after this. Her fingers spread over his back, nails digging. Her hips matched his steady rhythm. A drag and pull like the tides. A rhythm the kiss followed . . . increased.

Moisture cleaved his naked chest to hers, the patch of hair stirring her nipples as successfully as his fingers and his tongue had. She moaned in delight and frustration, plunged her fingers through the mussed locks on the crown of his head, and directed him lower.

He wrenched his mouth from hers and nibbled down the arch of her neck, a rich sound creeping from his throat. His chin brushed her ribs, the scrape of stubble making her shudder. Flicking a molten, heavy-lidded glance at her, he stared through golden curls untamed by pomade. Stared until her cheeks heated and pleasure thumped at the apex of her thighs.

Weak lid drooping, his gaze slithered low. Again, he displayed his wicked smile. "This, *ma chère fille,* is what you wanted." He bent his head, she tilted hers, watching her erect nipple disappear between his lips.

Sweet mercy. Elle gasped and closed her eyes to the sight of him looming over her, helpless to ignore the heat, the frank intimacy, of his touch. Scarcely aware of the lumpy mattress beneath her, rather, she felt suspended in air. Adrift on a sea of pleasure.

His mouth spread over her breast, his groan muted against her flesh. Animalistic, the things he did to her, the way he sucked her nipple between his teeth, rolled it beneath his tongue. Astounding waves of ecstasy combined with sharp stabs of awareness. Ah . . . he was right, she concluded, doing a slothful pitch into a bottomless pit of carnality, her arms tumbling to the bed, her legs splaying wide. He'd given her *exactly* what she'd wanted. Craved, she decided, her body burgeoning beneath his enthusiastic hands, his eager lips.

Juste Ciel, his remarkably skilled teeth.

Sensation, both literal and fanciful, pressed in upon her. Noah's hips grinding into hers in a gradual figure eight. The crisp hair on his arms. The strain and release of muscle. His generous weight atop her, welcome and solid. Damp cloth covering his arousal, a part of him she had never imagined, in all her dreams, would be so long, or hard. His hands stroking the sides of her breasts, curling to cup them, kneading, drawing them into his waiting mouth. Callused palms gliding along her stomach, seizing her waist. Fingers plucking at her nightdress, tugging it higher. His tongue warming her, his lips welcoming her. His touch robbing her of thought or purpose, command or design.

Mental pictures providing taste and smell. Fields of green, dark, red wine, sapphire clouds. A stormy blue-black sea stretching to the horizon. A slender boy nudging spectacles high atop his nose, his smile comforting and compassionate.

She invited the images into her mind, opened her legs to invite the man she loved into her body.

Pounding. Her heart slamming against her ribs. *Pounding.* Her pulse ringing in her ears.

Noah jerked atop her and cursed beneath his breath.

Dazed, Elle watched him search for his spectacles, frown to find them missing. He straightened, his knees hugging her waist as he sat astride her. The hand he dragged through his hair trembled. His chest rose in rapid catches beneath a dangling strip of cloth, the tattered end tickling her breast. Bewildered, he looked completely bewildered. Funny, Elle had figured *she* was the confused one.

The pounding inside her head started again. Then she realized someone pounded on the door.

Chapter Thirteen

Except for the heavy footfalls on the staircase outside, the room sounded ghostly quiet. Elle hiked to her elbows and glanced at Noah. Slowly, his look slid past her chest, to her hips, still wedded to his. He stared for a long moment, then muttered a ragged oath, and rolled to the floor in one smooth motion.

Harsh bursts of air spurting from his lungs, he strode to the window, his stride noticeably unsteady. He flipped the curtain aside, pressed his nose to the pane. "Caleb, I think," he said, his breath fogging the glass. "Looks like he's swaying on his feet." He swabbed the circle of vapor away using the ball of his hand. "Blessit, he lets everything upset him."

Elle waited for him to turn, maybe even finish what he'd started, but he showed no sign of doing either. Drawing the scooped neck of her nightdress to a modest level, she lifted her bottom and yanked in an awkward attempt to cover her legs. A deafening rip filled the silence. With a sigh of dismay, she fingered the tattered piece of material. "Well, we can't all be as composed as you. Regardless, don't worry. He won't go to Widow Wynne's. See I'm missing and put two and two together. He's not that suspicious.''

Noah turned, a sharp torque from the waist. "Right where he's headed," he snapped, sounding both shamed and flustered. "He's looking for me, and he knows I'm stalking you like some damned bloodhound." Again, he peered out the window, knowing good and well he couldn't see a darn thing.

She rubbed her eyes, breathing in the smell of rainfall and man. A part of her wanted to tell him to go straight to hell on *his* sharpened pencil, since it appeared he would not act civil about what had transpired between them. Instead, she considered his ramrod posture, the tangled mat of hair on his head, feeling disappointed and unsatisfied. It took considerable effort on her part to keep her hands where they should be—tidying her disarray—and not where they wanted to be. Tracing the muscled ridges of his back, cupping the round curve of his buttocks. He had an extremely nice physique, sleek with just the right measure of muscle. Lean, but graceful, the way he was put together.

Scooting to the edge of the bed, Elle wriggled until her feet touched cool heart pine. Her knees wobbled when she put weight on them, but they held. Her toes curled from the chill. "Why do you suppose this is?"

She watched his fingers knot as he dropped his brow to the pane. A sweep of air through the window fluttered the trailing end of his bandage. "Why, what?"

Her feet's soft pad reverberated through the room. She stooped to grasp his spectacles, moonlight sparking off metal. Thankfully, he'd put no cracks in the lenses. "Why do you suppose we"—she pressed her lips together, figuring how to say it—"we react like this? I never felt this, hot and . . . and *itchy* about Magnus. About anyone."

A minute passed. Thunder rumbled in the distance. "How do I know? Happens to people every day."

She traced the wire frames with her fingertip, remembering

what he had done with them. "Much like your married lady friend, isn't it? I'm not ignorant of life's basic truths. Most men have a lover and a wife. Extreme appetites, Christa told me."

He tapped the pane: three hard knocks. "You shouldn't be listening to Christabel. And, you're wrong about Caroline."

"Oh yes, I witnessed, firsthand, how wrong I am." Even now, if she let her mind sink its claws into the picture, she could see his hand folded in both of *Caroline's*, the woman stroking his fevered brow.

Another knock. "You don't know what you witnessed."

"No matter. I kept her from your bed tonight. In fair recompense—"

All at once, he stood before her, his hands closing about her shoulders. "Don't say that." He shook her. "Don't even think it."

"How can I not?"

"I told you, before. I've never touched her"—his gaze lingered on her breasts—"like I just touched you. Never touched her at all. Whoever wrote your father's report wrote lies." His fingers tensed, cradling her skull. "The desire I feel for you is more than I've felt for anyone in my life. Nothing has ever come close. No one has come close."

For a long moment, they stared, caught in a world of their creation, a world Elle wanted to delve into, even as the rational part of her mind rebelled, begging her to remember they would not be a part of each other's lives much longer.

Lifting her hand, her wrist brushed the front of his trousers, his flesh rock-hard.

His sensual pout emerged, top lip curling. *"Stop."*

She blinked, unable to utter a sound.

"Stop looking at me like that. A look like . . ." He shook his head. "Do you want me to go completely mad and—and tear your clothes off?" His gaze flicked down, then shot up. "What little you're wearing, of course."

Sinful images stormed her mind. Her lips curved against her best judgment.

He stumbled back. "Dammit, Elle."

"I can't help it. If it makes you feel any better, part of me thinks this is all a very bad idea. That part"—she shrugged—"I'm inclined to ignore. I usually do."

"For once in your life, listen to what the discarded fragment of your brain is telling you, because you and I are not going to happen." His eyes cut away. "Don't make this out to be something it isn't. You'll only end up hurting us both."

"What do you make it out to be?"

He wedged his shoulder against the bedpost and crossed his ankles, staring past her, the wheels in his mind spinning as he reasoned in his systematic, professorial way. All right, two could play this game, she asserted, and struggled to allow her features to slide into lines of indifference. Hard to do when he stood before her half-clothed, hair mussed, charmingly undone. She chewed on her lip, fighting the urge to touch him.

As a clock counted each contemplative second, his eyes lightened, his fists unfurled, and his splendid arousal withered. Her hold over him, whatever it constituted, diminished with each annoying tick. "Elle"—he tapped the bridge of his nose, threw a quick glance at the spectacles dangling from her fingers—"I think we should stay far, far away from each other."

The edges of her temper crisped and curled. "That's what you came up with? Stay away from each other?"

A spark of fury lit his gaze. "What the hell do you want me to do? To say? I can't answer every question, find a solution for every problem. That blessed professor nonsense is a myth. I thought you understood better than anyone." He wrenched his ankles apart and took a fast step forward. "Understand *this*. I want you. I sit awake, night after night, crammed in a stiff leather chair, lust eating me alive, picturing you twisting beneath me, or God help me, beneath another—" With an angry torque, he swept his hand across the marble-topped bureau. The troublesome shelf clock struck the floor, a deafening shatter. Shards of glass glittered amidst the raindrops blowing in the open window. "Forget him and let this . . . situation between us die."

"*Him?* You believe"—she flung her hand toward the rumpled bed—"this is still some sort of youthful obsession? A child's heart in a woman's body?"

Over his shoulder, his tormented eyes met hers, his chin lowering in what she had to assume was a positive reply.

"Maybe you're right. Maybe everything I feel *is* for that boy. The one who walked me to the doctor and held my hand while the doctor set the splint, who helped me speak his language and protected me until I could do it well enough to avoid getting knocked around in the schoolyard. Maybe I'm yearning for *him.* Some befuddled retrospection because I see him when I look into *your* face. A figment of my foolish, sentimental imagination and not you at all. That's exactly what you expect from me, isn't it, Professor? Fickle, flighty Elle Beaumont."

Noah flinched and jammed his hands in his pockets, as if the words he had practically begged her to utter disturbed him. "No, no, that's not what I expect from you at all. It's just this"—he wagged his elbow in a slow circle, the enticing play of muscle in his back catching her attention—"attraction between us can't work. It doesn't make sense if you take a moment to examine it. *We* don't make sense. We're too different, you and I. And, the lure, the excitement, well, passion and—and love, love which comes from deep inside, are different beasts. Love is, love makes intimacy special. Inversely, lust roars around in your chest like a bear, clawing and slashing its way out. I guess I don't know . . . honestly, I don't know if one has much to do with the other."

Realizing she should tell Noah Garrett where he could stick his bungling rationale, she instead prolonged her departure by fidgeting with his spectacles, slipping them on her face. The room melted into ribbons of black and white. Seeing the world through his eyes deepened the ache in her chest. Swallowing hard, she forced herself to say, "Then, what just happened between us was simply a spontaneous reaction to a—what would a scientist call it—some kind of primitive stimulus?"

He dropped to his haunches and began to place shards of glass in his cupped palm, his firm bottom resting two inches above the floor. "All I'm telling you, blessit, simply asking you, is to think. Use your clever little mind. Be sensible for once. You're too intelligent not to understand what I'm saying. We're oil and water, Elle, we don't . . . mix."

She felt her heart shatter like the clock at his feet. "When have you ever known *me* to act sensibly, Professor?"

"Exactly what scares me," he replied, the words hard-edged and determined. Gravely determined.

Of course, she wasn't an impartial judge, but her feelings felt indisputably genuine, shades darker than those she'd felt as a child. Conceivable to imagine she would have admitted it, but Noah's painstakingly methodical movements—selecting the largest piece of glass first, a considerate pause, another choice—told her just how much he cared to listen. Despondent, she lifted his spectacles from her face and found him watching her, rotating a jagged shard between his fingers. A strange, almost fearful expression shaped his features. Then he averted his gaze, ending any argument she hoped to make.

Dazed and unsure, she dropped his spectacles on the wash-stand, navigated a pile of research books in the living area, and descended the staircase, head held high, posture as rigid as his, *damn and blast*. Pausing at the bottom, muddy water seeping between her toes, she faltered, looking over her shoulder.

Noah stood on the landing, hands gripping the paint-chipped railing, a wooden slat biting into his lean stomach. A drop of water glistened on the edge of his clenched jaw.

Tell me, she pleaded, struggling to decipher the emotions sweeping his face. *Something, anything*. In answer, he dipped his head, wagged it slowly back and forth.

Noah watched her walk away, *let* her walk away, her aggrieved sigh yanking his stomach to his knees. He wanted to go after her, drag her into his bed, and make astounding love to her. Wake after presumably the best night of sleep he'd experienced and see her sweet smile, hold her hand, and talk with her. *Just talk.* Gulping for air, he threw back his head, and expelled the choked breath. Hand trembling more than he liked, he dug into his pocket, lifted the scrap of muslin to his nose. The ever-present earthy scent, a touch of lemon and honeysuckle.

He cursed viciously. A wrathful swipe across his lips didn't help. Her taste lingered, strong enough to stir his groin. And his sheets, hell, his entire bedroom, smelled of her. Couldn't go there.

The door slammed behind him. He tripped over a textbook, skidded across glossy pine, and sank into the chair he slept in most nights, where dreams of Elle slicked his skin to worn leather, had him jerking awake and reaching for her.

His dreams had ballooned to intense proportions, incredibly vivid, although he could rationalize them, or at the very least, his reasons for having them. He had recently read a commentary by an Austrian psychiatrist who speculated that dreams revealed a person's deepest desire in its most blatant form. Made sense, because having Elle naked and writhing beneath him represented Noah's deepest desire at present. Nonsensical, but true.

He sloped forward, hands going to grip his knees. Dreams he could dispute. Scientifically, if this psychiatrist could be believed. The agony crowding his chest, he had no argument for. Even worse, he feared his feelings as he'd never feared anything in his life. When he'd turned to see his spectacles perched on Elle's pert nose, her lovely eyes distorted by the lenses, it wasn't desire that galloped through him like a high-kicking mule.

Somewhere in the flat, a branch slapped a windowpane.

Tipping his head, he watched a spider spin a web around the aged kerosene chandelier and realized he was in deep trouble.

I'm falling in love with Elle Beaumont.

He could not define in exact terms—precise classification at that point would have been a blessing—how he knew it to be true. Besides love for his family, he did not completely fathom the emotion. Or welcome it.

Just the same . . . far too many factual incidents for a scientist to ignore. His heart slamming out of control when she got within fifty feet of him, his gaze hawking her as she crossed the street, his ears perking when she delivered a lesson to one of her students.

He yanked the scrap of muslin in two and flung the pieces to the floor. Zach spoke the truth. Emotions were *not* rational. Love didn't require precise classification. Hadn't the past month—getting to know his brothers again and unearthing the affection hidden deep in his heart—taught him that lesson?

It had, but familial love he *wanted.*

Somehow, Elle had worked her way under his skin. Or, dear God, had she been there all along? He slumped, dazed. She loved sunrises and chocolate ice cream. He liked sunsets and vanilla. She thrived on chaos. He loathed chaos. She dreamed impossible dreams. He renounced impossibilities of any kind. He was boring and predictable, she fairly glowed with dynamism and vigor.

There had to be a rational solution. He snapped his fingers and bolted from the chair, striding to his mammoth desk. Squinting, he shoved aside the latest Sierra Club *Bulletin* and an empty specimen bottle, grabbed his notebook, and flipped to the first blank sheet. Plundering through the papers littering his desk, he located the silver fountain pen he had received for five years service with the fisheries commission.

Walking backward, his legs bumped the chair, and he dropped into it. Bringing the notebook close to his face, he drew a line down the middle of the sheet. Things he admired about Elle went on the right, things he despised on the left. He began writing, his hand sweeping the page. Dismayed to see the right list growing considerably longer than the left, he ripped the sheet out and wadded it into a ball. It hit the floor with a crinkle.

He tapped his pen on the notebook and decided to approach the problem from a different angle. In the same fashion he would a research project, outcome certain but procurable by various methods. *Outcome: Mind free of Elle Beaumont.* The pen moved swiftly, until he had two pages of concise clarification and a systematic strategy for avoiding Elle—thereby reducing his engrossment, as he politely termed it.

Rubbing his head, which had begun to ache, he sank against the worn leather. Fine. Good. He had listened to the warning signs—like any decent researcher—and devised a plan. He would throw himself into his work and spend time with his family. No more kisses. Blessit, no more *anything* that involved touching her. No more daydreams—actual dreams he couldn't hope to control. No more considerate gestures. Eating dinner with her or repairing her shutters was forbidden. He had been planning to mow her grass; he would ask Caleb to do it for her.

Also, he thought discussing the situation with Caroline might help. Perhaps, he could secure her assistance. Glancing at the plank-and-beam ceiling, he pictured the tangle of fragrant sheets covering his bed. His fingers tightened around the fountain pen, in cool contrast to his skin. Lifting the notebook an inch before his eyes, he scribbled one last notation.

Maybe it wasn't crucial, but he listed it anyway. Less urgency to tell Elle—which, remarkably, he found he really wanted to do—if he recorded it. After all, what purpose would it serve to tell her the astounding taste of her on his lips, the exquisite feel of her in his arms, had erased the few sexual experiences in his past like chalk dust from a blackboard? He snapped his notebook shut.

No need to tell her. No need at all.

Chapter Fourteen

Her mother's cameo caught a spark of sunlight as Elle pinned it to the collar of her faded percale blouse. Stepping from her father's office, she wondered if he would have missed it if she'd taken it long ago. Instead, she had waited for him to offer it to her. Today, her father's solicitor, Mr. Hobbs, had done just that, while snidely twisting his waxed mustache, never realizing this small piece of jewelry would serve as the sole legacy from a devoted father to his wayward daughter.

It would surprise Mr. Hobbs, and anger her father, she supposed, to know she had nullified the additional codicil two days before the reading. Reaching into her trouser pocket, Elle fingered the scholarship-acceptance letter. She had telegraphed her agreement and had received a reply from Savannah that morning. The committee anticipated her arrival in New York City in no later than seven days. She had applications to submit, a lesson of study to prepare, and an award luncheon to attend. And, she had to prepare Savannah to manage her women's school during her absence. Perhaps the activity would keep her mind from straying to impossible dreams, even if her heart seemed captured for life.

Leaning against the staircase railing, she tipped her face to a cloudless blue sky and drew a breath. Her lungs pinched, and she released the air on a determined sigh. In the distance, a familiar voice filtered past the thud of ships edging the dock. A white-hot wave of heat—totally unrelated to the merciless sun beating down on her back and shoulders—lit her from the inside out. Closing her eyes, she strained to hear his words over the hammering of her heart.

"... quantity *and* size. Blessit, Zach ... need both. You volunteered ... stupid questions ..."

Warm laughter traveled the distance, stroking her senses. Lids lifting, she watched Zach pitch a fish at his brother's head. In turn, Noah pivoted, stuffing a thick book beneath his armpit, and snared it in one hand. "Nice try," she thought she heard him say between gusts of wind.

She stared, helpless not to, wishing he stood a little closer, wishing fewer people crowded the street. Wishing the memory of his body pressing hers into a lumpy mattress would leave her mind for one blasted *minute*. She quelled the urge to shade her eyes, instead leaned out farther. Inches closer in her heart, miles away in truth.

Noah poked inside the barrels of salted fish circling the *Nellie Dey*'s steep gangplank, then turned to scribble in his book. A lock of hair fell into his face, and he flicked it back. Zach yelled a number, which he noted with a slight incline of his head and another furious scratch. An image of those long, sun-kissed fingers trailing over her shoulders, teasing her breasts and hauling her hips against his, forced her to wedge her knees against the wooden railing to steady herself. To add to her humiliation, her nipples pebbled beneath her shift, an abrasive reminder her of her weakness.

Panicked, she hit the boardwalk at a near run. Between swaying carts loaded with putrid oyster casks and stacked piles of lumber, she caught occasional glimpses of the man she had worked diligently to ignore.

Something seemed different. His black bib trousers were wrinkled. Sloppily rolled sleeves capped his elbows, and dirt stains soiled his knees. And his hair, curling airily about his head, lacked hat or pomade, and needed cutting. His appearance didn't keep Meredith Scoggins from yelling his name and crossing the street in a flirtatious, eager stride.

A buckboard hauling ropes and net halted with a shuddering screech, completely blocking Elle's view. Cursing her foolishness, she dodged a small boy sitting cross-legged on the boardwalk, a calico kitten wrapped in his shirttail. The kitten swiped at her ankle as she passed. She didn't feel the scratch; she felt nothing but Noah's hands upon her. For eight days and fourteen hours, they had avoided each other. Except for one mischance. Four days ago, leaving the post office as he entered. He had grabbed her elbow to keep them from colliding and had stared for a strained, impassioned moment into her face. They had jerked apart and stalked off in opposite directions.

At least *she* had gotten her mail.

Worming her way through a crowd of fishermen entering the Nook, she stumbled into a foul-smelling body. Her gaze traveled from the mud-caked brogans nudging her low-heeled boots to the patched bib trousers stained with sweat and amber whiskey. Sean Duggan stood before her, meaty legs thrown wide, rage mottling his cheeks. His hands flexed into fists by his side. "I've been waiting to talk to you, *Miss Ellie,*" he snarled, spittle flying from his mouth. Ale rode the breath buffeting her face, a repulsive comrade for the stale liquor seeping from his clothing.

He swayed on his feet, and a chill streaked down her spine. She pressed the small of her back into the post and tilted her chin. "What can I do for you, Mr. Duggan?"

"You lil' scrawny bitch," he growled, talking a step forward, seizing her wrist. His fingers were as thick as sausages, the nails rimmed by dirt. He squeezed hard, until she feared her bones would snap. She grimaced and breathed through her mouth, fighting the abhorrence churning her stomach, the pain swimming up her arm. Her knees trembled, but she stared into his red-rimmed eyes, ignoring the discomfort and the stench, daring him to do more than this on a public street. He did not have the privacy of his home to lay an abusive hand on a woman half his size.

"You'd better step away, Mr. Duggan. I'm fixing to scream bloody murder, and in the event you don't know, I can scream louder than a child with a finger caught in a bicycle spoke. The noise is certain to alert Zachariah Garrett. His office is just across the street. Family friend, if you recall. Wouldn't take kindly to this"—she twisted her arm, his sweat coating her skin—"brutality."

Sean's gaze flicked toward the constable's office. He released her, but did not step away, slapping his palm against the post above her shoulder. "You think I don't know what you done? I know where Annie went to. Home to that whining momma of hers. And you helped her. Now I got a house to keep and a stove to tend. Victuals to buy. My own child ain't gonna be born here." Leaning in, his hot breath licked her face. "You shouldn't be sticking your damn, high-pointin' nose where it ain't wanted."

"Excuse me, but I think you'd better do as Miss Beaumont requested, or I may have to scream as well. I live in Chicago, among many desperate souls, so I guarantee I've had more experience. Besides, I *love* to draw an audience."

Sean growled and stumbled. Elle edged around him, flicking a glance at her savior's placid face.

"Never look a rabid dog in the eye, darling," Caroline advised with a calm smile.

"Come on." She linked her arm through Caroline's and whisked her down the boardwalk. Their heels clicked on the pockmarked planks, the only sound for several minutes. Halting in front of Tilly's net store, Elle jerked free and gasped, "Why?"

Caroline raised a brow, her gloved fingers fluttering around the package in her hand. "Why?"

Elle threw her hand out. "Why have you been trying to befriend me all week? Suffering cats, you've come to my house, stopped me on the street and . . . and today, you help me out of a"—she struggled—"a disagreeable situation. Why?"

"Because I like you."

"Like me? You don't *know* me."

Caroline smoothed her hand over her frilled bodice. "I know Noah well enough, and he likes you. Quite a good recommendation in my book."

Elle felt the pounding in her head lower to her chest. "Yes, you know him."

"And you love him, so you think you must hate me."

"I—"

A group of rambunctious sailors shuffled by, singing in slurred voices and stamping their dirty feet, the first lazy days of spring upon them. Elle watched the Nook's swinging doors swallow them up, then turned toward home, neglecting to ask if Caroline wished to accompany her.

"What did I stumble upon back there?"

Elle increased her pace. "Just another reason for me to leave this place," she muttered beneath her breath.

"What did you say?"

"Nothing."

"Darling, you have to tell someone what happened. That drunken man is a menace."

Elle halted, a sudden burst of apprehension shaking her in her frayed boots. "You mustn't say anything about what you saw today, Mrs. Bartram. *Nothing.* Sean Duggan's problem is with me and no one else. I don't want—No—" Snapping her lips together, she marched away.

Caroline's shoulder brushed Elle's as she stepped in beside her. "You don't want Noah getting involved, is that it?"

Turning into Widow Wynne's weed-choked front path, she

kicked the gate open, and crossed the yard. Caroline stayed right with her, her unflagging gait kicking up bits of grass and straw. Frustrated and confused, Elle snatched her skirt high, taking the porch steps at an unladylike gallop. She glanced back to find the annoying woman grinning at her.

"*What?*" she snapped, Caroline's amusement chaffing.

"You've got dash, darling. Just what Noah needs, if he'll only realize it."

"Sorry to disappoint, Mrs. Bartram, but Noah isn't going to bother with anyone who doesn't have gills. You see, my father wasted his money sending for you."

Caroline's smile dimmed. "I never took any money from your father, Miss Beaumont, and I never intended to. I came for my own reasons, mostly."

"I'm sorry. Noah told me about the two of you being ... friends." Glancing at her feet, Elle scrubbed a spot of mud off the toe of her boot. "I've confused the issue enough as it is. I don't need to speak without thinking and make it worse."

"Darling, how have you confused the issue?" Caroline shifted her umbrella-shaped skirt to the side and perched on the step.

Elle settled hesitantly beside her. "It's not Noah's fault I keep mistaking the boy I knew with the man I don't. That's all I meant."

"Are the boy and the man very different?"

She plucked a withered azalea blossom from the bush by her side and twirled it between her fingers. *Different?* In her mind, she saw Noah bending over her, raw desire darkening his eyes, his lips parting before covering hers. "Sometimes I look at him, and I think my childhood friend is still there. Somewhere. Other times, the way he stares at me, the way he touches me, the bitterness on his face ... I don't know who *he* is."

"A man who desperately wants to make love to you and is fighting it like the very devil, that's who."

Elle crumbled the bloom between her thumb and forefinger, pollen dusting her skin. "After all the women he's, I mean, well"—she cleared her throat—"why does he get angry with me?"

Caroline covered her mouth, but not soon enough to keep a howling bark of laugher from escaping. She had never witnessed Noah Garrett looking *twice* at any woman. Handsome and successful, women naturally flocked to him, and considered him an eligible bachelor in Chicago's social circle. And, beyond doubt, being a man, he had accepted an indiscreet offer or two, but nothing matching Miss Beaumont's presumption. Nothing at all. *Poor dear*, Caroline thought, and struggled to hide her smile.

"Laugh if you want. If you only knew . . ." Elle ripped another bloom from the bush, her voice dropping to a whisper. "He's very *experienced*. I don't know why it seems to disturb him to lust after *me*. I'm not trying to trap him into . . . into anything. Far from it. I have a life to live. Plans and dreams. Not some grand fish experiment, maybe, but important just the same."

Caroline gulped for air, propping her head on her knees.

"I'm glad to be a source of amusement for you." She flapped her hand, rebuffing Caroline's inane gesture of apology. "Don't worry, I'm used to it. Everyone's always regarded my feelings for Noah as nothing but fodder for gossip. A joke to tell as I strolled by, usually trailing in his footsteps. When I leave they'll say I did it because of him, I guarantee."

"Are you planning a trip, Miss Beaumont?"

Elle's mouth formed a startled circle.

"I'm sure you don't need my advice, or want it for that matter, but if you love him, you'd better stay and fight for him. You won't be the first woman who has had to, I can assure you. No man on earth wants to admit falling in love, darling. No man I've yet to meet, anyway. They all need a . . . what shall we call it, kick in the seat of the trousers to set them in motion.''

Elle murmured.

Caroline leaned in, caught a trace of honeysuckle. "Again, please."

"Noah doesn't love me, I said."

"Are you sure?"

"Of course I'm sure!" She exploded off the steps and began pacing in front of Caroline, the frayed hem of her cycling trousers bumping her slim ankles. "He thinks we don't mix. Like oil and water, he said. I'm too frivolous, too foolhardy. And believe me, I tried, at least I did years ago, to conceal it. Think first, act later, that sort of thing. Aim to do all this planning before the actual doing." She dropped to her knees beside a tilled square of soil, picked up a rusted spade, and stabbed it in deep. "Didn't work at all."

"Try to put yourself in his shoes, Miss Beaumont. After all that happened here, Noah is overly cautious. What he reveals and what he hides are very important decisions for him. To me, he's this little boy protecting a precious vase. He's so afraid the beauty of it won't last, he smashes it to bits just to ease his trepidation." She lifted the package of embroidered handkerchiefs to her lap and considered giving Elle one to wipe the brown smudge from her nose. "You mustn't take his word, all those silly reasons you two don't *mix*, gracious alive, as scripture. If you want him—"

"I don't want him." She snatched the spade from the ground, flinging dirt on herself. "I don't need him. I have lofty ambitions, ones that do not concern Noah Garrett one tiny bit." She angrily dusted her blouse, rubbing the stains in. "Pointless, discussing this. He's turned me away at every corner. For my entire life, Mrs. Bartram. *Juste Ciel,* even *I* have a breaking point, some reasonable idea of when to abandon a sinking ship."

Caroline smoothed her finger over the wrinkled corner of

her package, pondering her words. "Are you leaving soon? On this adventure of yours?"

Elle's head swiveled in her direction. She looked like a rabbit trapped in a snare. "Will you tell him?"

"Will *you*?"

Her look grew unfocused as her fingers danced over the garden tool. Then her back stiffened, and she gave her head a firm, terse shake.

"You're a grown woman. What you tell Noah or don't tell him is your choice and no one else's. Despite this, I have to tell you, I don't agree. I've seen the intimate glances the two of you share. Gracious, a person would have to be blind not to. And trust me, darling, it's a rare boon to be able to communicate with another person without speaking. An attachment of such depth doesn't wither, or die." She curbed her counsel at seeing suspicion fill the young woman's eyes. "I suppose you'll just have to find out for yourself. Noah will, too."

The wind swept a stray curl into her face, and Elle snatched it back. "I can't endure watching him leave again, Mrs. Bartram. My decision is not an impulsive one, nor is my destination perilous. Regardless, my leaving is better. For both of us. He won't have to feel guilty about ... about ..."—she groped for words—"anything that's happened. And I can finish something, something I *want* to finish, and should have a long time ago." Looking away, she added, "Pipe dream or not."

Caroline sighed, wondering how she could help two of the most headstrong, gun-shy people she'd ever chanced to meet. Noah's love for the little hellcat was as obvious as those spectacles perpetually perched on the end of his nose, yet they certainly didn't help him see what loomed right before his face. And Marielle-Claire, the way she looked when she talked about him, all warm and tender, it almost made Caroline want to squirm.

There must be something she could do *and* keep her promise. Caroline wedged her finger beneath the package's ribbon and gave it a meditative tug. If she could only make the girl trust her. It couldn't hurt, if nothing else, to know where she planned to run off to. Then, Caroline would try to knock some sense into Noah's thick skull. "Miss Beaumont," she asked, shattering the melancholy silence, "could you do me a small favor?"

Elle flinched, pulled from a daydream that had left her eyes overbright and her cheeks aflame. "If I can," she said weakly. *Trust.* "I want you to tell me about your school."

Noah couldn't help but wonder what she wore beneath those clinging cycle trousers. Since he'd peeked in her window and seen the lacy yellow frippery hanging from her bedpost, he imagined it beneath everything.

He winced as the blade sliced into his skin. Dropping the knife, he brought his finger to his lips, the sour taste of blood filling his mouth. He swore, sick and tired of Elle's blessed undergarments monopolizing his thoughts.

"What is wrong with you?" Zach pitched a fishtail over the side of the dock. "You've been in a fog for the last hour."

Noah turned, unobtrusively wiping his hand on his bib trousers. What was wrong with him? *Hell.* He'd seen Elle gawking from across the street and had barely contained the impulse to . . . "Nothing's wrong with me," he snarled, and slammed his notebook atop the oyster barrel. "Just thinking about some materials Tyre McIntosh told me he needs for the lab, that's all."

"Wouldn't have to do with Ellie leaving her daddy's office earlier and standing on the boardwalk and watching us, could it?"

He ripped a sheet from his notebook and wadded it into a ball. "For God's sake, Zach, drop it."

"Fine, I'll drop it." Zach shrugged his shoulders and tossed Noah's slide rule in a bleached wooden bucket. "Consider it dropped."

"Easy there."

Zach glanced up, eyes full of mischief. "Boy, are you touchy."

Flinging the wad of paper into a rusted rubbish tin, Noah felt a scowl crack his blistered cheeks. He sucked brackish air into his lungs, the clamor of approaching ships and ravenous seabirds and rowdy fishermen adding to the tempest of confusion in his mind. How could the scent of honeysuckle be stronger than the stench of fish? How could he have slept less the past week than he had the week before the Woods Hole laboratory opened, when he had been more nervous than he'd been in his life? How could he want her so badly, a woman completely dissimilar to any he had reasoned would make him happy?

"You coming for dinner tonight? Caleb caught a mess of cat. Promised to fry them up and make hot pepper corndodgers."

Noah looked toward the sunset spill sliding into the horizon. Waves thumped against the pilings; a fine mist dusted his lenses. He concentrated, searching for the contentment the sea usually brought.

"Dinner, Noah?"

He shook his head, gestured to the satchel by his feet. "Going to Devil for a day or so. I want to explore the mud flats on the south side of the island."

"You sure?"

He nodded, not sure of anything.

Zach patted his shoulder, then headed down the dock, the sectioned planks rocking beneath his feet. Shouldering his satchel, Noah stuffed his notebook inside the front pocket and made his way to his skiff. Recklessness had him setting sail under more of a pinch than he would have liked, the lines twitching in his hands.

He could not spend another hour in the coach house, knowing Elle slept less than a hundred yards away. He had woken from a particularly vivid dream the night before and actually ended up at her back door, hand raised, prepared to knock.

Excuse me, but I hoped to make desperate love to you.

He tugged the sheet and guy with a muttered oath. He had packed enough provisions for one day, maybe two. Long enough to figure out what to do about Elle. He had to do something. The avoidance part of his plan wasn't working. With each passing second, she became more difficult to resist. Listening to her melodic voice seeping through the thin walls of her schoolroom drove him mad. Only the day before, he had watched her step onto the boardwalk, her lovely bottom swinging on the upsweep, and, standing right in the middle of the street, he'd grown stiff as a board. As he jerked a square knot in the line, the gash on his finger split open and started to bleed.

Ah, yes, for the first time in his life, his span of attention equaled Rory's.

The wind whipped his shirt against his chest and the heart beating forcefully beneath it. Hanging his head, he sighed, truly miserable. His rigidly constructed life had not been the same since he'd returned to Pilot Isle. He feared it would never be the same again. Feared he did not *want* it to be the same.

Two days. Two days to decide how to tell Elle he had fallen in love with her.

Chapter Fifteen

A jarring noise pulled Elle from the first genuine sleep she'd had in days. Swaying, she hitched to her elbow and blinked into absolute darkness, the glow from the gas lamp at her side a distant memory. She patted her chest, realizing she had fallen asleep in her clothing. Must be the jigger of whiskey Christabel and Caroline had forced on her at dinner. Throwing her hand to the floor, she searched—

"Enough of that, sweet," Noah said and slid the glass out of reach with the muddy toe of his brogan. Her eyes grew accustomed to the darkness as her gaze traveled his long, lean body. He dropped, grabbed her by the waist, and pulled her into his arms.

"What . . . whe—"

He seized her words and her mouth, wrenching her into a tempest of emotion. Desperation and loneliness raged; passion consumed her. She groaned low in her throat and melted into him. Demanding and rough, the kiss bruised her lips *and* her soul. She surrendered to the love she felt for him and the need she could no longer contain. She delved deeply, devouring— lips and teeth and tongue—as he devoured her.

He circled her wrists, his fingers tangling in her cuffs, and pressed her against the chaise longue. "Blessit." Chest heaving, he lifted his head, a look of complete bafflement crossing his face. "Not here ... I didn't plan to ... oh, hell."

Moving quickly, he pulled her to her feet, dragged her down the hallway, and out into the moonlit night, grumbling beneath his breath along the way. Something about inquisitive brothers knocking on doors and how on this night, of all nights, she had to be inebriated.

"I'm not inebriated." Unfortunately, she followed the denial with a loud hiccup.

He groaned but didn't reply, nor did he look at her or slow his pace. Exhilarated for no good reason, she leaned in and sniffed his sleeve. Woodsmoke and a hasty dash of soap. No hint of liquor.

Trying to track his lengthy stride, she stepped on the rough edge of a shell, and gasped in pain.

Pausing, Noah swept her into his arms, looked both ways, then sprinted down the alley leading to the docks. His heartbeat thudded beneath her breast; his brisk stride rocked her in his arms. He lifted them, a subtle shift that brushed her mouth against the underside of his jaw. Quite helplessly, she kissed him, her lips lingering long enough to moisten the dried salt on his skin.

Noah groaned and halted in the shadowed recess of the seamstress's shop, braced his elbows on the whitewashed wall, and lowered his mouth to hers, trapping her in his heated embrace. She hardly had time to loop her arms around his neck and thread her fingers through the hair curling over his collar, before he pulled away, his breath batting her cheek.

"I want to talk with you. Just talk," he said, a shudder working its way down his arms. "Not here. Not this." Peeking from their hiding place, he loped across the street, pressing a tender kiss to her brow. *"Not yet."*

She shivered at the intensity of his words and the alluring

images they brought to mind, wondering how her clear sense of purpose had vanished so easily into the balmy darkness.

Gazing over his shoulder, she found a deserted street. Other than the oyster factory, Noah's laboratory was the only structure on the eastern end of town. The lab stood tall and proud against a twilight sky, the wooden shakes recently fitted to the roof gleaming. Aching deep inside at the look of completion about the place, she pressed her cheek to his chest, the warmth of his skin seeping past cotton and into her heart.

Stepping onto a narrow, little-used dock, he halted beside a skiff secured and bobbing. He rolled her from his arms, his muscles tensing as he slid her down his body. Lids fluttering, he lowered his head. *Yes.* She tipped her chin, welcoming the aroused rush of blood between her thighs, the quick tightening of her nipples. Oh . . . her body remembered, even if her mind labored to forget.

Mint and ripe apple riding his breath. Close . . . *closer.*

He jerked, a frenzied oath muffled behind the hand he swiped across his mouth. *"Chrissakes,"* he whispered and steadied her with unsteady hands. Yanking his spectacles from his pocket, he hopped into the skiff, avoiding her blatant regard.

Never thinking to ask where he took her, Elle watched him work the lines, the muscles in his arms bulging beneath blue cloth, each movement exposing his chest through the open neck of his shirt. Knees beginning to tremble, her gaze dropped to his flat belly, material tucked haphazardly into form-fitting black trousers. She blinked, curled her fingers, nails biting into her skin. A mismatched button on his trouser fly gaped, revealing a tiny patch of skin. *Juste Ciel,* she thought, and squirmed, a forbidden thrill racing to her nether region.

Lifting her head, she encountered eyes the color of a stormy sea. The lines hung slack in his hand; his throat pulled in a long swallow. With a gradual movement, he extended his hand, palm up, fingers spread in invitation.

For a moment, she considered turning tail and running. From

the persecution of his blasted rationalizations and the incredible
power of his touch. She feared him in an elemental way, yet
he remained a part of her, as essential as the blood coursing
through her veins. Taking whatever he offered would not alter
her love for him. Taking would only serve to heighten the pain
of leaving him.

And, leaving him would be unbearable no matter what she
did.

"I just want to talk with you, sweet. Please, come with me."

Decided by the faint tremor in his arm and the vulnerability
etched on his face, she linked her fingers through his, closed
them in possession. Stepping into the skiff, she ignored the
warning her mind insisted on issuing: *The words he wants to
say aren't likely to be ones you wish to hear.*

Settling her between his thighs, Noah's arms came around
her as he searched for the lines. The determined desperation
in his movements sent a glimmer of feeling, *his,* through her.

Under a billow of white canvas, the firm flex of muscle at
her back, Elle tipped the crown of her head to his collarbone
and struggled to hold her apprehension at bay. She had willingly
placed the power in his hands. If this was not how she had
pictured their relationship ending, her clothes damp and clinging from the spray of water, her hair curling wildly about her
face and neck, her hands clenched together to keep from reaching . . . well, at least she had made the choice. Finally, even if
the decision ended in grave error, *she* owned her life. Her
future.

His chest expanded, then his hot breath tickled the nape of
her neck. He cleared his throat; his arms tensed. *Oh, heaven,*
was he going to tell her he didn't want her in his life? Tell her
he was leaving, and they had no future? *We're like oil and
water, Elle, we don't mix.* Was he going to destroy her again?

She jerked, rocking the skiff against a cresting wave.
"Easy," he whispered beside her ear, and drew back before
he found himself tasting. She smelled different tonight, expen-

sive and exotic. Almond and honey, a rich scent weakening his already weak resolve. "What's the new fragrance?"

"Caroline gave it to me, said you would . . ." Her explanation withered.

Had she dabbed the perfume between her breasts? Groaning, he tried to keep his focus, remember his purpose. He had planned precisely how he would tell her he loved her. Knew *exactly* what he would say. He had spent the last two days thinking about her every waking moment. Dreaming about her every sleeping one. He wasn't sure about the particulars, where they would live, and when they would get married, but he knew he didn't want to live without her. Could not live without her.

The final determination had arrived last night. He had woken, shaking and screaming, the dream returning in ghastly fragments. Elle in the skiff with Leland and her father . . . a wave tipping them . . . her body tossed beneath the white-capped waves . . . a rapid descent into the depths of hell.

Expelling a terse breath, he fit her to his chest, his hands slipping on the lines, the awkward position making a laborious sail of a calm, easy one. He didn't care; he wouldn't let her go again.

She shifted, and for a moment, he feared he held her too tightly. Then, her lips grazed his neck, an arousing flutter, and he feared nothing at all. Her tongue, hot and rough, flicked his earlobe, her teeth digging in just enough to hurt. He leaned into the touch, his body kicking into gear, a frenzied rhythm it did not take long to find.

Kissing his jaw, she swayed to the side, *Christ,* searching for his mouth. Her arms wound around his neck, giving him a plentiful view inside the gaping neck of her blouse. Of its own accord, his hand crawled higher, his knuckles, then the back of his thumb, brushing her taut nipple. She was exquisite, the wonder of her more extraordinary than all his dreams. Needing to prove she was real, he pressed his palm against her thumping heart as his fingers cupped her breast in blatant ownership.

She reared and sought his lips, found them parted and ready.
*Stop her before she makes you forget what you're supposed
to be doing.*

"Sweet"—he grasped her wrists, pulled her arms by her
side—"please help me here." He struggled to speak clearly.
Blessit, he struggled to catch an even breath. Throwing a glance
off the starboard side, he saw they had almost reached the
island. Another five minutes, and he could put his feet on
firm ground, move a thinking distance from the warm, sweet-
smelling bundle of seduction in his arms. "I can't think when
you touch me." *Damn,* why had he gone and admitted *that?*

She laughed softly—an empowered laugh that scared him a
bit—and did something he had never imagined her doing, even
in his wildest dreams. She reached between his legs and slid
her finger into the mismatched buttonhole he had caught her
staring at on the dock. Not a bold touch by any means, more
of a grazing, playful stroke.

By God, it was the most erotic caress he'd *ever* imagined.

Seizing her chin, he found her lips and plundered, passion
threatening to consume him. She tasted of whiskey and citrus
of some kind. She tasted glorious, and for a brief instant, he
didn't care if he sailed them off course and out to sea.

Beneath her exploration, her innocent discovery, he swelled
and throbbed. She unsnapped buttons, and he held his breath,
his trouser fly spilling wide. Groaning hoarsely against her
mouth, he lifted his head, and sailed them into shore as skillfully
as he could with her hand closing about him, gently at first,
then with a determined rhythm. His thin underdrawers presented
little defense against her touch.

"Am I hurting you?" Her mouth skimmed his neck, a moist
slide, her teeth catching, nipping.

He couldn't speak, but managed to shake his head as the
skiff beached in the shallows. His collected plan, his grand
design, disappeared in the sensual mist enveloping them.

Reclaiming her lips, he swept her into his arms, climbed

from the boat and stumbled across the sand, never breaking contact. She worked the buttons of his shirt, one by one, then palmed the exposed skin, her thumbs teasing his nipples. A woman had never touched him there and if she had, he definitely wouldn't have imagined it shooting a white-hot burst of heat to his loins. A woman found pleasure there, he had assumed. Of course, his lovely vixen would find a way to arouse him to the point of madness on her first try.

"What are you doing to me?" he asked in a rushed whisper, approaching the glowing driftwood fire, shadows flickering across the towering dune. The ocean rushed into the shore, and somewhere in the distance, sand locusts croaked. Nothing penetrated but the sound of her blouse crinkling against his arm, the whistle of air past her lips.

She dipped her head and laved his nipple, tangling her fingers in his chest hair. She'd gone wild and he loved it. "I want to know your body"—she sucked the hardened bud between her teeth—"as well as I know my own." She shoved his shirtsleeve past his wrist. "Better."

Before he lost the use of his brain and his vocal chords, he forced her eyes to his. He loved this woman. It all but knocked him from his feet to realize just how much.

"Elle, I—"

She shook her head, covering his lips with her finger. Then she replaced her finger with her mouth. Aggressive and sure, doing all the things she knew he liked. He could not deny her.

Not when he had, quite possibly, wanted her forever.

He walked the required distance, his makeshift pallet coming into sight. Cradling her against his chest, he dropped to his knees, the packed sand cushioning their fall. Her legs sprawled; he smiled. He liked the strange trousers she had worn of late. Liked them a helluva lot.

She tore at the cloth hanging from his shoulder, bucking her hips. He shrugged, let her strip the damp cotton from his arm. Slanting his head, he deepened the kiss, taking her lower lip between his teeth and tugging, a sudden image of her lips tracing his rigid arousal filling his mind.

"I want to press your body against mine. Feel every naked inch of you," he rasped and started at her collar, working the bone buttons free one by one. Wanting to . . . *God*, he stopped himself from cupping her breasts. This time, he would wait until nothing stood between them.

She complied, guiding his hips up, tugging his trousers down, while her lips traversed his cheek, his nose, his brow. Tentative pillages, light nibbles and licks, a whirl of sensation snaking into every exposed pore, setting fire to every nerve ending.

Although their fingers faltered often, it seemed easy to divest each other of clothing. Boots, he toed off. She wore none. Her divided trousers, he managed quicker than he could a complicated dress. She wore a simple shift, no corset in sight. He had dressed in a hurry to get to her and wore nothing but a pair of worn underclothing. She had no stockings; he had no socks.

The first touch of skin against skin sent a wallop of shock to his senses. He lifted just enough to allow a glimmer of moonlight to cross her naked body. Overwhelmed, he could do nothing but stare—and appreciate his good fortune. She had grown into an incredibly beautiful woman.

"Noah." Embarrassed, she reached for his spectacles.

He shied away, emitting a husky laugh. "Oh, no, sweet. No way. I waited too long for this not to see clearly."

Her hair a wild, crimson riot flowing over his tattered blankets, the curls meeting ivory sand. Her breasts plump and capped to perfection, rosy nipples budding beneath his ardent scrutiny. Her slightly rounded tummy, the bellybutton so utterly feminine he wanted to smile. The need to smile vanished, the need to touch outweighing all else as his gaze dropped to her hips. Creamy skin and a round birthmark on her pelvic bone. Below, a swirling tuft of reddish brown between her thighs.

Shapely, and leading to a pair of slender, surprisingly lithe legs.

"You're perfect," he said, and lowered his body to hers, the wind rustling the sea oats above them. "Simply perfect."

"No." A soft denial, followed by a breathless exclamation as he fully covered her.

He wrenched his spectacles off and flung them to the sand, kissing her cheek, her lips, her neck, wanting . . . wanting *everything*. His hand moved to her right breast, his lips to her left. "Yes. Yes, you're perfect." Then he set out to prove it by catching her nipples between his lips and his fingers, lavishing them as he had dreamed of doing. *Oh, God, he was . . .*

Dying. She was dying.

The man she loved lay atop her, firm muscle to her sleek softness, half breaths rattling from his lungs with each slow grind of his hips, his fingers and teeth, his lips, all over her, everywhere at once. He groaned and in an instant of raw understanding, she realized his need matched hers.

Gliding her hands past his shoulders, she marveled: He found *her* perfect? *Juste Ciel. He* was perfect. If she could only get another look at him, a real, five-minute look. A vivid picture of his body bloomed in her mind, and she arched into the motion of his hips, capturing a whimper between clenched teeth. His hand had strayed, his fingers delving into the tight curls at her apex, a place forbidden except during bathing, and even then, under evidence of a heated blush.

He combed and stroked, diligently seeking, oh, merciful heavens . . . *seeking.* She stiffened and went on alert when he found what he sought.

"Trust me." His lips captured her earlobe, his breath sweeping inside. "I'm here, I'll always be here."

Shaking her head, she dug her heels into the sand, twisting the blankets into a snarl, inching away from his hand. She didn't believe him . . . could not give him what he sought . . .

not at all certain what he sought. It frightened her, the ease with which he molded her, a lump of clay in need of shaping.

Perhaps sensing her hesitation, he returned to her mouth and began kissing her deeply, seducing her, using whispered words and a velvet touch. Struggling through a dense cloud of half-formed pleasure, she could only follow his guiding commands. As his tongue began to match the rhythm of his hips, liquid heat rose from the tips of her toes, flowed up and out her fingertips.

She trembled, blood pounding in her head. "Please," she begged, unsure just what she begged for.

With an answering movement, his fingers renewed their probing assault. She recorded it all in dazzling awareness. A ravenous nip to the side of her breast . . . a rough tongue laving . . . bristly hair chafing the smooth valley. Sliding his hard thigh between hers, he gradually forced them apart. Blinding sensation, each one of greater magnitude than the one before. She didn't know where it would stop or how to stop it, could only hang on to him, a splash of color staining her lids.

She clutched his shoulders, dug her nails into his skin as his finger worked inside her moist folds. Desire clashed with fear, hunger with indecision. *Tell him no,* her mind screamed. But she followed her body's will, arching, crowding into him, and sending him deep inside her.

"Blessit, you're so warm," he whispered against her breast. He moved to her nipple, sucking sharply, drawing her in. "So wet." His finger retreated, and she whimpered. "Let me pleasure you." Then he plunged. Again, and again.

A deafening roar, a mad pulsing. Mindless, breathless. A masculine scent on the hand she lifted to her face, moisture and sand on the arm she threw over her eyes. The hammering fury of the ocean, the hammering fury of the man she loved. She shuddered, then shuddered again, her toes curling into the sand. She moaned, perhaps she screamed. However loud, whatever sound, it pealed in her ears.

"I'll be here," he coaxed, his voice shaky and thick, his touch direct and unrelenting.

Snagging both hands in his hair, she guided his mouth to hers.

He didn't follow, instead kissed his way *down,* swirling his tongue, lewdly, in her navel.

"Why?" She rocked onto his finger as it slid deep. His thumb found the erect nub nestled in her curls. She felt his tongue glide past her hipbone, suckle softly on the inside of her thigh.

"I want to taste you, know every crease in your skin." The words blurred on a labored breath. "I would never hurt you. Trust me, sweet."

She did trust him, even as, unbelievably, his mouth replaced his finger.

One moment of suspended shock, then she broke apart, scattering in a thousand different directions. Need overwhelming reason. Delight overwhelming fear. She thrust her hips and demanded. Ecstasy, pure and undiluted, scorched a wide path, clearing her mind of everything but the reality of him caressing the most intimate part of her, his fingers working in delicate tandem. She gasped, needle pricks of pleasure striking her, jettisoning her into a world of shrouded gratification known only to those who sought to grasp it.

Cool air brushed her skin, and she blinked, dazedly found Noah poised over her, his weight held on his elbows, his gaze ravishing her, setting fire, inch by inch. She writhed, his aroused flesh nudging the moist folds he had just vacated. He met her eyes, his as dark as she had ever seen them. The raw hunger in his look sent a dizzying burst of longing straight to her toes. Her knees swayed; her legs fell flat. Had her heart ever felt this complete, her body this sated, her mind this calm?

A smile of masculinity flickered on his face. Hands cupping her face, he leaned in, his mouth capturing hers in a long, deliberate kiss. She met each thrust of his tongue, desiring equal partnership in their loving. He growled his approval, slanting his head, and taking all she offered. Strange how the taste of her only knocked her desire a notch higher.

"Did you like it?" A razor nick on his chin held her attention, as did the gradual parting of his swollen lips. Without doubt, God had never created a more handsome man.

"Sweet?" he prompted, curt gusts spurting from his lungs.

She closed her eyes, making a sound like a purr. "Hmm-umm . . ." Flopping her arms wide, she burrowed her fingers knuckle-deep into silken sand, uncaring that she lay before him, naked, and complete.

His thumb smoothed her eyebrow, his hand trembling against her temple, passion building inside him, she could tell. "I've never, well . . . I didn't know if you would like it. God, I wanted you to." His arm slid under her bottom, angling her hips as he settled against her. "This will be even better," he promised, his breath stirring the curls at her temple.

"Not possible." She sighed.

She felt his slow smile against her cheek. "Just watch." This said, he seized her lips, a kiss of savage possession, of mastery and crude compulsion. More blatantly sexual than any he had given her. Gone was the seductive, patient lover, the childhood friend. In his place, a man whose need had risen above his level of restraint.

Elle should have figured how he would take her comment. Even as a boy, Noah had appeared apathetic about swimming contests or boat races, the most unconcerned of the bunch. Until dared. Caleb had defied him and suffered defeat, time and time again. She had never seen anyone work harder, by honest means, to win.

And now, he used his incredible tenacity, his talented lips and fingers, to drive her wild. She blinked into a midnight sky nestled with winking silver stars. As she stared, the world tilted on its axis.

"Where next?" His gruff query rang in her ear. "Here?"

He caught a tingling nipple between his teeth and nibbled on the erect tip. "Here?" His fingers slipped through the fissure of her thighs and entered her slowly, once, twice, then a complete, teasing withdrawal, moisture slicking her skin. Sweet heaven, what had he done to her?

He pressed his sex against her folds. "Here?" he asked, each word he spoke more husky than the last.

She dragged her hands from the sand and clutched his shoulders. *"Yes."* A memory of her fingers circling him, followed by an image of them *joined,* shattered her coherence. Moaning greedily, she urged him to sink into her. With everything she had.

He made a guttural sound and pressed her into the blankets, his lips taking possession. A creeping thrust; his hold on her tightened. Lifting her hips, she took him deeper. She hid her face in the crook of his neck and breathed in the mix of soap and sea clinging to his skin.

"So long, I've wanted you for so long." He captured her startled cry as he embedded himself inside her, hip to hip.

Her body bloomed in response to the unfamiliar fullness, each petal unfolding. Quickly, the sharp edge of pain subsided, outweighed by a flush of pleasure. Smiling, she looked into his face. A muscle in his jaw jumped, a circle of white surrounded his mouth. He tilted his head and swallowed hard, obviously controlling his reaction.

Her hands skimmed his back, coming to rest above the rounded crest of his bottom. Tentatively, she moved her hips, a fresh torrent of desire claiming her.

His lids fluttered, his eyes meeting hers for the first time since he'd made her his. "Are you all right?" He pressed a feather-soft kiss to her cheek.

Amazed by the gratifying feeling of completeness, and so *all right* she could not believe it, she nodded. Grasping his waist, she made an impatient movement he could not help but understand. "But I think you need to . . . work harder . . . to win this bet of yours, Professor."

He laughed hoarsely and complied, the muscles in his buttocks bunching as he teasingly withdrew so far she feared he would pop out. "Yes, ma'am," he said, before claiming her lips and doing a gradual, glorious slide.

Tender movements became fierce, amused expressions solemn. Restraint broken, he set a furious, steady pace, surging into her, each stroke seeming to touch deeper than the last. She rose to meet him, lost in a tide of tactile awareness. Whiskers scraping her cheek . . . teeth closing around her inflamed nipples . . . muscles, damp and hard, flexing beneath her fingertips . . . hips bumping, bruising and rough. Savage and untamed, fighting for subsistence, for the most basic gratification. And every place she hungered, he found, touching, licking, driving, tensing.

He raised her knee to his waist. She lifted her leg, locking her ankles behind his back, marveling at the wonderment of him thrusting, filling her completely.

"Ma chère fille." Low and ragged, the once-loved designation brought her closer, ever closer to the edge. For the second time.

"I'll be there, with you. Always," he whispered next to her ear.

A swift crest, a headlong dive. Harder, then harder again. The wind whipped the blanket against their hips, sand pricking their skin. Searching, she thrashed and whimpered. Answering, his finger found the nub of flesh he had teased before. Keeping his pounding rhythm, he touched her there, purposely.

And she exploded.

"Thank God, only so long I could think of fish," he said over the odd ringing in her ears. The ground shifted, and she slammed her lids to stay conscious, arching into him, digging her heels into his calves, clasping him to her. Heartbeat to heartbeat, slick skin to slick skin. They fought for the same air, not enough for either of them.

As she floated to earth, he called her name, his body shuddering. Driving deep once more, he buried his face into her hair and gathered her close, panting. For a long moment, they lay silent and dazed, limbs tangled in an intimate, moist jumble. Tremors shook him, passed to her.

Suddenly, he lifted his head, his gaze part-feral, part-docile. A bead of sweat crossed his cheek; a rapid pulse beat double time at his temple. Lazily, she smoothed her finger over the bulging vein, swept the drop of water away with her thumb. He leaned into her touch, his lids fluttering, the scarred one drooping. She smiled. She hadn't noticed before, but his nose was peeling, and his cheeks were freckled from the sun. The dark circles beneath his eyes attested to his lack of sleep.

Had she ever looked at him this closely? Would she ever again?

Releasing a weary sigh, he rolled to his back, pulling her with him, pressing her into his side. He brushed her hair from her brow and laid a soft kiss on the crown of her head. "Better than candy," he murmured and yawned.

Fulfilled, she snuggled against him, the muscles beneath her cheek relaxing as he slipped into sleep. The arm around her went slack, the other lay across his belly, his slim, well-shaped fingers splayed wide. She searched for his hand, linked them. Automatically, his tightened in possession.

Forever, she would treasure what they'd shared, even if it *had* been the biggest mistake of her life.

Because, how long would it be before Noah began to regret?

Chapter Sixteen

Contentment. Completion. The first of either Noah had truly felt in twenty-seven years of living. Before this wondrous night, he had never experienced heartfelt desire, never understood what it meant to hold the woman he cherished in his arms as he made love to her, her tremors of release shaking him to the core of his being. He had never slept in the same, well ... never spent the entire night with someone, naked limbs tangled.

He liked it; he liked it a lot.

He smiled, amazed by his stupidity. He had actually believed he could reason his way out of loving her. Staring at the sapphire blaze streaking the sky, he realized Elle was no longer chaste. But then, neither was he.

His shirttail fluttered about his waist, a gusty breeze dried his damp skin. Since he had woken to find her draping his chest, her light breaths teasing the patch of hair, her hand clutching his, he'd struggled to remember a time before her. Panicked, the notion had struck hard. He had left more than two loving brothers behind ten years before.

He'd been a fool, even if she had been merely a young girl of fourteen. He stooped to grasp a conch shell, dusting off bits of sand. What if he had returned to find her married to Magnus Leland? A cinnamon-headed child bouncing on her round hip, another man's baby suckling at her breast. Another man suckling at her breast. Noah cursed and flung the shell into the waves. She was *his*. He would waste no more time on regrets and fear.

It wasn't entirely his fault, he reasoned. He had always been rather possessive of her, fiercely protective and unable to shrug off the sense of responsibility he felt. In some fashion, he had recognized the bond between them.

But she had recognized the love.

Dammit, how could he have known he would never find another woman to match her, that she would be the one to fill the emptiness inside him? How could he have known he would never *try* to find another? With all Elle's foolishness and flippancy, practically chasing him down the street on a daily basis, he hadn't dared lower his guard long enough to find out.

Now, he would put the past behind him. Forge a solid relationship with his brothers, with Rory. Let the wounds of distrust heal. Take a chance on the future. Take a chance on love.

Love.

Icy water lapped at his ankles as he walked forward. The wave retreated; coquina shells pricked the pads of his feet. Why hadn't she told him she loved him earlier? It had been a long time since he'd looked into her vivid green eyes and known for sure she did. Maybe leaving like he'd done had killed her love. Perhaps she had confused her fondness for a childhood friend. He had certainly accused her of it enough times.

He dropped to his haunches, his trousers getting soaked to the knee. He thought women always said those words after coupling. During, maybe. Elle hadn't said anything even remotely maudlin that he could recall. Of course, he could have missed three little words, if she'd whispered them, or mumbled them against his neck or something.

Sighing, he drew his hand across his whiskered jaw, sniffed at the sensual aroma of almond and honey and woman. He sought to disprove the cold lump of suspicion collecting in his gut, the familiar fear of rejection, yet he could not.

Only once before had he loved someone and trusted them blindly—and Caleb had betrayed him, at least in his adolescent mind. He should have stayed, let his brother beat him to a bloody pulp, if necessary. They could have solved the problem a week later, not ten years.

And now, because of idiotic mischance, he had to gather the courage to tell—

"Noah?"

He wrenched around, landing flat on his bottom. "Chrissakes!"

Elle stared, wide-eyed, for all of ten seconds, then slammed her hand over her mouth and burst into gleeful laughter. She had slipped on her shift and nothing else. Fading moonlight flowed through the thin material, silhouetting her body well enough to stir parts of his that he had assumed were satisfied.

He shoved to his feet, his trousers, minus underclothing, sticking to his legs like wet parchment. He could not tear his gaze from her, aching at her unaffected loveliness. "You think scaring the life out a person is funny, huh?"

She shook her head, yet choked for breath, the laughter still bubbling.

He took a step forward. She took a step back. She broke into a run, and he was right behind her.

They stumbled up the beach, a faltering gait in the ankle-deep sand. He caught her about the waist, swung her off her feet, and against his chest. "Forfeit," he growled next to her ear, recalling a childhood game.

She giggled in delight, this woman who never giggled, the sound rumbling beneath the palm of his hand. "If you remember correctly, Professor, I never yield easily. You'll have to torture me first."

Her teasing, languid tone sent a spike of desire to his loins. He swelled and hardened against her round bottom. "What kind of torture do you have in mind, sweet?" Her heels knocking helplessly against his shins, he seized her shift and tugged it to her hips in bunched fistfuls.

She gasped, not able to form a coherent reply when his fingers teased, delving into the patch of satiny curls, spreading, exploring, penetrating.

"Is this adequate punishment?" he asked, finding a bare spot on her shoulder and sucking greedily.

Her head lolled forward, then back. She purred in reply.

He swung her into his arms and slanted his mouth across hers, realizing he was in wretched shape if a weak feline growl had the power to set him off.

Her shift fluttered to the ground. His shirt followed. He settled her atop the twist of blankets, then stripped off his trousers, his movements impatient and jerky. Passion clawed at him, a ravenous beast demanding nourishment.

He fell to his knees; she spread her legs. Chest to chest, hip to hip, he entered her in a sure, swift stroke. Uninhibited, they mated like wild animals in the dawning light. *Animals.*

Something Noah had never compared himself to.

Elle fished a threadbare sailor's cap from Noah's satchel and settled it over his face. He'd already blistered his skin, trudging around the island in improper clothing.

Throwing his shirt across his chest, she watched it rise and fall on a languid breath. He was exhausted, his cheeks darkly stubbled, his normally neat clothing smudged with dirt. Tawny hair hung past his ears, far longer than usual. A memory of her nose embedded in the thick strands as he plunged into her curled her toes into the sand.

Nonplused, she concentrated on the calm break of waves against the shore, the shrill call of seagulls in search of food, the rustle of sea oats carpeting the sand dune behind her. Even after a hurried, frigid swim in the ocean, she could smell the carnal scent of their joining on her skin. Even after washing her mouth with salty water, she could taste him. Sliding Noah's satchel to the side, she slumped against the dune, groaning at the unwelcome friction between her thighs.

They had made love *three* times. Once while waist-deep in the ocean. An hour ago, no more. How could she want him again so soon? How? *Juste Ciel.* She had not expected this.

Elle had understood the mechanics of copulation. Vaguely. An indistinct, yet defined, sense of what happened between a man and a woman in a darkened bedroom. He positioned his sex accordingly; she complied, stiff and sacrificing beneath him. This information circulated at every sewing bee and quilting circle, crossed every coverlet at every church picnic. Naturally, the married women stopped talking the minute she, unmarried and ignorant to the reality of wifely duty, entered their line of sight. Until her engagement to Magnus Leland. She'd had no mother, and they had felt obliged to educate her.

Mrs. Scoggins had explained in shadowy terms how thinking of household chores made the act go quicker. Widow Wynne had listed excuses she could use to avoid *it* altogether. Jewel Quattlebaum had detailed the necessary pain involved in a reporter's concise, unemotional manner. Only Lilian Quinn had made it seem like intimate relations did not rival tooth surgery.

Thankfully, lovemaking seemed nothing like those women's descriptions. Love made it truly wonderful. She swiveled her head, needing to feel him near. Long feet, a slight dusting of hair on each slim toe. Sturdy legs covered by a pair of salt-crusted trousers. A muscular arm folded over his belly, the other stretched from his body, fingers nestled in the sand. Her breathing accelerated. She had touched much of him, with her hands, and later—at his urging—with her lips and her teeth. His sex had lost its wonderful rigid shape, of course, but she could still see a firm outline beneath clinging cotton.

Who would have imagined that circumspect Noah Garrett, the first to hesitate and weigh all the options, would have taken her with such confidence, such lewd boldness? As if he knew exactly what she needed and held no misgivings about giving it to her.

It excited her—in a secret place Noah had brought to life— to picture him, staid and fussy, buttoned up and pressed down, precise speech and polite bearing, panting and plunging into her, passion stealing air from his lungs, rational thought from his mind. Amazed her to find she could set him aflame, shatter the composed façade he presented to the world.

She stretched her hand out, then folded her fingers into a fist and jammed her bottom into the hot sand, forcing her arm to her lap. He needed to sleep. And she needed to conclude what this night, and this morning, had done to her. How it had changed her life, her plans for the future.

Leaning over him, she rolled his cuffs past his ankles, shading as much skin as she could. She loved him, but he had not said he loved her. Luckily, she didn't think she had said it, either.

Could he love her? She traced a faded scar on the sole of his foot. She had seen indefinable lights, tender sparks of emotion flaring in his eyes. Especially the last time they made love. They had left the water still joined, and he had brought her on top of him as they attained bliss. If there were the slightest chance he loved her, she would forgo the scholarship, and persuade Noah to take her with him. She remembered seeing a university in Chicago on the list of those offering women's programs.

Her hand stilled; apprehension flooded her. What if he didn't want a wife who attended university? What if he didn't want a wife at all? He had made love to lots of women. Maybe this meant next to nothing to him.

She sat back on her heels. She could go with him anyway, make a life with him, somehow. She preferred this choice to the wretched one of never making love to him again, never talking and laughing with him again. They could have a modern relationship, much like the one she suspected Christa and Caleb had. Except, Caleb had asked Christa to marry him more than once, and she had refused.

Determined, Elle shoved aside skepticism and decided to love him. She had never been one to leap off the track once she put herself on it. And she had put herself on this track years ago.

Pulling her watch from her pocket, she checked the time. Another half hour, and she would wake him. She glanced overhead, the sun a bright, blinding ball in the sky. Looking at Noah, she saw his cap shaded his nose and cheeks, but not his lips. Red and swollen, they looked well loved.

When they got home, she would make a baking-soda paste for his skin, spread salve on his chapped lips. She snapped her fingers. Maybe he had some in his satchel.

She searched the shallow outside pocket. Two pencils, a metal measuring tool. Opening the larger section, she found nothing but a notebook and a leather-bound manual of some sort.

Normally not a meddlesome person, she took the notebook out, wanting only to see what he had been studying the last two days. She flipped the cover, turned a page. A surprisingly garbled scrawl detailing migration habits for a type of fish she'd never heard of. On another, he had drawn a rough sketch of the beach and back bay, marked off specific sections, and given them complex names. She leafed through sheet after sheet of scientific terms, facts, and figures.

Wishing she had taken a biology class during her lone year at university, she turned a page and froze. He'd written *Outcome: Mind free of Elle Beaumont* in sloppy block letters and underlined it.

Twice.

Her jaw dropped as she skimmed the lines of text. *Work longer hours. No more kissing. No more touching. No more daydreams. Eating dinner or repairing her shutters is forbidden.* A circled notation reminded him to ask Caleb to mow her grass. She dug her toes into the sand, a furious quiver working its way down her legs. Obviously, he had intended to read her this list when he brought her to Devil. His raging lust had simply gotten in the way.

Elle would have laughed if a sharp wedge of pain hadn't driven the breath from her body, had her doubling over trying to suck in air. A dull buzz sounding in her ears, she placed his satchel beside her and laid the notebook on top. Dazed, she covered him with the blanket wadded by his feet, knowing he would swelter, but at least his skin wouldn't crisp.

She trudged toward the water, readied the skiff for sail, found the strength to shove it through the bucking waves, then struggled to climb aboard. She licked her finger and held it into the wind. She could make it to the dock in less than fifteen minutes, pack a bag, and have Stymie shuttle her to Morehead City in time for the four o'clock train. Send a telegraph to Savannah and ask her to meet the train in New York City.

I'll be here, with you. Always.

She released a harsh bark of laughter, let the ache of deception claim her. Tugging the lines taut, she sailed from one dream and toward another.

For six months after leaving Pilot Isle, Noah had slept in deserted rail cars and abandoned shelters, curled into a ball, fearful and tense. The dreadful experience had honed his instincts, razor-sharp, and when he woke, he knew instantly.

Elle was gone.

He blinked into muted light, flipped his sailor's cap from his face, and swore. Blessit, he was burning up. Shoving the thin blanket from his body, he rolled to his knees, prayed Elle would be sitting there, a smile of happiness, of acceptance, gracing her lovely face.

A bead of sweat coursed down his cheek, another down his chest. He shook his head and calmed his breathing. *Think, Noah, think.* Always been easy before, but now . . .

He stumbled to his feet, his stiff trousers crinkling. For a step or two, he followed the set of petite footprints, remembering his first day back on Devil. He felt for his spectacles. No pockets. Hell, he didn't even have his shirt *on.*

He squinted, glanced anxiously around him, and turned a full circle. Where could she—

Two things struck.

His skiff, although he couldn't see clearly, no longer appeared to be on the shore. And his satchel lay in a spill, his notebook sprawled open beside it. Dropping to his haunches, he brought it close to his face. *Dear God,* he thought, the notebook sliding from his fingers. In the distance, the harsh grunts of a nest of white ibis filtered through his bafflement.

Hadn't she known? Why hadn't she trusted him? He had begged her to, told her he would be there for her. His list . . . it didn't mean anything. Nothing at all. Just an asinine way to try to expunge her from his system. Blessit, he *loved* her. Didn't she know? Did she think he had experienced with another woman what he had experienced with her? Impossible.

Wrenching his head back, he located the sun. Elle couldn't have left more than three hours ago. Four at most. She would send Zach or Caleb for him, then he would straighten this mess out. Tell her he loved her and explain the silly damned list. Plan in mind, he set about folding the blankets, spreading his campfire ashes, packing his satchel. Slipping his arms through his sleeves, he lifted his wrist to his nose, and inhaled deeply. The smell of her was enough to drive him wild—the smell of *them* enough to weaken his knees. He hoped he could persuade her to stay at the coach house tonight. He would grovel if necessary.

A resounding shout above the crash of breaking waves. The wind ripped at his shirt as he turned toward the sea.

Caleb sailed into shore in a spritsail skiff of his design—one he had promised to make for Noah—his brawny arms working the lines. He glanced up the beach once, his lips parting, words Noah couldn't catch over snapping canvas.

He looked beyond Caleb and saw Zach, sitting in the stern of the boat. Noah fumbled for his spectacles, slipped them on his face. The troubled look hardening Zach's usually agreeable features triggered a frenzied squall in his stomach.

He stood, rooted to a blistering spot of sand, trying not to let his imagination get the best of him. But . . . *both* of them? Why had *both* his brothers come to fetch him? Like they performed some mission of mercy or something.

Zach reached him first; Caleb lingered by the skiff, clearly hesitant. Without saying a word, his brother dropped a wrapped bundle in his hands. Fingers unable to do his bidding, Noah started to loosen the piece of cloth, then halted abruptly, staring.

He fondled a worn buttonhole, a faded blemish. "Where did you get this?"

"Where did you leave it?" Zach's tone held a faint thread of anger.

Once, the material had been pale blue, now it was the color of chalk. And stained with blood from his split eyelid. "The docks. Or Stymie's sloop, maybe. He ferried me to Morehead City that night. I changed into a shirt I grabbed from a clothesline." He swallowed hard, fighting the dread creeping higher. "Where did you get this, Zach?" But he knew, oh, he knew. Elle had kept his shirt for all these years. The shirt he'd been wearing the night he left Pilot Isle.

He wasn't sure *what* that made him feel. Queasy, impatient, fearful.

"Little bro', you know where I got it. She left you a coat, too."

"Left? Where is she?"

"How the heck should I know? Wherever she went, your friend Caroline went with her, so she's not alone, thank goodness.'' Zach retraced his steps, his stride chafing and furious. Nearing the skiff, he called over his shoulder, ''I don't know why Ellie wanted you to have that. You'll have to ask her, if you ever get to.''

Noah yanked the worn cloth away and flung it to the ground, staring at the book in his hand. He had only seen it once, but he would never forget what his mother's diary looked like. Not when her secrets had cost him so much.

Why had Elle left it for him?

It took him a moment to understand. This way her way of saying good-bye.

''Are you going to go get him or do I have to?'' Zach banged the skillet to the stove. A tarnished silver ladle followed.

Caleb slouched in his chair, hung his head over the hard wooden back, and groaned low, where Zach couldn't hear it. He drummed his dirt-smudged fingertips on his thighs, knowing he should have washed up better, and wishing the aroma of dinner cooking—fried ham and sweet potatoes from the smell of it—did something besides make his gut twist. He didn't want to face his little brother across the scant width of a kitchen table. Not right now. Ellie had been gone for three weeks and each day proved worst than the last.

''I don't like going there,'' he finally said. Shamed him, yes, because only children feared the burying ground. Shamed him, but it was true.

''I don't care what you like, Cale. Go get him. Truth be told, he's like Rory in my mind. If he doesn't eat here, I don't know if he eats a'tall.'' Zach slammed a bowl of gravy to the table, rocking Caleb's glass of tea back and forth. ''From the weight he's lost, I know he isn't eating anywhere *but* here, that's for sure. And what about the stunt he pulled with Sean Duggan, knocking him unconscious on the docks, us having to pull him away. Whatever Mrs. Bartram wrote in her letter . . . Lord, I believed Noah was going to kill the man. Someone has to talk some sense into him.''

Caleb grabbed the wobbling glass in both hands, condensation coating his palms. Only June, but already hot enough to melt glue off every hull plank he slicked. He'd been working double time to get Noah's skiff ready, hoping it would lighten his brother's black mood a smidgen. ''I don't know what to say, don't you see? I don't understand women. I've been asking Christa to marry me for nigh on five years, and she always says no. Holy Mother Mary! What do you want *me* to say?'' He gulped a mouthful of lukewarm tea, drops dribbling down his chin. ''Anyhow, thinking about him and Ellie, well, it kinda makes me uncomfortable.''

Zach wedged a knife between the pan edge and a cake of corn bread, snapped his wrist, and popped the steaming loaf onto a chipped blue plate. ''It makes you uncomfortable to imagine your brother in love?''

Caleb wiped his fist beneath his chin and squirmed against the unforgiving seat. ''Yeah, I guess. I mean, it is *Ellie*, after all. Professor spent the night on Devil with her. God knows what they did.''

Zach wedged a piece of corn bread into his mouth and chewed, a lazy smile growing. ''Doesn't take God to figure that one.''

''Stop. I don't wanna hear this. Practically my little sister you're talking about.''

Propping his hip on the counter, Zach folded his arms, and settled his stoic gaze on his brother. *Damn,* Caleb hated that benevolent look. ''I never understood Noah either, Cale, if it makes you feel any better. Less than you, safe to say. Always a step ahead of me, a step ahead of any child I had ever met. And then Momma died, leaving me to raise him. I tried the best I knew how. And when the two of you . . . well, I figured giving him some time to think was the way to fix things.'' He cupped his elbows in his hands and squeezed hard. ''Let emotions settle.

Only, he had the hurt fixed in his heart, so deeply fixed, there was no way to budge it. Every day that passed, he built these walls around himself, holding us out, feeling betrayed and alone. And, he's doing it again, only this time with Ellie.''

"Maybe she'll—"

"She won't come back, not while he's here. You heard what he told us, the blasted list she saw. Lord, what's she to think? That he's doing what he did his whole life—running from her.''

Defeated, Caleb scooted his chair back and rose, his shoulders hunched. He rubbed the nape of his neck, trying to remove the stiffness. "I'll go. I hate that danged burying ground, but I'll go.''

"Just listen if he wants to talk. Simple.'' Zach turned to the stove. "Besides, I have to pick up Ellie's friend, that city woman who's running the school while see's gone. Savannah. I can't remember her last name. I invited her for dinner, felt like I should. Had to convince her not to ride her bicycle, knowing she would have to ride it back at night. Told me she lived in New York, so I shouldn't worry.'' He jammed a dishrag in the waist of his trousers. "Anyway, I don't care what you do, Cale. Or how you do it. Drag him here if you have to. I'm not letting him withdraw from this family again. And you're going to help me, even if you have to visit a haunted graveyard to do it.''

Caleb shouldered the screen door open. "Not funny, Zach. Lotta spiders in that creepy place.'' The door smacked behind him as he stalked across the porch, Zach's laughter trailing him.

She could be pregnant.

Settling back, Noah rested his head against the gnarled wisteria vines circling the oak's trunk, wondering a little angrily if Elle had considered that fact. A wall of heat shimmered even in the shade; he muttered an oath, wiping the dampness from his brow. Three times posed significant risk for an unmarried woman. He hadn't minded taking it, or asking her to. He had assumed they would wed soon after. Blessit, every day spent imagining a child growing inside her pushed him closer to the edge of madness.

His child.

Closing his eyes, he let the unbidden images flow, accepting the agony as his due. To save his sanity, he allowed this painful process twice a day. When he woke, invariably reaching for her, and again in the afternoon, after stocking the laboratory library or draining blessed fish nets. Nights were unbearable unless he labored to the point of exhaustion. Which should cover him tonight . . . he had just finished a twelve-hour shift on the *Nellie Dey*.

He searched for a comfortable spot, leaves crackling. Dappled sunlight danced over his unlaced brogans and seared his skin through his clothing. High above, branches stirred restlessly—restless discontent he understood.

Easily, his fingers found the marks in the tree trunk. Like he did every day, he traced them: *Elle loves Noah*. Christabel had carved the words when he was fourteen, disfiguring two trees in the burying ground—which most people avoided unless lowering a loved one into sacred earth—and every tree in the schoolyard. It had taken her an entire summer to complete the project, she'd once told him. Naturally, he had been mortified, completely and horribly mortified. Now . . . now he wished some of them read *Noah loves Elle*.

He did love her. More deeply than he had believed possible.

Would she have left if she'd known? Would it have made any difference? He had proven it their night on Devil, in a thousand different ways. Or assumed he had. He had imagined her spirited lovemaking spoke the same of her feelings. But, a nagging question burned: What had her intentions been that morning? Had his damned list completely changed them?

Her betrayal, even if the fault lay at his doorstep, cut deep as Christa's marks in the oak he rested against. He questioned ever trusting her, ever trusting *himself*, again.

Behind him, the shrill creak of the iron gate sounded, followed by a heavy tread on the dirt path. Noah leaned out and felt a frown spread. He watched Caleb chart a hesitant course through the graveyard, dodging the shell slabs with devout consideration. Somewhere in the back of his mind, he remembered his brother's fears: spiders and haunts. Dammit, didn't his family realize he wanted to be left alone?

Caleb halted, his fists diving into the pocket of his bib trousers. He stared at the vaulted brick Noah propped his left arm upon. "You shouldn't be leaning all over someone's final resting place, should you?"

Noah spared the worn tombstone a glance. "Navy captain, dead for fifty years. Truly, I don't think he minds the company."

Caleb fluttered leaves and twigs with a halfhearted kick. "Zach made dinner. Wants you to come home."

"I'm not going anywhere, Cale. I don't feel like talking, and I'm not hungry."

"Have you eaten today?"

Noah tilted his head, incensed for no good reason. "What is this? The damned Inquisition?"

"I don't even know what that's supposed to mean, so I won't get mad about it. But, you'd better not think to push me too far, little bro'. I've had about enough of your bull roar the last couple weeks. A beating wouldn't hurt you any as far as I can see."

Noah swore beneath his breath, a vulgarity he'd never said to his brother, never said to anyone.

Caleb jerked him up by the front of his shirt, brought them nose-to-nose. "Listen, you half-witted fool, I don't want to do this again. I lived through it once already. With Zach, after Hannah died. Crazy fits and black moods, not eating and not caring. If it hadn't been for having to care for Rory, Zach woulda died.'' Caleb abruptly released him, then grabbed Noah's wrist to steady him as he stumbled over a gnarled root. "Ellie ain't dead; therefore, the reason for this gloom don't make sense to me. If you want her, find her. Quit lolling in grief that ain't real. Real is the stone slab Zach puts flowers on every week. That's life lived without someone.''

Noah jammed his arm against the tree, supporting his weak knees. "You don't understand, Cale.''

"Hell, I'm sure I don't.''

He yanked a piece of moss from the bark and mashed it between his fingers. "I gave her all I had to give . . . and she left anyway.''

"Yeah, you gave everything. Good aims are all fine and dandy, but did you say the words?''

Noah didn't have to ask what his brother meant. Flinging the crumpled greenery to the ground, he growled, "No.''

"Aw, hell, you *have* to say the words. Women expect it. Ain't bad once you whisper 'em a few times to yourself. Then, they'll come spilling right out, even when you wish they wouldn't.''

"I never got the chance to say them.'' He frowned and plucked at another bit of moss. "Not literally anyway.''

"Literally? I guess that means you never actually said it.'' Caleb laughed and rocked back on his heels. "Funny how you can be so danged smart in some ways and dumb as a brick in others. Don't you see Ellie ain't a little girl anymore, trailing after you like a lost pup? She's all grown-up.''

Noah cut his eyes toward Caleb. "What the hell do you mean by that?''

He threw his arm over Noah's shoulders, a stretch when he stood inches shorter. "I mean, little bro', you've joined the ranks of the unlucky souls who have to work for a woman's affection. About time, cause you never had to work for Ellie's before. Guess I don't know much about women, confusing creatures I'll admit, but I do know this much . . . they delight in the niceties. Little presents. A lace handkerchief or a colorful hair ribbon, maybe pretty flowers or a tin of fine powder. Walking on the side closest to the street, so's mud doesn't splatter their new dress, which you remember to say you like when you pick 'em up. All those fancy words you think to yourself but never reckon you'll have to actually say aloud. It won't get you far to keep quiet, I tell you. Gotta come right out and make a fool of yourself."

Noah wrenched away, snatched his satchel from the ground. "That's the most ridiculous advice I've ever heard."

"Maybe it is." He shrugged. "Only, who has a woman and who don't?"

"Woman?" Noah slapped bits of dirt and dried leaves from the wide shoulder strap. "Blessit, you can't even get yours to marry you."

"Mighty true, but at least I know where mine is."

Noah clenched his fists and took a furious step forward. "I could find Elle if I wanted to. I have some ideas about it, you know."

Caleb walked backward, shaking his hands, a silly smile on his face. "I'm sure you do, Professor. You always did have plenty of *ideas*."

"Elle left Pilot Isle with a woman who has been my friend for years. I know where Caroline lives, and she probably has a good idea where Elle is living. Jesus, don't you think I could find her if I wanted to?" Actually, Noah had telegraphed Caroline three times. She had refused each request, once going so far as to advise him to stew in his own juices. "She left me, Cale, meaning she doesn't *want* to get married. That's the end of it. What do you want me to do? Drop to my knees before her and beg, give her the opportunity to rip my heart out completely?" He kicked the gate open and stalked down the sidewalk, Caleb right on his heels.

"Marry? Damn, you gotta tell 'em you love 'em before you start asking. Though it ain't worked yet for me." He clapped

Noah on the back. "No wonder you messed this up. Like I said, smart in some ways, dumb in others. Makes me happy to know I've got more brains than you about something."

"Know? You don't know anything." Noah shrugged from the irritating grasp and crossed the shell-paved street at a trot. He could see Zach's steep hip roof just ahead, the wooden shakes that needed replacing catching dying rays of sunlight. Might as well go over there, he grumbled, all this talking had made him hungry.

Caleb jogged beside him, panting raggedly. "Hate to disagree . . . but I do know one thing . . . little bro'."

"Yeah, what's that?"

Caleb halted in the middle of the street and patted his chest, a smug grin plumping his cheeks. "Stopped by the post office on the way here, and I know I got a letter from your lady friend, Mrs. Bartram, right here in my pocket."

Chapter Seventeen

Elle passed a boisterous group of young men wearing odd-looking shirts she had come to find they played football in. Acknowledging their subtle leers and soft whistles with a steady gaze, she refused to let them intimidate her. South Carolina College had eight female students in the fall of 1898, and horse-faced or winsome, they elicited a fair share of attention.

Attention she could live without for the rest of her days.

Slipping her watch from her pocket, Elle gave it a quick glance and gasped. Lifting her skirt above her ankles, she took the steps to the college of science at a near run. She couldn't afford to arrive late. She had petitioned the dean for entrance to this class, a first-year biology course, and he had agreed, albeit reluctantly.

Hushed voices echoed off the high ceiling as she entered the auditorium. With an airy swish, the door closed. She glanced around, found Piper Campbell, the only other woman in class, and slid in beside her.

Piper leaned in. "I thought I was going to have to search the halls for you."

Elle loosened the string binding her books and pulled the

biology text from the stack. "I had a meeting with Dr. Collins. He doesn't think I can handle his European Chronicles class. After four years of accepting female students, I can't believe this university still expects us to take nothing but literature and domestic economy. Simple bookkeeping is about the only class they'll approve without a fight."

"Collins?" Piper snapped her fingers. "Ah, yes, the one who wears a pince-nez and cracks his knuckles while he lectures." Her smooth ivory features tightened, a determined look Elle had come to know well after daily discussions about the faculty's lack of confidence. "Your duty is to go in there and score the highest mark, knock that dandified goat on his fussy bottom."

Smothering a smile, Elle said, "No, no, Pip, I'll knock Professor Laurent on *his* bottom. When I signed up for his course, I neglected to mention I spoke French for the first ten years of my life."

At the front of the classroom, a loud clap silenced the hum of conversation. Professor Stanford, the youngest faculty member on campus, climbed three stairs to the platform and halted behind a decrepit lectern. Clearing his throat, he smoothed the glossy thatch of hair on his head. "Students, I've made a slight adjustment to the syllabus, one I hope you will appreciate." He propped his elbows on the podium, where he would keep them the entire lecture. "I've asked a former colleague, a doctoral candidate teaching an advanced oceanography class at this university, to speak once a week on elementary marine-science topics. I firmly believe an introductory class should present a wide variety of subjects to enable you to choose your next course with a clearer understanding of your interests and talents."

Professor Stanford announced his guest lecturer's name, and Elle's vision blurred. She gripped the edge of the splintered desk, the crazed kick of her heart all she heard.

Noah crossed the small stage, his hand extended toward his colleague. He had a notebook—the *same* blasted notebook—

tucked under one arm, the familiar leather satchel looped over a broad shoulder. She drew him in like a long, cool drink of water, then spit him out.

Close-cropped hair parted slightly off center, jaw square and clean-shaven, cheekbones prominent in a lean face, lips parting to reveal straight, white teeth. His formal attire—striped trousers, black sack coat, gray waistcoat, and four-in-hand knotted over a butterfly collar—befit a scholar.

"My, my, will you take a look at him," Piper whispered, her normally barbed tone thick as honey.

Elle vaulted to her feet, her textbook thumping to the floor.

Noah looked up from the lectern, his spectacles catching a glint of light, concern crinkling the skin around his eyes. He heeded the lapse, his features smoothing. "Miss"—he glanced at his notes, then back with a half smile—"Campbell or Beaumont?"

She could have killed him, dashed down the aisle and pummeled him with her bare fists. If every female student didn't suffer at the emotional outburst of another in this world where they were watched so closely, she would have, *damn and blast*.

"Beaumont, Marielle-Claire. Sorry to disturb, *Professor* Garrett," she said through gritted teeth, then smacked her bottom to the wooden bench, the hard spank exactly what she deserved.

A responding spark of anger lit his gaze; his smile flattened into a thin, harsh line.

She glared. He nodded.

Across twelve rows and two dozen students, they waged war.

"Welcome aboard, Garrett. Hope you're settling in. Unpacking the modest library I seem to remember you carrying with you years ago? I'm sure the jars of sand and rusted anchors are on the way." Martin Stanford leaned a shoulder against the doorjamb of his guest lecturer's office, his brilliant blue eyes lit with impish humor his students would have been shocked to see. That his colleagues called him Marty, a man once known as a flagrant profligate, would also have come as a surprise. "By the bye, you want to tell me what the little scene was in the lecture hall earlier?"

Noah crushed his fountain pen in his fist, cursing his earlier slip. Thank God only two people in the room had noticed. "Excuse me?" he asked, and raised his brow in virtuous arrogance, hoping the ruse would work.

Marty dropped into a chair and hooked the heels of his square-toed oxfords on the desk. Noah had never seen an educator alter his personality so dramatically before his students. "Come on, Noah. I may not know you well, after all, you weren't the most gregarious fellow in my residence hall, but I know you well enough. Quite a show. I actually believed Miss Beaumont was going to leap from her chair and claw your face to ribbons." He whistled, lips pursed. "Scared me, my friend."

Me, too, Noah thought with pride and dismay, recalling the furious flush staining Elle's cheeks.

Marty rocked his leg in time to a personal tempo, patiently waiting. Finally, he said, "The silence is killing me. Fortunately, I don't have another class for two hours."

Noah sighed and dropped his pen to the desk, slipped his spectacles off, and buried the heels of his hands in his eyes. "She's a family friend." He rubbed hard, seeing stars. "Is that enough?"

"Not nearly."

"Sorry, but it will have to be."

Marty's feet hit the floor. "You contact me out of the clear blue, a terse telegraph asking me to bring you on for a semester, *and* help you fund a research project on the coast. Admittedly, in light of your stellar reputation, your arrival provided somewhat of a coup for me, as I took all the credit for inviting you and for creating the research project." He waved his hand in dismissal. "No thanks are necessary for my selflessness. Glad to accommodate an old university chum. Without complaint, without question.''

"Thank you. From the bottom of my heart, Marty," he muttered, and replaced his spectacles, returning to his work. He had to formulate a lesson plan for the oceanography course before four o'clock. And . . . until he figured out what to do about Elle, he wasn't clueing Martin Stanford in on anything.

Marty hummed a ditty and tapped his foot in time to it. "I'm Miss Beaumont's advisor. Worked with her a lot this semester."

Noah's head came up, greed overriding caution. He had missed her; blessit, he'd just about gone blind from it. Spent countless hours worrying and dreaming . . . and, a time or two, wishing he could curse her judgment as he cursed his. Damned helpless, he could not deny the impulse to ask, "Is she a good student? Is she happy?"

A wide, cat-got-the-cream smile bowed Marty's slender lips. "Talkative, temperately disruptive on occasion. Slides in right under the bell, but notably intelligent and enthusiastic. In fact, she's impressed quite a few of the program's detractors, of which there are many at this institution. At any institution accepting female students, I would imagine. Dane Cossin—you remember him don't you, came down in '94—anyway, he asked her to assist in his World Geography class. Grade papers, take notes, those types of duties. For that old cuss, a weighty honor."

"Cossin?" Noah jerked forward. "Wasn't there a rumor about a liaison with one of his students in Chicago?"

"No, the scandal involved his son, Daniel. Mathematics department. Dane is seventy if he's a day."

Noah frowned and slumped back, wishing Marty would get the hell out of his office.

"Is she a former student?"

"No."

"Had to ask." Marty shrugged, the first sign of chagrin. "I didn't think so. Except for formal functions, I've never even seen you in the company of a woman. But, I had to ask, you understand. Being a female student's advisor carries a peremptorily higher level of responsibility than I am used to.''

"Give me her class schedule, Marty."

His gaze sliced back, round and startled. "I can't do that."

"Yes, you can. If you don't, I'll find a way to do it myself. Make it easy on me, an old university chum."

Marty abruptly unfolded from the chair. "What *is* this?"

"I'm going to ask her to marry me. I'm quite certain that's all you need to know." There, he'd said it. And, as Caleb had predicted, it hadn't stung much. Only a slight twinge of discomfiture. The next time he said it, it probably wouldn't sting at all.

"You're in love?" Marty stumbled. *"You?"*

"What do you mean, *'you'* ?" Noah slapped his hand to his knee.

Marty opened his mouth, closed it, and muffled a cough. "I can see ..." He fluttered his fingers, not even bothering to hide his incredulity. "I can see you living in a decrepit house surrounded by sharks' teeth and driftwood, some bundles of archaic netting. But a wife? And marriage?" His arm stilled in midair as he stared past Noah's shoulder. "Come to think of it, I *did* see a lot of interested women flocking around you in Chicago, but you never gave them a second look. Actually, I'd started to wonder."

"I never gave them a second look because of *her.*" *I think I've loved her since I was twelve years old,* he silently added, too private a comment to make to anyone but Elle. Besides, it made him sound like a lovesick fool.

"Hell's bells, you must have it worse than I ever did."

"Have pity on me. I do." Noah slid a sheet of paper across the desk. "And either you give me her schedule or I follow her around campus, starting with your class on Wednesday morning." He tapped his pen. "Would the news you've invited a deranged marine biologist to teach in your esteemed department enhance your sterling reputation, Professor Stanford?''

Marty grabbed the pen and scribbled hastily. ''You're lucky I have a crack memory. Besides, can't stand in the way of true love, now can I? I'm a romantic fellow, really. Always have been.''

Noah linked his fingers over his twitching stomach muscles, hoping it would all be this easy.

Elle opened the door and peeked inside. Holding her breath, she crept along the deserted hallway, hugging the wall. The two hours the library remained open after dinner seemed the safest time to study; she felt sure Noah would eat in the faculty hall, then stay for the customary cigar and brandy. In the day since he'd shown up in her science class, she had not caught a glimpse of him. And she had looked. Around every corner, beneath every shrub. Releasing a jittery giggle of hysteria, she wondered if his appearance at the university symbolized nothing more than the mercilessly ironic will of God.

Turning into a small back room, she noted the scent of dust and leather. A comforting scent she would always associate with learning. Maturing. Heaviness settled in her chest, and she searched her mind for the source. Ah, yes. Now, she would also associate it with *him*.

Settling at a table hidden behind shelves of books devoted to Roman history, she blinked the mist from her vision. Muttering a vicious oath, she swiped at her eyes. Why did this have to happen? When she had finally decided leaving had been for the best? Turning her head, she stared out a window overlooking the quadrangle. Pine straw and horse dung littered the grassy expanse; the wind snatched at students' hats and pulled at the pages of their textbooks. Elle pressed her fingers to the pane, feeling detached and despondent, her heart and mind working against each other.

Merciful heavens, what could she do to forget him?

The sharp shriek of wood signaled someone taking the other chair. She swiveled on the smooth seat, thinking to ask for privacy.

Noah. Elbows propped on the stained planks, rolled cuffs hitting him high on the arm, wrinkled neckpiece twisted between his fingers. He ruffled curls already mussed, his sun-kissed features angled in earnest regard. His lips softened into a half smile, faint and sorrowful, the corners tipped low. Hushed voices and heavy footfalls faded as his bewitching, pure scent overwhelmed the stale odor of aged parchment and learning—all crowding the air she breathed.

She almost lifted her hand to adjust his crinkled collar, dazed by the surge of longing that set her heart beating like a drum. "What are you doing here?" she whispered, her hushed tone not induced by their erudite surroundings.

He searched her face, considering. She saw a hint of sadness cross his, but his façade of a smile crept higher. "The best spot in the library. Quiet, an agreeable window."

She gripped the edge of the table and leaned in, close enough to see a tiny circle of stubble he had missed with his razor. "That's not at all what I meant, and—"

"What have you got there?" Frantic, but trying hard to conceal it, he dropped his neckpiece and reached, using a slim finger to rotate her textbook. *"Basic Discussions in Biology.* I used this once. In a class two years ago. What chapter does Marty have you reading?" When the silence lengthened, he said casually, "I could tutor you . . . if you need help."

A thousand memories passed through her mind. Carefree evenings spent at his mother's kitchen table, fireflies flitting outside the screen door, pencils scattered across a cream-colored cloth, his hand guiding hers, gray eyes watchful and expectant. All the love she felt for him, absolute and powerful and unwelcome, flooded her being. Blind with panic, she grabbed the textbook and shoved her chair into the wall.

Reacting quickly, he grasped her wrist, the bones shifting beneath his fingers. "Don't run, sweet. Please, don't. *God, I've missed you.*" The sight of her fear—raw, gut-wrenching fear—eroded his weak confidence. "I've only seen fear on your face once before, when I blacked out in Caleb's skiff . . . the night we found your father. That emotion was *for* me. It"—he let her hand slip away—"it really hurts to be the cause."

Cautiously, she perched her bottom on the edge of the chair. Her throat trembled beneath a lace collar; a quiver shook the cinnamon curls brushing her chin. Noah wanted to press his lips to her pulse and love her with his heart and body. Share his soul with her.

Blessit, he would do it this time. He would show her she was not alone.

Forcing his hands to his side, he tried to disregard how beautiful she looked, sitting there in a new dress. "I'm sorry for shocking you in class. I'm also sorry for sneaking up on you today." Tried not to imagine what she wore beneath the butter yellow material.

"Caroline told you where to find me, I suppose." She linked her fingers and squeezed, presenting the crown of her head.

"After my fourth telegraph, plus two from Zach, yes, she finally did. You mustn't blame her. I left her no choice. Since then, I've been going crazy trying to get the lab on its feet and get to you."

She lifted her head. "Get to me? Why would you want to get to *me?*"

"Elle, I"—he tunneled his hand through his hair—"I need to talk to you. Desperately. There are things I need to say. Words best spoken in"—glancing over his shoulder, he looked back to find a rosy flush staining her cheeks—"private."

"I thought this might be why you'd made this journey." Her voice dropped. "I'm not pregnant, Noah. Thank God, for both of us. So you can go to Pilot Isle or Chicago or wherever it is the fish need you with a completely clear conscience."

He glanced down in dismay. He had *hoped* to find her pregnant. What would she think about that? "If you're trying to hurt me, you're doing a fine job of it."

"I'm, I'm not trying to hurt you."

"Doesn't matter. Nothing hurts as much as it did when you left. You didn't even think to tell me you planned to return to university. I woke up on Devil *alone,* Elle. Reaching for you."

"You don't have to tell me how much not knowing hurts, how much being alone hurts."

"Is that what this is? Revenge for my leaving?" He leaned in, the scent of almonds and honey fueling his desire *and* his anger. "I wish I had never left you. I wish I had given you your first kiss, been the one to hold your hand and dance with you the first time, see you through university and the opening of your school. I wish . . . oh, hell . . ." He banged his fist on the table.

"No use in wishing, Professor. We're like oil and water, you and I." Her lower lip trembled; she swiped her knuckles across it. "You're the one who reminded me time after time, in your subtle, diplomatic way. Congratulations. Now I believe it."

His hand shot out. "You *don't.*"

She flinched, dodging the contact. "Yes, I *do.*"

He wrenched his spectacles off and gazed into her eyes— green and wild and tormented. "My whole life it seems you've been able to recognize my feelings, better than my family even. You could look into my face and see everything. How is it you can't now?"

"I used to be able to see everything, you're right. Now . . . now when I look at you, I see *us,* together, kissing and . . . touching. Like the night on—" She flinched and her textbook smacked to the floor. "Why did you come, Noah? *Why?* I told you not to feel responsible about what happened between us. You were right when you begged me to forget the boy I loved.

I've done it. You should do the same and forget the girl you protected."

"I did say that, didn't I?" He laughed raggedly and scrubbed his hand over his jaw. "I once said far too many things." Before she could move, he'd leaned halfway across the table, cradling her face in his palms. "Blessit, I hadn't planned to say this for the first time in my life in a damned library, of all places, although the irony isn't lost on me. However, another night isn't going to pass without you hearing me say it. The last two months I've said it in my dreams. Tonight I want to say it to you." He leaned in until their mouths brushed. "I love you, Marielle-Claire Beaumont. I'm deeply, hopelessly, helplessly in love with you."

Then he kissed her. And felt love flow from his heart.

Against his, her mouth formed one word—*no*—as anguish etched her face. With a pained cry that cut clear through him, she wrenched to her feet and rushed blindly from the room.

Staring at the strand of hair wrapped around his finger, he realized he did not know where she lived, and, she had sprinted into a dark night. Shoving from his chair, he raced along the narrow hallway, slapped the door open, a rush of cool air cuffing his face. Slipping on a smooth marble edge, he cursed leather soles, inferior vision, and lack of foresight.

"Elle, stop!" he shouted, ignoring the alarmed looks of a group of students.

Chest hitching, he caught her as she turned into a dim passageway bordering two faculty residences. She pivoted, shoving at his hands, fat tears streaming, dampening the curls hanging in her face. "Easy, sweet. There now. I'm here." Leaning against the rough bricks, he wrapped his arms around her, and drew her close to ease her trembling.

"No," she choked, and slumped against him, the crown of her head slipping perfectly beneath his chin.

"Tell me why my loving you is a terrible circumstance."

He turned his face into her hair. *Lemon,* he remembered, and inhaled deeply.

"I know what happened that night wasn't"—she burrowed her cheek against his chest, her muffled sob tearing into his soul—"what you planned and . . . you don't know how to make it right. It's nagging at you . . . to make it right. Make me fit somewhere proper, somewhere decent. It's your way."

He cupped her chin, forcing her watery gaze to his. "You think my love for you is born of guilt? I don't feel *any* guilt over what happened between us. I'm incredibly awed by the beauty of what we shared. And I'm admittedly starved, actually somewhat desperate, to touch you again, but guilt?" He shook his head.

"Your list—"

Laughing softly, he fit his brow to hers. "Oh, sweet. Forget that ridiculous list. I've been making those since the day I defended a disheveled French immigrant in a crowded schoolyard. I've made a thousand, at least."

"If you have, you hid them well."

A renewed burst of love swelled his heart as a renewed burst of desire swelled things elsewhere. He had not been lying when he'd said he was starved. For the feel of her beneath him, arching to meet his thrusts, eagerly grasping his hips, and guiding his movements. Taking command in a manner unknown to him before her. His heart pumped in remembrance. Sixty nights alone, dreaming and wishing for her touch, her witty conversation, her harmonious companionship, had proved to be an excruciatingly torturous experiment, one he never, *ever,* wanted to repeat.

Losing sight of his purpose, he lowered his head, thinking only of tasting. . . .

Oh, no, he's casting his spell.

Proof of his hunger pressed into her hip, hard and long, as his mouth skimmed her cheek, his tongue flicking, stoking. Her thoughts scattered. Frantic and aroused beyond measure, she shoved against his chest, then repeated the action more forcefully.

Swearing, he backed off. "Elle, for God's sake, you're killing me. Tearing my heart from my chest." He drew a shaky breath, let it rush out. "I need you. Blessit, I love you. How can I prove it to you?"

She covered her ears, the pounding of her heart deafening. "You're confusing passion with love. You see, I went to the psychology section of the university library when I first arrived and spent an entire afternoon reading about . . . intimate relations. A classic example of misplaced affection, confounded by our childhood relationship. Also, I know it's odd because, at one time, I would have sold my soul to hear you say the words you said to me tonight. I prayed to hear them, dreamed of hearing them. Only, I don't want to hear them now." She babbled and could not stop. "I can't depend on you. I have to depend upon myself. I've been trying to heal, trying to find my way the past few weeks. Trying to decide what I'm going to do with my life, now my family is gone. You have your life planned, successful career, loving family. I'm alone now, and—"

He grabbed her shoulders, his fingers digging into her skin. Throat working furiously, he glanced at his hands. Jerking them back, he wrenched around to lean stiff-armed against the wall. His frenetic breaths echoed in the silence; a tremor rippled his spine.

Had she imagined the glint of tears in his eyes? In the muted darkness, it was hard to tell. "Noah? Please understand. I think, I think it would be better for both of—"

"Please," he said, an anguished, inaudible plea, "don't say any more. I'll go crazy if you do." His fists clenched, his knuckles scraping the wall in what must have been a painful movement. "Not your fault. I don't know what I expected . . . after all I've said . . . the warnings . . ." His head dipped low, and she watched him struggle, the muscles beneath his shirt bunching, quaking. "Just before you left, I figured it out, what it means, the rarity of this bond between us. I know the timing isn't perfect, blessit. It's horrible. You've started university again and, and have your future mapped out. Hell, I intended to tell you how I felt that night on Devil, had every word planned, but you stopped me, kissed me. I never got my thread of thought back."

"You're a child with a new toy. You don't—"

He slapped the wall. "Don't presume to tell me what I feel. Don't you dare."

She swallowed, heartsick, and surprisingly, a tad angry. "It's too late." She added harshly, "*You're* too late. Time will take care of this, for both of us."

His head turned. "You little fool, time won't take care of a damned thing." He glared, his features settling into an intractable expression she recognized from having seen it so many times on Caleb's face. It was the first moment she remembered thinking the Garrett brothers looked anything alike. "You'll marry me, Elle. Within the month. I'm not waiting any longer for you to come to your senses."

"Not waiting?" she sputtered, misty red coloring her vision. Taking a step forward, she jabbed her finger into his shoulder. "Well, you'll have to wait a long time." Jab. "I'm not marrying you." Jab. "This is my life, Professor, and you have no say. And thank you, but you can keep your romantic proposal."

He captured her hand before she could utter another word of protest. "I love you, and I'll do whatever it takes to make you believe it. Get down on my knees, if necessary. Every day for the rest of my life. Swim the length of the Atlantic Ocean. Lasso the moon. You're the first person I've ever belonged to, and I'm not letting you give me up."

"No." No use. He didn't hear her, suddenly occupied with nibbling from her wrist to the tip of her longest digit.

"Yes," he said, and sucked her index finger into his mouth, rolled his tongue around her ragged nail for good measure.

As if it were happening to someone else, she watched him make love to her hand. The same sweeping tilt she experienced when he kissed her, an earth-shattering shift, rocked her where she stood.

"This is what I want to do to your entire body, sweet. This is what I *will* do. I promise you."

A weak sound rose from her throat. A scorching flush of need and embarrassment flamed her face. The juncture between her thighs caught fire, her breasts swelled, her nipples scratched against her corset. Desperate, she curled her fingers and tugged.

Stepping back, he leaned against the wall, hooking his feet at the ankles, a deceptively calm pose when she could see his knees trembling, his chest rattling. Taking his time, his gun-metal gaze traveled from the tips of her new leather boots to the ends of her recently trimmed hair. A triumphant smile curled his lips. "You want me as much as I want you. I can see it, don't try denying it. And you love me, even if you don't want to."

"Yes, I want you."

Raw hunger replaced confidence. His stance stiffened as he pushed off the wall. "Spend the night with me. Come to my house."

She walked back a step, stumbling over an uneven brick. He followed, his depraved expression exposed by a strip of moonlight. Helplessly, she whimpered.

He squinted, his hands falling to his side. "You're terrified of me. Completely terrified."

"I am," she agreed, pride yielding to honesty.

A look of naked sorrow swept his face, making her feel the guilty party. "I'm sorry. I shouldn't have come here, forced myself upon you. I just figured"—he closed his eyes and touched the bridge of his nose—"what happened . . . on Devil . . . you left because . . . I thought you felt enough for me to want me to come to you, that you only needed to hear me say the words. I assumed my foolishness was keeping us apart." He turned and walked into a gaping recess of shadow. "I guess that's what my limited experience with women gets me."

Lacking a defined reason, she raced forward, catching his crisp sleeve between her finger and thumb. "What did you say?" Impatient and confused, and as always, impulsive. "What did you just say?"

His gaze slid her way and he blinked. As he remembered, a bright flush she could see even in the dim moonlight flooded his cheeks. "Nothing." He fingered the neat golden arch above his ear. "I didn't say anything."

"How you touched me, I, well . . . you were confident . . . clever." She worried her bottom lip between her teeth, a movement he watched with the blind attentiveness she knew him to possess. "How many?"

His frown deepened, creasing his cheeks. "Elle, this isn't something we should discuss."

"Why? You've never kept secrets from me before."

"Secrets?" He expelled a choked groan. "It isn't a secret."

"Then tell me. I want to know." She swallowed, preparing for the worst. "How many? Too many to count?"

"Too many to *count?*" He leaned in, searching. "Is that what you think?"

She nodded with a jerk of her chin.

"Sweet—"

"It's all right. You don't have to tell me. We're not children anymore, whispering under a spread of scrub pines, dangling our feet over the side of a dock."

She heard the bricks shift beneath his feet. A rock cracked the wall. "Two." His labored sigh echoed along the passageway. "In college, a professor's daughter. Engaged to a very wealthy man her father had selected for her. She was testing the waters, being rebellious, I suppose. She made her interest known, and I accepted her offer. One time, at her father's summer cottage. Later, in Chicago, a woman I met at a university function. Widowed, attractive, not interested in an attachment I would not offer. There were other, well, times I could have taken more, given more . . . but a nagging sense of discontent always held me back.''

Elle flicked her lids, found him watching her, his eyes guarded and wary. "Once with her, too?''

He jammed his hands in his pockets and shook his head.

The balm of unmitigated relief dulled the pain of imagining him with another woman. "Now I understand what Caroline meant.''

"What Caroline meant," he growled and knocked the toe of his oxford against the ground. "I want you to know, the things we did, most of them were as new to me as they were to you. If it appeared I was overly confident or possessed a great degree of knowledge, well . . . I didn't really know, I''—he lifted his head, a wicked smile growing—"I guess it was just beginner's luck.''

"I'm scared," she blurted, startled to hear the confession.

His smile dimmed. "I can see that. It hurts me to see it. Hurts badly.''

"Everything's all mixed up in my mind." She pressed the heel of her hand to her throbbing temple. "My father attempted to determine my future, guide my hand. He told me so often that my choices were foolish, sentimental, and preposterous. I've come to wonder if he's right.''

"Blessit, Elle, he's not right. I told you the same thing, and I wasn't right either. You knew, the little girl knew. She was wise and brave, and I loved her as much as I love you.''

"You don't understand. I'm not a girl anymore, living on dreams of the future and believing in your love above all else. I can't pin all my hopes on you. Give you my heart like I could before. I just can't.''

"Time? Do you need time?''

She bowed her head, the uncertain look on his face bringing to mind the boy she'd cherished. *Damn and blast,* it made her want to shout at the unfairness, the gross irony, of life.

When she failed to answer, he rocked from one foot to the other. "I'm going to the coast for a few days. Research at a commercial fishery in Georgetown. I had hoped to ask you to come with me, somehow schedule around your classes. I can see now, that won't happen."

"Will you come back?"

Tilting her chin, forcing her gaze to his, he bit out, "You're slow to get the idea, sweet. I'm not leaving South Carolina without you."

"But—"

He stopped her denial by capturing her lips beneath his, a kiss of gentle honesty, not persuasion. Entirely too vulnerable to this side of him, she bloomed beneath the caress, unconsciously urging him to deepen it. "I can't live without you," he murmured, then slanted his head, assaulting her from another angle, his hands sliding into her hair to cradle her head. He tasted of citrus and mint, wonderful, appealing.

Time slowed. Angling, he leaned against the wall and spread his thighs, fitting his hips to hers. She followed every movement, mirrored the thrust of his tongue, the rock and grind of his pelvis. Somewhere, the clang of a church bell and a horse's shrill whinny resounded. It meant nothing, the world outside. For her, there was only his thumb sliding beneath her collar, pressing against her pulse. His lips suckling her cheek and moving lower. Liquid heat, a shower of color—red, green, and gold. Her low mewl of assent. Her hands tugging at buttons, seeking what she knew he could give.

At the ingress of her finger through a loosened buttonhole, he set her from him. "Either we stop now"—he sucked air into his lungs—"or we make love on the blessed ground."

"What?" She blinked, her vision blurred.

His jaw tensed. He fisted his hands by his side. "I'm sick to death of alleys and beaches. I want to lie with you on my bed, your bed, *any* bed. Wake next to you. Hear you breathing in the middle of the night. Curl our feet together under the blankets. I want to be more than your lover. I want to be your husband, the father of your children. I want you, forever.''

She couldn't stifle her startled gasp, just as he could not stifle the spark of anger. ''I'm leaving for Georgetown at dawn, sweet. When I come back, I'll find you. Don't think to run from me again.''

''My life is here, why would I run?'' Foolish to act confident with her knees knocking together.

He thumped his chest, for once, brute strength and mulishness. ''Your life is with me. Don't ever forget that.''

Dazed, she could only figure it was not the right time to argue. She walked from the alley, not even sure which direction she took. Stepping behind her, he grasped her hand, and led her to the library, where they retrieved his spectacles and her textbook. Not a word passed between them.

Noah dropped her off at the boardinghouse the female students shared, left her standing on the front porch with nothing more than an authoritarian glare of possession and a light, lingering kiss on her cheek. Elle watched him stride across the withered lawn, his tall form blending into the darkness.

Stark exhilaration raced through her, followed closely by sheer terror. Merciful heaven, against her wishes, or *because* of the thousands she'd once exacted, it looked like Noah Garrett meant to have her.

Chapter Eighteen

The first gift arrived the day after he left. A square bundle wrapped in brown paper and sitting on the top step. He'd scrawled her name across the front in his now-familiar script; a yellow ribbon, one she had inadvertently left on Devil Island, held it together.

Slumping to the stoop, she unwrapped the paper with trembling fingers, an autumn gust tugging at the loose knot of hair on her head. Her eyes stung from lack of sleep, from twisting and turning, replaying everything Noah had said to her and wondering if it could possibly be true.

Deep inside, praying it was true.

Carefully, she opened the tin box, trying to deny the quiver of excitement in her stomach. It was the first gift a man had ever given her, outside a modest present or two for her birthday. Nudging the swath of velvet aside, her breath caught. Her mother's brooch lay amidst the plush maroon folds. Hands shaking, she pinned it to her collar, blinking past the mist clouding her vision. She had sold it the day before she left Pilot Isle, to help pay expenses. Promising to keep it in her family, Mrs. O'Neil, the jeweler's wife, had paid a fair amount.

How had Noah known how much it meant to her? Or that she sold it?

Elle lifted the scrap of material to her nose, wishing it captured his scent. She could clearly see his elegant fingers arranging the piece of velvet just so.

A square slip of parchment fluttered from the box. Heart racing, she grabbed it.

> Sweet,
>   This belongs to you, as I do.
>   I love you.
>
>   Noah

Elle replaced the velvet and closed the dented lid. With wooden movements, she followed the hallway to her set of rooms and collapsed on her bed in a rare fit of misery.

She missed her morning classes.

Two days turned to four, four to six, six to eight. Her tension mounted with each package she found on the step, each hour that passed waiting for Noah to leap from behind a pine tree or pop his head from beneath her desk. As he had no doubt known would happen, her resistance melted as well, her love for him increasing each time she read one of his hastily scrawled notes.

First the return of her mother's brooch. Then Noah's pilot coat wrapped around a set of leather-bound books she had admired, weeks ago, in the mercantile window on Pilot Isle. A parasol with pink-and-green ribbon loops came the next day. Or was it the shot silk dress, trimmed with black-velvet bands and guipure lace? The loveliest item of clothing she had ever seen, one she plainly had no place to wear. Sighing, she set the hat on her head. This morning's gift, trimmed with roses and a striped fabric, perfectly matched her parasol.

Noah had wonderful taste in women's apparel. With an angry kick, she scattered a pile of burnished leaves. Better to spend her time worrying about what she was going to tell him when he returned than imagining how he had come to have such good taste.

I love you, and yes, I'll marry you.

No, no, that sounded brazen, as though her earlier rejection had been a deceptive feminine ploy. But, she had to have an answer. Soon. He had begun asking her in his daily missives. Blatant queries, often underlined for emphasis. *What church shall we say our vows in? Should we go to Pilot Isle and do it there?* His methodical certitude made her smile and laugh aloud, her classmates looking on in stupefaction. Who but Noah would think to champion his cause, fact by listed fact, while never even showing his face?

How had he known it would work?

Curiosity killing her, she had risen one morning at the break of day, and watched Professor Stanford creep into the yard and place the latest gift on the step. Although she should have resisted, she'd leaned from her window and called to him. He had lifted his head, his face turning all colors of red in the dawning light. Since then, he had avoided her gaze in class and had not called on her to answer a question once. She expected to score a high mark in biology.

A sudden gust tugged at the lapel of Noah's pilot coat and sent a shiver down her spine. Elle shoved her hands in the pockets, drawing the wool close. She leaned her cheek against the scratchy material and sniffed, berating herself for her foolishness. She punished herself by wearing it when it presented such an inescapable sense of closeness to him. Hmmph. He had probably anticipated her reaction. She had to remember the man did nothing by chance.

Closing her fingers around the apple in her pocket, she brought it to her mouth and took a healthy bite. Kicking pinecones from her path, she thought Mrs. Holden really needed to hire someone to—

Elle stumbled to a halt, the apple halfway to her mouth. She spun in a small circle. A black-and-white cat crossing the yard at a dawdling pace, a grocery cart rolled past, the driver lifting his hand in greeting. Dropping the fruit to the ground, she walked forward. Carved in the trunk of the only dogwood in the yard: *Noah loves Elle.* Not deep etching, like Christa's. This was a hasty attempt. She brushed the letters and raised her hand to her face. A raw scent clung to her skin; her fingertips glistened. Moist, the bark was still moist.

Calling his name, she completed another turn, even tipped her chin, and searched the thick copse of branches above her head. A sudden burst of emotion . . . longing, trepidation, inevitability. He was close; she could *feel* him. She sprinted across the yard, blades of grass snagging in her bootlaces, leather soles skimming the scatter of leaves. The wind sucked the lace curtain inside her bedroom window. She snatched the screen door wide. She had closed it before leaving for class.

The air felt cooler in the hallway, a pale burst from an electric bulb lighting her way. Tiptoeing, she reached her door. Something different. . . . She sniffed. A cloying odor, syrupy and floral. Hair on her arms rising, she twisted the beveled knob, the door swinging in without a murmur.

The gasp came fast, although she tried to call it back, clamping her hand over her lips. Candles covered every vacant surface, flames wavering from the air flowing through the window. Rose petals, red and yellow, littered the heart-pine floor and the unmade bed. Elle closed the door and slumped against it. A faint sound, a whistling release of breath. Cautiously, she turned her head.

Noah sat in a chair in the far corner, arms folded over his chest, feet propped on the rattletrap desk she and Mrs. Holden had moved from the attic. She stepped closer, saw he slept deeply. Candlelight lit every angle of his whiskered cheeks,

silhouetted the gradual rise and fall of his chest. His frock coat
lay in a tangle on the floor; his fingers gripped his neckpiece.
The edges of his waistcoat curled, revealing a snowy white
shirt unbuttoned past the point of decency, and, *oh* . . . a wealth
of dark chest hair showed.

Drawing the wrinkled cloth from his hand, she unbuttoned
his collar, and dropped them to the desk. He murmured and
sighed. She brushed his hair from his brow, slid his spectacles
from his face, and placed them on a shelf above his head. Only
after she had covered him with a thin woolen blanket, making
sure his feet did not poke out, did she take a long, leisurely
look. Perching on the edge of her bed, she stared, marveling
at her good fortune. Noah rarely let anyone see him like this—
splendidly ruffled, utterly undone. She could look all she
pleased, caress freely if she chose to. The notion of touching
him sent a molten rush through her body.

The candles dripped wax in melting plunks; the world
retreated behind lace curtains and dying sunlight. The low
flames bathed them in warm brilliance, creating an island of
solitude and understanding. How could she have ever imagined
living without him? Pride, her damnable pride. Simply because
he had not discerned his love as promptly as she would have
liked. True, he had rejected her impassioned ardor at one time.
But he had also been her closest confidant, her strongest ally.
Wasn't that worth its weight in gold?

Laying her lovely hat on the floor, she curled into a ball,
sinking into the feather mattress, rose petals sticking to her
skin. Propping her cheek on her arm, she blinked, yawned. In
response, Noah mumbled her name, once, softly. Beautiful.
Beautiful and brilliant, and he claimed to love her. She started
to rise, to go to him, thinking only to slide her hands inside
the gaping neck of his shirt, press her lips to the tender area
behind his ear, an act which never failed to drive him wild.
She wanted to drag him to her bed and shock him with the
strength of her desire.

Shaking her head, she determined to watch him until he woke from his deep slumber. They had time enough for everything.

For a long moment, Noah stood beside the bed, staring at the woman who meant more to him than life itself. The sun had set, leaving only a few sputtering candles to caress her skin, her hair, a glorious, rusty spill across the cream sheets. Funny, now that he had let her love into his heart, he could not bear to live another second without it.

When had Elle come to belong to him so completely? The first time he saw her, in the schoolyard? From that day forward, she had certainly thought *he* belonged to *her*.

Curled on her side, she stretched, innocently raising her skirt, baring a slender thigh he knew the shape of very well. Her dated cambric drawers did not hide much, not nearly enough. He remembered her wrapped around his waist, firm muscle tensing with each thrust. Groaning, he raked his hand over his face. Blessit, he had to keep his mind free, clear. He needed to talk to her, wanted . . . *oh, God,* to explore the exceptional bond between them. He wanted to hear an accounting of every minute of her life.

He wanted to drink her being into his soul.

As if she witnessed his struggle, and wished to destroy his good intentions, her mouth parted on a sleepy sigh, her tongue sneaking out to touch her bottom lip.

Blessit, what was a man supposed to do?

Pressing his knee into the mattress, it sank deep. Feathers, he realized, and smiled. He had never made love on a feather bed before. With a gentle sprawl, he lay behind her, pulled her against his chest. Elle was, if he remembered correctly, a very deep sleeper. Proving that, she shifted, crowding her buttocks against his groin, all the while humming low in her throat, her sensual kitten growl. The sound, and the press of her bottom, shattered the last of Noah's noble intent.

Nudging her hair aside, he placed feather-soft kisses along the nape of her neck, searching for, and finding, every hidden nook behind her ear. Hitching to his elbow, he caressed her jaw, her temple, traced her arched brow with the tip of his tongue. The scent of her drove him wild. The faintest hint of lemon and crisp autumn. And roses, he thought, smiling as he peeled a velvet petal from her cheek. He unfastened the buttons on her practical blouse, wondering if she had worn the dress he had given her. He would have liked to give her lace-trimmed underdrawers, something secret and naughty for him alone. He had no word for the piece of clothing he pictured her wearing for him.

Breathing heavily, he tugged her sleeve past her wrist, set his lips to the naked skin at her shoulder, his hand rising to cup her breast, heavy and warm in his palm as his thumb searched. She wore a corset, strangely enough. Stiff and unyielding, he pondered how to go about getting it off.

"Let me help you," she whispered, and turned her head, her mouth finding his, her tongue stroking, begging for entry. She tasted of apple, sweet and ripe. Knocking his hand away, she quickly worked the ties on her corset, jerky movements that sent her elbow into his ribs.

He harbored no theory of denial, no theory except one concerning the quickest way to get inside her. There would be time for finesse and kind words later, time to strip off every piece of clothing, and pay homage to her lovely body. Now, he *needed* her surrounding him, tight and moist and hot. Needed her badly. Her little moans of urgency, delicious sounds raising his level of confidence, convinced him rapidity would work for her as well.

He tore his mouth away and rolled her beneath him, her corset flopping open. Her thighs spread, and his hips slid into place, a consummate fit. "I'm sorry," he rasped, his lips pressed against the side of a freed breast and moving higher. "I want you too much to wait."

She laughed, a deep gurgle that set her nipple quivering beneath his lips. "Wait? Merciful heaven, Professor, I don't want to wait. Hurry up and get your clothes off."

"Oh, sweet." He moved to the other nipple, pebbled it beneath his tongue, his fingers working in fevered conjunction. "A little clothing never hurt anyone." In impatient fistfuls, he drew her skirt to her waist, dismayed to find more than one layer. Her drawers were simpler, the matter of a knotted tassel or two. Promising to buy her new ones, he snapped the ties he could not easily undo.

Cooperative and eager, she went right to the heart of the problem, loosening the buttons on his trouser fly. Their lips met in furious, compelling hunger, their fingers trembling and slipping over buttonholes and ribbons. She removed fabric, grasping him, fingers curled. Her teeth sank into his shoulder as she roamed the length of him . . . and back. Delirious with desire, he closed his eyes, his weight held on his elbows, his fingers tracing the curves of her body. Had he taught her to touch him in this fashion, a firm, assertive glide from tip to juncture? He must have, but he could not remember. Right now, he could scarcely remember his name.

Hand pressed to the small of her back, he angled her hips. Lowering his lips to her ear, he instructed her to wrap her legs around him and hold on.

With a sweep of her thumb over the rounded tip of his arousal, a daring stroke that came close to ruining his fine purpose, she let him go, her arms clasping, legs circling and locking. His hand drifted between her thighs, found her moist, swollen, and warm. He dipped deep, plunged, preparing a passage that seemed ready. He teased, finding pleasure in her candid response. He wanted, no, he *needed* to see her need matched his. She tipped her head, throat muscles jumping as she swallowed. He glanced at the door, closed, but who knew how much sound would travel through it?

In a sudden movement, she raised her hips, bumping against

the heel of his hand. The moan started deep, threw her eyes
wide, rendering them dark, dark green. Acting quickly, he
captured her groan of pleasure in his mouth and entered her in
one smooth stroke.

She gasped, and together they found a fast, sure rhythm. Her
muscles tensed, then tensed again, her nails digging into his
back. She called his name, thrashing and bucking, wild and
ungoverned.

"I love you," he said, his mind shutting down. Pulling her
close, he thrust once more, hip to hip, thigh to thigh, and uttered
a hoarse cry, flooding her with everything in his heart and his
body. Every muscle strained and snapped like a taut band, leaving
him limp. He kissed her, weak and clumsy, not certain if she
responded. Still clasping her to his chest, he rolled to his back,
moisture slicking their skin, their harsh breaths filling the room.

Elle slumped across him, her arm a deadweight beneath. He
stretched, found his trousers circling his knees, snarled and
damp. His shirt hung off one shoulder. Rose petals matted his
cheek. And, oh yes, he remembered, shifting with a groan, Elle
had clawed his back mercilessly. He drew much-needed air
into his lungs, the scent of their joining filling his nostrils.

Damn, how hot their passion flamed. Incredible.

"Juste Ciel. I'm dying," she said, her voice cracking. She
plucked at her skirt. "Good heavens, I still have my clothes on."

He smiled, pressing a kiss to her brow. "Actually, I ripped
your drawers off, ruined them, I'm afraid. I'll buy you a new
pair, I promise."

"Drawers? Who cares about drawers? I can't even feel my
arm."

Noah laughed and lifted enough for her to pull her limb free.
Not wanting to let her go, he gripped her waist, and brought
her atop him. A dazed look ruled her face. Her lids slipped
low as her head flopped forward. "Sleepy," she mumbled.

He tightened his hold, cherishing the secure weight of her.
"It's all right. I'll be here."

"Love you," he thought he heard her whisper between a sigh and a yawn.

He checked the urge to kiss her. A stray tear he could *not* check streaked down his cheek. "I love you, too." Mere words did not even begin to describe what he felt. "Too much."

She hummed in response, a drowsy, sated vibration.

Footsteps echoed in the hallway; Elle tensed against him, lifted slightly. "Hush, sweet. There's nothing to fear. I locked the door." He brushed his lips over the top of her head, the springy curls catching in his whiskers. "Besides, we're getting married. With this going on, and not likely to wait for a wedding ceremony, I figure the sooner, the better."

She brought her hand to his chest, trailed her fingers through the hair she appeared to like so much. "When?"

He sank into the mattress, exhaled in relief. "How about this Saturday?"

"Saturday?"

"Preacher Ellis has been notified, the church in Pilot Isle reserved. Caroline's arriving on Friday afternoon. Christa's baking some kind of cake and throwing us a party or something. I bought our train tickets last week and—"

Elle reared, snatched a pillow from the bed, and cuffed him in the face. "You planned all this, never even bothering to ask me first?"

Feeling a twinge of anger, he jerked his trousers to his waist, hastily buttoning his fly. "Yes, blessit, I did. I told you I wasn't waiting any longer. Chrissakes, after this"—he gestured to the tangled sheets and scattered rose petals—"how can you argue? It's the only sensible option." *Uh-oh.* He realized after he said it that this would never be the best argument to present to Elle Beaumont.

"Why, you . . . oh!" She rolled to the floor and started pacing by the bed, her hands fisted on her hips.

Noah scooted, resting against the rosewood headboard, beginning to enjoy this. The sight of her stomping around the room, bottom swinging beneath wrinkled satin, bosom bouncing beneath nothing at all, caused a miraculous erection to spring forth.

She glanced at him, glared actually, her gaze sliding down his body. She came to a sudden, shuddering halt. "Oh, no, Professor. Not again. Not as long as you're making all the decisions and not even asking me what I'd like to do. Stubborn, arrogant . . ."

He laughed and leaned over the side of the bed. Straining, he slipped his thumb inside the ribbon surrounding the box he'd hidden beneath the side table.

She raised her head from drawing her sleeves to her shoulders, her blouse still gaping, breasts rising on each furious breath. Her eyes widened when she saw what he had in his hands, lashes fluttering. She could not contain the flush of excitement across her cheeks or the way her fingers danced down her stomach to her waist. A rush of pleasure warmed him. So, she'd liked his gifts.

Grinning like a lovesick fool, he nudged the tiny package toward the edge of the mattress. "This is the last one." He winked and crossed his ankles. "This week, anyway."

She took an eager step forward, a shy half step back. "You shouldn't have bought me all those gifts."

"I can return them, if you don't want them."

"*No.*" Her cheeks reddened; her head lowered. "I mean, of course, I like them. I love them." She touched the flowing green ribbon circling the box. "It's just . . . I never . . . thank you."

"You're welcome." He shoved it beneath her hovering hand. "Go on, open it. Before I decide to pull you back into bed."

She looked at him then, dead in the eye. Her hunger caught him by surprise, and he reached for her. Grabbing her gift, she skipped to the side. "Oh, no, you don't, Noah Garrett. Patience, you must have patience. Remember how you always used to preach the sacred value of patience?"

He flopped against the headboard, banging his shoulder on the rounded edge. "In the future, don't listen to my preaching."

Smiling wickedly, she climbed onto the end of the bed, settling Indian-style next to his feet. Her skirt hooked over her knees, gaping wide, giving him a wonderful view.

He knocked his head against the bedpost. "You're killing me."

She glanced down. A mischievous glint appeared as her gaze lifted. "Good," she said, and loosened the elegant bow. Sliding the ribbon free, she set it by her side with care. "This one is prettier than the others."

"Yes." He swallowed and struggled to breathe normally. "The store wrapped it."

She pushed the brown paper aside and stared at the silver jewelry case in silence. Wildflowers and roses embellished the casing. A touch of feminine nonsense, but he had guessed she would take pleasure from it. Watching her outline the ornate design, he felt a moment's unease, a pang of uncertainty. Dammit, he wanted nothing more than to make her happy, to give her anything she desired.

She lifted the lid, a whisper of air slipping past her lips. "Noah . . ."

He rocked forward, squinting to bring her expression into clear view. "Well?"

"Juste Ciel." She lifted the ring from its velvet perch, the round emerald catching a ray of candlelight, throwing a blazing spark to the coverlet. "Oh, my," she said, and slipped it on her finger, tilting her hand back and forth in the meager light.

"I looked and looked, searching for the perfect ring, one that *felt* right. But they were too fancy or too plain. Too big or too small. Too ugly." He shrugged, his cheeks heating. "Until I saw this one. The stone is the exact color your eyes turned the first time we made love. After the night on Devil, it was burned into my mind. And . . . I knew, I thought, I mean, you would . . ."

She launched herself at him with a cry of delight. "I love it. Oh, Noah. I love *you.*" She hooked her arms around his neck, feathering sloppy kisses along his jaw. "I always have, as you and everyone else in Pilot Isle knew."

"Thank God." He tightened the hold, enjoying the soft plumpness of her breasts.

She laughed, sending a hot rush of air across his skin. "Did you ever doubt it?"

"Once or twice."

Her delight faded. "Do you have to go to Chicago soon? How will we ... what will we—"

"Chicago? Good God, what kind of marriage do you think this is going to be? I'm staying *right here,* in South Carolina. We'll decide where to move after you graduate. You're not getting away from me again. I rented a house large enough for a family of ten, just around the corner on Senate Street. Marty is thrilled beyond words to have me teach the next four terms. Coupled with a research project on population dynamics of planktonic systems and making love to you as much as I can handle, I'm going to be incredibly busy."

"Marty? A house? Planktonic systems?" She blushed, her voice lowering. "Making love?"

"Never mind that, sweet." He flipped her to her back, settled in to kiss her soundly. "Right now, I think we have more important issues to worry about. Issues on, what shall we say ... the rise."

She nodded. "History thesis due in two days. Biology exam next Thursday."

Determined to win this round, he slanted his lips over hers, nibbling and licking until she moaned low in her throat, her thighs splaying wide. "I'm not sure I can help with the history thesis, but I know I'm a fair science tutor."

"Are you certain, Professor?"

"Positive *ma chère fille.*"

And, as any good biologist would do, Noah set out to provide concrete proof.

Author's Note

Readers familiar with the Outer Banks may recognize Pilot Isle as Beaufort, North Carolina. Indeed, I loosely based my setting there, thanks in large part to information provided by the kind ladies at the Beaufort Historical Society.

I incorporated artistic license in these areas, mostly calendar changes, which I hope the reader will forgive. In 1902, the second Federal fisheries laboratory in the United States was completed in Beaufort—still there to this day. Woods Hole, the first, was established in 1871, actually placing its construction before Noah's birth. But I know he would have wanted to take part, so he did. The scholarship Elle received I based on the ones given by the American Association of University Women, founded in 1882. They bestowed their first loan, much as I described it, in 1901, three years later than Elle received it.

The lifesaving program is a marvelous part of the Outer Banks history and well worth further research. Also, the University of South Carolina, in 1898 called South Carolina College, did admit female students. As an alumna, I wanted Elle to be one, too!